Nevada Testament

ALSO BY WIL MARA

Frame 232
The Gemini Virus
The Cut
The Draft
Wave

The Nevada Testament

A Jason Hammond Novel

Wil Mara

Sagittarius Publishing
A Division of Sagittarius Media LLC
New Jersey

This is a work of fiction. All of the characters, organizations, and events portrayed in this novel are either products of the author's imagination or are used fictitiously.

THE NEVADA TESTAMENT

www.wilmara.com

Published by Sagittarius Publishing
A Division of Sagittarius Media, LLC
New Jersey

Library of Congress Cataloging- in-Publication Data (TK)

Produced in the United States of America

10 9 8 7 6 5 4 3 2 1

Acknowledgements

So many people to thank on this one, wow...where do I start? Thanks to Jan and company at Tyndale for helping to get Jason Hammond off the ground. To all who read early drafts and gave great suggestions—Patti, Jane, Susan, Kari, Lisa, Michele, and Heather (now a novelist in her own right). To Tracey Miller, Scott Menho, Serena Boyd, and Fernando Gibson, all of TMA, for whom my gratitude knows no bounds. Kudos to the wife and da' brats, of course. To Andy and Scott for letting me talk about this story until even I couldn't take it anymore (get ready for the next one, boys—yeah, you heard me). And to He who wired me up to do all this in the first place.

To paraphrase the greatest band ever, I get by with a lot of help from my friends.

Dedication

To those who know what to throw overboard
when the storms come.

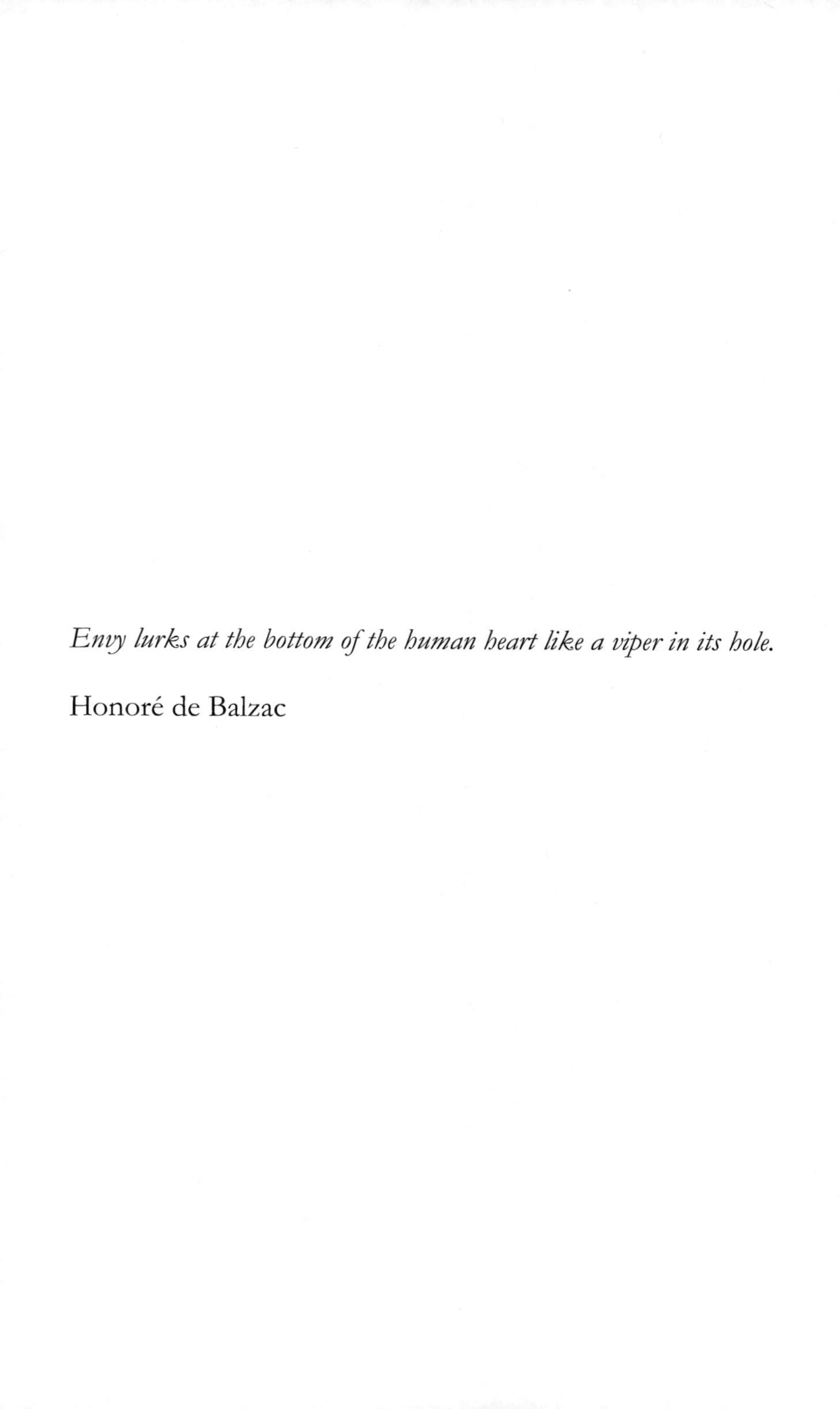

Envy lurks at the bottom of the human heart like a viper in its hole.

Honoré de Balzac

Prologue

Las Vegas, Nevada
October, 1970

CHASE WHEELER WAS SMILING when he entered the busy casino kitchen; he knew what was coming. As soon as the mostly-immigrant staff spotted him, the catcalls began—*Ice cream man! Ice cream man! There he is!*

Chase was tall and gangly and fresh into his twenties, still struggling with acne and the other echoes of adolescence. He waved like the Queen of England at the playful mock-adoration of his co-workers. This had become part of the joke. In his other hand was a bowl of Baskin Robbins banana nut ice cream covered in plastic wrap.

"Don't let it melt, ice cream man!"

"Be sure that spoon is sterile, ice cream man!"

"Remember to tuck the napkin into his shirt, ice cream man!"

Chase laughed. He'd been working at the Desert Inn for just over a year and had come to like these people very much.

"Wish me luck," he shouted back, "I'm going up!" This announcement earned him a round of applause.

He passed into a tiny alcove. There were tall shelves stocked with dry goods on either side, and the door to a service elevator at the back. He pushed the button and waited, his boyish grin fading away. The door slid aside and he stepped in. As it closed again, the busy-kitchen noisiness faded to silence.

He shut his eyes and breathed deep. Then he removed a small key from his pocket and inserted it into the control panel.

He pushed the button for the penthouse, and the car began rattling upward. His heart was pounding. When the door opened again, he saw a young black man of superhuman size, dressed in a guard's uniform complete with sidearm. The brief hallway behind him terminated at a locked door. There was a folding chair tucked in a corner, and a rolled-up magazine lay on the floor next to it.

"Come on," the man said, waving Chase forward with both hands. He had never formally introduced himself, and the uniform bore no nametag, so Chase had given him a nickname—The Big Scary Guard. Chase had learned quickly that anonymity was the law of the land up here, so everybody needed a nickname.

"IDs," Big Scary demanded, and Chase took out his wallet. He was required to produce two—his driver's license and his Desert Inn employee card. He had forgotten the latter once and received no small measure of grief for it. Since then, he left a reminder note on his dresser at home.

Big Scary inspected each ID as if he'd never seen them before; as if Chase didn't come up here every day at the same time with the same bowl of the same ice cream. Big Scary even went so far as to hold the IDs up so he could compare the photos to the actual person. Chase said nothing, just prayed he wasn't transmitting any signals that would expose how nervous he was. Today's visit represented a significant departure from the routine, although no one but Chase and his host knew that.

Big Scary handed the IDs back and turned to the door, unlocking it with a key that was attached to his belt by a retractable wire. He pushed it back and stepped aside so Chase could pass. Then it was closed and relocked per procedure, which always felt like walking into a prison cell at the start of a very long sentence.

The anteroom was nearly as spartan as the hallway. The main furnishings were two well-used desks, both battleship gray. They had rotary phones and were covered with piles of folders and papers, and there were cheap wooden cabinets on the walls above them.

A man was seated at each desk when Chase came in. Both wore conservative business suits, had equally conservative haircuts, and appeared to be in their late thirties or early forties. Just like Big Scary, neither had ever formally introduced himself, so Chase gave them names based on their personalities as well—Jerk A and Jerk B.

"Well, if it isn't the Good Humor Man," the one on the right said. This was Jerk B, and he struck Chase as a classic example of the kind of person who found himself considerably funnier than anyone else does. "Here to make your delivery, Good Humor Man?"

"Yes."

"Did you sanitize the bowl and the spoon as per the boss's directive?" asked Jerk A. He had received the higher designation because he was the older of the pair and appeared to be in charge.

"Yes."

"And that is banana nut? *The* banana nut?"

"Yes." *We have over fifty gallons of it in the freezer downstairs per your boss's orders*, Chase thought. *What other kind would it be?*

"I need to see it."

Chase came forward and held it out. Jerk A looked it over, taking longer than any reasonable person would need to inspect ice cream.

"Exactly eleven ounces?"

"Yes."

"And where's your uniform?" Jerk B asked, now as somber as his partner.

"I'm sorry?" Chase was currently wearing his Desert Inn attire, which bore the casino's logo on the shirt pocket and was made of the most uncomfortable polyester on the planet. "I'm already in my—"

"I mean your Good Humor uniform!" Jerk A shouted, followed by a fresh explosion of laughter. "The one with the little hat!" He slapped the desk repeatedly, consumed by his own comic brilliance. Jerk B permitted himself a tolerant smile.

"I'd better get in there and give this to him," Chase

said, "before it melts."

"Go on," Jerk B said.

There was another door on the opposite side. Just as Chase reached it, Jerk B reminded him to ring the little bell on his ice cream truck when he went in.

The next room wasn't much bigger than the service elevator, and it was lit only by a dim red bulb on the ceiling. It reminded Chase of the darkroom that his Uncle Pete, a professional portrait photographer out in Seattle, had in his basement.

Chase closed the door and temporarily set the bowl on an empty shelf. The one just below it held several cardboard boxes and bottles of isopropyl alcohol. He took a handful of paper towels, dampened them with the alcohol, and wiped down every exposed inch of skin on his body. The towels were then discarded in a small trash can with a foot pedal. The next step was to cover his shoes with a pair of disposable booties, then put on rubber gloves and a dust mask.

When he took the ice cream in hand again, his heart was hammering. He knew it was nothing more than a prop this time. When he opened the second door, the red light shut off automatically, and he found himself enveloped in cool darkness. He stepped inside, shut the door quietly, and waited a moment for his eyes to adjust. There was no source of illumination here, but the heavy shades that had been installed to cover the windows still bore a pale glow from the blazing Nevada sun.

The other physical adjustment he made—one that had become a necessity since that first day—was to breathe through his mouth instead of his nose. The musky stench of human excrement was awful. It was the odor of bus stations and public restrooms and hospital beds magnified exponentially. He had heard that there were rows of glass jars filled with urine lined up against the far wall. But he had no way of knowing this for certain because he had never been over there. In the eleven weeks since he had been given this assignment, he had only been able to determine two things—the centerpiece of the room was a large hospital bed with nightstands on either side, and there was a large television positioned at the foot of the bed for the occupant's entertainment. Chase had come to feel that the occupant in question was, in fact, not only the real centerpiece of the room, but of this entire floor of the Desert Inn, of the hotel itself, of several others in town, and of countless other business interests around the world. Chase thought this because the man who lay not more than ten feet away from him was one of the wealthiest people in human history.

He became aware of the man's slow, wheezy respiration. Then the voice, thin and reedy and still colored by a Texas accent. A voice that had not been heard by the public in decades. The voice of Howard Robard Hughes—

"Chase?"

"Yes sir."

"You brought the ice cream?"

"Yes sir."

"Please set it down on the table here. Set it on the corner nearest to you, with a one-inch margin on both sides of the right angle."

"Yes sir."

"I've laid out a pathway for you."

Chase translated the word 'pathway' as a succession of fresh Kleenex tissues from one of the dozens of boxes that were also supposedly kept in this room. Hughes's fear of germs were already legendary in the media. Chase Wheeler was one of the few people who could provide firsthand testimony to the accuracy of those reports.

The fact that Hughes had gone to the trouble of laying out the tissues not only touched Chase but also told him that Hughes had gotten out of his bed. Chase took this as a very good sign. He had grown to genuinely care about the man with a kind of selflessness that the billionaire's other minders could not fathom. Hughes's fortune meant nothing to him; he had been born on the lower rung of society's ladder and had never known anything else.

His vision reached a point of clarity where he could at least make out the line of tissues. He followed it to the nightstand and set the bowl down. As he tried to position it according to Hughes's wishes, he bumped a glass filled with water. It struck several others, causing a series of silvery notes to ring out.

"Oops—I'm sorry about that, sir."

He estimated that he was no more than a few feet from Hughes now, and the reek of the man's living decay was wretched.

"It's there," Chase said finally, "with the plastic wrap still on it."

This statement, as well as the one that preceded it, was technically a violation of procedure. The rule was that you could not speak to Hughes unless he spoke to you first. At the moment, however, Chase didn't care. The sympathy he felt for the man was overwhelming. He had also gotten the impression that Hughes regarded him differently from the others; a way that was special. When he began with this routine, he knew Hughes had already tried out several others on the kitchen staff. And the reason Hughes had settled on him was because Hughes felt he could trust him. Chase believed this because Hughes had said as much. He was fully aware of Hughes's capacity for ruthlessness. He knew, for example, of the cold-hearted manner in which Hughes destroyed the reputation of Maine politician Owen Brewster, who tried to embarrass him during a Senate wartime investigation. Hughes emerged from the incident unscathed and saw to it that Brewster lost his seat in the next election. In spite of this vivid example of Hughes's power and vindictiveness, Chase felt no real fear of him.

Through the inky darkness, Chase could just see Hughes reach over and touch the bowl of ice cream. His fingers squeaked on the clear plastic.

"Thank you for bringing it, Chase."

"You're welcome."

A long pause followed, segmented only by Hughes's unsteady breathing. Chase had grown used to these random breaks in their discourse. Early on, he thought Hughes was simply drifting in and out of sleep. He had since come to understand that the man followed his own sense of timing and felt no concern for the way it might inconvenience others. It would not have mattered to Chase under ordinary circumstances, for Hughes would have dismissed him after the ice cream was set in place. But the last few visits had been anything but ordinary. There had been additional instructions each time, all of which lead to the final request Hughes made now.

"Did you take care of the things I asked?"

"Yes sir, I did."

"Exactly as I described?"

"Yes."

"And you found a place?"

"Yes. It's in—"

"No, don't tell me. I can't know."

"Yes sir."

Another pause. Then the sound of rustling fabric. Hughes was removing something from under his pillows.

"It's ready. Come and take it, please."

Chase moved forward until his knees made contact with the bed. He groped gingerly through the air until he felt a sheaf of papers. As he went to take them, his fingers brushed over those of his employer. The latter were hard and bony, the skin stretched tight. There was no direct contact because of the rubber gloves. But enough sensitivity remained to make Chase think about the grinning plastic skeleton that hung in the corner of his old high school science class.

"Be careful with it," Hughes said. "You know what it is."

"Yes sir. Your will."

"My last will and *testament*."

"Yes sir."

"It's more important than ever because I don't know how much longer I'm going to be around."

"Please don't say that, sir."

"It's okay, Chase. It comes to all of us eventually."

"I know, but...still."

"Keep it hidden like we discussed and don't say anything to anyone," Hughes told him. "Not even your family."

"I won't."

"And don't you read it, either."

"No sir."

"You won't be safe if you do."

"I won't read it, I promise."

"Some very powerful people are going to be very angry with what I put in there." He cleared his throat before adding, "The same people who've been keeping me here for the last four years."

"I—I'm sorry?"

"The public thinks I've become a recluse, Chase. I guess that's true by all outward appearances. But it's not by my own choice. I'd walk out of here right now if I could. I'm being held captive."

"By who?"

Chase immediately regretted asking this, afraid he'd stepped too far outside the protocol. He braced himself for a scolding, but no amount of emotional fortification could have prepared him for what Hughes said next.

"By some people who are trying to bring this great country of ours down," Hughes replied.

****

At first Chase thought he'd misheard it.

"You think I'm crazy." Hughes said through the darkness.

"No sir."

"Yes you do. You think I'm delusional from all those codeine injections they're giving me, right?"

Chase knew of the rumors about this but had prayed they weren't true. His hatred of the men outside increased a hundredfold now that he had confirmation.

"I have heard about those injections, yes."

"I haven't had a shot in almost two weeks."

"You...you haven't?"

"I've been pretending I have a cold so they won't give them to me. It's too dangerous at my age to receive them if I'm sick. I needed the time to get everything written down. I've been working on it for awhile now, writing and rewriting. I can't remember the last time my thoughts were so clear. But my window of opportunity is closing. They're getting suspicious because no one has a cold for this long."

"Well...no, I guess not."

"You still don't believe me," Hughes said flatly. "I can hear it in your voice. Am I right? I need to know I can rely on you, so I need to know you believe in what I'm saying."

"It's hard because...you know, America—"

"Because we're so powerful? Economically? Militarily?"

"Well...sure."

"Chase, the nation that runs the world changes all the time. Don't make the mistake of thinking any country gets to sit on that throne forever. In 1500 it was Spain, but two hundred years later it was France, under Napoleon. A hundred years after that it was Great Britain. Do you know anything about the Achaemenid Empire?"

"No sir."

"Five hundred years before the birth of Christ, they were the most powerful civilization in history. They had more than fifty million citizens, and their influence stretched from modern-day Turkey and Israel in the west to Pakistan's Indus River in the east. They freed slaves, built roadways, ran a reliable postal system, and most of their citizens were prosperous. They were much more powerful in their day than we've ever been in ours. Yet only the historians remember any of this."

"I've never even heard of them," Chase said.

"Yes you have," Hughes shot back quickly, "But today we call them Iran."

"Oh my God."

"'Oh my God' is right. When it comes to global power, they're not even in the top ten anymore."

"And that could happen to us?"

"It's already happening, and they asked me to be a part of it because of my money and my connections. But I wouldn't do it. I guess this sounds a little corny and sentimental, but I have great affection for this country. I wouldn't have been able to do the things I've done anywhere else but here. My father wouldn't have made his fortune, and I wouldn't have made mine. But the problem with being a great nation is that it stirs up jealousy and resentment everywhere else. Sooner or later, someone gets tired of it and decides to take action."

"And there are people like that doing things to us right now?"

"Yes."

"They sound crazy," Chase said.

"I thought so too. Much too crazy to really accomplish much. But now I'm starting to see things happening out there, things that are going on right under our noses. But we won't realize it until it's too late. The scale of what's been planned...you wouldn't believe it."

Chase suddenly felt sick to his stomach. He no longer had any doubt Hughes was being truthful. The man had never been so lucid and articulate. This was not the eccentric hermit they wrote about in the newspapers. This was someone in full control of his faculties.

"Who are they, Mr. Hughes? And how are they doing all of—"

"There's no time to explain that now, Chase. It's all there in those papers. Please—I'm trusting you."

"You can."

"I hope so. You have to bring them to a probate court immediately after I'm gone."

"Yes...yes sir."

"The court will need to verify the handwriting."

"Okay."

"Hide it now, in your clothes like we discussed."

Chase went folding the pages into thirds, a simple task that his shaking hands made all the more challenging. Then he reached around back, lifted his shirt, and tucked them into his pants. Dropping the shirt again would provide the necessary cover, he hoped.

"I did it."

"Good."

Hughes let out a long sigh. "I guess that's it."

Chase hesitated, feeling the urge to say something more.

As if sensing this, Hughes said in the most defeated voice Chase had ever heard, "Go on, Chase. Take care of this for me."

"Yes sir."

"Thanks."

****

When Chase reappeared, Jerk B said, "If you spend anymore time with him, people'll start to think you're a couple." The stupid grin was back in place. "They'll be wondering when the two of you are going to send out wedding invitations!"

Chase laughed along this time, hoping it would provide the necessary distraction. Jerk A, however, was watching him with a kind of malignant suspicion and seemed to have missed the joke. *They don't like anyone getting too close to him*, Chase thought, and not for the first time. *He's their golden ticket, and they don't want anything to mess that up*. Chase was all but certain the handwritten pages that were tucked in the back of his pants would lay waste to whatever plans these two had made concerning their foreseeable futures. *I have to get out of here.*

He held up the empty bowl. "He still makes me wait while he eats it."

"Yeah? Does he also make you feed it to h—"

"He didn't do that before you started coming," Jerk A said. He leaned forward, his eyes thinning in a prosecutorial glare. "He didn't do that with any of the others before you, either."

Chase looked away, then regretted it. Hadn't he heard on some TV show that breaking eye contact was a sign of guilt?

Then a flash of inspiration struck.

"It was probably because of what I said a few weeks ago."

"And what was that?"

"When I went in with the ice cream, I asked if I should take away the dirty bowl from the day before."

The Jerk twins seemed confused by this revelation.

"I guess it was the word 'dirty' that bothered him. Y'know—the idea that a dirty bowl had been sitting there all that time. So he asked me to stay while he ate, then told me to take the bowl with me when I left."

Jerk B looked to Jerk A in the same way a child looks to a parent for a reaction before they decide on their own. Jerk A, Chase saw with some relief, was mulling over the idea.

"At first I thought it was weird," Chase went on, intuitively understanding that he had to retain control of the conversation if he was to close the deal. "But then I remembered about his fear of germs and all that." He snickered and twirled his finger by the side of his head. "Crazy."

Jerk B didn't wait for his colleague's reaction this time. His eyebrows rose in delighted surprise at this show of impertinence from the lower ranks.

Jerk A, however, maintained his careful scrutiny, apparently operating on the theory that Chase would give a sign of culpability if he waited long enough. Chase had never known such anxiety, and it took all the strength he possessed to maintain a casual bearing.

"Go on," his interrogator said at last, motioning toward the exit with his thumb. "Just get out of here. And going forward, we'll decide if there are to be any changes in procedure."

"Yes sir," Chase said politely.

****

Eight days week later, Las Vegas police went to the top floor to the Desert Inn and found it abandoned, with no indication of where Hughes and his entourage had gone. Five days after that, they opened a missing-persons report on Chase

Michael Wheeler. No one made any connection between the two incidents at the time.

Chase was never found—nor was any kind of documentation concerning the dispensation of Howard Hughes's vast estate following his death in April of 1976.

One

Henderson, Nevada
Present Day

RANDY MILLER MADE a quick left into his kitchen as another bullet zipped by. He went past the refrigerator adorned with his kids' watercolor paintings and school announcements and monthly lunch schedules, sweeping several of these items off the stainless steel surface and sending dozens of plastic ABC magnets clattering to the floor.

As he drew closer to the doorway on the other side, he took note of the silverware drawer. It held several large knives, and for a brief instant he considered going for one. The idea was just as quickly dismissed; there wouldn't be enough time. And somewhere along the farthest reaches of his mind he remembered a movie in which one of the characters had warned against the stupidity of bringing a knife to a gunfight.

A muted cough from the silenced pistol sent another shot within inches of his head and splintered the doorframe. He gasped and dove through it at an angle and let out a wrenched scream when his bare knees slid across the hall carpet.

There was a nightlight in the wall next to an accent able, and he slapped it from the outlet as he scrambled to his feet, casting the hallway in darkness. Then he took off in a mad sprint for the far end, knowing he posed an easy target as long as he remained in such a confined space.

The basement door came up on the right, and he yanked it back to form a barrier, hoping beyond hope that his pursuer would slam into it face first. He thought about going down there, maybe finding something he could use as a weapon. But a quick mental inventory told him there was nothing that would serve that purpose. Then again he wasn't trying to fight this guy—he was trying to lead him out of the house and away from his family. *If it does come to a fight,* Randy thought, *I'll do it.* He was a large, physical individual who, in spite of having an essentially peaceful soul, knew how to use his hands when necessary. But he'd just as soon avoid any such confrontation. He knew why this lunatic was here, and his only objective now was to keep him clear of Jeanine and the kids. He could deal with the other part of it afterward.

The hallway ended in an intersection—to the left was a staircase to the second floor, to the right was the door into the garage. He had already formulated a plan that involved the latter. There was a cordless phone out there. He would grab it and dial 911. He wouldn't even have to say anything—emergency services would trace the location and police would be on their way in minutes. *And if this nut follows me, I'll go out the side door and into the yard while we're waiting.*

Just as he wrapped his hand around the doorknob, however, he heard his wife's first scream. The first coherent thought that squirmed through his fear was, *How did he get up there so fast?* Then he heard the shooter step into the hallway at the far end, and Randy lunged left as three more shots came. Then the kids cried out too, both of them.

He reached the top of the steps and kept going. Allie and Mark's bedroom doors were wide open. Even though Allie was only ten, she already had a well-developed sense of privacy and kept her door closed at all times. Some of the items on her dresser had been knocked to the floor—her jewelry box, several of her stuffed animals, her iPod.... The sight of this drove up Randy's anger until it was level with his trepidation. The very fact that this animal might have violated his little girl's personal space made him feel murderous.

Another shriek—this time it was Allie—told him they were all in the master bedroom. He sprinted to it, pushed the door back, and found them there—his wife and children, cowering in the presence of the most horrifying human being he had ever seen. The man—who was currently living his life under the name of Robert Grant—was bullishly large, the eyes dark and cruel, and his long hair pulled tight and rolled into a ball at the back. For all that, he was also clean-shaven and had a healthy pallor that seemed oddly out of place. Randy had the fleeting thought that this made him seem like a highly successful individual—a successful *criminal*—which was all the more unnerving. Grant held his weapon out as Randy's family clung to each other.

Randy held his hands up, barely aware that he had also begun crying. "Okay, okay! Don't hurt them, please!"

Grant swung his weapon—a nine millimeter—around until it was inches from Randy's nose.

"Where are they?" he said. It was the voice of one whose programming did not include a sense of humor.

"Th-they're not here."

"Where *are* they?" He thumbed the hammer back.

"I swear to you they're *not…here*…."

Grant took a step forward, his face twisted in a snarl, and used the weapon to strike Randy on the side of the head. His wife and children exploded in wails as he went down. Then came a vicious kick to the kidneys. Randy let out a scream and twisted like a worm on hot pavement.

Grant stood over him. "Pay attention."

Randy turned, his face screened with sweat. "Okay…yes."

The gun was aimed again, this time toward someone on the bed. Randy couldn't see who.

"No! Please!"

"You have five seconds to tell me where they are. After that, I start killing your family while you watch. Five…."

"I swear they're not here. I swear it!"

"Four."

"Come on, please! I *swear to God* they're not—"

"Three."

"PLEASE, NO! PLEASE DON'T!" He was sobbing like a child now.

"Two."

"Jesus, *no!*"

"One."

Randy screamed out "*THEY'RE AT MY BROTHER'S HOUSE!!!*" but half of this was cut off by a shot that spat from the barrel with an accompanying flash. There were collective shrieks from the others…and then an icy silence. Randy got to his knees to see which of the three had been taken from him, knowing that if he survived this night he would have the image of the lifeless body burned in his memory for eternity.

He saw the bullet hole, which did not run through any of his loved ones but instead tunneled into the wall a few inches above his wife's head, and his first thought was, *How could he have missed?*

"That's to let you know I'll do it," Grant said conversationally. "Now, are you lying to me about the pages being at your brother's house? Because if I think you are, here's what I'm going to do—I'm going take the pleasure of killing all of you, and I'm going to start by age, youngest first."

Randy Miller had never known such blazing terror. "I swear he has them. "He's a lawyer, and he has a safe in his office. I thought they'd be best kept in there when you…when you started calling."

Grant studied him close. "Even if I believe you, that still doesn't solve the problem we have here."

"What? What do you mean? I don't want the pages anymore. They've been nothing but trouble. You can have th—"

"I'm talking about the four of you."

When the implied meaning sunk in, Randy's level of panic went into the stratosphere. Somewhere in the midst of this rocketing alarm he realized this guy wasn't just a brute—he was a sociopath.

"You're going to kill us all? That's not going to get you the p—"

Grant leaned in and backhanded him across the face, sending Randy spinning to the floor again. A pain brighter than a thousand suns blossomed in his jaw, but a memory broke through it as well—his high school psychology course. At the urging of the class, the normally prim Mrs. Donner had spent one memorable afternoon talking about homicidal tendencies. The kids had never been so absorbed, such was their youth and the naïve comfort of knowing they would surely never encounter anyone like this.

Realizing he was now at the mercy of such an individual—and that the next people to see him and his family would probably be whatever civic officials discovered their bullet-riddled bodies—Randy was overcome by a surprising sense of liberation. *If we're all going down*, he thought, *he is too*.

He looked under the dresser and saw exactly what he prayed he would see—the two squash rackets he and Jeanine had hidden there after they caught Allie and Mark using them in a living-room 'swordfight.'

He got on all fours and let out an agonized moan. Although the pain was still sparkling in his head like fireworks, the moaning was nothing but theater. *Please let this work…oh please God, please let this work....* He swayed a moment, creating the illusion that he was disoriented, and moved closer to the dresser.

Grant said, "I'm sorry, but I have to." Then came the click of the hammer being set into place again.

Randy reached under the dresser and wrapped his fingers tight around one of the handles, then pulled the racket out and brought it up in one fluid motion. It struck Grant's forearm the moment he fired. Randy did not pause to evaluate the results, but rather drew the racket back and swung again. This is where he got lucky—the long side of the oval frame connected perfectly with Grant's mouth, which had formed into a perfect lowercase 'o.' The gun tumbled from his hand as he clutched the point of impact. Randy did not have even a split second to enjoy this bit of good fortune because his attacker recovered quickly and lunged. Randy rolled over, took the gun in hand, and fired off a wild shot of his own. It whistled past Grant's head and shattered the dressed mirror into a million pieces.

Grant turned and raced from the room as Randy kept firing. Drywall exploded in chunks, spraying everywhere. Randy went out into the hallway, fired one more, then screamed, "*I'm calling the police right now!!!*"

He could heard the back door being thrown open, and when he returned to the bedroom he saw his assailant sprinting across the lawn. He considered firing another shot or two, then thought better of it. It was unlikely he could hit the target at this range, and he wanted to preserve whatever ammunition was left in case the animal came back.

He said breathlessly, "Where's my cellphone? We've got to call 911." He kept shifting his gaze from the door to the window, as if Grant might reappear any moment. "Jeanine? The cellphone? Where is—"

He turned and found her holding Allie tight against her chest and sobbing. Randy went cold when he saw the blood spreading rapidly across the child's nightshirt.

Two

JASON HAMMOND STOOD on the sandy margin between the bay and the jagged, vine-tangled palisade at the northern end of his New Hampshire estate. He stood there and wished he was just about anywhere else.

The boathouse, the dock, the zigzagging wooden steps that led up to the rest of the property—all were worn to the point of near dysfunctionality. As someone blessed with more money than he would ever need, he wasn't worried about the financial demands of repairing or replacing these things. It was the emotional aspects that troubled him on this clear, windy afternoon.

He was dressed casually, in jeans and a button-down shirt with the sleeves rolled up. The lagoon-sized portion of the Atlantic Ocean that was trapped in the rock-walled cove behind him gyrated sluggishly, and a few dozen gulls sailed around overhead. One would occasionally swoop down and pluck something out of the water as the others cried out their resentment.

He had a spiralbound notebook in one hand and a pencil in the other. A part of him burned to just make the decisions and be done. Another governed him not to do anything in haste. And underlying all this conflict was the most powerful desire of all—to do nothing. But the only other living occupant on the property had nagged him relentlessly until he committed himself. That was the essence of Noah Gwynn these days—nudging, pushing, pulling, nagging...whatever it took. *We're not related by blood,* Jason thought on many occasions, *but we may as well be. He's the closest things to family I've got left.* And

Noah had been focused on "bringing the estate back into the land of the living," as he put it, for the last month and a half.

Noah believed there were only two approaches. The first was to faithfully re-create what had always been there—have the builders use the same materials and follow the same blueprints that Jason's late father had drawn up long ago. The second was to tear everything down and start fresh—all new materials, all new designs...all new everything.

The latter strategy was the more reasonable for reasons obvious enough. The property would be safer, more durable, fully modernized, better suited for life in the 21st century, etc. And, of course, giving the property a new face would be "…more conducive to focusing on the future," as Noah had said several times. The unspoken caveat there, delivered with the man's usual gift for diplomacy, was *…and letting go of the past.*

Jason looked from one landmark to another—the boathouse, the steps, the dock, back to the boathouse. With the wind blowing his hair every which way, he went over to a large, weather-smoothed boulder and sat down. Even the boulder held memories—he and his family used to set their towels on it after a swim. The sun would heat it like a stovetop, and everything dried quickly. This image brought a flood of others. He had, in fact, been fighting them back them all day. But this time he let them come, and figures began to move before him in a ghost play.

The first was his mother, smiling and radiant as she maintained that rarified balance between girlish and matronly. She wrapped in a terrycloth robe, her face protected by sunglasses and a wide-brimmed hat. Holding her hand was a seven-year-old version of himself, replete with a perfect tan and his normally black hair lightened ever so slightly by repeated afternoons in the sun. He—or, rather, his mother—kept it styled in a Beatlesque moptop, as was acceptable for virtually all small boys. They strolled along the shoreline, examining the soppy border that separated land and sea. They would pause occasionally, and his mother would crouch down to point something out. They would then discuss what they had found, and in a way that never struck the little boy as tiresome or dull. She would cover the natural history—what every creature ate, where it lived, how it related to others in its world, and so on. But this was the concrete, and she also wanted her son to understand the abstract—their delicacy, their inherent beauty, and their value.

Then came an image of Jason's father, from whom he had inherited his lean, athletic build and satiny black hair. Jason was perhaps twelve or thirteen in this vision, which put his father somewhere in his early forties. They were both in bathing suits, t-shirts, and baseball caps. The time had come, Alan Hammond decided, to begin teaching his son how to negotiate the open seas. He had a traditional sloop at the time, a J-24 with a single foresail. They were standing on the dock, and Jason's father was pointing out the craft's every detail. The vocabulary alone was formidable—mast, boom, tiller, winch, chainplate, jibsheet, shroud…. Alan Hammond did not possess his wife's oratorical gift, but the sheer depth of his knowledge kept the boy absorbed. And Jason was excited, not just because he was being groomed for an obvious rite of passage but because he and his father were getting along like best friends. This had not been the case in recent times, for Jason had reached an age where he began to truly understand the scope of his father's wealth and, more pointedly, grow uncomfortable with how his father had acquired some of it. This had led to heated exchanges that often resulted in long periods of silence between them.

From there came the remembrance of the night he spent talking with his sister. He was sixteen, Joan eighteen, and it came at the end of a particularly tense week between him and his father. His mother had been doing volunteer work overseas and was thus unable to her fulfill her customary role as mediator and peacekeeper. This latest quarrel had peaked in a shouting match followed by Jason storming out of the house and coming down here to cool off. Joan had always made a point of remaining neutral during these episodes, but on this evening she surprised her brother by taking up their mother's diplomatic duties.

She sat down a few feet from him on the sand and just listened. After most of the rage had blown out of him, they were able to engage in a real conversation. The topic that night was the conflict between excessive profiteering and staying true to one's beliefs. Jason said he could not resolve it to the point where he was able to accept all of their father's practices. Joan offered her thoughts here and there. Then she got an inflatable beachball from the boathouse, and they rolled it back and forth as Jason's anger gradually tapered off. The subject soon turned to other issues, and by morning Jason felt as though he had undergone an emotional purge.

Tears threatened, as they did so often now. Jason had never been much of a crier, yet no more than a day or two passed without an episode of some kind. He kept the grief to himself, releasing it only when he was certain Noah was nowhere near. He knew Noah loved him, and the feeling was certainly reciprocated. But he couldn't bring himself to share the suffering; not with Noah, not with anyone. Sometimes he wished he could, because the weight of it was unbearable. The emptiness, the confusion, and, worst of all, the longing...the terrible, endless longing. He didn't even realize one person could feel such pain and survive.

He got off the big rock and went to the boathouse. The door opened with a dry creak. Inside was a disorganized mess of fishing poles and rotting nets and styrofoam buoys and crab traps. And there in the corner, deflated and filthy, was the beachball in question.

Like everything else in here—and on the rest of the estate, for that matter—it had not served a useful purpose since time out of mind.

****

"Tell me honestly, how's he doing?"

Noah didn't want to lie to Darren Redeker, friend and neighbor of the Hammond family for decades.

He stood in Jason's office, located on the first floor of the estate's enormous main house and dominated by an L-shaped mahogany work station. It was a cramped former a sitting area that went largely unused by the Hammond family back in the day. There were papers and folders everywhere, and an Apple computer with a massive screen.

Noah fingered open the microblinds to see if Jason was anywhere in sight. "I just don't know, Darren. Some days he seems perfectly fine, but on others...."

"The last time we spoke, you said he was attending services again. But I haven't seen him there lately."

"He *was* going, then he stopped. And he won't tell me why. When I ask him about it, he won't give a direct answer."

"Did something happen?"

"If it did, I certainly wouldn't know." Noah sighed heavily. "I thought he was completely back on track where his faith was concerned. I thought that issue was closed. I guess not."

"Hmm...well, what's he doing with himself otherwise?"

"No idea there, either. I think he's still itching to keep up his role as homegrown superhero. Fighting evil, bringing the bad guys to justice. It makes me very uneasy. I mean, please don't misunderstand—he *is* a superhero in many ways. He's donating more money to charitable causes than his father ever did. He's directed the company to work on new projects that have the sole function of making the world a better place, like child safety devices and advanced medical technologies. And I can't tell you how many times he's read about someone's misfortunes in the newspaper or on the Internet and, like a magician waving his wand, made their problems disappear. And always anonymously, too. He's stubbornly devoted to that crazy idealism everyone else loses when they grow up. When you combine that with his wealth and that big brain of his, he's like a character in some fantasy movie. But this *isn't* a movie. This is real life."

Redeker laughed. "You have to admit, Noah, some of the things he's done have been unbelievable. Michael

Rockefeller, Amelia Earhart, and now the Kennedy thing...wow. Nobody thought the truth behind the assassination would ever come out. Jason did the whole nation a service with that."

"And almost got killed in the process."

"So what would you prefer he be doing?"

"Something that won't put him in the path of danger all the time. Like going back to school and finish up his degree. Go for the Ph. D. and become a professor of history like he talked about before Alan, Linda, and Joanie were killed. When he was a kid, I couldn't get him to shut up about history. Ancient Greece, the Mexican Revolution, the Renaissance, the Gilded Age. Even recent periods like the Sixties fascinated him. I'd love to turn him back to all that."

"Does he do any studying these days?"

"Not really. Not for the reasons he should be."

"That's too bad."

"And if he won't do any of that, I'd like to get him to take more of an interest in the business. His father spent forty years building an industrial empire, and Jason regards it like a Mac machine. Keeping him focused on it is like pulling a mule up a hill."

"Why do you think that is?"

"I think he's trying to avoid the harsh realities he needs to face here. Mainly that his family is never coming back, and that the world is moving on. If he doesn't keep up with it, it's going to move on without him. He has to accept it all and live in the present."

"Is that why you're having him redo the place?"

Noah nodded. "Absolutely. It's just a starting point, but it's an important one. The estate looks exactly as it did on the day they all died. And I think that's what he wants—to keep it as a kind of museum. But that's unhealthy and unrealistic. He *has* to live for today, not yesterday. He can't see the road ahead if he's looking in the rearview mirror all the time."

Noah thought he spotted some movement at the top of the grassy hill that overlooked the inlet. It turned out to be a lone heron strutting around in the late-afternoon breeze.

"A lot of people don't come back from a loss of that magnitude," Redeker said, "Some just fall apart. I've seen my fair share of suffering. And look who I'm talking to—this isn't unfamiliar territory for you, either, considering the loss of your—"

The rest of his comment was cut off by a call-waiting beep. Noah held the phone back and peered over his glasses. He did not recognize the number, although he could tell from the area code that it was somewhere in Nevada. A friend from his Boston youth had moved there a few years back, and they spoke from time to time.

"Darren? I'm sorry, but there's another call coming in. Can I get back to you?"

"Of course. Take your time."

"Thanks."

****

Noah thumbed the FLASH button.

"Hello?"

At first there was nothing but static and road noise, as if the caller was standing near a busy highway.

"Hello?" Noah said again. He gave it a few more seconds, then moved his thumb to the OFF button. Just before he pressed it, a voice came through the speaker—

"Hello?"

Noah tensed at the clear terror in the man's voice. "I'm here," he said. "Who is this?"

"Are you Jason Hammond?"

"No, I'm his personal assistant, Noah Gwynn. Personal assistant, housekeeper, you name i—"

"You have to help us, please. I need to talk to Mr. Hammond."

"All right, who—"

"We really need help, badly."

"Okay, but I can barely understand you."

"Please—" The man paused to take several rapid breaths.

"Who are you?" Noah said firmly. "And where are you calling from?"

More staccato breathing, almost gasping now.

"My name is Stuart Miller. I'm an attorney from Reno, Nevada."

"Okay, Mr. Miller, and how can I help you?"

"My brother, Randy, was attacked the other night. His whole family was. Some lunatic with a gun. My niece was shot."

Miller broke down following this last admission, his cries rising to a childlike pitch.

"Oh no—is she all right?" Noah asked.

"We don't know yet. She's alive, but…." His sobs were segmented by a series of nasal hitches. "We don't know. But we need help. Please, can I speak to Mr. Hammond?"

"He's here, Mr. Miller, but…I'm sorry if this sounds impersonal under the circumstances, but what does your situation have to do with him? Shouldn't you contact the police?"

"We already have. They said they couldn't guarantee our protection."

"Our?"

"I'm part of this, too."

"Part of what?"

There was another pause here while Miller reigned in his emotions. The hiss of nearly three thousand miles and the cacophony of road noises returned.

"I think it has something to do with Howard Hughes's lost will," he said finally.

Noah felt his stomach drop, and the urge to roll his eyes was overwhelming. The words he wanted to say hung there on his lips—*I'm sorry, but Jason doesn't handle such matters anymore*. But as he had been instructed by Jason to pass along all such messages....

"Can you say that again, please?"

"Howard Hughes and his lost will. That's why they were attacked."

"Umm—that doesn't sound quite on the level to me."

"I know it's hard to believe. Trust me, I know. But I can prove it. I can prove that what I'm telling you is the truth."

"How's that?"

"Are you near a computer?"

"Yes…."

Miller instructed him to open the web browser and do a Google search. Eleven articles came up, all from the previous day, and all from legitimate media outlets in the Las Vegas area. A family of four was attacked in their suburban home in the middle of the night. The parents refused to comment on what might have motivated their attacker. Then, after their daughter was treated at a local hospital, they disappeared. The attending emergency-room physician urged them to return because the little girl's condition was far from stable. Regardless, no one had heard from them since. The police were looking.

Noah was still not convinced. Perhaps Miller had seen the same articles and sensed an opportunity. Very convenient, his call. And strange that none of the journalists had mentioned a brother.

But Miller expected this and told him the whole story. By the end, Noah believed him.

And wished he'd never answered the call in the first place.

Three

"I'VE GOT A VISUAL," Jason said from behind the controls of his Gulfstream roughly six hours later. Excitement was surging through him like a magic elixir. "Just like in those pictures online—a little outpost in the middle of the Nevada desert. The middle of absolutely nowhere."

"Okay." This was Noah's voice in the headphones.

"It doesn't look so bad. All those lights twinkling in the night. You know what it reminds me of? Those government stations tucked away in New Mexico. Like Area 51, with all the alien bodies they keep in the freezers."

"Right."

Henderson Executive Airport sat eleven miles south of downtown Las Vegas, in a vast flatland nestled in the McCullough mountain range. The location was chosen in 1969 specifically for its remoteness. Although always a public facility, it was originally intended to appeal to corporate and private flyers rather than any of the major airlines. It was purchased by Clark County in 1996, which invested more than $30 million in upgrades.

"Jason, are you sure you want to do this?"

"I'm sure."

"There's still a lot that needs to be done back here."

"The estate's not going anywhere."

"And this security process these people want you to go through...I have a very bad feeling in my gut. Maybe you should come back and let the police sort it out."

"You always get a bad feeling in your gut," Jason said. He checked the gauges again—altitude, airspeed, fuel pressure, water temperature—and set a hand on the throttle. "I agree it's a little unusual. But I can understand their reasoning."

Noah sighed. "You know what to do if you get into trouble, right?"

"Yes, of course."

As he drew closer, he saw that there were only two roads in and out of the area.

"And what if the emergency plan doesn't work?"

"Then I'll have to improvise."

Another voice crackled through the headphones—a male's, flat and businesslike.

Jason said, "Noah, that's ground control. They're giving me the green light to descend, so I have to go."

"No chance of you changing your mind?"

"Nope."

****

After a landing that was smooth and uneventful, Jason taxied to the assigned hangar, grabbed his backpack, and went to the arrival desk to take care of some routine paperwork.

He exited the terminal twenty minutes later and headed toward the parking lot. The night air was cool, crisp, and eerily still. No crickets chirping like those along the overgrown fringes of the estate. A coyote did howl in the distance, and under different circumstances Jason would've found this bit of desert kitsch amusing. He checked his watch—2:14 AM.

Following the instructions Stuart Miller had given, he walked through the parking lot until he reached the corner farthest from the terminal entrance. There were only a few cars out this far, and no other people in sight. He found the license plate in question on a small black sedan. There was nothing noteworthy about the alphanumerics—DR7 546. They were printed over a simple graphic of the snow-capped Sierra Mountains. The word 'NEVADA' ran in capital letters along the top, and the motto 'Protect Lake Tahoe' was at the bottom. He went to the front passenger door, saw no one inside, and tried the handle.

Locked.

The first pangs of nervousness began. The instructions had been to open the door, get inside, and wait.

Maybe it was the back door, he thought, but at the same time he knew this was nonsense. Stuart Miller had been very clear on each step.

The back door was also locked, as were the two on the driver's side. He leaned down and peered through the windows. The contents of the vehicle were as unremarkable as the plate number—a styrofoam Dunkin Donuts container in the cup holder, a pair of red plastic dice hanging from the rearview mirror, and a nylon gym bag in the back seat, unzipped and pulled open. A pair of white sneakers and a squash racquet were visible.

"Mr. Hammond?"

Jason turned and found a stranger about ten feet away. He was tall and lanky, with the kind of longish, weather-worn face common to people who have spent their lives exposed to the elements. He didn't have a cowboy hat, but the rest of the outfit fit the image—dusty boots, faded jeans, big silver belt buckle, plaid shirt, and a denim jacket with sherpa lining. Then there was the handgun. It did not have pearl handles or a cylinder that could be spun by the flat of the hand. This was a modern weapon—Jason recognized it as an IMI Desert Eagle to be exact. He also knew it was capable of blowing most of his torso into bloody fragments with one shot.

"That's me," he said. It came out more like a croak, as his throat had turned as dry as an old flue. "Can I help you?"

"Come with me, please."

"Umm…this wasn't part of the plan."

"There's a new plan. Come with me."

The man stepped back and waited. With little choice, Jason went. As he walked forward, he searched for security cameras. There were none. *Did this guy remove them? Shoot them from their perches before I landed?*

"The gray minivan," the gunman said, "over there."

It was another few spots away; Jason had passed it en route to the sedan. He did not notice then what seemed so significant now—there were two other figures inside; one in the front passenger seat, the other behind the wheel.

The gunman guided him to the big door on driver's side. Then he told him to put his hands on it and spread his legs. Following this, he proceeded to frisk Jason from head to toe.

When he was finished, he said, "Okay, get in."

Jason did as he was told. The interior light, he noticed, did not go on when the door slid back. Of further concern was the fact that the van was parked between two other large vehicles—a pickup truck on one side and a jitney on the other—in an unlit section of the lot. This made it impossible to clearly see any physical details of the other two men.

He got into the seat, set his backpack on the floor, and reached for the belt. Then he saw that the man in the front passenger seat had turned around and was also holding a weapon.

"If you're going to kill me now, I'm not going to bother buckling up," Jason said flatly.

"No," gunman number two said, "strap in." He had a bushy mustache that went down to the edge of his chin and scraggly blonde hair that poured over his shoulders. *He looks like one of the Allman Brothers.*

The man who had led him from the black sedan got into the seat beside him.

"Give me your cellphone, please," he said.

"Shouldn't we get acquainted first? You already know my name. It doesn't seem fair that I don't any of know yours."

"We'll do that later," the driver impatiently, speaking up for the first time. Jason looked to the rearview mirror and found the most sinister set of eyes he had ever seen. "If it's even necessary," he added, "which it may not be."

Nice welcoming committee, Jason thought. *Charles Manson behind the wheel, the lost Allman brother sitting next to him, and the Lone Ranger to my right.*

Moving slowly, Jason reached into the pocket of his windbreaker and removed his phone." Do you mind my asking why you want it?"

The Lone Ranger retrieved it gingerly, never taking his gaze away from his guest, and set it into the pocket of his own jacket.

"We just don't want you making any unauthorized calls."

"I see."

"And the backpack," Charles Manson said.

"I'm on it," the Long Ranger replied. He lifted it into his lap and unzipped all the compartments. "There's a laptop, spiralbound notebook, some apples, an iPad, and papers from the flight."

"What about...anything else."

"No—" More digging around. "I don't see anything like that."

"I have a wallet on me, too," Jason said, "if that's what you're looking for."

"No, we don't need to s—"

"Yeah, let's have a look," Manson said.

The Lone Ranger set the backpack down in the last seat, well beyond Jason's reach. Then he held out his hand. "Okay, let's have it."

As soon as Jason gave it to him, it was passed to Manson. Jason could not see what the latter was doing with it, but his heart began hammering. There was over two thousand dollars in cash and a half-dozen credit cards with sky-high limits. He could hear Noah screaming in his mind—*Are you crazy?! Get out of this! Push the button! PUSH IT!*

Manson snapped the wallet shut and handed it back. Jason went through it quickly—everything was there—and replaced it in his pocket.

"Okay, so you're not robbing me and you're not shooting me. So what's the plan? I don't want to sound like an ungrateful guest, but unless you're going to do a colon search next, I'm assuming we're not just going to sit in this parking lot all night."

Manson started the engine, and the lost Allman brother opened the glove compartment.

"You need to put this on," he said, holding up what appeared to be an ordinary sleepmask.

"Again, may I ask why?"

"Because you can't see where we're going."

"Of course not."

He took the mask and slipped it over his head. Never a good sleeper, he had tried several of these over the years. Most were useless in that they did not shape themselves to the natural contours of one's face, allowing light to shine around the edges. This one, however, had fine aluminum ribbons running under the silky material, just pliable enough to be formed and reformed, yet stiff enough to hold their position.

"Pardon me, Mr. Hammond," the Lone Ranger said, "but I have to do this…." He pressed gently along the aluminum strips to assure a tight fit. "Please don't try to remove it during the ride. I don't want to have to handcuff you, but I will."

"Oh, don't worry about that," Jason said. "I love surprises."

****

No one spoke during the journey, which, in Jason's estimate, took about an hour and a half. Someone switched on a radio at one point and surfed from station to station until he found a classic rock channel. The missing Allman brother mumbled along to Steely Dan's 'Josie' in a rough baritone. *Turns out he doesn't have such a great voice after all*, Jason observed, *which explains why they never put him in the* group. The guy also didn't know all the lyrics, so he filled in the gaps indiscriminately.

They pulled onto a gravel driveway and stopped. The engine was shut off and the doors opened, filling the interior with a frosty gust. Jason was taken under the left arm and led out. Then someone else set a hand on his right shoulder. A fairly unsavory memory flashed through Jason's mind—an online video clip he once saw of a blindfolded Pakistani man being led into a plain room, where a hooded executioner waited with a scimitar. According to the captions, which were translated from Urdu via English subtitles, he was being punished for aiding an American intelligence team in their hunt for a local terrorist leader. After a ridiculously theatrical pronouncement by the swordsman, the captive's head was separated from the rest of him.

After about thirty steps, the Lone Ranger—Jason was quite familiar with his voice now—said, "Watch it, there are stairs here." Jason kicked out cautiously and bumped the first one. Then he went up, a door was unlocked with a key on a ring of many others, and he was led inside. What hit him first was the distinct odor of home cooking—chicken specifically, rubbed with a variety of herbs and now slow-roasting in an oven.

He was guided to the right (carpeted room), then left (hardwood floor), then left again (narrow hallway, judging by the acoustics), and finally right again (more carpeting). He was put in a chair with armrests and told to wait. Then a door closed behind him without being locked.

"Mr. Hammond?" This was a new voice, although not altogether unfamiliar, "I'm going to take the mask off now. You might want to cover your eyes."

Stuart Miller removed the sleepmask gently, staring down at his guest with genuine concern. The room was, as Miller had implied, copiously lit. An overhead fixture burned several bulbs, and there were lamps on three different tables. There was, however, no natural light—as Jason's eyes adjusted, he saw that the windows had been covered with heavy blankets.

Miller was plain-looking enough—medium height and build, conservatively cut brown hair, wire-rimmed glasses. He wore a decent suit with the tie pulled loose and the top button undone. He could've passed for a corporate accountant or a school administrator as easily as an attorney, save for the haggard, unshaven complexion and a selection of stains on his shirt.

But it wasn't Stuart Miller that gripped Jason's attention—it was the couple sitting on the couch directly across from him. Randy and Jeanine Miller looked as though they had been dragged through the bowels of Hell. On the surface, they appeared to be the textbook working-class couple. He was in jeans, a plaid shirt, and a nameless brand of brown suede shoes that would need replacing in a month or two. She was in cotton Capris, a pink t-shirt, white sneakers, and ankle socks. These, Jason sensed, were everyday Americans, fundamentally honest and decent, moderately educated, and devoted to their domestic agenda. They did everything together, from Friday night movies at home with a big bowl of popcorn to weekend road trips with the kids. Jason sensed all this not in Jeanine Miller's relatively inexpensive jewelry or the grease under her husband's fingernails. It was in the way they clung to each other like two refugees, the dark half-moons that fatigue and sleeplessness had drawn under their eyes, and the crushing distress that dogged their expressions. All signs of the strain that would naturally come to ordinary people who found themselves far removed from their comfort zone.

Randy cleared his throat.

"We're, uh…we're sorry we had to bring you here this way." His eye contact was sporadic, and his hands were red from the constant wringing. "Please understand that we didn't feel we had a choice. We know about you, but we don't *know* you."

"I understand."

"This man…this nut…." He looked up at nothing in particular as a tear broke free and rolled along his cheek. "He's been after me for awhile. Now he's after *us*."

Stuart stepped in and handed him a tissue. Randy patted his face with it, then blew his nose.

"I'm sorry, I'm sorry."

"It's all right," Jason said. "Why don't you tell me what happened? I read the articles online, but I'm sure there were plenty of details left out."

"Yeah, okay." He took a deep breath to compose himself. "It was the other night, about two in the morning. I got up to go to the bathroom, and then I went into the kitchen to get a glass of water because my throat was dry. Our kitchen is at the back of the house, and when I went to put the glass in the sink, I saw through the window that someone was running toward the house in the backyard. We have a motion-sensor light back there, and it flicked on. The intruder was enormous, and he already had his gun out." Randy went back to his hand-wringing. "I knew immediately who he was and why he was there. I mean, I didn't know his *name*...but I knew who he was right away."

"The man who'd been calling you about the Hughes pages you found?"

Randy nodded. "That's right."

"Then what happened?"

"He went onto the deck, shot through the lock on the back door, and came inside."

"Did you try to confront him?"

"No. I don't keep a gun in the house, so I knew I wouldn't have a chance. I decided instead to let him see me—I knew it was a risk, but it was the only way—and then try to lead him back out again. That way, he wouldn't go near…he wouldn't get upstairs to…to..."

Randy covered his face and sobbed like a child. His wife put an arm around his back and held him tight as her own tears streamed out.

"I think your brother told me the rest," Jason said gently. "You don't need to repeat it."

"Thank you."

"Before we talk any more about the papers, I hope you don't mind my asking, but how is your daughter's condition?"

Randy took his hands down. His face was damp and pink. "She's uh…she's…."

Jason's heart stopped. *Please don't say she's died. Please, no….*

"She's stable at the moment," Stuart said, resuming the role of family spokesman, "but...."

"But what?"

"She needs to return to a hospital in case there are further problems. In case the wound develops an infection or something."

Jason looked back to the parents, who now appeared to be on the verge of a breakdown. In that instant, he saw it all.

"You can't go back because he's looking for you," Jason said, and it wasn't a question. "This lunatic—he's been searching for you. Is that it?"

Randy nodded.

"How do you know this? How are you sure?"

"I do personal injury law," Stuart said, "so I have contacts in all of the local hospitals. This lunatic's been calling around, asking about Randy and Jeanine. Pretending he's a friend or family member or whatever."

"Does anyone have any idea who he is?"

"No. He never shows up in person. Just makes the calls."

"And where is your niece now?"

Stuart looked away.

"Stuart," Jason demanded, "where is she?"

"She's here."

"In this house? Right now?"

"Yes."

"*What*?!"

"I know."

Jason turned back to the parents. "She needs professional care! A gunshot wound is nothing to mess with."

"I know," Randy said. "Believe me, I know. But we can't…I don't want to take the chance. If we expose ourselves…."

"All right, I think I can help you here. I have a friend named Noah. He's the one Stuart spoke with when he first called. I can have him—"

Randy was already shaking his head. "No, we can't."

"Why not?"

"Because we don't *know you*, Mr. Hammond. We can't trust anyone right now. How do we know you aren't—"

Jason put a hand up. "Listen, I could've had the police here any time I wanted." He snapped his fingers. "Just like that, I could've had them storm this house and take all of you into custody."

With the mildest touch of arrogance, Stuart said, "Come on, you were frisked, your cellphone battery was removed, and your backpack was taken from you. How could you—"

"Do you have the phone?"

"What?"

"My cellphone. Do you have it?"

"Well...yes."

"All right, get it out."

"I don't think I should give you—"

"You don't have to give it to me, just get it out. I want to show you something."

Stuart took the phone from his pocket and held down the power button.

"It's on."

"All right. Now watch."

Jason held out his left hand, palm down. There was a large class ring on the fourth finger, gold with a red stone. With his other hand, he pressed the stone twice. Each time there was a muted click.

"Now wait," he said. The phone rang seconds later.

Stuart—"What the heck?"

"You'll want to give that to me," Jason said. "Believe me, you don't want to let it go to voicemail."

Stuart did as he was told. Jason flipped the phone open and put it on speaker.

"Hello Noah."
"What's happening?"
"All's well at the moment."
"You're in one piece?"
"I am."
"We're they rough on you?"
"No."
"How's the little girl?"
"We're discussing her right now, so let me call you back."
"Call me back?"
"Yeah. Just give me a minute. I'll explain later."
"Okay."
Jason set the phone on his knee and pointed to the ring. "This is part of a new product line the company is developing. 'Panic Jewelry' we're calling it. It's intended mostly to minimize child abductions, but anyone can use it."
"Wow," Stuart said.
"I'm not a spy for the government or a hired thug like the guy who's trying to get the Hughes pages from you. I have no agenda and no allegiance to any organization. It's just me, guided by what I hope turns out to be a fairly accurate sense of right and wrong."
He rose and went to the other side of the room, where he sat on the coffee table in front of Randy and Jeanine.
"I believe I can arrange for your daughter to get the medical care she needs. And no one will know about it—everything will be anonymous, and she will be protected. You all will. But you're going to have to trust me. Can you do that?"
Randy and Jeanine Miller looked to each other, wordless lines of communication buzzing between them. Then Jeanine looked to Jason and nodded.
"Yes," she said, reaching out and taking his hand as the tears began anew. "Please help us."
Jason smiled. "I will."

He called Noah back, and they worked out the arrangements for about fifteen minutes. Then he replaced the phone in his pocket and turned to the others.

"Okay, it's all set. An ambulance will be here in about an hour. It will take all of you to a private care facility, where your daughter will be listed under a false name. It'll be a male name for better cover. There will be some other bogus information as well—eightysomething years old, born in another state, different medical condition, and so on. Not that any of the paperwork will be seen by the public. But if it does, the odds of someone figuring out the truth behind the lies are pretty slim."

"How can we trust the people at this place?" Randy asked.

"They deal with high-profile figures all the time—actors, athletes, politicians. Discretion is part of their business. If they sold anyone out, they'd've been shut down long ago."

"What about the insurance company?" Stuart said. "They'll have to know—"

"There won't be any insurance company involvement."

"What?"

"The bills will be taken care of."

"By whom?" Randy asked. Then his eyes widened. "No, Mr. Hammond, no. We can't ask—"

"You didn't ask, so don't worry about it. Besides, it's already done. It's in motion and can't be stopped."

"Please, Mr. Hammond, at least let us—"

"You can call me Jason, and it's really okay."

Randy Miller stared at him, lips pressed together hard. Then he threw his arms around him in a hug that was so abrupt it almost qualified as an assault.

"Hey, easy there," Jason said, smiling and hugging him back. "People will talk."

****

Stuart gave Jason his backpack and led the group into a small, elegantly furnished dining room. Cold water bottles were procured from the kitchen, and everyone sat.

"Okay," Jason began, opening his MacBook, "since we've got limited time, let's talk about these pages. Randy, please tell me everything you can remember—how you got them, how this guy came to know about them, the whole story."

Randy said it began in November of 2004, when he was working on a demolition crew in Las Vegas. The Desert Inn was owned by Vegas magnate Steve Wynn, who wanted to raze the remaining tower in order to build a larger and more modern resort called Le Rêve.

Randy was alone on the top floor one afternoon when he entered the suite occupied by Hughes from Thanksgiving of 1966 until almost exactly four years later. Hoping to find some copper piping or other valuables, Randy broke away pieces of the drywall and eventually found a stash of crumpled legal paper. Smoothing them out, he examined the scribblings—which included aeronautic diagrams, large financial figures, and references to dozens of notable people—and wondered if Hughes was the author. Some quick Internet research to conduct handwriting comparisons convinced him that the sheets were genuine. In time, Randy also came to believe there were details about a will.

He knew the pages were worth something on the basis of Hughes's authorship alone. But he was earning good money in those days and decided to hold off selling them, feeling that their value would only increase over time. So he kept them in a safe in his basement, where he planned to let them sit until it came time to one day fund his children's educations.

Then came the financial crash of 2008 and the many years of agonizing hardship that followed. In 2006, Randy had achieved his lifelong dream of launching his own small construction business. By 2010, however, he had lost over 70% of that business. He was forced to release half his workforce and reduce the rest to part timers. But even with these emergency measures, drastic action was required to stay afloat by 2014, so he made the agonizing trip to the basement of his dream home—for which he was barely covering the mortgage—and retrieve the Hughes pages. He scanned the three that appeared to be in the best condition, wrote up a brief description, and launched a separate eBay auction for each.

The reaction was immediate and overwhelming. Bidding wars broke out, driving the price beyond even his wildest hopes, and emails began pouring into his inbox. Some offered generous sums if he would end the auction early and sell the pages in private. Others wanted to know where they came from and how he had acquired them. And a few asked if he had any more that he hadn't listed yet.

"I posted the answers to these questions right on the auction site," Randy said glumly. "I know now that that was my biggest mistake. A few days later, reports about the pages started to show up in the media. They were on the Internet first, then in newspapers. After that, a few local television stations here in Nevada reported it."

"And there were other reports on television in Texas," Stuart added, "all speculating the same thing—whether or not the pages had anything to do with Hughes's estate."

"Hughes was born and raised in Houston," Jason said, "so that's understandable."

"That's when I started getting scared," Randy said. "I thought about closing the auctions and letting everything cool down. But I needed the money badly, and the bids kept going up."

"How high?"

"I set the starting price at five hundred. I thought that was too much, but I figured I'd begin there and see what happened. On the last day, all three were over a thousand. And then a bid came in the last minute of all the auctions—*three thousand dollars each*."

"Someone wanted them pretty bad," Jason said. "And I think we all know who it was."

Randy nodded. "The guy calls me on my personal cellphone after the auction closes—I still can't figure out how he got the number—and wants to know about the other pages. I said I didn't want to sell them in a single lot because I'd make more by auctioning them off individually. But he kept pushing, saying 'Name your price, name your price.' Between that and all those news stories, I realized I had something pretty big. I should've just taken his offer and been done with it. But I was desperate to make as much as I could. And I was curious, too, so I went on the Internet and began reading about the battle concerning Hughes's estate following his death."

"I'll bet you were stunned."

"Totally blown away," Randy said, sweeping his hands in the air for emphasis. "Thousands of people were involved—relatives, business associates, judges, lawyers, the IRS...."

"Everybody wanted a piece of the action," Stuart said.

"People who hadn't been in contact with Hughes for decades came forward with their hands out," Randy went on. "There were billions of dollars at stake. And yet..."

"He didn't leave a will behind," Jason said.

"That's right. I thought maybe there was something about a will in those pages, so I began reading them more closely. And when I looked at some of the scribble from that perspective, a lot of it wasn't scribble anymore. A lot of it began making sense."

"Was there anything signed?" Jason asked. "Like a formal declaration page with a signature and date?"

"No, but a lot of the stuff he wrote down—it had to be for a will. It's the only explanation."

"So what did you do then? Did you try to sell the other pages?"

"No. By this time, the guy who won the first three auctions was calling me every day, sometimes four and five times. I finally got sick of him and told him I'd get the cops involved if he didn't cut it out. That's when he started getting nasty."

"At this point," Stuart cut in, "we just thought he was some rich nut who collected Howard Hughes stuff. Someone who wasn't used to hearing 'no' for an answer."

"And then the threats began," Randy continued. "He started by saying he'd ruin me financially, which was pretty funny considering how close I was to being broke already. And I figured it was all a bluff anyway, just something guys like that said. A grown-up version of a temper tantrum. But then he called and read off my bank account numbers, credit card numbers, recent transactions, everything."

"Unbelievable," Jason said, shaking his head.

"At this point I was more angry than scared, which was *also* dumb. Manly pride, I guess. Anyway, I finally told him I was going to call the police and get a lawyer."

"That's when he decided to pay you a visit, right?"

Jeanine Miller reached over and took her husband's hand. She wasn't crying anymore, but she was close.

"Right," he said.

****

Jason spent the next twenty minutes on the phone, his Bluetooth headset tucked into his ear. He worked at the laptop at the same time, navigating through several sites.

When the call was over, he said to the others, "I had Noah contact some people we know at eBay. As I suspected, the account that thug opened in order to place the bids was created through a proxy server for anonymity. They weren't able to trace its origin, and it hasn't had any activity since. No traces, no footprints, no trail. Not surprising." He turned directly to Randy and Jeanine. "I'm convinced at this point that you're dealing with more than one person, and that pretty powerful. I can all but guarantee it's not some screwball with a fetish for Howard Hughes collectibles. If I had to make an educated guess, I'd say that punk was acting on behalf of someone who stood to lose a great deal if a genuine Hughes will suddenly surfaced."

"And who might that be?"

"Well, that's part of the problem," Jason said. "All those people you mentioned before—politicians, business associates, relatives—it could be any of them. Or a combination thereof. When there's money like this involved, pretty much anything goes. But the most likely culprit or culprits are the remaining Hughes heirs. They potentially have the most to lose, namely their entire fortunes."

"So what's the next step?"

"I think it's time you showed me the pages. I assume you've got them with you?"

Stuart looked uncertain, but Randy didn't hesitate—"Yeah, let me get them." He was out of his chair before his brother had a chance to protest. He returned moments later with a large leather portfolio.

"All forty eight are in there."

Jason felt a tingling throughout his body as he took the portfolio in hand. He knew it wasn't appropriate under the circumstances to be so charged up, but he couldn't help it.

Stuart said, "Randy, don't you think—" but was immediately cut off.

"I know what you're going to say, and don't bother. I just want them out of our lives."

Jason could sense they'd had this argument before. "If these turn out to be real," he said, "and I'm sure they are, I'll give you the three thousand apiece for them that you were supposed to get, for a total of a hundred and forty-four thousand. In fact, I'll round up to a hundred and fifty just to keep it neat. Will that settle the matter?"

Stuart looked at his brother with the faintest trace of a smile. "You can't ask for much more than that!"

Randy shook his head. "That's...unbelievable."

Someone stuck their head into the doorway that separated the dining room from the kitchen. It was the Lone Ranger.

"The ambulance is here," he said.

Jeanine rose and gave Jason a kiss on the cheek.

"Thank you for everything."

"You're welcome. Take good care of that little girl."

"I will."

Randy put his hand out for Jason to shake. "I just don't know what to say."

"Don't worry about a thing. It's my problem from here on."

"I hope you don't live to regret it the way I did."

Jason nodded. "Me too."

****

Now it was just him and the lawyer.

Stuart said, "You're a pretty amazing guy."

Closing his laptop and slipping it into his backpack, Jason replied, "Just trying to inject a little justice into an unjust world." He put the portfolio in the knapsack and zipped it shut.

"Can I give you a lift back to the airport, or perhaps somewhere else?"

"That depends—do I have to wear a blindfold again?"

"I think we can go without it this time."

"Good."

As Jason started toward the door, Stuart stopped him by placing his hand on his chest.

"Look, we both know this isn't really where it's going to end for my brother and his family. The people who are after those papers will find them sooner or later. So I'm going to ask you just one favor, and I'll give you anything you want in return."

"What's that?"

"Nail these animals before they nail us."

Jason saw in Stuart Miller's eyes the kind of restrained rage that is borne from a combination of boundless love and white hot terror. A rage he knew all too well.

He smiled and said, "You bet I will."

Four

THERESA RICHTER STARED into space for a time, her mind working. Sunlight slanted through the blinds, illuminating the large Nevada state seal stitched into the carpet. On the other side of the desk, a smallish, elegant woman of Asian descent sat watching her.

"I should keep my distance on this," Richter said, "don't you think? This new business about Howard Hughes's will?"

"I really don't have any opinions on it at this point. Still too many unknowns."

"Oh come on, Kelli, you've been my most trusted advisor all these years. In so many ways, I owe my political career to you."

"No no...."

"Yes yes. Come on, be straight. Give me a 'heavy dose of reality,' as you like to say. Do you see any trouble here?"

The woman sat thinking, her hands together in an A-shape in front of her delicate lips.

"Is there anything in the will that could hurt you?" she asked.

"I don't believe so."

A nasty feeling churned in Richter's stomach; this was the first time she'd ever lied to Kelli Nashamura. Lying to her constituents from time to time made her uncomfortable enough, but lying to the woman who'd given her so much and asked for so little was sickening. *Then again, maybe it's not a lie after all,* she reminded herself. *The truth is that I really don't know.*

"Howard and I got into it a few times in the early days of my career," Richter said. "I was just starting out and wanted to prove myself, and he was vying to become Vegas's heir apparent, buying up every property he could get his hands on. I did a few things, not strictly by the book, to get in his way. Things that helped me move up the food chain. I know Howard was furious about some of those things, and he could be quite vindictive."

"Everyone does things like that at the start, Reese." This had been Nashamura's pet name for her for years. "We can whitewash all that if need be, turn the public's attention to his mental state at the time. But could there be anything *really* bad in there?"

Richter shook her head, relishing the opportunity to be completely honest with her again. "Like did I sell heroin to schoolchildren in order to finance my first campaign? No, nothing like that."

"Okay, good."

"But if Howard really did leave evidence behind of my wrongdoings, then there goes the sterling reputation we've worked so hard to create. And right after that, the support and my funding is out the window, even at this late stage of the game. Once all that's gone, I'm—"

Nashamura's hand appeared. "Stop right there."

"Hmm?"

"That's never going to happen to you."

"How can you be so sure?"

"Because I won't let it."

"You can stop the will from being found?" Richter asked.

"I'm just talking about *you.* You're not going to lose anything. I'll see to that personally, whatever the cost in time, money, and energy."

"I can't allow you to do that."

The hand again, waving this time. "We're not going to debate it. As long as you still want the future we've been building all these years, I'm going to see that you get it."

Richter shook her head. "I'll truly never understand why you're doing all this for me."

Nashamura leaned forward. "I can't run for the presidency in this country because I wasn't born here. But because of my inherited wealth and power, I can have an impact on who does. I believe that this nation, for all its flaws, is the greatest on Earth. The very concept of democracy is magnificent. And yet, how many women have held its highest office? Not one. We came so very close in 2016...so very close. But as I always say—"

"Close isn't close enough."

"That's right. You know I'm not some ax-grinding feminist, but I do believe that the right woman in the White House would bring a fresh perspective that this country desperately needs."

"And you have never moved off your position that I'm that woman."

Nashamura appraised her. "Have *you*?"

"There are days when I admit my confidence wavers." Richter smiled. "A *little*."

"It's normal to have self-doubt from time to time. Perfectly normal. But you have always loved power, Reese. I didn't have to know you in your early days to see that. Am I right?"

"Yes, true."

"And you are highly intelligent."

"I...yes, I am."

"And it would be safe to say your hands are relatively clean in comparison to others in this business?"

"For certain."

"And your heart—you believe your heart is in the right place where the future of America is concerned?"

"I believe I have a vision for America that could lead us into our next age of greatness."

"Then what else matters?"

"It's not my only motivation, though. And you know that. I also want to cleanse my soul of some of the things I did early in my career." She grinned. "This business hasn't completely eradicated my conscience."

"That's because, deep down, you're a decent human being. That probably comes from your background. You started off with nothing in life. Struggling through poverty either destroys you or it makes you stronger. Maybe you weren't penniless like me, but you didn't have much."

"My mom was a homemaker, my dad was a plumber. Both were alcoholics, and neither knew how to hold onto a dime."

"And I used to sleep in the forest, eat things that crawled on the ground, and wash myself in a stream. And yet, look at us now—I own several international businesses, and you're the governor of Nevada."

"Not bad."

Nashamura leaned forward. "You're on the road to the top, Reese. I've seen it before, so I recognize it. Don't be self-conscious about your humble beginnings, because the rest of the world will be bowled over by them. It's the classic rags-to-riches story, and it really only happens here. It's a strength, not a weakness. And when the nomination comes around next week, it's your name they're going to call. I'll make sure of that. Your popularity ratings are already unprecedented; more than sixty-five percent in some parts of the country. If we do everything right, it'll be an afternoon stroll to the White House."

Richter considered this for a moment, then said, "How wonderful that would be."

Nashamura shook her head. "No—how wonderful it *will* be."

Five

THE MAN THE POLICE wanted in connection with the assault on the Miller family stood in front of a cracked and spotted bathroom mirror in the Starlight Motel. The Starlight was located a few miles from the Strip, in a part of Vegas that law enforcement generally avoided. They combed the area the day before, but nobody seemed to know anything. That's why he chose to hide out here. Everyone had their secrets, so they knew the value of keeping their mouth shut.

He had already cut his hair—the ponytail was history, and what remained was respectably short around the sides. Now he went about putting the finishing touches on the new color, which was a much lighter shade of brown with red highlights. He set the applicator down, turn his head left and right, and decided it looked okay. It would be another few minutes before he could rinse out the excess, so he used the time to shave off his goatee. He felt no emotion toward this radical alteration of his appearance; he'd done it many times.

He cleaned up thoroughly, stuffing the evidence into a plastic bag and tying it tight. It would be dropped in a random dumpster later. Then he took a long shower, soaping and washing off twice. He towel-dried the new hair and got back in front of the mirror. The style would be simple now—swept back at an angle on top and minimalistic on the sides. Very collegiate, very nonthreatening. It took several attempts to get it just right. Then came the colored contacts, eclipsing his natural gray with a modest hazel. Last were the glasses. He had several pair on hand and ultimately settled on round rimless. Now a stranger stared back at him. An ordinary man, a dad perhaps, with some sort of rivetingly dull white-collar job. He wondered if he was a bit on the large side for this role, but perhaps the character had been a star athlete in school and still took pains to keep himself in shape. That was believable.

He went to the bedroom, where the television was tuned to local news with the sound off. All the shades were drawn, fending off most of the late-morning sun. There were several outfits laid out on the bed, and he picked the one that seemed to best fit his new persona—jeans, a white dress shirt, and a tweed blazer. A pair of loafers completed the picture. *Loser casual*, he thought. As he dressed, he watched a report of an apartment building that had caught fire during the night. Twenty seven people had been killed, mostly from the gas explosion that came later. The news station kept playing a cellphone video someone took, which shook wildly when the gas ignited. "*BOOM*!" he said when the building blew apart, chuckling. Then his cellphone, lying on the table next to his laptop, buzzed twice.

"Yes?"

"Give me an update."

The man's voice was astringently anonymous, and that made him nervous. From the beginning, there had been no accent and no regional quirks in the vernacular. There was some type of minor speech impediment—a faint slurring that was only occasionally detectable—but that didn't give anything away, either. Millions of people had imperfect articulation. Otherwise, the tonal austerity made any kind of identification impossible.

"I've got eyes and ears all over the place, working around the clock."

"Leads?"

"Nothing yet, but I'm confident."

"I don't share your confidence."

"People disappear every day, it's not a big deal."

"Not people like this. They're not government agents. She's a soccer mom, he's a laborer. They're nobodies."

"That means they'll be easier to catch in the end."

"You'd better be right."

"I should tell you, though, that there could be a new wrinkle on a different front."

"Which is?"

"A guy named Jason Hammond."

The caller made no reply to this.

"I checked him out on the Internet. Rich guy, worth billions. He goes around solving big mysteries in his spare time; when he's not doing charity work, that is. He's the one who got to the bottom of the Kennedy assassination about two months ago. It was all over the news."

"And why are you worried about him?"

"Because he's in Vegas now. He landed at Henderson in the middle of the night. I've been watching all the airports in case the family tried to leave. One of my contacts recognized him when he arrived."

"Maybe it's a coincidence."

"I doubt it, and you know why? Because the Kennedy thing wasn't his only success. He's the one who also figured out the disappearances of Michael Rockefeller and Amelia Earhart, and brought down quite a few people in the process. He's a Boy Scout, and we don't need any Boy Scouts."

"You have to find out if he's here because of the will."

"I'm already working on it."

"If he is, then he needs to be stopped. You understand what I'm saying?"

"I think so, yes. You should know, though, that it won't be easy. Or cheap. And it wasn't part of our original agreement. I'll do some things for you beyond my pay grade, but not that. That's extra."

"Just find out why he's here, Grant," the caller said. "I need facts."

"I'll get them."

"This is an unfortunate development."

"I realize that."

"If you hadn't failed to get those notes from that family, we wouldn't be in this position."

Grant stiffened with anger but did not respond.

"You may have complicated the issue through your ineptitude," the caller went on.

"If so, I'll fix it."

"Now that I consider it, I would not be surprised if the Miller family contacted Hammond after you failed to obtain those notes, and that's why he's involved now."

"We don't know that for sure."

"And you're willing to risk everything on that hunch?"

Again, no response.

****

'Robert Grant' was not his real name but rather the latest in a progression of aliases that stretched back decades. There had dozens over the course of his criminal career. He'd been foolish with them in his younger years, going for the dramatic with things like 'Lucifer' and 'Falco.' Then he realized this childish folly simply drew unwanted attention, so he moved in the opposite direction with pseudonyms that were just inches away from 'John Doe' or 'Bob Smith.' They had to be interesting enough to seem real, yet plain enough to be overlooked. He sometimes browsed the Internet for lists of common first and last names until he found a pair that felt right. The results were always satisfactory.

He slipped into the tweed blazer, turned off the television and the laptop, and returned to the bathroom for one last look in the mirror. The fictitious person was there, but he could still see the real one beneath. And what he saw rattled him. The lines were deeper, the blemishes more numerous, the skin less supple. He had never given much thought to his age before. He was frankly amazed he'd lived this long. Forty-seven wasn't particularly old these days, but he never believed he'd make it out of his twenties. Then came thirty, then forty. Now fifty was bearing down fast. And he was beginning not only to see it but *feel* it—knees that creaked like dried wood when he got up in the middle of the night, eyes that couldn't make out the small print anymore, muscles that hesitated before executing even the smallest gesture. There were compensations for these problems, but they wouldn't suffice forever. And in his line of work, they weren't just annoyances—they were liabilities.

He massaged his chin and cheeks a few times before pushing these thoughts aside. Then he gathered what he needed and went out.

Six

OTHER THAN THE FACT that it was also a hotel, the Four Seasons in downtown Las Vegas bore little resemblance to Grant's current residence. Jason's Valley View Suite included a private study, bedroom with walk-in closet, marble-floored full bath, pantry with a private service entrance, and dedicated dining area that could comfortably seat six. He had made the reservation under the false name of a married couple. He had matching ID for himself and, upon check in, told the concierge that he and his wife would carry their own bags up later on; they were going out for breakfast first. And like Grant, he had disguised himself. In this case it was a simple Ralph Lauren cap and Ray Bans.

He sat at the desk in the study, hunched over one of the Hughes pages with his reading glasses on. He was also peering through a jeweler's loupe. The other pages were in a scatter at various points around the room. Most surrounded him in a horseshoe pattern or lay on the credenza nearby.

His iPad was propped up in its foldout case, and Noah's round face was on the screen.

"You should finish your breakfast," Noah said. The egg-white omelet and fruit assortment sat nearby on a room-service cart, barely touched.

"Mmm."

"You can't do anything on an empty stomach."

"Sure, I know."

"And I'm glad to see you're taking care of those pages, valuable historic documents that they are."

Jason sighed and looked up. "And I'm glad a whole load of really smart people spent time, money, and energy developing Skype so you could nag me from the other side of the country."

Noah put his hand up. "I'm sorry."

"No, it's all right. I'm just kidding around. Here, look—" He reached over, forked off a piece of the omelet, and stuck it in his mouth. "See? I'm eating like a good boy."

"How many pages did you say there were in total?"

"Forty eight."

"And you've gone through all of them?"

"Only briefly. Now I'm going over each one more carefully, trying to decipher what's here." He picked up the one he was currently inspecting. "Listen to what Hughes says about Elliot Roosevelt here."

"The president's son?"

"Yeah. He wrote, '*Roosevelt knew all along that we were greasing him with women and booze leading up to his recommendation of the D-2.*' The D-2 was one of Hughes's experimental warplanes, and he wanted to sell it to the government as a successor to Lockheed P-38. '*He let us wine and dine him for thousands, then he turned rat during the Brewster Hearings to protect himself.*' After this he added in a scribble—*Maybe include the photos of Roosevelt that we took in his hotel room after the Manhattan party.*"

Noah shook his head. "Charming."

"Hughes's reputation for vengeance was widely known and obviously well deserved. He also wrote a detailed list of what he determined to be the amorous inadequacies of actor Mickey Rooney, who was making time with Ava Gardner while Hughes had detectives shadowing her."

"Real nice."

"Isn't it?" Jason hunched over the loupe again.

"Is his handwriting really so small that you have to use that thing?"

"In some places, yes."

Noah cleared his throat. "So listen, about the boathouse and the sea steps and so on—I've got the contractor bugging me for an answer. What should I tell him?"

"Tell him I haven't decided yet."

"I don't think he's going to like that."

"He'll like it when we pay him."

"You're definitely going to do something down there?"

"Yes. And if not there, then in another part of the estate."

Noah rolled his eyes; he'd heard this one before. "Should I tell Antonio the same thing? That you haven't decided on the—"

"The China oil stock?"

"Yes."

"Tell him to purchase half a million more shares," Jason said. "Do it in varying increments and over the next six weeks so it doesn't draw attention. He should offer 12% under the current asking price, then set the stop-loss at 15%, moving up 2% every time the stock grows another 5%. That should leave plenty of room, not that it'll be needed."

"Aren't you concerned the Chinese government will tighten down their currency again? That's what I've been reading online."

"They can't afford that at the moment. They need foreign investment, if for no other reason than to have greater liquidity. They've played around with their currency so much in the last few years that some investors have begun parking their cash elsewhere. So the leaders will behave for awhile. And as more members of their younger generation continue to abandon the agrarian regions for more industrialized areas, the demand for oil will grow. The government will have to meet those demands or risk becoming more dependent on outside sources, which they won't want to do."

"Oh, okay."

"It's a nation that has prided itself on a large degree of self-sufficiency and a quiet kind of isolationism for thousands of years. If they've got oil under their feet, they're going to try to get to it."

Jason almost added that this was a lesson he had learned from his father, having overheard it while walking past his office one afternoon. But that would spawn a much longer—and, Jason thought, highly unwelcome—conversation.

"I'll let Antonio know," Noah said.

"'Kay."

After a moment, Noah added, "You really do have a head for business, Jason. This could so easily become a career for you."

Jason knew he was fishing for a response of any kind, but this too was a conversation that could wait for another day. He examined a few more lines on the Hughes page and jotted down some comments in a spiralbound notebook. Then he fell back in the chair, removed his glasses, and rubbed his eyes.

"How frustrating," he said.

"What is?"

"There's so much stuff here, but I can't find a common thread. Does any of this refer to a will? Maybe. But I haven't come across anything I can really grab hold of. I'm finding plenty of Hughes's engineering calculations and diagrams, financial figures in amounts you wouldn't believe, and more of those gossip-column revelations. Lots of shorthand-type scribblings, too. He loves to use initials—'D.S.' and 'R.T.' and 'Z.L.' But who knows who any of these people are? He even abbreviates inanimate objects. I've seen four references to a 'Bldg. G.' Hughes owned about a thousand buildings, and in all the material I've got on him, I've never come across anything about a 'Building G.' Then there's 'SManch.' I had to invest about a half hour puzzling out that he was talking about the 'Spring Mountain Ranch' here in Vegas that he purchased for his wife, Jean Peters, in the '60s. Yet I haven't seen the word 'will' written once. Then again, just about everything here could have something to do with a will. He was such a secretive person, it's no surprise that it all seems so random. I'm sure it all made sense to *him*."

"Do you honestly believe there's a will out there somewhere?"

"I do. Remember, he did write others that we know about. He drafted one in May of 1925 when he was only nineteen. Both of his parents had died at that point, and he inherited the fortune his father made from the Hughes Tool Company, not to mention the company itself. The will was pretty standard, drawn up by Howard with the help of an attorney. All provisions were laid out carefully, very correct and proper. But no signed copy was ever found. He did another around 1930, and another in 1938. A handwritten codicil to the '38 will was found in '39, but not the will itself. In 1947, he made an updated version with the help of an assistant named Nadine Henley, who went on to become a very powerful figure in his organization. She later recalled working on it with Hughes, but said that he procrastinated endlessly when it came to signing it. During the 1950s, he discussed the disposition of his estate several times with his then-wife Jean Peters. It was around then that he began talking about leaving the bulk of it to the Howard Hughes Medical Institute. Billions of dollars. *Billions.* But again, no signed paperwork."

"Crazy."

"Yeah, but the point is a will was on his mind all his life, so I find it impossible to believe he didn't leave one. Think about who benefitted the most from the fact that a signed will was never found—the IRS, his relatives, and all the lawyers. The IRS got millions, another huge chunk was distributed among twenty two cousins after endless court battles, and the rest went to the army of lawyers who were involved. That's pretty strange considering Hughes said many times he didn't want his family getting anything—yet another reason I believe they're the ones behind the hiring of that lunatic who attacked the Millers. At this point, it's the most reasonable explanation. Also remember that Hughes loathed paying taxes. His hatred of taxes in particular was legendary. Noah Dietrich, his confidante and righthand man for more than three decades, said that every wealthy person he ever knew hated paying taxes, but no one hated it more than Howard Hughes."

"Hughes's righthand man was also named Noah?"

"Yeah," Jason said.

"That's quite a coincidence."

"Tell me about it. *Twilight Zone* kind of stuff."

Jason held up one of the pages and pointed to a line near the bottom. "Anyway, check this out—down here, Howard writes, '*86% to the Institute.*' Just one random comment, and yet think about how many lives that would've changed if it had been included in a legally viable document. Here's another—'*0.5% to Jean P.*' I'm sure he meant Jean Peters. It was his last marriage and the closest he ever got to a normal, domestic life. Not that there was anything normal about Hughes at this point—he was heading into the darkest stage of his mental illness. But Peters was, at heart, a very caring person, quite different from the Hollywood starlets Hughes had been dating throughout his younger years. She wanted a home, children, all of it, and she was very patient with his eccentricities. And even though Hughes was a lousy husband—he remained in seclusion during the last few years of their marriage, communicating only through handwritten notes like these but never actually seeing her—he was very generous with the divorce terms and always spoke highly of her in the years after. I'm not surprised he wanted to leave something for her in his estate. But again, that begs the question—where are the formal documents? What happened to them?" He shook his head. "I simply cannot believe he didn't leave a will. It's my belief that someone, or more likely a group of someones, went out of their way to make sure it never reached the courts."

"Perhaps."

"All these people he talks about, with their dirty little secrets.... Perhaps he was going to expose all this information right along with the distribution of his holdings. Like I said, he could be a very vindictive person, particularly when it came to those who betrayed him. Of all the names I've encountered in these papers so far, there is one common thread—they're all people who tried to stick it to him in one way or another. Any one of them would've had good reason to make sure the will was never found."

"And they were all powerful, influential."

"That's right." Jason rubbed at a growing ache along his forehead. "I mean, I'm not stupid—I know he's not going to write, '*And then I'll leave the will taped to the back of the painting in my study*' or whatever. Of course he wasn't the type to do that. But come on—there must be something somewhere...."

"Maybe it's just not those pages."

"If that's the case, then the Millers' little girl took a bullet for nothing." Jason closed his eyes and took a few deep breaths. "Have you heard from them?"

"Yes. She's holding steady. I think she's going to be all right."

"Thank God."

"Exactly. And hey—if there really is no clue in those pages as to where the will might be, maybe you should consider letting all this go and coming back home."

Jason ignored this and surveyed the mess before him. Then he shook his head. "For such a brilliant aviator, Hughes had an awful sense of direction—his writing's all over the place. First he's in the lines, then he's out of them. Then he's in the margins, then on the back. Sometimes he writes sideways, once in awhile he goes on a diagonal. Half the time I can't even figure out what he's trying to say. Aren't people who suffer from OCD supposed to be addicted to neatness and organization and structure?"

"I think that's right."

Jason sighed. "All right, I'm going to rest for a little while. I'll talk to you later."

"You have a nice comfortable bed here, y'know."

"The bed here is comfortable, too," Jason replied, "but thank you for your concern."

Then he said *g'night* and turned off the iPad before Noah could say anything further.

****

The defining event of Jason Hammond's life began as a simple family vacation. The Hammonds were trying to escape the merciless New England winter by spending a few weeks in and around the Bahamas, specifically Bimini, Abacos, and

Nassau. They all brought work along, as workaholism was a standard component of the Hammond philosophy. The father, Alan, had started life with nothing and reached billionaire status by his mid fifties, and the day-to-day demands of running his empire were interminable. Jason's mother, Linda, was a physician who devoted her energies to missionary work. His sister, Joan, had also gone into medicine as a pediatric nurse and, like her mother, lent her skills exclusively to charitable causes. Mother and daughter planned to one day open a hospital in one of the African locales they frequented. And Jason was doing post-graduated studies at Harvard with the goal of earning a doctorate in history and one day securing a professorship. He also hoped to use some of the family's philanthropic funds to build a school in the same third-world region where his mother and sister would establish their medical center.

Jason was the only one who survived the trip. He chartered a plane in order to leave two days early when he heard that Pulitzer Prize-winning biographer and historian Doris Kearns Goodwin was giving a lecture and Q&A. This was on a Tuesday, and on Thursday evening he received the chilling news that his family's single-engine Cessna, piloted by his father, fell into the Atlantic Ocean less than a hundred miles off the coast of Miami. Only bits of wreckage were recovered, but no fuselage and no bodies.

Jason cut himself off from the world and sank into a deep depression that lasted years. He became an obsession with local media, who interviewed old friends, former classmates and professors, and employees of the Hammond empire who previously reported to his father but now, at least on paper, reported to him. The businesses continued to run, but not as profitably as before. Stock prices dropped, and although they eventually bounced back, they never reached their previous highs. Since Jason remained in complete seclusion—some journalists, in fact, began referring to him as a 'modern-day Howard Hughes'— no one was sure who was making the decisions. If it was Jason, then it seemed he had inherited much of his father's acumen—but not all of it. Others theorized that the man behind the curtain was Noah Gwynn, the family majordomo and, by and large, a mystery figure in the equation.

Noah was the only other person aside from a handful of loyal servants who remained on the estate. He had met Alan Hammond in elementary school during their Boston days, joined the military with him as a way of paying for college, then lost touch after their four-year service was completed. They reunited eleven years later when Alan was well into his first million and got word that his old friend was living in a YMCA. What followed was a harrowing two-year pingpong of rehab and relapse that nearly concluded with Noah taking his own life. He finally reclaimed the mantle of sobriety through Alan's tireless support. Alan then offered him a permanent, albeit somewhat nebulous, job on the estate; 'property manager' was what they told the IRS each year. Noah was given his own cottage a short walk from the main house, a generous salary, and, in time, *de facto* membership into the family. He had been there when Joan and Jason were born, when they took their first steps, had their first dates, and got their first cars. Neither child had ever known a time when Noah wasn't part of their lives. Yet neither knew the mind-bending events that almost brought him to ruin.

Noah became the sole observer of Jason's dark journey following the accident. He saw himself as the closest substitute to a family that Jason had left. But it was a precarious arrangement, for he never forgot that he was still an employee of the company and, as such, technically a subordinate. Furthermore, Jason was a grown man, not a child, and thus didn't need to be coddled. The bottom line for Noah, however, was that he loved Jason as much as any father loved his son, so he went about attending to him within the bizarre reality that came to surround their two wounded souls; a reality that would've been impossible to understand by anyone else.

Noah continued his duties as 'property manager' following the accident, assuring that the bills were paid, the meals were cooked, and the laundry was washed. He also acted as the conduit between Jason and the handful of individuals at the helm of his father's global business interests; an arrangement that boiled down to Jason making the most important decisions and then Noah communicating them. While Noah was often frustrated by Jason's unpredictable bouts of procrastination, he was also impressed—and occasionally encouraged—by Jason's occasional brilliance.

Noah also worried about his physical health—Jason kept himself in good shape and worked out every day, although when he was stressed he would go on wild eating binges—as well as his mental health, as Jason had never spoken to him about the loss of his family or the emotional turmoil that followed, and he refused to seek professional help or even take mild medications. But he did have a pressure valve, one that Noah had noticed very early on.

Jason had always loved a good mystery. As a boy he would read every novel in the local library, watch every television show, see every movie. It was an addiction. When both of Jason's parents were too busy to play with him, Noah would create little mysteries for him to solve. These usually involved some item that had been 'stolen' and then hidden somewhere on the estate. These were some of the happiest memories of Jason's formative years—and among the few that had no direct connection to his family since neither of his parents possessed his fondness for mysteries, nor did his sister. Noah would later theorize that this was one of the key reasons Jason was drawn back to them after the accident. And when he did, he did it in typically full-throttle fashion.

Less than two years after the accident, Jason emerged from his self-imposed exile by traveling to New Guinea in a quest to solve the disappearance of Michael Rockefeller. The son of New York governor and future vice president Nelson Rockefeller, Michael had been in the Asmat region to study the local culture. While on the Eilanden River, his pontoon boat overturned. After drifting for a time in a dugout canoe, he tried swimming to shore and was never seen again. He was declared legally dead in 1964, and in the late '70s his mother paid for a private investigation that produced no conclusive results.

Jason took it upon himself to launch another at his own expense and soon found remains that, after DNA testing, were positively identified as those of the missing heir. This stunning achievement triggered a media sensation, as did his subsequent recovery of Amelia Earhart's downed plane and his unearthing of the truth behind the assassination of John F. Kennedy. With each success came greater notoriety—which he disliked—as well as the desire to seek the next epic challenge—which Noah disliked. Noah worried that Jason was using his newfound 'career' to avoid the greater priority of directly addressing his grief so he could reach a point of inner peace—and get back to his true calling in the world of academia.

****

Jason slid up onto his elbows, breathing hard and slicked with sweat. It took a moment to remember where he was and why. He checked the clock on the nightstand—1:37 PM—and got to his feet. Then he went into the bathroom, soaked a cloth with cool water, and pressed it against his neck and cheeks.

The face in the mirror looked haggard and drawn; much older than its calendar years. It didn't have to be this way, he knew. He didn't even want to imagine what Noah would say about the dark half-moons that had taken up residence under his eyes, the lines that were engraved across his forehead, and the neglected hair that bore the earliest strands gray and was rarely kept nearly as neat as it had once been.

He returned to the study and got behind the desk. He finished inspecting the sheet he'd had when Noah was on the iPad, whose screen was now a glossy black dead zone. He recorded more of his own comments and observations in a spiralbound pad as he tried to decipher Hughes's scattershot thinking. He spent the next two hours going through other pages and became more convinced than ever that these were, in fact, the scratch notes of Hughes's final covenant.

"But where is it?" Jason said aloud. "Where did he *put* the stupid thing?"

Starvation set in after another hour, eclipsing his growing frustration. He picked up the phone and hit the button for room service.

"Hello, this is the kitchen," a woman said cheerfully.

"Hi, I'd like to order something, please."

"You're in Room 232?"

"Yes."

"Okay, and what would you like?"

"I saw on your menu that you had brook trout almondine?"

"That's correct."

"And that it's sometimes unavailable?"

"Yes, would you like me to check to see if we have it today?"

"Please."

"Okay, one moment."

Jason looked to the window, where the curtain was parted just enough to reveal a sunny day outside. Then he turned back to the page he'd been studying. His focus, however, wasn't fully there at first; he was seeing it without really seeing it. That was about to change.

"Hello? Sir?"

"Yes?"

"Yes, we do have the brook trout available."

"Great."

"So you'd like an order of that?"

"Please."

"And what would you like for your sides?"

"What are the choices?"

The woman began to recite the list, and Jason listened intently for the first few moments.

Then he saw it—written sideways and all but covered by a hastily rendered diagram of a primitive jet engine—

Final copy to C.W.

His mouth fell open.
"Sir?" the woman asked. "Are you still there? Sir?"
She tried a few more times, then gave up.

Seven

A WHITE LEXUS COUPE pulled into the driveway at 533 McInerney Lane in the Las Vegas suburb of Summerlin. The house was an impressive two-story colonial, one of six homes that sat on a cul-de-sac in this mostly-upper-class neighborhood. From the outside, it possessed all the requisite charm—wraparound porch, copious landscaping, intricate stonework. The Lexus itself was an essential component, on par with the BMWs and Volvos that sparkled in the surrounding driveways.

The kid who got out of the coupe, however, seemed out of place. He was a lean and muscular twenty two, clad in faded jeans, a plain t-shirt, and sneakers. It would've been easy to presume that the car wasn't his. His father's, perhaps, or he maybe he was delivering it following an annual tuneup at the dealership. A closer inspection, however, revealed that the jeans and t-shirt and sneakers were all designer brands, as was the Omega chronograph and the Cartier diamond earring.

Danny Rudd scanned his surroundings without being obvious about it; a skill he had mastered in recent years. He had a Burger King bag and large soda in one hand. With the other, he took out his iPhone and deftly worked his thumb across the screen. The app he launched was of his own authorship. There was an image of an old-style traffic light—the kind with eyelids over the bulbs—but no labels or other wording. The program had been designed for him and him alone, and if anyone else discovered it, they would have no clue as to its purpose.

Noting that the green bulb was still glowing—as it had been each of the other nineteen times he'd check it since he went out to get lunch—he returned to the home screen and replaced the phone in his pocket. A green light meant the house's security field had not been violated. Yellow meant minor movement had been detected but the identity of the intruder could not be determined. And red meant a full breach had occurred—and, most likely, he could never return to the property. Rudd had learned long ago that paranoia was critical to survival in his line of work.

He hurried up the steps, unlocked the door, and went in. The home was equally splendorous on the inside. The dining room, fully visible from his vantage point in the foyer, had a French moderne table surrounded by eight hand-upholstered chairs. On his other side, the flatscreen television in the living room nearly covered one entire wall. There was an entertainment center beneath it, connected wirelessly to eight Bose microspeakers that had been fitted around the room to the point of near invisibility. Rudd took no notice of these or any other amenities. He had seen them a thousand times and was bored of them.

He relocked the door and expertly worked the security keypad. Then he went down the long hallway between the living and dining rooms. There was a small accent table with a Bible on it. The latter had been here when he moved in seven months ago. He had never opened it and never would, although he had set soda cans on it a few times, as evidenced by the rings on the cover. He opened a door on the right and started down, turning first to actuate the lock with the same practiced dexterity.

The basement was fully finished, with painted sheetrock, wool carpeting, recessed lighting, and more electronics. Rudd passed through three other rooms before reaching the gym. He did spend some time in here each day, as evidenced by the pungent stench of perspiration that had fused with the rug and ceiling tiles. He opened a louvered door on the opposite side and went into the only unfinished room in the house. The cinder blocks were fully exposed here, as was the stud framing that held up the wall of the previous room. Piles of dirty laundry lay in little mounds by the washer and dryer, neglected for weeks. And to the left of that stood a pair of sliding doors.

Rudd moved one of these doors aside. The contents of the closet were common to any home—seasonal jackets on hangers, a black umbrella, a box marked 'CHRISTMAS DECORATIONS,' a selection of board games on the top shelf, and an open cardboard box stuffed with athletic equipment that included a baseball bat, two ancient gloves, a half-deflated basketball, and a pair of cleats smeared with dirt.

Rudd took a sip from his soda and stepped inside. When he slid the door shut, there was a pronounced 'click' as the two magnetic plates rejoined. This also activated an electric circuit that Rudd had installed during the first week of his occupancy. Now in darkness, he took out his iPhone again and launched another homebrewed application. Like the first, it featured a single image—a combination dial of the type seen on safes and school lockers throughout the world. He spun the three digits into place, and a small button with the words 'OPEN SESAME' faded into view. Rudd pressed it, and there was another click—this time from the corner opposite the first. He set his palm against the back wall and slid it aside.

The small room he entered now had a distinctly sinister feel to it. It was dimly lit and had the faintest traces of static in the air. There were twenty flatscreen monitors attached to a grid of interconnected aluminum tubes. Beneath this was a long desk with a single keyboard and mouse. To the right was a table with nine different CPU towers. There were several other devices around them, all blinking madly. Wires and cables slithered behind and beneath everything, relatively out of the way but too abundant to be completely obscured. The image on the monitor in the upper left corner changed every few seconds—different rooms in the house or various angles outside, all with a time stamp in one corner.

Rudd checked this monitor first as he pulled the chair back and set down the Burger King bag. Then he went about inspecting the others while unloading the bag's contents—a Baconator, French fries, onion rings, and a hot fudge sundae.

One screen exhibited his efforts to hack into the accounts of a relatively new bank in Arizona that was located in a fast-growing community of Eastern transplants, mostly well-off retirees. He had discovered some years ago that if he skimmed a small amount from each balance—say, $200—none of the account holders would bother calling the authorities. Most of them didn't even seem to notice. The bank's insurance would eventually cover the losses anyway, and the administrators went to great pains to keep such incidents quiet so as not to drive off future customers. Rudd had harvested more than $400,000 from 120 different institutions in the past year alone, and that cash was now parked in an offshore account in Nassau under the name of a limited liability company that didn't exist. On another screen, he was altering the tax records of a construction firm in Lake Tahoe to create the illusion that they were trying to defrauding the IRS. No one in this particularly company would realize it until mid April following an anonymous call from the individual in the competing company who had hired Rudd in the first place. Rudd had already received $25,000 for this and would get a second and final payment for the same amount when the inevitable audit was launched. A third screen displayed his favorite and most original project—a virus designed to paralyze the climate controls of a busy local restaurant that had insisted on charging him full menu price for a badly undercooked ribeye and watery mashed potatoes.

He unwrapped the Baconator and took a bite, then stuffed a splay of French fries into his mouth.

"Nice diet."

Rudd screamed, jumped, and spun around in one frenzied motion. His hands clamped onto the ends of the armrests as his eyes widened into bright circles.

The figure that stepped from one darkened corner was the size of a pro wrestler.

"Easy, sport. It's just me."

Rudd studied him for a long moment.

"Grant?"

"Yeah."

The chair creaked as the kid leaned forward for a better look.

"Maybe this will help," Grant said, removing the glasses. "There, see?"

The fear in Rudd's face dropped into a look of irritated relief. Shaking his head, he said, "Yeah, sure. There's never anything to worry about when you're around." He then swiveled back to his desk and took another bite of his burger. "So how'd you get in here?"

"Good magicians don't show you how they perform their tricks."

"Seriously, I'd like to know."

"I'm sure you would."

Grant stepped forward and appraised the monitor bank. This appeared as a casual gesture, almost indifferent. But he had entered the house only moments after Rudd left and had in fact been studying Rudd's current activities very carefully.

"Quite an operation you've got," he said. Rudd didn't reply to this; he loathed small talk. "Such a naughty boy."

"Well, you'd know all about that, wouldn't you?" Rudd delivered this line with an air of authority, but the truth was he knew very little about the man—and as someone who used information the way other terrorists used guns and bombs, this drove him out of his mind. Grant always appeared out of thin air, then disappeared with the same spectral agility. Rudd had secretly taken photos of him on three separate occasions but had yet to make an identification. The fact that Grant seemed to changed his appearance as often as ordinary people changed their clothes didn't help. Rudd noticed that he never left any physical traces, either. He never gave Rudd anything on paper, never rendered anything in his handwriting, never even touched anything. Thus, a DNA sample would be impossible to secure short of yanking one of his hairs out or running a Q-tip through his mouth. Rudd was certain he'd end up with several broken bones if he tried either. Grant also had no discernible accent, used no obvious regionalisms in his speech, never made any references to his past, and never mentioned any of his other underworld associations. Rudd no longer even believed 'Grant' was his actual name. All he knew for sure was that this was one of the most skilled and experienced criminals he'd ever encountered. And although Rudd had never experienced it firsthand, he sensed that Grant was, in spite of his refined demeanor, the most dangerous. Whenever they had one of their brief meetings, Rudd always felt like a mouse in the presence of a very large and ill-mannered cat.

"So what do you need?" he asked.

"Information."

"On?"

"An individual." Grant continued to examine the profusion of illegal activities that were unfolding before him.

"Do you have to do that?"

"I can't help it. I'm fascinated."

Rudd sighed. "Okay, what individual?"

"A guy named Jason Hammond."

"There are probably five thousand Jason Hammonds. Can you be a bit more specif—"

"His home's in New Hampshire, but he's here in the Vegas area at the moment. At this point I'm assuming he's staying in a hotel, and I'm willing to bet it's not one of the seedier ones because he's about as rich as it gets. I'm also willing to bet he's not using his own name, but then again maybe he is. Go into the data banks of all the four- and five-star dumps in the area and get a list together of the people who checked in last night."

"That's going to take a little time."

"Got a date?"

Rudd shook his head and turned back to his keyboard. He pressed a hot-key combination with three fingers, and nineteen of the twenty screens went blank. Only the one in the upper left, monitoring the property's security, remained unchanged.

Rudd then set to work, the keys rattling like popping corn as he typed with impossible speed. He first created a list through data from a fashionable travel site, filtering the search results within a twenty-mile area and narrowing it to only four- and five-star establishments. He sorted these by the most recommended locations first, then bookmarked the page. He then went through each hotel individually, starting with their home page, exposing their IP address, and then burrowing into their private network. Within fifteen minutes, lists of current guests—along with information such as their home addresses, license-plate numbers, and credit-card data—began appearing on the other screens. There were hundreds of names.

"Can you compile all of that onto one screen, then sort it by columns?"

Rudd tilted his head in frustration and turned back to him. "I can, but that, too, will take some time. It's not like all these data systems are naturally compatible. And by the way, what kind of payment can I expect for this unsolicited job?"

"How much do you want?"

"What's your ultimate objective?"

"I need to know where this guy is staying, nothing more."

"A thousand."

Grant chuckled. "Let's try that again."

Rudd's turbo-typing came to a halt. "You could always get someone else to do this."

Grant looked away from the monitors for the first time and appraised his host with a thin smile of bemusement.

"Yeah, I could. I could also pass word to the Feds that I know the whereabouts of the last still-at-large member of the Green Devils. How much did you end up costing the Pentagon before you were through shredding those hard drives? Over twenty-five million, I think I read? Very appropriate for someone with the screen name 'Mess-U-Up.'"

Rudd's face drained of all color, and his smug hacker's arrogance went with it.

"How could you possibly know about that?"

Grant patted him on the shoulder. "I told you, a good magician does not reveal his secrets. Oh, and also don't forget about your parents. As respected diplomats, their reputation would probably take quite a hit if you went down. Just imagine the shame."

Rudd said something else here, but it came out as an unintelligible croak.

"So let's be reasonable, okay?" Grant went one. "I'm feeling generous today, so I'll give you half of your proposed fee—five hundred bucks. How's that sound?"

Rudd nodded and turned back to the keyboard.

Eight

JASON SAT AT the suite's dining-room table—now covered by piles of papers and folders—with his hands pressed against his forehead to keep a growing migraine at bay. They always came when he read for too long without a break. But that, he had already decided, was a price he was willing to pay at the moment. His fingers were thrust deep into his inky black hair, elevating the forelocks into a spider-legged mess.

"Okay…" he said to Noah's image on the iPad, which was propped on its stand. Then he checked the clock on the wall. "It's almost midnight...great."

"I'm exhausted."

"One more," Jason said, holding a finger up.

"You've been saying that since ten. I'm starving, too."

"Just one more. There *is* only one more!" He tapped his finger on the spiralbound notebook that lay next to the laptop. "*One.* Terrific...."

Noah groaned. "And that would be?"

"Calvin White."

"Okay."

They went to their respective keyboards, and a moment later Jason said, "He was one of the engineers who worked with Hughes when they were building the Hercules H4, aka the Spruce Goose. This is according to what I found on Google."

"That's what's on Yahoo, too."

"Born 1937, died 1999 from pneumonia."

"Yeah."

"Anything else? Anything to tie them tighter?"

More Internet surfing underscored by the plastic ratcheting of their mouse wheels. Within the rectangular frame of the iPad, Noah shook his head.

"No, nothing."

Jason dropped back into his chair, flipping his pencil down and closing his eyes. "Okay, I'll keep on it. Go get something to eat before you pass out."

"Thanks."

Noah disappeared from the screen, leaving behind the static image of a well-stocked bookshelf.

Jason zoned out for a time, reducing his respiration to a near-tantric state. Then he gazed across the piles of dusty municipal records, brown-edged newspapers, and other referential minutiae he'd gathered during the day. It hadn't even been a *full* day—since his discovery of Hughes's cryptic 'Final copy to CW,' only about ten hours had passed. But it felt like days.

The search had begun on the Internet, then moved to books, magazines, newspapers, aeronautics journals, tax records, and finally a full set of employment records borrowed from the Clark County municipal complex. The clerk there was an efficient, bespectacled woman in her thirties. Jason told her he was writing a book on the history of defunct casinos and hated himself for the lie.

He compiled a list of seventeen people in the Hughes universe bearing the initials 'CW'—and by midnight all had been dismissed as nonstarters. One was a rival Hollywood producer from Hughes's RKO days. Another was a young, aspiring actress Hughes had dated for a week or so and then discarded when the next pretty face come along. There was a switchboard operator who had worked at Hughes's personal office on Romaine Street in Hollywood, but Jason couldn't even find evidence that the two had ever met. This was dispiriting but not surprising—in the later stages of his life, Hughes was reclusive almost to the point of nonexistence. His second and last wife, actress Jean Peters, had no personal contact him during the final years of their marriage, and most of the top executives in his organization had never even seen him.

The only 'CW' prospect that seemed to have any real potential was Charles Wilson, the Secretary of Defense under President Dwight D. Eisenhower's. Hughes's engineering firms had been awarded many military contracts during World War II, so the two men would have known each other. Jason's optimism deflated, however, when he could find no evidence of a substantial relationship; certainly nothing that suggested Hughes would trust Wilson with his last will and testament.

Jason scanned the list again. Each name had been rendered in his meticulous schoolboy print, and each now had an equally neat line through it. About halfway down, an image flashed through his mind—a smiling Princess Diana in a powder-blue blouse, standing in front of a flagstone hearth.

"Why does that keep coming to me?" he said out loud.

"Are you talking to me?" Noah asked. He had returned to the iPad.

"Huh?"

"You just said, 'Why does it keep coming to me?' Are you asking *me* that?"

"Oh, no. I'm sorry, just talking to myself. I've been getting this recurring picture in my head."

"Of?"

"Princess Diana of Wales. It's from the Eighties or early Nineties, with the dark eyeliner and all that. She's wearing a silk blouse, baby blue, and standing in front of a large stone hearth."

"Your mother and father knew her a little bit, y'know. Not close friends, but friendly."

"Yes, I did know that."

"Okay. So...?"

Jason shook his head. "The image came to me several times today. I'm sure I got it from one of the books I was using for research, or something on the Internet. I'll bet I could find it online if I looked. What I can't understand is why it keeps surfacing. It's clearly floating around my subconscious for some reason. We've both studied psychology, so I don't need to tell you the subconscious works."

"No, I'm well acquainted."

"This is a message being sent from the deep down. Remember when I said I found myself humming that Beach Boys song, 'Warmth of the Sun,' while I was in the middle the Kennedy thing?"

"Yeah."

"Brian Wilson wrote it immediately after hearing that Kennedy had been killed. And I knew that, but I wasn't thinking it at the time. I figured it out later on. These things come from places we can't access on a conscious level, but they still have significance."

"It was just a song, Jason. Your brain simply made a connection."

"I know, but this vision of Princess Diana is particularly persistent. It came to me several times today, but I have no idea why." He considered it again, tried to conjure some meaning from the dust, but nothing materialized.

"You've been researching Diana's death on and off for awhile now. Maybe it's just something that got caught in the filter, so to speak."

"Maybe."

"Or it could be your mind's way of telling you—"

Jason was already nodding. "I know, I know. That I should give up on this Hughes business and come back home where it's nice and safe."

"Yes."

"Well, not yet." Jason began looking over another sheet.

Noah stared hard at him, his jaw visibly tightening. "Fine—so what are you going to do now?"

"I don't know. Get some rest, I guess. I'm tired."

"Okay," Noah said, "then good night." He moved off the screen.

Jason sat there for a time, unable to muster the motivation to get up. Then he forced himself, pushing his body forward with a groan. He fell onto the still-made bed and was out in seconds. Dreams came in full, vivid color, as they always did.

This time, however, they were good ones.

****

According to conventional wisdom, there are two types of human sleep—non-rapid eye movement, *aka* 'NREM,' and rapid-eye moment, *aka* 'REM.' NREM is divided into three stages, whereas REM has just one. On average, a person goes through a full cycle involving all four in a span of between seventy and a hundred minutes, and it is during the last—REM—when dreaming occurs.

Precisely ninety two minutes after Jason collapsed on his bed, he snapped awake and sat bolt upright, his eyes shifting frantically as he tried to retain the images. They lingered without too much difficulty, and the grin that had faded earlier curved back into place.

He scrambled to his feet and went into the dining room's *de facto* work station, pulling the chair around to one particular stack of papers. These were tax records for Hughes's employees during his time in Las Vegas; 1966 to 1970. They were yellowed with age and separated into two piles by fresh rubber bands; the dried-out originals had snapped before Jason even left the Clark County complex. The top pile—i.e., Hughes's executive staff—was considerably thinner than the bottom—i.e., everyone else. Jason had only examined the former, figuring Hughes would have had no contact with anyone in his organization below a certain degree of influence. Now he wasn't so sure.

He thought about calling Noah, then decided against it after checking the clock—1:47 AM. He set the top pile aside, pulled the rubber band off the other, and began finger-walking through the pages. He guesstimated there to be at least a thousand. Mercifully, whoever had compiled them back in the 1970s had done so in a relatively orderly fashion—each page was in the same position, so all the names appeared in the same place at the top left. An hour later, his notebook list of 'CW's had eleven new entries. Forty two minutes after that, he launched an Internet search on the sixth name down, which led him almost immediately to an archived article from the November 1970 issue of the *Las Vegas Sun.*

"Oh my God," he said in a whisper.

****

"Okay, slow *down*," Noah said, back on the iPad again. His wispy silver hair was frazzled out in some places, and his robe sat crookedly on his shoulders. "I'm still half asleep here. The name's 'Weller'?"

"Wheeler," Jason said, his face aglow from the laptop screen. "Chase *Wheeler.*"

"And who was he?"

"A kitchen worker at the Desert Inn, where Hughes lived in the top floor. I think he was a busboy. He was twenty one."

Noah paused, then ran a hand over his face. "A busboy," he repeated.

"That's right."

"You seriously believe—"

"It's perfectly logical."

"Not to me."

"Princess Diana. I told you—the subconscious."

"You're not making sense."

Jason turned to him. "Remember I said that I kept getting that image of Diana—"

"—standing in front of a flagstone hearth in a blue silk blouse."

"Right. Well, I had a dream a little while ago where I saw the rest of it. The hearth was in a cottage in rural England—I don't know the town or village—and a married couple lived there. They were farmers or something. The hearth was in their kitchen, Diana was standing in front of it, and the couple was sitting at a table nearby. One of those rough-hewn tables, like something out of *Lord of the Rings.*"

"I still don't—"

"That couple, Noah. They were just ordinary people."

"So?"

"They were the princess's friends."

"Good for them."

"No—I saw a television interview with them after she died. I don't remember their names, but they said she used to visit them from time to time. Like once or twice a year."

Noah shrugged. "So what?"

"She needed someone to *confide* in, Noah, and she didn't feel as though she could trust anyone in her own world—the one in which she had to be a royal figure. So she became friends with this couple. They weren't rich or powerful or influential or anything. Ordinary people with no stake in the game she was being forced to play."

"How do you know they weren't lying?"

"Because they had pictures of her. One of them was of her standing by that hearth in the blue blouse, but there were others, too. The couple showed them during the interview, and some photo expert confirmed that they were real. Photos, letters...a lot of stuff."

"Well, yes, that's pretty unusual."

"She asked the couple to keep their relationship a secret, and they did. But after she died I guess they felt it was okay to come forward. Everyone in the princess's inner circle was shocked because no one knew."

"So you think this busboy, Chase Wheeler—"

"—was the same way, yes. Just an everyday person, down toward the bottom of Hughes's company ladder. But that's exactly the type of person Hughes would've turned to. He was always doing things like that. Remember the rumors about the handful people who *did* have direct contact with him during the last years of his life? How they manipulated him by doing things like withholding his codeine? How they got him to sign away TWA? One biographer called it 'The financial rape of the 20th century.'"

"I remember that, yes."

"I'm sure he didn't feel like he could trust any of these people with his will. I've read through his notes several times now, and there was no mention of him leaving a penny to any of them. I don't care how much dope they were pumping into him, I'm sure he realized he couldn't leave the will in their care. So he would've needed someone outside the circle. And it would've been someone who wasn't obvious."

"And you say this Wheeler kid went missing?"

Jason looked back to the article. "Yes, in November of 1970. He went to work one day, and no one ever saw him again. According to police, he—"

Jason's mouth fell open.

"What's wrong?"

"November of 1970...that's when Hughes disappeared, too." He shook his head. "That's when he left Vegas for good. Wow...*wow.* That can't be a coincidence, it just can't be. No...I'm onto something here, I can feel it."

Noah agreed, but had no intention of saying so.

Nine

THE PARKING LOT that was visible from Jason's window was nearly full, save for a few spaces along the perimeter. Most of the vehicles spoke to the status of the hotel's clientele—Jaguars, BMWs, Lexuses, Range Rovers, etc.

One in particular, a black Mercedes coupe, sat in the farthest corner, well away from the glow of the buzzing fluorescents and the oscillating security cameras. It blended perfectly with its lot-mates but was, in fact, unique in two respects. First, it was the only one that had been rented under a false name. Second, it was the only one that presently had an occupant.

Grant sat behind the wheel wearing a pair earbuds. The wire that ran down to his lap connected with what was, by all appearances, a standard iPhone. In reality, the device was linked wirelessly to a hub in the trunk that was receiving signals from the nine bugs he'd planted earlier in the day, while Jason was busy at the municipal complex. The false iPhone also acted as a master controller, enabling Grant to switch from bug to bug as needed.

He'd been keeping notes in a pocket-sized pad. Now he took out his actual phone and tapped in a five-digit number, followed by the pound sign. The call was answered on the first ring.

"Yes?"

"He's definitely here looking for Hughes's will—and he's making progress."

"What kind of progress?"

Grant recounted the major developments—the discovery of the scribbled 'CW,' the failed Internet searches, the trip to Clark County municipal, and the inspired discovery following Jason's dream of Princess Diana.

"He came up with the name 'Chase Wheeler,'" Grant said at the end, purposely dropping it like a brick. There was a long pause from the other side.

Then—"I have no idea who that is."

Grant smiled. *He's never stumbled before. Never. Okay...I'll play along.*

"Apparently he was some kid who used to work at the Desert Inn back in the '70s."

"As I said, I've never heard of him."

"Hammond's probably barking up the wrong tree, then. Anyway, what do you want me to do now?"

"Exactly what we discussed."

"You sure about that? Hammond isn't the kind of person who'll go unmissed like some wino sleeping by a dumpster somewhere. He's got money, connections, and a degree of celebrity. It won't be easy afterward."

"You're not getting paid to do easy work. Can you make it happen or not?"

"Of course I can."

"And you won't make a mess of it like you have everything else?"

Grant fantasized about reaching through the phone and choking his current employer until the man's eyes popped out.

"No."

"Then follow through."

****

After the call ended, Grant began going through a checklist he'd developed from his past forays into the macabre trade of contract murder.

He also made a mental note to do some research on Chase Wheeler.

Ten

FOUR HOURS LATER, Jason was still in the process of doing just that. He scoured the Internet specifically for information on Wheeler's disappearance using every combination of search words imaginable, but was able to unearth just two references, both from the archives of the *Las Vegas Sun*.

The first—the article he'd seen already—was little more than a minor blurb with few facts. The reporter spoke with the two detectives that had been assigned to the case, who in turn had spoken with Wheeler's mother and sister and confirmed that Chase had simply gone to work one morning and never returned. The latter described the boy as a quiet and friendly individual who'd never made an enemy in his life. The officers were unwilling to comment further since the investigation was ongoing, but they did ask anyone who might be able to provide a lead to come forward.

The second article, a followup piece published eleven days later, stated that Wheeler's abandoned car had been discovered in a stretch of open desert along the western fringes of the city, but had been cleansed of any useful evidence. Thus, authorities speculated, Wheeler's abduction was likely the work of professionals. In the last paragraph, an anonymous source within the LVMPD described the chance of finding Wheeler alive as "...basically zero." Jason decided the next move was to go through the town's records again to see if the original case file could be found.

He dressed quickly and went out.

****

Las Vegas's municipal complex was a postmodern steel-and-glass monstrosity that occupied a full block of the city's business district. At the visitor's desk, Jason found the same clerk that had helped him the previous day.

"Back for more research on your book?" she asked, and the eyes behind the bookish glasses took on a bemused sparkle. The name on her faux-gold tag read 'Christie.'

"Absolutely," Jason said. "I hope you don't mind."

"Not at all. How can I help?"

"I'm looking for the file of a police investigation from awhile back."

"What year?"

"1970."

"Oh wow, that *is* awhile back. All right, let's see what we can find."

She took him to a tiny office and got behind the computer, then asked for whatever details he could provide. He repeated what he knew so far, and she typed along fluidly.

She paused and tapped a finger on her lips. "Hmm…I'm not seeing anything here. I entered the victim's name first, which is really the best starting point with a search like this. Then I tried his mother and sister, and the detectives you mentioned. There's nothing coming up in our cloud."

"How could that be?"

"Well, it's really not unusual. Even though we've been online for years, we haven't had the chance to convert all of our paper to digital. Budgetary restraints have slowed the process, and the necessity of prioritizing which files get converted first probably means this one is still sitting in a box, waiting its turn."

"Is there any chance that box is in this building?"

"Maybe." Christie rose from her chair. "Let's take a little walk."

She led him through an echoey corridor that, Jason learned, was colloquially known as the 'wind tunnel' because so many local politicians huddled here with each other and blabbed for hours on end. Then they went down three flights of stairs to a security door. A six-digit code unlocked it, and the storage area beyond was cool and quiet. Christie flicked a single switch, and a long line of overhead lights came on. There were thousands of boxes stacked on what appeared to be miles of shelves.

Noticing the like-new condition of the cement floor and cinder-block walls, Jason said, "I assume this area doesn't get many visitors."

"No. Like I said, we've had financial difficulties getting these files converted. We'll get to them all eventually."

"Do you have any idea where the one I'm looking for might be?"

Christie grinned. "Have faith, Mr. Hammond."

She did not consult any kind of diagram or map, nor did she glance at any of the Post-Its that were affixed to the end of each shelf. She simply led him down the path between numbers six and seven. Stopping about halfway along, she turned and made circles in the air with her open palm. It looked like she was polishing an invisible window.

"These are the missing-persons files for the years '68 through '72," she said.

They were typical storage boxes of the period, cheap cardboard with faux woodgrain exteriors and white lids. Months and years had been written on the front of some of them—'1/68 to 3/68,' for example, was rendered in faded magic marker on the first, which sat on the top shelf to the left.

"If the file you're looking for is anywhere, it'll be here."

Jason smiled. "Great, thank you."

"Now, you should know that you can't take any of these out of the building. And that's because—"

"—technically, many of them are still considered active."

"Right. The one that you're interested in, for example—unless Mr. Wheeler turns up alive in a cabin in Idaho or his body is found, the case will not be officially closed for a long time."

"And yet you're letting me look through these because they're considered longshots, right?"

"Well, we don't like to think of them that way, but...yes, that's essentially it."

Her cellphone vibrated at just that moment, as if it had been waiting for her to finish her sentence. She took it out and read through a text message.

"I'm sorry, I have to get back to my office. If you need anything further, let me know."

"Okay, thank you."

****

It didn't take long for Jason to find the boxes from the correct timespan. There were three in total, all nearly bursting from dry rot.

He set gently them on the floor, removed the lids, and began fingering through the files. Some were in standard manila folders, others in goldenrod envelopes, and a few in hanging folders of varying colors with their plastic tabs still attached. Whoever had packed them away all those years ago seemed to have been in a hurry.

As Jason watched for the name 'Wheeler,' other words flashed by that were impossible to ignore, such as *rape* and *beating* and *manslaughter* and *suicide*. He saw the phrase *child prostitution ring* on one loose page that was sticking up at an odd angle. On another—a carbon copy on an almost translucent sheet of onion paper, its typeface faded to a dusky purple—was a vivid description of a mutilated body that had been discovered in a dumpster. *This is a ledger from* Hell, Jason thought.

The names on the labels were not in alphabetical order, nor were they arranged in a common line like the Desert Inn's tax records. The height of his frustration, however, came when he reached the end of the third box without finding any file pertaining to the Wheeler case.

He looked over those that were still on the shelves to see if he missed one from the period in question, but he hadn't. He theorized that the Wheeler file could be in some other box.

It wasn't completely out of the question considering the haphazard nature in which these files had been stored. He peered down the corridor in each direction and recalled his earlier estimate that there had to be thousands of boxes in this room. Then he dropped his head and took a deep breath.

One more time, he told himself. He would go through the three boxes that were on the floor around him just once more before launching into the unthinkable task of going through all the rest. He went slowly, flipping back single page after single page. *Maybe it was shoved inside another file...or it slipped beneath another...or it's facing a different direction...or—*

There it was—a manila folder with 'Wheeler, Chase / Disappearance' typed on an ordinary piece of paper, which had then been cut into a strip and glued to the tab. The folder was even in relatively good condition.

With his heart pounding, Jason pulled it out and flipped it open. Then he froze.

"You can't be serious," he said wearily.

There was nothing inside.

****

He strode briskly through the wind tunnel with the folder in hand and frustration racing through every vein.

He reached Christie's door, which was open a few inches, and went to knock. Then he stopped to compose himself. There was no point in spewing his anger in her direction. He closed his eyes and took a few deep breaths, then rapped twice very softly.

"Yes?"

"It's Jason Hammond."

"Hey, come on in."

He stuck his head through the opening and found her at her desk with a sandwich in hand.

"I'm sorry," Jason said. "I didn't know you were having lunch."

"No, it's fine." She set the sandwich down and waved him in. "Please."

"Thanks."

As soon as he stepped inside, she said, "What happened to you?!"

"Huh?"

"You're a mess!"

He held his arms out like a scarecrow and made a cursory appraisal of himself. His clothes were covered from top to bottom with dusty smudges. The jeans were bad enough, but his pale green Polo shirt looked as though it had been lying on a busy highway.

"What were you doing down there? Wrestling with the rats?"

He smiled. "Just a little clerical archaeology."

"Well, you've got it everywhere." She opened a drawer. "I think I have some disinfectant wipes you can use...."

"No, please. It's okay."

She looked up. "You don't want to clean yourself off?"

"I will when I get back to my hotel. For now, there's a much bigger problem."

"What's that?"

He held the file up and tapped a finger on the label.

"Look at what I've got here."

"You found it!"

"Yeah, except—" he let it unfold into a long rectangle "—it's a little light on content."

"It was *empty*?"

"It was indeed."

"Were the papers somewhere else in the same box?"

"No, I looked. Nor were they in any of the other boxes from the same time frame. And they weren't in any of the other forty-two boxes I dug through, either."

She held her hand out, and he passed the folder over to her. She looked at it front, back, and inside, as if maybe the paperwork was hiding in a fourth dimension accessible only through the folder itself.

"This is really strange."

"Do you think there's any chance the contents are still down there somewhere?"

"It's possible. When I started working here, I did some of the digital conversions myself. Very boring work—feeding sheets into a scanner, checking a screen to make sure they were readable, then shredding the originals. Every now and then I'd find a few that were out of place."

"But the percentage was pretty small, right? Even smaller when it came to the entire contents of a file?"

"Very small."

"As in...so small it's not really worth considering?"

"Not quite like winning the lottery, but along those lines."

"Terrific." Jason shook his head. "Let me ask you, how secure is that storage area?"

"Very. You saw the door with the electronic lock. Even if it wasn't there, you still have to get into this building, past the guard at the front, go through the wind tunnel, down the stairs, and so on. *And* you'd have to know which box to look in. Not to mention there are cameras everywhere. Why? Are you thinking someone stole the material?"

"Possibly."

"Well, that would be a really stupid thing to do. We'd have it on video."

Jason nodded. "How long have the cameras been in operation?"

"About five years."

"That's all?"

"Before that we had an old videotape system. And we didn't keep most of the tapes. After a time, we just recorded over old ones because of—"

"Budgetary restraints."

She pointed at him. "Now you're getting it."

"Okay, well, I guess that's it then. Thanks very much for your help, I appreciate it."

"I'm sorry it didn't work out for you today, Mr. Hammond."

"Not your fault. And I apologize if I came across a little terse. The information I needed was pretty important."

"If I learn of something that might be helpful, I'll let you know."

"Thanks."

He started to go out, then stopped at the door and turned back.

"Hey, let me ask you something."

"Shoot."

"I was reading an article about this case in an online archive from one of the local newspapers, and it mentioned the two detectives who were working on the case. One was named Merv Griffin, of all things. The other was Robert Sanchez. Is there any chance—"

He stopped when he saw her break out in a broad smile.

"What's funny?"

"I knew Rob Sanchez. Very well, in fact."

"Really?"

"Yeah. Merv Griffin passed away in the mid '90s from emphysema, and I never met him. But Robert used to come in her all the time up until last year. Very funny—always joking, always smiling."

"Why only until last year?"

"He died too, I'm afraid. Peacefully, though, in his sleep. Very different from his partner."

Jason's shoulders dropped. "I'm sorry to hear all that, for all sorts of reasons." He scratched behind his head and looked around. *Now what?*

As if reading his mind, Christie said, "You could try his daughter."

"Whose daughter?"

"Robert Sanchez's. She took after her daddy and became a detective, too."

Jason pointed downward. "Here in Vegas?"

"That's right. Her name is Lisa."

"Oh, wow—terrific. Is there any chance I could trouble you for—"

She already had her Post-It pad out and was scribbling on the top sheet. She peeled it off and handed it over.

"That's her cell number. I'm sure she'd be happy to talk to you."

"Thanks, I really owe you for this."

"Just be sure to mention me on the acknowledgements page of your book."

For a split second, Jason had no idea what she was talking about. Then he remembered the lie, and the guilt came forth in a flood.

"Sure," he said with a quick nod. "No problem."

Eleven

PARKED ACROSS THE STREET, Grant watched Hammond exit the municipal complex. When he saw how filthy Jason's clothes were, he thought, *He's been digging.*

Grant also noted that he hadn't carried anything out of the building. It was hard to know whether this was good or bad. He wished he could've followed him inside, kept a closer eye on him. That would've been risky, though. All those cameras. And cops.

When Jason got into his car, Grant turned up the volume on the false iPod. The bug he'd planted days earlier was located just beneath the driver's seat. It was a modern omnidirectional, the same as those he'd scattered throughout the hotel suite, and he marveled at the sound quality as Jason took out his cellphone and make a call. It was like sitting in the car next to him.

Following a conversation from only one side was usually challenging, but in this case Hammond's enthusiasm made it fairly easy. Grant took out his notepad and began scribbling—*Lisa Sanchez...friend of 'Christie'...daughter of one of two detectives in Wheeler case...both now deceased...Hammond laughing...they're getting along...Hammond found Wheeler file but it was empty...Sanchez surprised...she can talk to Hammond as soon as he wants...Hammond asks for address...programs it into GPS....*

The call ended, and Jason started the car. Then he pulled out of the lot and headed south.

Grant followed him.

****

Sanchez lived in a sparsely populated suburb within view of the McCullough mountains and not far from the airport where Jason had landed days earlier. Her house had been built from the same blueprints as numerous others in the neighborhood, with traditional high-desert features like ornamental ironwork, cultured stone elevations, and a Spanish tile roof. The construction was reasonably new.

Parking at a discreet distance, Grant took out a small telescope and watched as Jason went to the arched entryway and rang the bell. Lisa Sanchez answered a moment later, and they had an amiable opening exchange. Grant could not get a good look at Sanchez through the screen, but he did manage to make a quick appraisal when she pushed the door back to let Jason in—small and compact, with short brown hair atop a roundish, smiling face. She was wearing jeans and a t-shirt along with a pair of canvas work gloves.

Grant watched them go into a room and sit down. He assumed this was the living room, but it was hard to tell for sure because of the loose-weave curtains that hung in the large front window. Either way, he knew his opportunity here was limited.

He got out of the car and went around to the back. His disguise this time was of a much younger man, in a sweatsuit and sneakers. Sunglasses and a UNLV cap completed the illusion. He opened the trunk and removed a backpack, which he slung over his shoulder.

With his heart beating rapidly, he approached the house.

****

"I was going to apologize for my appearance," Lisa Sanchez said, removing her gloves and gesturing toward the smudges on Jason's shirt, "but it appears I'm not the only one making a mess of themselves today." She was small and compact, with short black hair and an infectious smile that struck Jason as similar to that of a happy child. He sat across from her, a large coffee table between them. A cowhide mat covered most of the table's surface, with a three-wicked candle in the center inside a stone bowl. These accents perfectly complemented the Santa Fe stylings that pervaded the rest of the sun-brightened house.

"I was digging through the archives at the municipal building," he said, "and got carried away."

"Ah. And I was out back collecting wood for the stove before the day's heat became unbearable."

"Stove? You mean for nighttime?"

"That's right. I take it you've noticed the radical temperature swings in our part of the world. Boiling during the day and frosty at night. Welcome to Nevada."

Jason nodded. "I'm from the Northeast, where the cold season is cold all the time, and the hot season is hot all the time. What you've got here is crazy."

"I know, the human body really isn't built for it. Speaking of cold, would you care for something to drink?"

"That'd be great."

She went into the kitchen and returned with a two full glasses of ice water, each with a lemon wheel floating on top.

"How's this?"

"Perfect," Jason said. "Something smells nice in there, by the way."

"I'm baking two pans of M&M cookies."

"Oh?"

"I don't really like them that much. I just make them for the neighborhood kids. My husband always used to do that." She shrugged. "Maybe it's a way to keep him close to me. I don't know."

"He passed away?"

"Yes, six years ago, following a battle with pancreatic cancer."

"I'm sorry to hear that."

"He put up a good fight. We both did, but in the end, you know...."

"I'm truly sorry."

"Well...life doesn't always deliver what we want, right?"

Jason shook his head. "It truly doesn't."

"In the meantime, I focus on my job. I not only love it, but it helps keep the pain away."

"It's necessary to have something like that."

"Absolutely. So what can I help you with? You want to know about Chase Wheeler?"

"I do."

"And a possible connection to one Mr. Howard Robard Hughes?" Her emphasis of Hughes's name was accompanied by a raised eyebrow.

"How did you know—"

"I checked you out online before you got here. Remember, it's what I do."

"Of course."

"There was an article speculating that that's why you came to Nevada."

"It's on the Internet already?"

"It is."

"Unbelievable."

"I also know about the papers that were found by the demolition worker, and how his family was attacked."

"That was appalling," Jason said. "Going after a family like that, shooting their daughter. Pure savagery."

"Are you in touch with them?"

"I am."

"And is she okay?"

"She will be. But for awhile it was touch and go." He took a deep breath. "So, knowing what you know of the situation, what do you think?"

"Well, let me ask you first—*is* the lost will of Howard Hughes the reason why you're looking into the Wheeler case?"

Jason paused here. He liked Lisa Sanchez very much already, and there was no reason to believe she wasn't trustworthy. But past experience had developed a tendency toward wariness and caution.

"I'm not sure yet. At this point I'm still trying to draw that connecting line."

"It's an intriguing possibility. A *very* intriguing possibility. I know the case well because it was one of the few my father never solved. When I was little, he would let me sit in his lap and we'd go over all sorts of cases, and this was one that always held his attention. I'm sure I don't have to tell you it went cold pretty quickly. That's what makes these new developments of yours so interesting. The fact that someone is trying so hard to get those papers back tells me there are still figures in the shadows who want them to remain unfound. That strikes me as highly significant."

"I couldn't agree more."

"My father and his partner—"

Jason grinned. "Merv Griffin?"

"Correct. Oh man, the misery my dad put him through for that name. Anyway, they never considered a Hughes connection. Yes, Chase worked for that crazy old man at the Desert Inn, but so did about a thousand other people. Chase was just a member of the kitchen staff, and even then he was a newbie. I think he'd only been there a few months. Can I ask you *why* you think there's a connection?"

"There was what appears to be a mention of someone with the initials 'CW' in Hughes's notes," Jason said. He decided to stick as close to the truth as possible, while remaining selective about which pieces of the puzzle to reveal. It occurred to him that this wouldn't be particularly difficult in light of the fact that the puzzle was far from complete in the first place. "I checked into other possible 'CW's from Hughes's universe and none of them panned out. Plus, Chase disappeared just days after Hughes took flight from here to the Bahamas. That, I think, is also very noteworthy."

"They wrapped him up in a stretcher and took him down a fire escape in the middle of the night, right?"

"Correct."

"Y'know, now that I think of it, dad and Merv did talk about Hughes a little bit. But they never felt they had any reason to dig deeper. Frankly, people disappear in this town all the time. And Hughes...well, I don't think he was a murderer. He was just a strange duck."

"He was a *very* strange duck," Jason said. "The things I've learned in the course of my research are mind blowing. I'm sure you've heard your share of stories too."

"I know he dropped into Vegas clear out of the blue in 1966 and bought up every property he could. I know he went ballistic when the government started carrying out weapons tests in the desert. He was convinced he was going to wake up one morning with that emaciated body of his looking like a Cajun steak. I know he once purchased a local television station just so they'd play the movies he wanted to watch at night. The most expensive DVD player in history. And I know that his vacated suite atop the D-I reeked of urine and human decay in spite of the fact that he was one of the most neurotic germaphobes of his day."

"And—" Jason added "—he was known for being unpredictable when it came to picking his friends, which is why a connection with Chase seems like a real possibility. There are records of him making deeply personal confessions to girls who were one-nighters, signing contracts with men whose names he couldn't remember, and giving generous gifts to people he met once and never saw again. When he went into seclusion, he surrounded himself with—"

"Members of the Mormon faith because he considered them the most upright," Lisa said.

"Exactly. That's quite an honor to bestow upon any one group in such a broad, sweeping fashion. He basically handed control of his life to them."

Lisa was nodding. "The 'Mormon Mafia,' they were called. My dad knew a few of them. You can't believe how tight-lipped they were about their boss."

"I'll bet Chase Wheeler got inside," Jason said. "If Hughes really wrote a final, signed will, Chase was just the kind of person Hughes would've given it to for safekeeping. Young, naïve, trustworthy, and under everyone else's radar. Think about it from Hughes's perspective."

Lisa was nodding. "Possibly, yes."

"What can you tell me about Chase?"

She leaned forward, elbows on her knees and hands together. "Well, I'll have to dig up my dad's old files to get the full details, but I do remember a few things. I know Merv and my dad interviewed just about everybody in his life—his friends, co-workers, former schoolmates. And then there was his immediate family, which consisted of a mother and a sister."

"I read about them in the *Sun*."

"His mother, Vallie, worked as a cashier in a grocery store. She was beautiful in an Old World kind of way, with an elegance that had faded over time. She was also a bit heavy for her age. But mostly, she was just a very tired soul. One of the most broken-down people I've ever met. She loved her son so much, and she deteriorated after he vanished. Every day that passed without the case being cracked, another inch of her was chopped away. She used to call my dad at all hours, crying like a child."

Jason shook his head. "Horrifying. And the sister?"

"Her name was Denise, and she was very different from her mother. A real spark plug. Not passive in the least. Tough, outspoken, take no prisoners. If they'd found the person or persons responsible for her brother's disappearance, I honestly believe she would've killed them with her bare hands. A very angry young girl with a huge chip on her shoulder."

"You mentioned Chase's father, but I didn't see anything about him in the articles."

"He was gone by then."

"He abandoned them?"

"No, passed away. Gambling, drinking, smoking. I don't think he touched drugs; he wasn't really from that generation. But he did everything else, and he did it without limit. He had a massive coronary, dead before he hit the casino floor. It was mostly the bottle that got him, but his gambling debts were huge, and that wears on you in a different way. He got himself arrested several times on purpose just so he'd get thrown in the county tank where the loan sharks couldn't get him."

"Ugh, what a mess."

"He destroyed his family, plain and simple. Vallie loved him, and that was a big part of her undoing. It's like drugs—they drag you to ruin, and yet you're smiling the whole way down. He couldn't keep a job, couldn't hold onto a dime. Vallie and Denise were suffering long before Chase disappeared."

"No wonder Denise was so angry."

"Exactly."

"And what about Chase's car? I understand it was found?"

Lisa nodded. "In the desert on the west side of town. It had been ditched in an old construction site, one of a hundred future casinos that ran out of investors before the first wall went up. Someone left it in a Quonset hut under a tarp along with a half-dozen others. The only reason the authorities learned of it was because some guy had wandered in there looking for old cars to restore. What they call a 'picker' these days. He eventually tracked down the owner of the property, who knew about every car except Chase's '66 Plymouth Valiant. That's when my dad got the call."

"And there was no useful evidence inside?"

"Well, that's impossible to say."

"What do you mean?"

"The authorities couldn't find anything back *then*. But with today's technology, I'll bet we could. DNA analysis and chromatography and UV lights to reveal blood stains, all that."

"So you're saying the car isn't around anymore?"

Lisa let out a one-note laugh that sounded more like a bark. "No, that thing's long gone. It was a tired old wreck that could barely crawl forward when Chase had it. His mom eventually gave it back to the town. But they couldn't sell it at the auctions no matter how hard they tried. They kept it for a few years, then unloaded it for scrap. I'm sure it's sitting deep in landfill somewhere." She paused, then added bitterly, "Probably just like Chase himself, poor kid."

"Can you tell me anything about him as a person?"

"As far as my dad could determine, he was very sweet. Not the sharpest knife in the drawer, if you know what I mean, but *good.* Always minded his business, did what was expected of him, never complained. He was a hard worker, took a real interest in the job even though there didn't appear to be anything interesting about it. Dropped out of high school to earn money to keep the household going. Vallie was buried under bills and the other lingering debts of her whackjob husband. Chase didn't have much time for friends, but those who knew him said he was quiet and easygoing. He smiled a lot, I remember someone saying that, which is a heartbreaking thing to hear for some reason. But he simply was not the kind of person to make enemies."

"And no one ever got even a whiff of who might have done it?"

Lisa shook her head. "Nope. The people responsible were good. Very good." She took on an expression of dire import. "And I'll tell you something that is to remain just between us."

"I promise."

"There were times during the investigation when my dad got the distinct impression he was dealing with powers well beyond the reach of the LVMPD."

"Why's that?"

"Just a hunch, mostly. But his hunches were rarely off the mark. Remember, he was someone who had been at the game for years and knew exactly how it was played around here. There were many dark forces at work in this town, and there still are. Never forget that, Jason. When there's this much money in one place, you're going to attract a bad element—people who are powerful, people who are ruthless, people who are used to getting their own way. There were moments when it seemed to my father as though there was an invisible hand at work, thwarting him, manipulating him. He knew every crook and every thug that squirmed under every rock in Clark County, and suddenly they all seemed to lose the power of speech. That's rare even in a place like this. I'm not the least bit surprised that the file you found turned up empty. It's nearly impossible to accomplish something like that."

"Which is exactly why I think Chase had a connection to the will," Jason said. "If Hughes did give it to him and one of Hughes's cronies found out, I have no doubt Chase's life would've been forfeit."

"And from *that* angle," Lisa said, "there would've been more than enough cause for my dad to have Hughes and his people investigated. No doubt about it."

"Are any of those people still around? Any of his so-called 'Mormon Mafia,' for example, that I could speak with?"

"Highly doubtful. Remember, this is going back to 1970. That's another generation ago. The majority of them are dead now; dead and buried. They were grown men at the time."

"What about Chase's co-workers? Do you think I could track down some of them?"

"Maybe. I go back through my dad's notes and see what names I find."

"And what about Vallie and Denise?"

"Vallie was in her fifties, so I guess there's a tiny chance she's still alive. It's highly unlikely, though. But Denise was just nineteen at the time Chase disappeared, so she's probably still in the land of the living."

"Do you remember where they lived? The address?"

"On Gold Strike Boulevard. Number fifteen, if memory serves. Gold Strike is in North Vegas—but be careful if you go there. It was a rough area then and it's a rough area now."

"All right, thanks." Jason rose, and his host did likewise. "Thank you for *all* the information."

"Sure. And hey, would you mind keeping me updated on your progress? I'm still very interested in this case. It would mean a great deal to me personally."

"I certainly will. It looks like I've got a lot of work ahead."

"Yes you do."

When they reached the foyer, Jason said, "If there really is a connection between Chase's disappearance and the lost will. I'll find it. Then we can both expose whoever's responsible."

"That'd be great," Lisa replied, "But remember—whoever's behind what's happening now, I can tell you based just on seasoned instinct that they're the type of people who don't like being messed with. You need to be *very* careful."

Jason nodded. "I will be."

Twelve

AS JASON WALKED back to the car, a rush of excitement rolled through him. The dates of Wheeler and Hughes's disappearances...the missing file from the municipal archives...Lisa's comment that her father felt as though there were unseen forces trying to hamper him.... *There really is something here, I know it.*

When he reached the sidewalk, he removed his blazer and tossed it through the open window onto the passenger seat. Lisa was right—the weather swung in very broad arcs out here. The jacket had been necessary when he left the hotel this morning. But now the desert sun was beating down with a vengeance. Walking around to the driver's side, he rolled up the sleeves of his shirt. Getting behind the wheel felt like climbing into an oven. He put the windows up again and blasted the air conditioner.

As he pulled away, he thought about what came next. It was time, he decided, to interview a few key people. Nearly half a century had passed since Chase disappeared. Many of the peripheral players were probably long gone, but a few had to be around. Some of Chase's fellow kitchen staffers, for example. Most of them must've been fairly young at the time; a busy casino kitchen wasn't ideal for the middle-aged labor class. And Chase's family—his mother was a longshot, but his sister wasn't. If Lisa's description had been accurate—aggressive, opinionated, bitter—then Jason doubted he'd have any trouble getting her to talk.

Back on the road, traffic had thickened considerably. Highway 15 had two lanes on each side, and there was nothing dividing northbound from southbound except a pair of solid yellow lines. Once he got into the flow, he moved into the left lane and floored it. The speed limit on this particular stretch was seventy five, but even when he put ten on top of that he drew a line of impatient, lunatic motorists bearing down on him. He resigned himself to the right lane and decided to call Noah for an update.

What happened next happened quickly.

****

His phone was in the inner pocket of his blazer. Keeping his eyes on the road, he reached over and tried to locate it with his hand. He found the shape of it first, a hard rectangle enveloped by the jacket's fabric. When he tried to slip his fingers inside, the phone vibrated—or so he believed for the first moment. Then he realized the buzzing was too loud and too harsh. *And I never set it on vibrate anyway....*

He looked over in confusion, and there in the footwell of the passenger side was a small, ash-gray rattlesnake. It was coiled tight, head raised, ready to strike. The tail was going so fast it was nothing but a blur, and the animal's pink, forked tongue waved about lazily.

Jason jerked his body back in terror, and in doing so he gave the wheel an involuntary turn. Then came the mad blare of a horn, and he looked up to see that he had drifted into the opposite side of the highway with a casino bus bearing down fast. The driver, who looked equally petrified in the giant window, was trying to wave him off. They spun their steering wheels at the same moment and missed each other by inches. Jason slanted across his original lane and continued unabated into the next, striking a pickup truck loaded with greenish, pressure-treated pilings. The truck swerved and smashed into the guard rail, and the tie-down belts snapped like rubber bands. Pilings flooded out in a chaotic wave, striking Jason's car in thunderous rhythms and smashing both windows on the passenger side. The impact also nudged him into the left lane again.

He glanced briefly at his traveling companion, who was now more agitated than ever. It also seemed longer and ropier than before, making Jason wonder if half its length had been previously tucked under the passenger seat. Then the heart-freezing truth occurred to him—*There's more than one.*

A second rattler was gliding by his colleague among the scatter of safety glass. The first one watched him angrily for a moment, as if offended that his personal space was being invaded, then turned its gaze back to Jason. It opened its jaws just slightly and let out a forceful hiss that sounded like air escaping from a punctured tire. The second snake responded by coiling and setting its tail in motion. The sound of both rattles going was like a hive of bees harmonizing in communal fury.

I've got to get to the shoulder and get out of this thing, Jason thought through his boiling fear. With his hands shaking and other drivers honking and screaming obscenities, he looked frantically to his right and found an opening in the flow.

Then something touched his ankle.

Reflecting on the incident later on, Jason wondered if he could've avoided everything that happened next if he just remained calm. But with his nerves rapidly disintegrating, his body was on a kind of hyperactive cruise control that nullified the capacity for calm and measured thought.

He saw the third rattler—or at least the head of it—for only an instant. Then his right leg came up in a reflexive spasm. Somewhere in the back of his panic-hazed mind was the idea that he could yank up the other one, crouch on the driver's seat, and still guide the coasting vehicle onto the shoulder. This plan, however, was cancelled before it even got going—his knee struck the back of the steering wheel, and the car veered to the wrong side of the highway again. This time it was not a casino bus barreling down the fast lane, but rather a long-range rig traveling at Mach speed. Jason had just enough time to see the driver reach up and pull the chain that activated the loudest horn blast he'd ever heard.

Now acting on pure instinct, he twisted the wheel further left and narrowly avoided the collision—but this also put him into the next lane on that side, where a minivan was zooming toward him like a missile. Just one word flashed through his mind—*children*—and he decided in that instant to make the only choice he could morally accept. He gave the wheel a final spin and jammed the accelerator, and the car broke through the guard rail with surprising ease. It left the Earth's surface for a few seconds, sailing soundlessly through the air, then landed hard in a sloping gully populated with boulders and scrub brush. He tried desperately to regain control, hoping he could get some traction in the sand if he laid on the gas again. But to no avail—the car bounced off the unforgiving surface, rolled once, then came to rest on its roof in a hardpan streambed that had not seen water in ages.

Still strapped into his seat and hanging upside down, Jason now struggled simply to maintain consciousness. But this too proved futile, as the world around him faded until the darkness prevailed and all was quiet.

Thirteen

HE REGAINED consciousness a short time later, his eyes popping open as if his power switch had been flicked on.

He looked around the room and took stock of his surroundings—the knit blanket, the blinking machinery, the privacy curtain. *I'm in a hospital....* Then he saw Lisa Sanchez staring down at him.

"Didn't I tell you to be careful?" she said. She had changed into fresh jeans and a t-shirt.

For the briefest moment, he had no clue what she was talking about. Then it all came back in a rush—the snakes, the highway, the guard rail....

"How long have I been here?"

"About five hours."

"What about the others?"

"Others?"

"The other people on the road. Was anyone...?"

"No, no fatalities."

"Injuries?"

"Do you remember the couple in the truck?"

"With the pressure-treated poles in the back."

"Yeah. The husband hit his elbow on the gearshift pretty hard. It was one of those tall shifters common to old trucks. Then the elbow went into his wife's side."

"Are they okay?

"They're fine, just some aches and pains to deal with for a few weeks. The wife was pretty mad."

"Can I see them?"

"They've already been released."

"Well, I want to pay for any expenses they incurred. Everything—the medical costs, the damage to the truck and its cargo...."

"I'm sure they'll appreciate that. And I'm sure the rental agency will be equally grateful for the same kind of generosity, considering the car you were driving is totaled."

"I had full insurance on it."

"Smart move."

He took a few deep breaths. "And what about me? Before I look, am I still in one piece?"

"More or less. You sustained a mild concussion and a bunch of scrapes and bruises. You look like you've been in a street brawl, if you really want to know. But mostly it's your left shoulder. That looks like an overripe plum."

It was covered in gauze and white stain tape. When Jason tried to move it, the pain flashed through him with bright immediacy. It felt like a bag full of broken glass.

"Okay, that really hurts."

"It's going to for awhile. They'll give you something for it."

Which I won't take, he thought, adhering to his lifelong no-drugs-unless-there's-no-alternative policy.

"It's a miracle you weren't bitten by one of your slithery friends," Lisa went on. "They were Mojave rattlers, which are highly venomous. I've hauled away a few dead bodies courtesy of their venom. Nervous little things."

"They're not the only nervous creatures I've riled up," Jason said. "Clearly there's someone out there looking to throw a blanket over my curiosity."

"I was listening to the scanner after you left, and as soon as I heard about the accident, I called into the station and told them you'd been over for a visit. They immediately sent two squad cars because they were afraid I'd be targeted next. They went around talking to some of my neighbors, but no one reported seeing anything."

"Professionals, as we discussed."

Lisa nodded. "It looks that way."

"I'll bet it's the same lunatic who went after the Millers."

"Possibly. And by the way, not being bitten isn't the only way you got lucky. You might have noticed that we have a lot of open space around here."

"Yeah, I've noticed. If someone fell asleep behind the wheel and went off the road they'd probably run out of gas before they hit anything."

She laughed. "That's a good way of putting it. And if you'd crashed in the middle of nowhere, you could've been lying there for hours, maybe even days, before anyone found you. It happens more often than you might think."

"I believe it."

"I should probably also mention that the your little brush with death has also done wonders to further enhance your celebrity status."

"Oh no...why do you say that?"

"You were recognized by a few people, some of whom felt compelled to whip out their cellphones."

"Great."

"There are already a bunch of photos on Instagram and Snapchat and at least two videos on YouTube."

Jason thought about Noah and the phone call that was coming. "Terrific."

"The price of fame, Mr. I-Solved-the-Kennedy-Assassination."

"Yeah, great. So I assume there wasn't a shred of evidence at the scene that's going to provide any kind of a lead?"

Lisa laughed. "Not a scrap. They found the bag the snakes were in lying on the floor in the back. It was old, which means it could've come from anywhere—thrift store, yard sale, whatever. Totally untraceable. They'll check it for DNA, but I wouldn't hold my breath if I were you."

"Well, there's *one* clue—if someone was willing to actually kill me and not care about who else I took out at the same time, then we're talking about ruthlessness on a grand scale. A person or group of people who have a lot to lose if that will turns up."

"I agree with your assessment."

Jason smiled. "Seems to be I've hit a very big beehive with a stick.

"And it's hard not to wonder who might be at the center of that hive."

Jason exhaled mightily. "Well, the list of people who wouldn't want the will found is pretty long, but the first and most obvious would be Hughes's relatives. Hughes made it clear many times during his life that he didn't want them to get a cent, so their fortunes would immediately be at risk. Then there's all the people he was planning to expose—politicians, businessmen, ex lovers, enraged husbands.... Lots of reputations to protect. I recognized a few names in his notes, but not all of them. There's also whoever was responsible for Chase's disappearance. Maybe just *finding* the will could be enough to crack that one. Fingerprints, blood stains, DNA, whatever. If anyone who was involved back then is still alive—which is not beyond the realm of the possible—then I'm sure they'd be happy to remain in the shadows."

"It seems like everybody rich has enemies," Lisa said. "No offense to you."

"None taken. And Hughes certainly had his share. Did you know he was partially responsible for Richard Nixon's presidency?"

"Are you serious?"

"In 1956, he loaned Donald Nixon—Tricky Dick's brother—over $200,000 so the guy could keep his failing restaurant afloat. This was when the Dickster was vice president under Dwight Eisenhower. Not long after Hughes made that loan, the Hughes Medical Institute received tax-exempt status. Gosh, how convenient."

Lisa shook her head. "Pure coincidence, of course."

"Of course. What makes it even more interesting is that Hughes had been already denied this status by the IRS—*repeatedly*. So anyway, Hughes's loan to Donald was kept a secret until right before the 1960 election. The resulting scandal may have not been the only factor that caused Nixon to lose to JFK, but it certainly had some kind of effect since the election was so close to begin with. And Hughes was pretty irritated that the public found out. Maybe he felt partially responsible for Nixon's loss, I don't know. But when Nixon prepared to run again in '68, Hughes sent a handwritten memo to one of his top lieutenants saying, '*I feel there is a really valid possibility of a Republican victory this year. If that could be realized under our sponsorship and supervision every inch of the way, then we would be ready to follow with Laxalt as our next candidate.*'"

Lisa's mouth fell open. "Paul Laxalt? Our former governor in Nevada?"

"You bet. Hughes dreamed of hand-picking a candidate and funding him all the way to the Oval Office. And it looks like he succeeded with Nixon, which probably turned every member of the Democratic Party against him. When it came to politics, he believed that everyone was for sale."

"That's unbelievable—and yet it's not. Not based on what's happening out there these days."

"Tell me about it. Nice little world we've put together here, huh?"

A nurse came in to check on Jason. She was an older woman with hair the color of aged piano keys and a tiny mouth that she kept in an affable smile. She asked very few questions and did so in a tone so low it was nearly a whisper, and her attention was focused on Jason the whole time.

After she left, Lisa said, "So what are you going to do when they release you?"

"I'm not sure yet. I'm thinking maybe—"

He was cut off by the trill of his cellphone, which was lying on the table next to the bed. Picking it up, he glanced at the LED screen.

"Who in the world...?" He showed Lisa the number, which had a 702 area code. "Does that look familiar at all?"

"It's the Vegas area code," she said, "but I don't know otherwise."

He shrugged and pressed the button. The conversation lasted about two minutes, and Jason did very little of the talking.

When it was over, he said, "You won't believe this."

"What?"

"That was Preston Hughes."

"You're joking."

"No."

"*The* Preston Hughes."

"Yes."

"What did he want?"

"He asked if we could meet as soon as possible."

Lisa's eyebrows rose in an expression of complete astonishment. "Well...I guess you *do* know what you're doing after you get out of here."

Jason shrugged. "I guess so."

****

Theresa Richter came through the front door of the governor's mansion at two minutes after eleven with a parade drum beating in her head. An answering machine blinking nearby held twenty-one messages per the red numbers on the LED screen. Those could wait.

She went up the spiral staircase, then down a long hall to the master bedroom. The lights came on gradually as she entered. Now she was in an impressive space that looked more like a living room or small studio apartment. She stepped out of her shoes, removed her jewelry, then shed her blazer and laid it over the arm of a white settee. The drink she mixed at the small bar was vodka and ginger ale with very little ice.

She took a long first sip and looked to the bed she had shared with her husband not so long ago...before the long and painful arc drawn by the unforgiving specter known as cancer. There were days when she could still feel his presence, and moments when she still spoke to him in small whispers.

She wanted to get under the covers and escape for a few hours. The limo would return to take her to the office by six thirty, so every moment of rest was precious. Nevertheless, she decided to take a quick bath first. She had a secret hatred of getting into bed if she felt the least bit unclean.

She finished the drink and began to unbutton her blouse when her personal cellphone rang. She cursed and reached down to dig it out of the blazer's inside pocket. One of her assistants, a blueblood named Toni, had developed the annoying habit calling her at home, late at night, to discuss the most trivial matters. Her true intent, Richter knew perfectly well, was an amateurish attempt to forge a personal relationship. She knew she'd been the same way when she was Toni's age, so she tried to be patient and understanding.

When she looked at the caller ID and saw that it was Kelli Nashamura instead, she breathed a sigh of relief and hit the 'ANSWER' button.

"Good evening," she said.

"And good evening to you. How are you feeling after such a long day?"

"Ready for bed, although don't tell any of my enemies that. They'll tell the voters I'm a slacker."

"No doubt."

"So what's going on?"

"Well, we may have a problem."

Richter paused before saying, "This guy Jason Hammond?"

"He's meeting with Preston Hughes, and at the latter's invitation."

Richter could feel a wave of heat break out across her chest, as it always did was she become stressed. This was the reason she always wore tops that covered her to the neck—she never wanted to her enemies to see that they were getting to her.

"That's not a good sign."

"No," Nashamura said, "it isn't."

Fourteen

JASON WAS RELEASED from the hospital about an hour later, and Lisa took him back to the car-rental agency. After a stern lecture from the manager—which included the assurance that Jason would not be welcome to borrow another vehicle if the second one befell the same fate as the first—he climbed into a black BMW coupe and headed to the hotel to do some quick research on his host for this evening.

There wasn't much, which came as no surprise. Secrecy was clearly a trait that ran through the whole of the Hughes clan; Howard was simply the most famous example of it. What did surprise Jason was Preston's Hughes's public image as the nicest rich guy this side of Warren Buffett. The few puzzle pieces that were available formed the image of a most unusual species of philanthropist—one who has given not just his money but also his time, talents, and energy. Preston Hughes had personally administered vaccine injections to Congolese villagers, nailed boards to new schools in Paraguay, taught business courses without pay in Detroit, and made a habit of randomly writing checks to ordinary people all over the globe who found themselves in dire financial straits through no fault of their own.

Jason also scrutinized what he often thought of as a person's 'family credentials,' and even there he could find no fault. Preston appeared to be a devoted husband, brother, son, cousin, and uncle, as evidenced by a rare, and yet surprisingly long and detailed, interview with his wife, Doreen, in a 1992 issue of *Cosmopolitan*. A Wikipedia entry stated that the couple had not had any children, and that Doreen passed away from esophageal cancer in 2006. There was a piece in the *Los Angeles Times* in which Preston made a public statement after posting bail for the drug-related arrest of a nephew, and another in New Orleans's *Times-Picayune* following the apprehension of a niece for possession of unregistered firearms. Jason already knew that Preston had been one of the original twenty-two cousins who inherited a share of Howard's estate following the long legal battle. What Jason was beginning to understand now was that, in the decades since, the man had crystallized into the patriarch and 'positive face' of the Hughes family.

But rather than provide Jason with reassurance, it cultivated greater suspicion. He had seen the type all his life—the pillar of integrity, a shining example of graceful humanity balanced with calculative, machine-like business acumen, at once able to generate unimaginable wealth from the helm of a massive empire and then provide comfort and succor to society's uneducated and unloved. People of this stripe had passed through Jason's early years in a tireless march, usually at the behest of his father. And while the younger Jason at first admired and even hoped to one day emulate them, such idealism fell from his eyes once he learned of the extramarital affairs, sleazy deals, ruined lives, and other ugly truths that were imminently found lurking behind the bright social veneer. By the time of his father's death, Jason's mistrust of such people had rooted itself so deeply that he was all but unable to separate the concepts of accumulated wealth and personal corruption.

****

Although he never put much faith in the supernatural, he took it as a bad omen that the address of his meeting with Preston Hughes, on the east side of town, happened to be located on Howard Hughes Parkway. And the venue in question—ten stories of glass and concrete that looked like a short row of upright phone books, each set slightly forward from the last—was named the Hughes Center. As he pulled into a spot near the front and began toward the entrance, he began to feel like Bilbo Baggins heading into the Lonely

Mountain.

The security guard in the atrium, stationed within a C-shaped desk and clearly expecting his arrival, was friendly enough. As Jason waited for the elevator, he took note of the businesses listed in the directory on the wall—a real-estate broker, fabrics manufacturer, rehabilitation clinic, orthodontist, import-export firm, and a few names that gave no clue as to the business in question, e.g., Simmons and Sons, Harper-Clarke, etc. And there, on the top floor (of course), was his destination—Hughes Gaming, LLC.

When the elevator doors parted, he found himself facing a long white hallway with hardwood floors and bright pendant lighting. There was framed art on either side, mostly abstracts, and some modern sculptures that stood almost as high as he did. With no one there to greet him, Jason took the initiative and went forward.

The hallway eventually terminated in a large single room. There were more framed images here, mostly glass-encased paintings of casinos that Howard had owned at the peak of his Vegas reign or modern properties that, Jason assumed, were part of Hughes Gaming in some fashion. A couch and coffee table were set against one wall with large potted plants on either side. Adjacent to this was a water cooler and mini fridge. What drew his attention most, however, was the desk—little more than a frosted pane of reinforced glass with four titanium legs—and, more to the point, the man working quietly behind it.

Jason had found several photos of Preston Hughes on the Internet, but none more recent than four years ago. It was somehow fascinating to see him now, in the next stage of the aging process—the gray having completed its invasion of the once-dark hair, the cheeks a little more withdrawn, the eyes a little more bulbous. Jason was also mesmerized by the physical hallmarks of the Hughes lineage. The head was narrow, with thick eyebrows and a smallish mouth. And although Hughes was sitting, Jason could tell he was taller than the average adult, and that his frame was fairly slight although not quite gangly.

He also did not possess the scant mustache that Howard had occasionally sported; the one that gave Howard a faint resemblance to a sideshow huckster. Preston Hughes, Jason decided on the spot, was the type who did not leave home until he was flawlessly groomed—daily shave, every hair combed into place, shirt starched, suit pressed, tie knotted tight. *Respectable, that's the illusion he has manufactured. Respectable.* Preston was writing with a ridiculously ornate fountain pen, and Jason couldn't help but wonder if the penmanship was similar to Howard's. *Does he occasionally forget to dot his i's and cross his t's? Does he only refer to people by their initials so no one else—*

He surrendered this train of thought when Preston looked up. There was puzzlement in his face at first, then he made the recognition and broke into a smile.

"Oh, Mr. Hammond! Hello! Is it that time already?"

Another genealogical connection was easy to make here—the voice was high and thin, although not as cackling or birdlike as Howard's. It also had the faintest trace of the family's well-known Texas pedigree.

Preston checked his watch in a manner common to men who have spent most of their lives in a suit—basically throwing his arm forward in order to free the wrist from the sleeve.

"Ah, I guess it is," he said, and rose from his chair.

As he came forward, Jason caught a few other details. In spite of Preston's advanced years, he moved with an easy fluidity, and with a posture that was ramrod straight. *He's taken care of himself,* Jason thought. *Or someone else has.*

Preston put out his hand and Jason took it. The pump was firm but brief, right out of the businessman's handbook.

"Thank you for taking the time to come out here. I know you're quite busy."

"It's no trouble," Jason said.

"Please, have a seat wherever you like. Would you care for something to drink?" He began toward the mini-fridge. "I have soda, juice, bottled water...." Jason expected him to add a caveat along the lines of, *But no alcohol, as I'm a bit of a teetotaler,* to clumsily demonstrate what a straight-up guy he was. This particular advertisement never came, however.

"No, thank you. I'm fine for the moment."

"Okay, good."

Jason settled into one of the two chairs in front of the desk. To his astonishment, Preston came over and took the other one. Jason expected him to get back in his leather executive chair as part of the standard psychological ploy to establish dominance. Jason had seen it plenty of times; he even witnessed his father use the tactic on occasion.

Preston groaned slightly as he eased himself down. "Ugh, nothing like getting old. And I'm sorry, I know these chairs aren't the most comfortable. I've asked the landlords to replace them with something better, but so far no luck."

"Landlords? You mean this isn't your property?"

"My prop—oh, you mean because the building is named after Howard?" Preston laughed. "No, believe it or not, I'm just leasing this space. I know, it's quite a coincidence. But it is. We've only recently gotten back into the gaming business in Nevada, so we needed an office, and this seemed like as good a location as any." As he gave the room a casual appraisal he said, "It's nice enough, I suppose. I'm not really here all that much."

"No? Then why are you here now, if you don't mind my asking?"

"We're looking into joining with another firm to build a pair of new resorts. One right here on the Strip and another in Lake Tahoe." Then he added earnestly, "I would be grateful if you kept that information to yourself."

"Sure."

"This area is beginning to see some growth again, now that the worst of the recession is behind us. With the infrastructural improvements that were made in residential areas over the last decade or so, plus the price of homes staying relatively low, people are starting to consider this area a good option. That said, we're also looking into expanding our real-estate holdings. Believe it or not, we still own much of the land that Howard had purchased back in the '70s—land that he was criticized for buying back then. Now it looks like a brilliant move on his part."

"He certainly was brilliant," Jason said. "No doubt about that."

"For all his faults, he had *some* type of genius going on up here." Preston said, tapping his temple. "Anyway, as I said, please keep that information about our real-estate ambitions to yourself as well, if you wouldn't mind."

"No problem."

"Thank you. I figured you'd know as much about the value of discretion in business as anyone."

"Why do you say that?"

"Because you have quite the impressive array of business holdings yourself."

Jason tilted his head with an expression that implied both amusement and perplexity. "I'm surprised you already know that about me."

"I confess I did a little bit of research, courtesy of the Internet, before your arrival."

Jason figured as much but was surprised by the frank admission. *And what else does he know? Has he taken a page from cousin Howard's playbook and planted spies everywhere?*

"But I must also confess," Preston went on, "that I knew a few things about you even before that."

"For example?"

"For example, as a little boy, your favorite author was Faulkner, your favorite flavor of ice cream was chocolate chip mint, and you had a crush on a neighborhood girl named Janet Riley."

"How...how could you possibly know all that?"

"Is my memory accurate? Was I correct on all points?"

Jason cleared his throat, which had gone very dry. "Yes, but—"

Preston laughed. "I knew your father a little bit. We weren't close, but we had some minor dealings from time to time. Hammond Industries used to manufacture surgical equipment, correct?"

"Yes."

"In the 1980s, the medical institute purchased several items in quantity."

"Okay, but that still doesn't—"

Preston held up his hand. "I know, I know. I got the information during a most delightful evening one summer around that time. It was in '85 or '86, I think. We were holding a fundraiser, and your father was good enough to make a very generous donation of $500,000."

"Really?"

"Yes. It was quite something—I sent him an invitation to him, hoping he'd give us $10,000 or so. Instead, he showed up in person with a check for half a million...and you."

Jason reached deep into his memory. "Was this in San Antonio?"

"That's right!" Preston slapped his knees and held them, his mouth hanging open. "Wow, that's some memory, son!"

Jason smiled as the images came forth. He remembered being in the airport in Portsmouth...the terrible food on the plane...the banquet hall sparkled with crystal and silverware...and a woman, older, with a round, pleasant face.... Her identity came back sluggishly, but when it did....

"That was your *wife*," Jason said without trying to conceal his astonishment. "Your wife spent most of the evening with me!"

Preston was nodding. "She took you by the hand, led you to the ice-cream station, and asked what your favorite flavor was. Then you sat on her lap as you ate it and told her about this book you were reading. *The Sound and the Fury*, I believe it was."

"Yes."

"And when she asked you how far along in the story you were, you said only about halfway because you were spending a lot of time playing with someone named Janet. When my wife asked if that was your girlfriend, you blushed and wouldn't tell her."

Jason had no trouble remembering Janet Riley. He had always been a sucker for brown eyes; a weakness that had not abated into adulthood. The last he'd heard, she married a language professor and moved to Europe.

"You and I only exchanged a few words that night," Preston said, "but I do remember you being smartly dressed in your suit and tie. You were so serious for your age."

Jason could not suppress a smile as whatever suspicions he held for this man began melting away. "Was I?"

"Very much so. You talked about your school studies, although I don't recall those details. But your father stood by as you did, beaming. He was very proud of you." Preston's grin faded away. "I am so sorry for what happened to him, Jason. And the rest of your family. I'm so awfully sorry."

Jason broke their eye contact and nodded. "Thank you, yes, it was...it was a phenomenal tragedy. And similarly, I'm sorry about you wife's passing. I only had the privilege of meeting her that one time, but she seemed like a great lady."

"She really was."

Silence lingered between them for a time, then Preston clapped once and said, "But enough of the past. Let's get back to the here and now."

"Okay, let's."

"I understand you had something of a close call today."

"I did, but I'm surprised you know about it already. Can we thank the Internet for that, too?"

"Yes." Preston gestured toward his laptop, which stood open on his desk. "There's a video on the YouTube site."

"That's an unfortunate symptom of modern technology. Nice to know countless bright minds spent countless hours and countless dollars developing such a powerful tool so everyone's privacy could be stripped away. That aside, do you mind my asking why were you looking for it in the first place? You obviously had to search."

Preston smiled. "Automatic notifications. I get them through Google."

"Okay. But why—"

"Jason, I've been following the situation since my cousin's notes turned up on eBay. It would be unforgivable for a man in my position not to keep abreast of such things."

Again, Jason found his candidness disarming. "All right, that makes sense. But then—and please forgive me if this sounds prosecutorial—did you have anything to do with the attempt to buy them?"

He watched closely for any change in Preston's demeanor—and he got it. The grandfatherly warmth vanished behind a tightened expression of nearly visceral irritation.

"No, I didn't. And thus I had nothing to do with what happened to that family afterward. I can understand how you could think I might be. And if there's anything I can do to prove otherwise, you tell me what that is and I'll do it. But I want to make it very clear that I am not, in any way, threatened by the possibility of Howard's will being found after all these years."

Jason nodded. "All right, then let me be the devil's advocate for a moment."

"Go right ahead."

"I'm sure you can appreciate how a person would find your last statement difficult to believe. I mean, let's face it, if the will surfaced today and none of Howard's family members was included on the list of benefactors—which is very possible, since Howard made no secret of his intention to keep his relatives out of it—then those who *were* supposed to receive a piece of his estate would almost certainly launch a lawsuit to recover their lost bequests, plus interest. And they would almost certainly win such a case. How is someone supposed to believe you wouldn't be threatened by this possibility?"

"I can only speak for myself, but consider this—when the twenty two of us received our share of the fortune, I was already fairly certain Howard didn't intend for us to get it in the first place. And I know he didn't want the IRS to take such a big bite, either. If the rumors are to be believed, his plan was to leave it to the Howard Hughes Medical Institute. Correct?"

"Yes, that's right."

"So I decided that the only honorable course of action was to use the funds in a manner as close to Howard's wishes as possible. I gave a sizable portion of my inheritance to the Institute and then took a seat on the board to see that the money was used wisely."

"I have to say, the Institute's work has been exemplary."

"Thank you. Those successes were achieved through the hard work of scores of talented people. A very large and very committed team. I'm sure you can relate to that."

"I can."

"So, as I say, it just seemed right to put the money toward realizing Howard's intentions. I'm not going to lie and tell you my wife and I haven't done well as a result of our windfall. We have lived better than 99.99% of humanity ever will. And I have always grateful for that. I also had the good fortune of making some wise investment decisions, from which I've reaped significant benefits. So if Howard's will ever did show up, I would be able to pay back my share of the inheritance, along with whatever interest has accrued, and still live out my remaining years in comfort. Further, I could rest easy at night looking back on the work that I've done with the Institute."

"A polite way of saying the will's abrupt appearance wouldn't have any significant effect on your life."

"Exactly."

"It would be a stretch, though, to make the same claim about others of your lineage."

Preston's face clouded over again. "That really would be, as you say, a stretch. It's no secret that some of them have not been as prudent with their privileges. Just as great wealth can enable you to achieve great things, it can also lead to *terrible* things. I'm sure this is also something you already know. Money is like any other power, with the results being determined solely by the user. I always liken it to fire—you can use it for warmth or cooking, or you can burn yourself to death. My family's indiscretions are well known to the public. Drugs, alcohol, prostitutes, embezzlement, tax evasion...." Hughes took a deep breath and released it with a weariness that came from a place deep in his bones. "Howard's fortune really has been like a poison to us in many ways. It has ruined any chance of us being a normal, loving family."

"And you've been the one cleaning up the messes," Jason pointed out.

"Not always. Sometimes they got themselves in so deep I was unable to help them. But when I could, yes. Someone had to be the glue."

"And you appointed yourself to that role. That's quite a burden."

"As I say, someone had to do it."

Jason leaned forward. "Okay, so why did you ask me here tonight? Surely not to unburden your soul."

Preston chuckled. "No, not to unburden my soul. The main reason I wanted to see you was because of what happened to you today. And I know this is awful to say, but one of the first thoughts that flashed through my mind was that someone in my family might have had something to do with it. I would like nothing more than to be able to dismiss such a notion as utterly ridiculous, but that would be burying my head in the sand. And I don't know the first thing about investigative work. But, considering the situation before us, I'm willing to wager that the same possibility has crossed your mind as well."

"It has, yes. And now you want me to give up my investigation, is that it? Maintain the status quo?"

"No, son, no. As I've said, I've been prepared for the possibility of the will's discovery from the moment I took my share of the fortune. I can live with that. What I cannot live with is the idea of someone being killed over it, and further that someone in my family might have a hand in such a crime. The Hugheses have been through countless nightmares, and Lord knows some members of my family have them brought it upon themselves. But I still care for them, and I still see it as my duty to do right by them."

"So what do you want from me?"

"If you do find Howard's will, please just let me know before the rest of the world finds out."

"Let you know?"

"Yes. Just a phone call or an email, whatever."

Jason's mind was racing, trying to calculate the contingencies both good and bad if he honored this request. Gut instinct became the predominant force behind his reasoning, and his gut was telling him this was a risky proposition.

As if sensing this, Preston said, "I'm not asking you to show it to me, Jason, or to tell me where you found it or anything like that. No details. Just a little advance notice so I can prepare to deal with the difficulties my family will face if the terms in the will turn out to be as you and I both believe. That's all."

Jason nodded. "Well...yes. I can do that much."

"Good—thank you."

Fifteen

JASON CAME OUT of the bathroom of his hotel room an hour later, wiping his hands on a small towel. He was dressed in drawstring pajama bottoms but was bare from the waist up. His normally well-toned torso was decorated with scrapes and bruises, and a fresh bandage had been applied to his left shoulder. On his forehead, three small butterfly closures covered a coagulated gash.

"Do you realize how lucky you are?" Noah said through the Bluetooth headset blinking steadily in his ear.

"I'm fine. Just a little banged up."

"And what about the others? What about the couple in the truck?"

"They're fine too, Noah. They were released from the hospital before I was. I talked to the husband on the way back from the meeting with Preston Hughes, and he and his wife are both okay. Which reminds me, I told him we'd cover the damage to his truck. Please take care of that, if you don't mind"

"Sure, great. Ruined truck, ruined rental car, a few people sitting in the hospital.... How much more has to happen? How many more people do you have to put at risk?"

Jason ignored him and eased his arms into a plain grey t-shirt. The right was no problem, but the left sent shockwaves in every direction.

"Jason, are you listening to me?"

"Yes, yes."

"How much longer until your luck runs out? And what happens when it does? Think about that minivan. Do you realize how easily you could've struck it head on? You probably missed by a millisecond. You could just as easily have killed everyone inside."

"I swerved purposely to avoid them."

"But what about next time? Will your reflexes be so quick? What if you grab the wheel and your hands are all sweaty from the fear and the adrenaline and they slip off? The next driver might be the one who has to swerve instead of you, and then *they'll* go through the guard rail."

"Your point is taken."

"Really? I'm not so sure about that. You have to *stop*, and I mean right now. Let the police take the case from here."

"They're working on a thousand other cases at the moment. They're not going to devote valuable resources to an ancient missing-persons mystery when they've got murders, thefts, and Lord only knows how many domestic violence calls to deal with."

He reached for the bottle of water on the nightstand. Ordinarily, he would pick it up with his left hand and remove the cap with the right. But when he went for it this time, bright agony exploded within the damaged musculature of the injured shoulder.

Noah, meanwhile, kept going. "And you don't have priorities? What about all the work you've started on the estate? I've got a dozen contractors calling me. You've been keeping them on standby for weeks and they're starting to get agitated. Painters, masons, landscapers, electricians...."

Jason tried for the bottle again with only his right hand, but it was shaking badly.

"These guys are ready to breathe some much-needed life back into this place," Noah said, "and you're going to tell me some forty-year-old mystery is more important to you than—"

Jason managed to get the cap off, but when he brought the bottle to his mouth it slipped away, bouncing in his lap and splashing him everywhere.

His face reddened with rage. "Enough, Noah! Okay? *Enough*. God save me from your relentless nagging!"

There was only silence from the other end as Jason closed his eyes and took a few deep breaths. Then he replaced the cap, set the bottle back on the nightstand, and went to his suitcase for a fresh set of pajamas. Noah remained mute during this time.

No sooner had Jason worked his way into the second shirt than a knock came at the door.

"Hang on," he said into the Bluetooth, "someone's here."

He went into the foyer and opened the door, revealing two uniformed police officers. Both were of good size and very young.

The smaller of the two, who had a peach-fuzz mustache, said, "We're sorry to disturb you, Mr. Hammond. Can we talk for a moment?"

"Sure." He took a step back. "Come on in."

The second officer, trailing close behind, had tight facial features splattered with freckles. "Thank you for your cooperation," he said.

"What can I do for you?"

"We wanted to let you know that we've completed our analysis of the evidence we found at the scene of your accident."

"And let me guess—nothing?"

Freckles shook his head. The name on his tag read, 'R. Gannett.' "Nothing."

Jason nodded. "In other words, a very professional job."

"I'd say so," said Peach Fuzz—'L. Faraday.' "And just so you know, we're treating this as an attempted murder now, and we'd be grateful if you could come down to the station and give a statement. Would you be willing to do that?"

"Of course, no problem."

"How soon?"

"How about first thing in the morning?"

Farady gave a single, definitive nod. "That's fine."

"Thank you, Mr. Hammond," Gannett added.

"Sure."

He shook both their hands before closing the door, then returned to bedroom.

"And what else are you planning for tomorrow?" Noah asked quietly through the earpiece.

"A few things."

"Such as?"

"I'm going to Vallie Wheeler's house."

"I thought the ER physician told you to rest."

"I was there for over four hours. I've had plenty of rest."

"Jason, listen to me."

He sighed. "Go ahead."

"You're getting in too deep with this one. Let the police take care of it."

"I told you, they're too busy."

"And *I* told you I'm busy with a thousand things here. I need help."

"Then get some help, Noah. Hire an assistant or something."

"You're kidding, right?"

"Why would I be kidding?"

"I need *you* here, not just anybody. I need someone to make the *decisions.*"

Shaking his head, Jason found the notebook he wanted and snatched it up. "I'm sorry, Noah, but I'm not coming back until I'm finished." He slipped into a light jacket, groaning as the pain reflared in his shoulder, and made for the door. "There's something really nasty going on here, and I'm going to find out what it is. A young man disappeared ages ago, a little girl was shot, and I was almost killed. These are dark people, and I have no intention of letting them succeed at whatever they're trying to do."

Another uncomfortable silence followed this resolute proclamation, and then Noah said without a trace of emotion, "Fine. I'll talk to you later."

"Sure," Jason replied.

He pressed the headset to terminate the call.

Sixteen

GRANT SAT AT the little table in his hotel room with his laptop open. On the screen was an eBook called *The Money: The Battle for Howard Hughes's Billions*, which he had downloaded from a server somewhere in China. He'd been reading it for the last two hours and was now fixated on the millions that each of Howard's cousins had received following the legal battle that raged throughout the Seventies and early Eighties.

With that much in your pocket, he marveled, you could do anything—*anything*. You could buy a hundred cars and a hundred homes and still have plenty left over. You could finance a revolution in a third-world nation. You could puppeteer a dozen politicians and manipulate legislation. You could become the controlling stockholder in a modest-sized corporation.

And you could escape—forever.

It had long been one of his dreams to just disappear and spend the rest of his days on a sun-drenched tropical beach. Maybe change his appearance and his name one last time, buy a condo along the fringes of Waikiki, and wind out his days sleeping with an endless succession of Polynesian women, drinking vodka tonics, and snoozing in a hammock between two palm trees. A dream life...yet altogether possible to transition into reality. None of his employers ever coughed up enough cash to put such a life within reach. And as he approached the dawn of his sixties he knew he couldn't remain in his current profession much longer. He frankly never thought he'd even see forty. Between modern investigative technology, the fickle nature of luck, and the unavoidable fact that even the best make that one critical error sooner or later, he figured his career would've come to an unceremonious conclusion long ago. Yet here he was.

His cellphone vibrated. As usual, there was nothing on the screen except 'INCOMING CALL.' He willed himself to answer it.

"Yeah."

"Hammond survived."

"I know that."

"You failed again."

"He got lucky, nothing more. *Very* lucky."

"A lot of your targets get lucky."

"We both know that's not true."

"Your past reputation aside, I'm starting to seriously doubt your ability to achieve your objectives anymore."

Grant clenched his teeth. "Look, he got *lucky*, and the Millers got *lucky*. Everyone gets lucky once in awhile. That's the way it goes in my business; in any business. This isn't some TV show where everything falls into place the way you scripted it. This is real li—"

"I don't need a lecture on reality. I need Jason Hammond dead, and I need those notes. Can you do that, or do I need to replace you?"

Grant felt something alight in the pit of his stomach that hadn't been there in ages—real fear. There was something about the phrase *replace you* that struck him as more than a simple implication of lost employment. There was a lethal edge to it, and there was nothing Grant hated more than being threatened.

"You won't need to replace me," he replied evenly. "I can get this done."

"I wonder."

"Don't."

Click. Dead line.

Grant closed his eyes and breathed deep. His overriding impulse was to smash everything in site. But he had been a rageaholic in his younger years, and that had been one of the central factors that led him down the path he now wished to leave behind. He had since learned that it was better to swallow one's immediate impulse and reform the anger in a more productive manner. Only then was it possible to take aim at the person or people responsible and reach a satisfying conclusion.

As the dark clouds dissipated, he opened his eyes again and found the laptop still there, the text of *The Money: The Battle for Howard Hughes's Billions* sprawled on the screen like a divine message.

In that instant, he saw everything he needed to do.

****

"This is all that comes up every time?" Rudd asked. "Just this?"

He was sitting at his desk with Grant's cellphone in hand, peering at the LCD display through a pair of rectangular glasses.

"Yeah...." Grant's voice was detached and dreamy because his attention was fixed on the monitors as he studied Rudd's current projects. On one was the savings account on a woman in Saratoga, Florida. On another was an inventory report for a shipping firm in Michigan. On a third was the tax return of a Walmart executive from Oregon.

Rudd reached over and entered a panic command to clear everything, then gave Grant as dirty a look as he felt he could get away with. He was in knee-length denim shorts and flipflops, with a reverse-negative image of the Beatles' *Revolver* album cover on his black t-shirt. The remains of a cheese steak lay in crumpled foil by the keyboard, and next to it was an empty Coke can.

Thumbing through the cellphone's menus, Rudd went into the log for recent calls and found it empty, which didn't surprise him. Grant erased the record of all calls immediately after they were made or received as a matter of habit.

"What about the number?" Rudd asked.

"What number?"

"The number you use before this 'INCOMING CALL' message comes back?"

"How do you know I call a number? How do you know it's not just a one-way situation?"

"It could be. But I've found that people in your line of work rarely do that."

"You have no idea what my line of work is, junior."

Rudd sighed. "Look, if you want my help figuring out who's at the other end, I'm going to need as much information as possible. Now, I'll ask again—what's the number you're using?"

Grant was mildly startled by Rudd's obstinacy. He knew he scared the daylights out of the kid. He was a master at sensing fear in others, and he drew enormous pleasure anytime he inspired it. But he had also begun to sense that Rudd wasn't anywhere near the gutless, pencil-necked dweeb he appeared to be. There was a steely, no-nonsense side to him that lay snoozing most of the time, but Grant had glimpsed it often enough to wonder if the whole college-kid persona was nothing but a way of getting others to underestimate him. If this was the case, then it demanded some degree of respect.

"I'll give it to you," Grant said, "but you cannot, under any circumstances, call it." He knew he was taking a massive risk here. He had been instructed not to make any attempt to trace the number.

"I won't need to call it in order to find out who has it," Rudd replied, shaking his head. "Hearing the voice on the other side will not help me in that regard."

"Good," Grant said, then recited the sequence. After Rudd jotted it down, Grant said, "I was told that any attempt to locate its origin would be detected. Is that possible, or was that a bluff?"

"No, it's possible; the technology exists. But it's very advanced." Rudd looked up at him with concern. "Do you feel this is something the person at the other end is capable of?"

Grant was embarrassed by the question, as it forced him to acknowledge how little he knew about his employer.

"That's hard to say."

"Do you have *any* idea who he might be?"

"If I knew, would I be here?"

Rudd sighed and handed the phone back. "Well, then this is going to take some time, mostly because I have no idea who or what I'm dealing with. I'm going to have to be very careful."

"How long?"

"I don't know," Rudd said with a shrug. "A day or so."

"That won't work."

"Well, it's going to have to work, because I can't magically produce the results you want like *that*—" he snapped his fingers "—when I've got so little to start with." His tone was sharper now, with an end-of-my-tether edge to it. "Look," he continued, setting his hands on the keyboard, "just look at this...."

One screen flared back to life, and he entered the number into a program that Grant didn't recognize. After a few seconds, a message scrolled out along the bottom—

OUT OF SERVICE

"See? Just what I thought—according to public records, it's not being used by anybody. Whoever your contact is, he's managed to utilize an unused number and reroute it without even the carrier detecting it. But where is it being rerouted *to*? That's very difficult to say. What he's got is essentially a proxy phone service through an established cell network, and that's not amateur-hour stuff. This isn't some high-school kid in his bedroom screwing around after his parents go to sleep. There's most likely an algorithm at the heart of it that leads the call down a different path every time. It's like the fabled riddle wrapped inside a mystery within an enigma. The NSA couldn't crack this one without putting their shoulder into it."

Rudd closed the application, revealing the desktop pattern beneath—the blurred image of a spinning roulette wheel.

"If this is some attempt on your part to make it seem like more work than it actually is—" Grant said.

Rudd's let out a groan. "It's not. Now please, just let me get on with it. The more time you spend yapping at me the less time I have to work on it."

He looked briefly to Grant, then away again. Closing his eyes, he blew out his frustration in a long, silent whistle.

"I'll contact you the moment I have something," he said calmly. "I promise."

There was no response from his guest for what seemed like a long time. Then Grant said, "If you mess with me on this, I'll finish you."

Rudd turned back, a response already formed in his mind. But it died when their eyes met and Rudd saw the madman that lay at the core of Grant's true character. Fear flowed through him like freon.

"I won't," he said.

"Smart boy," Grant told him, then was gone.

Rudd's heart didn't stop pounding for hours.

Seventeen

AS JASON DROVE through the depressing North Vegas neighborhood, Lisa's earlier warning echoed through his mind—*Be careful if you go there. It was a rough area then, and it's a rough area now.* Jason decided a second adjective was needed to complete the description—*depressing.*

Every home occupied a ludicrously tiny plot of land and was either a standard shotgun shack or, for the slightly better off, a craftsman-style bungalow with a compact second floor. In another time, each had a small parcel of front lawn; or, more precisely, two equal sections separated by a brief walkway. But most of those sections were now patches of dead earth, as were the rutted driveways that ran up the sides of each home. Some of the latter had vehicles that looked as though they hadn't moved under their own power in ages.

There was a playground on one corner, most of its equipment broken and rusting. On another, a basketball court with no nets was surrounded by a chainlink fence that had been partially ripped down. There was also a broad half-pipe for skateboarders, covered in so much graffiti that the bare wood was no longer visible. And when Jason turned onto Gold Strike Boulevard, he found a liquor store with a neon sign stuttering over a rolled-up security gate.

What he found most disheartening, however, was the feeling that this had once been a fairly respectable neighborhood. It didn't take a sociology professor to understand that this area had been conceived for those with limited means, almost in the spirit of Lyndon Johnson's 'Great Society' where, even if you didn't have much, what you did have still conformed to a certain livable standard. But that mindset had been lost somewhere along the way, and all that remained was a rotting corpse too big to bury.

His heart sank further still when reached Vallie Wheeler's home and found it shuttered. He parked in the street and went up the walkway. The mailbox by the door still had 'Wheeler' spelled across the front in cheap stick-on letters. He drew some comfort from the knowledge that Vallie had one of the bungalows. *At least there was that. At least she had some degree of status, no matter how minor, within her community.* The house also appeared to be in decent condition compared to its kin. The cream-yellow paint was smooth and uniform, and the wood under Jason's feet felt solid. Even the boards that covered the windows had been applied with care, cut to perfectly fit their rectangular cavities. There was nary a hint of grass on the paired front tracts, but neither was their any weed growth. *Someone continues to perform basic maintenance on this place*, he realized.

He went up the driveway—a parallel run of pavers—and came to a back porch that featured more plywood integument. The half moon that hung overhead afforded him only a faint view of the tiny backyard, which was surrounded by a waist-high adobe wall. He could see a decaying picnic table in one corner, next to a scrawny palm tree.

The sheet covering the porch door came off easily enough, and the door itself opened after a few hard jerks. *Great,* he thought, *now I can add breaking and entering to my growing list of petty crimes.* The door to the rest of the house, he was relieved to discover, was unlocked.

The smell hit him first, warm and heavy. There was a faint mustiness, which was unsurprising, but thankfully not the precarious bittersweetness of mold growth. And just beneath everything else was the lingering imprint of disinfectant.

He felt along the wall and found three switches. None worked, leading him to the obvious conclusion that the local electric company had pulled the proverbial plug on this residence some time ago.

He got out his iPhone and launched the flashlight app, then moved the slider to maximum brightness. He found that he was in the kitchen, one that looked as though it had been pulled from the pages a '70s home-design catalog—laminate flooring, Formica countertops, a mustard-colored stove and matching dishwasher. The cabinets were faux colonial with little white knobs, and the tweed curtains over the sink hung from thick plastic rings. A memory came to him—his maternal grandmother, now long dead, and the small ranch house where she lived on the outskirts of Boston. The last time he'd visited, still in his teens, he was struck by the 1950s atmosphere that she'd managed to maintain inside. She had more than enough money to do updates if she wished, so Jason figured she kept it in that vintage state because it reflected the era in which she was most comfortable.

But now, standing among the remnants of Vallie Wheeler's world, he decided his original assessment had been in error. His grandfather had died of a heart attack in 1954, and his grandmother mourned him in voluntary isolation until her own passing in 1988. *Although she continued to live according to the calendar*, Jason thought, *all true growth was put on hold...permanently.* The tragedy of her husband's sudden passing struck with such force that it essentially took her life as well. *And that's what happened here—when Chase disappeared, so did his mother's desire to live.* The simple fact that Vallie had never upgraded her kitchen was not necessarily proof of this, of course, but Jason suspected his theory was correct nonetheless. *Same situation exactly—one major traumatic incident, and all other progress grinds to a halt.*

He went next into the adjoining living room. Three of the four walls were paneled, and the fourth, which was covered in floral wallpaper, had a collection of unfaded rectangles where framed photos once hung. *Was Chase in most of them?* he wondered. *Did Vallie make this a shrine to her son?*

Jason moved the light around and found no further evidence that anyone had lived here in the first place—no discarded scraps of paper, no dangling wires from the cable or phone service, no storied carpet stains or scuffs on the wall. He could feel the grief that had unfolded with torturous lethargy. *Was this the room where Vallie first got the news that Chase was missing? Was it here that she made her last futile phone call to Robert Sanchez before swallowing the truth that all hope was lost?*

He continued into the main hallway. The front door of the house was to the left, and another door stood closed directly across from him. The stairs to the second floor were on the right. He assumed—correctly, he would later learn—that Chase's bedroom was on the second level, so he began heading up. The air was much warmer, and tainted with an aged, almost sorrowful quality.

Just as he reached the top step and saw that there were three more doors—one was open partway, revealing a ridiculously compressed bathroom space that somehow held a shower and tub along with everything else—a window shattered on the first floor. Before Jason even had a chance to turn around, it happened again.

He didn't notice the smoke until he reached the living room. Then he saw the flames, growing rapidly on the back porch and blocking his exit. He also sensed a chemical element in the air.

To help it spread fast—oh God....

Going back to the hallway, he shined the phone-light toward the front door. Smoke was already beginning to leak in along the bottom, and he could hear the flames crackling on the other side. Then the shatter of glass a third time, muted through the floorboards. *In the basement*, he realized.

He considered running up to Chase's bedroom and grabbing everything he could. Then came an image of the house collapsing in a dramatic conflagration while he was still in it. He went to the nearest window and kicked hard. The cheap glass gave way at once, but the plywood board, so efficiently applied, held firm. The fire on the back porch was now working its way into the kitchen, racing up the inside door and consuming the decorative curtains.

Jason kicked the board again with no result, but on the third blow it split up the middle and flew outward. Before he could climb out, he had to first remove the triangular juts of glass from the bottom of the frame. As he was working the largest one free, he spotted a man of considerable bulk on the sidewalk, walking away from the house at a brisk pace.

"Hey! Stop right there!"

The man looked back once before breaking into a sprint.

Jason took a few steps back, then charged forward and dove through the breach. But his timing was off, and several of the window's remaining teeth tore at once through his shirt and then the skin of his belly. Already screaming as he sailed through the night air, he hit the stony, hardpacked Earth on the shoulder that had been injured earlier in the day.

He writhed on the ground like a fish, the pain so fervent that it made him lightheaded. Then he struggled to his feet and took off running. The pursuit was short-lived, however—he passed no more than a few houses before acknowledging that the man had too great a lead to be caught. Now just a tiny figure in the distance, he crossed under the furtive glow of one last streetlight before making an abrupt left between two abandoned properties and disappearing.

Jason turned back and saw that the flames were rapidly enveloping the entire structure. Other residents were venturing out of their homes to have a look, a few holding up their cellphones to take pictures.

God forbid they use them to call the police, Jason thought, taking his own back out of its holster to do just that.

Then someone said, "There's no need for you to do that."

****

Jason turned. He was on the sidewalk by one of the shotguns—tiny porch, one door, screened windows on either side. It was in fair shape, although some of the siding had fallen away, revealing ragged strips of tarpaper.

The voice seemed to have come from the window on the right, but the shade was pulled most of the way down and the lace curtains were pulled together. But there was also a diffused, incandescent glow inside.

"Are you talking to me?" Jason asked.

"Yes—I've already called the police."

It was an elderly woman's voice. The speech was also somewhat slurred, suggesting she had some kind of impediment.

"How long until they come? This fire's moving pretty f—"

"They'll be here," she told him. "They're here all the time." The last three words were delivered in a weary, singsong manner. "I dial nine-one-one more than any other number these days." Number came out *nummer*.

Jason took a few cautious steps up the walkway, and the silhouette of the woman's head became visible. She was peering cautiously around the edge of the window.

"I'm sorry to hear that, Miss...?"

"Don't come any closer, or I'll call the cops on *you* next! Don't even *think* of coming in here! I don't have any cash or valuables!"

Jason smiled and put his hands up. "Easy, I'm not going to rob you. I just came here to—um...."

As with Lisa Sanchez, he wondered how much he should reveal.

"To do what?" the woman demanded. "I've got my finger on the redial button. All the cops know me!"

"That won't be necessary, I promise. I came here because I'm looking into the disappearance of Chase Wheeler."

"What does that have to do with you?"

Jason sighed. "It's a long story. Look, I'm very sorry to have troubled you. I'll leave you alone now and—"

He felt something warm run down his stomach and into his jeans, and he saw that the bottom of his white shirt was soaked with blood. He pulled it out, and underneath was a slice of about four or five inches, already puffing up with infection.

"You're hurt!" the woman said.

"Yeah...I guess I should go to a hospital."

The blood was running out in a persistent stream, which was doubly alarming since he usually clotted quickly. *That means it's deep*, he thought with growing alarm. *If it nicked an organ...oh no.*

"Come inside, quick!"

"Huh?"

"*Hurry*!" the woman screeched.

A series of locks were undone, then the front door swung back. Jason went in, and a towel was shoved into his hand. He pressed it against the wound as the woman led him to the small living room where she'd been talking to him out the window. She guided him into a chair and hurried off, returning a moment later with a bottle of Bactine. He got his first good look at her then. She was barely taller than he was as he sat. Her hair was pearl white, unevenly cut and hanging loose around an age-spotted face, and her glasses were ludicrously large.

"Let me see it," she said, hovering over him.

"Hang on—do you know anything about medical treatment?"

"I did some nursing in my better days."

Jason searched for signs of deception in those wildly magnified eyes, then removed the towel.

"Oh boy," she said, "that doesn't look good."

"It doesn't feel good, either."

"This is going to sting a bit, so get ready."

"Wait, shouldn't you—"

She sank to one knee and poured, and Jason let out a scream that could be heard in deep space. Then he fell to the floor and curled into a fetal position, each breath enunciated by a labored moan.

"Did that hurt?" the woman asked curiously, still on one knee.

"A bit, yes!"

"But you probably should have some more."

Jason put a hand up, "No, it's fine, thank you."

The woman tried getting to her feet but lost her balance and went down. The bottle tumbled from her hand and rolled away, its contents gurgling out with uneven splashes. She cursed and tried to rise again, and once she was up she did not attempt to retrieve the bottle but instead returned to the chair by the window. Then she let out a long moan of her own, her head drooping as exhaustion took over.

Watching all of this from a sideways angle on the floor, Jason said, "What about your carpet?"

"This isn't exactly the Taj Mahal, as I'm sure you've noticed."

Jason noticed—the furniture wasn't suitable for a thrift store, the ceiling bore several large water stains, and the rug on which he currently lay was worn so thin that most of the floral pattern had been erased. Add to that the co-mingled odors of liniment and rubbing alcohol as well as the use of low-watt bulbs, and it was one of the saddest homes he'd ever seen.

"No, I guess not." He took several measured breaths as the pain settled back to a manageable level. Then he noticed something that made him rethink his earlier assessment that the woman had a speech impediment. On the round table next to her was an ornate decanter about half filled with a golden fluid that he to be a member of the whiskey / scotch / bourbon family. Next to that was a matching rock glass, empty.

"My name's Jason, by the way. Jason Hammond."

The woman lifted her head and smiled. Her eyes were red-rimmed and glassy.

"Nice to meet you, Jason. I'm Helen."

No last name, Jason noted, *which is perfectly understandable.*

"Nice to meet you, too, Helen. Thank you for helping me."

"Are you feeling any better?"

"A little bit." He propped himself up on one elbow. "But I've got to get to a hospital. I think I'll need some stitching."

"That's probably a good idea. The wound is very deep."

"I know."

"How did it happen?"

Again he found himself hesitating while his internal censor went to work. "Like I said, I've been looking into Chase Wheeler's disappearance. I'm a...a private investigator." Yes, that was good; it was honest. *I don't want to lie to her*, he thought, partly because there was something about Helen that he liked, and partly because he was pretty sure she wasn't some secret operative working for the other side. "I was in the Wheeler house looking around when someone set the place on fire. I had to jump through a window to get out. That's why this happened."

Helen's boozy eyes widened, which made her look like something out of a horror movie. "Vallie's house?! That's the one burning?"

"I'm afraid so."

"Ooo—Denise isn't going to like that."

"You know Denise Wheeler?"

"Before she was even born," she said, unaware of the obvious error. Either that or she was being intentionally droll. In her present condition, however, Jason seriously doubted it. "Both of them—Denise *and* Chase."

"So then I guess you knew Vallie pretty well, too."

"Yes, we were good friends.... Very good friends...."

Her voice trailed off and she looked away, phasing into deep contemplation. Then she did something that struck him as both strange and eerie—she turned toward the decanter and stared at it with a peculiar kind of resignation that was at once resentful and acquiescent. She reached over and filled the glass nearly to the rim, her hand shaking so badly that a good portion the contents ended up on the table. And unlike the similar accident with the Bactine, this misstep irritated her greatly. She cursed again and lifted the glass with both hands this time, using one as a bottom support. Then she brought it in her lap and held it there.

"Vallie had a rough life, didn't she?" Jason said.

"Like you can't believe." Each word came out perfectly enunciated this time, anchored by the power of her anger.

"Is she still alive?"

"She died eight years ago."

"I'm sorry to hear th—"

"Voluntary overdose."

"Good God, no."

"Denise found her in her room. Not in this house here. In Denise's house. She was taking care of Vallie by then." The glass came up, Helen took a sip, and the glass went down again. "Vallie had had enough. She just couldn't take it anymore. I can't say I blame her."

"Because of what happened to Chase?"

"Because of all of it—Chase, her useless husband, the two miscarriages, the rape."

"She was *raped?*"

"While she was working in town, coming home one night."

"That's nauseating."

Helen nodded. "It certainly is."

"Was the man ever caught?"

"Men."

"What?"

"There were two."

"Please tell me that's not true."

"It's true."

"How...how can people *do* that to each other?"

"I've asked myself that a million times. You know what answer I've come up with? None. None at all. I have tried to be understanding all my life, but now, as the end approaches, I have come to the conclusion that some people are just *bad*, period."

Jason was shaking his head. "First the woman gets raped, then she loses her son. I can't imagine—"

"Wrong way."

"What?"

"She lost Chase first, then got raped."

Jason closed his eyes and took a deep breath. "Christ Almighty."

"All she ever wanted was a home and a family," Helen went on. "That's it. She wasn't looking for a Rolls Royce or a yacht or a townhouse in Paris. Just a husband, some children, and a place to love them." She took another sip, this time larger and longer. "I guess that was too much to ask."

"What do *you* think happened to her son?"

"I have no idea. He was as sweet as his mother. Never said a bad word about anyone, never did anything to get into trouble."

"Is it possible he just up and left?"

"No chance at all. Impossible. If you knew him, you'd understand why I'm so sure about that. He loved his family, even his lousy father. He worked day and night to keep that house going. And when he wasn't helping to pay bills, he was trying to pay his father's debts."

"Maybe one of his father's creditors got him, in revenge."

"Connie—that was the bastard's name—was already out of the picture when Chase disappeared. Died the year before with nothing to show for his sorry existence but a big stack of IOUs."

"A random attack? A mugging?"

"I guess that's always a possibility around here."

"But you don't believe it."

"No."

"When was the last time you saw him?"

"A few days before."

"At the house?"

"No, in town. I spent a lot of time there back then. Too much."

Jason nodded. "You saw him at the Desert Inn, where he worked?"

"No, one of the other ones."

"Really? Are you sure about that? I got the impression he didn't gamble."

"He didn't."

"So why was he in another casino?"

She shrugged. "Probably paying off one of his father's markers. Connie had them in every joint on the Strip."

"And which casino was this?"

"I don't recall. I went to a lot of them."

"Did Chase see you? Did you talk to him?"

"We talked a little bit."

"What about?"

"I asked him how his mom and sister were doing. I hadn't seen them in a few weeks. He said they were fine, which I knew wasn't true. Then I asked him how *he* was doing, and he said he was great. I remember he seemed really cheerful, even more so than usual. I figured it was because he had just gotten a car. It wasn't the greatest, but it ran. I did say, 'You're not here gambling, are you Chase?' And he said, 'No, ma'am, I don't do that.' And I'm sure he was telling me the truth. First of all, he wasn't the type of kid who lied to his elders. And second, he didn't have the money to gamble *with*."

"Did he say where he was going?"

"I didn't ask; it was none of my business. Like I said, he was always a good boy. I didn't worry about what he was up to."

Jason nodded. "And you told the police all of this when they—"

"The police never talked to me."

"What?"

"They didn't talk to anyone around here except Vallie and Denise."

Jason thought of Lisa's comment about her father dealing with powers that existed well beyond the reach of the LVMPD. Was this an example of that? Did someone go out of their way to limit the number of inquiries that were made? To make only the minimum and most obvious just for the sake of appearance?

"That's a bit odd, don't you think? Not talking to any of the neighbors?"

She shrugged again. "They don't come around here much now, they didn't come around here much then."

"A lawless land."

"Now you've got it."

Jason lifted the towel and saw that the blood was finally beginning to coagulate.

"Any better?" Helen asked.

"It's clotting, so that's good. But I still need to get it laced up. Is it okay if I bring your towel back tomorrow? I'll see that it's washed."

"You can keep it."

"Are you sure?"

"Yes, yes."

She finished off the drink and returned to deep-thinking mode for a moment.

"You would do Chase's sister a great service if you could find out what really happened to him. And Vallie would rest more comfortably in her grave, I'm sure."

"Do you know where Denise lives? I'd like to speak with her, but I haven't had any luck tracking her down."

Helen gave her guest one last evaluation with those boozy, horror-film eyes. In spite of her inebriation, Jason felt as though her powers of appraisal were in full working order.

"The address is 35 Gin Blossom Street, on the other side of town," she said, then pointed a finger at him. "And if you do anything to hurt her, I'll come after you myself. I threw a pretty good right cross in my day."

Jason smiled. "My intentions are purely honorable."

"Good."

She went to refill her glass with the same shaking hand. Jason moved to help her.

Eighteen

IN THE COURSE of his research on Hughes, Jason had come across dozens of photographs of Las Vegas in the late '60s and early '70s—a bustling, electrified metropolis whose vasculature throbbed with the tireless currents of hedonism. Driving down the Strip now, he couldn't help feeling a little despondent at the way it had grown even worse in the decades since.

He saw a group of young girls stumbling out of a limousine, their short, sparkling dresses tighter than Saran Wrap. A bit further on was a homeless man propped against a brick wall. The torn piece of cardboard resting against his legs had the words I AM PENNILESS, PLEASE FEED ME scrawled across the front. And the next corner, three prostitutes awaited their next clients. One of them looked to be in the latter stages of her career and was wearing more makeup than an embalmed corpse. Jason couldn't help but wonder where their parents were, what life journey had led them to this point, and how he could use his considerable resources to help such women rekindle their belief in themselves.

As the neon pageant gradually faded behind him, his thoughts returned to the conversation he planned to have with Denise Wheeler. He admitted he was not looking forward to it. She would already know about the destruction of her mother's home by then, and unless she'd been secretly praying for some kind of insurance payoff, she would not be in a particularly chatty mood. She probably wouldn't know that he was the one responsible for it—perhaps not for setting it, but for being there in the first place—but he would tell her nevertheless. And not just about the house but everything else as well. Then he would pray that she was willing to participate in some meaningful way. This would be the variable in the equation, for people were particularly unpredictable when it came to the past. With some, time had no real meaning and the wounds remained fresh. With others, the torment was stored in a part of themselves where, even if it could not be erased, it would at least be rendered relatively inert. If Denise Wheeler turned out to be one of the latter and had no further interest in the matter, then the difficulties that lay before him would increase tenfold.

His cellphone rang, and he grabbed it from the passenger seat. When he saw that it was Noah, he didn't answer right away but rather looked to the digital clock on the dashboard. *12:21 AM...that's 3:21 AM in New Hampshire.* He took a deep breath and worked the Bluetooth headset into his ear, then pressed the button.

"Hello?"

"Are you still at the hospital?"

Noah's tone was sharp and clear; not at all what might be expected of someone in the middle of the night. It was also not what one would expect of an employee addressing his employer, although Jason never cared about any of that. He had only ever thought of Noah as blood and loved him as such. Wherever the line of traditional etiquette lay, Noah had crossed it countless times. Still, Jason frosted whenever Noah's voice took on this knife's-edge tone.

"No, I'm in the car on the way back to the hotel. Shouldn't you be slee—"

"How many stitches?"

"What?"

"How many stitches did they have to give you?"

"Eleven."

"That's just terrific."

There was a brief silence, then Jason said, "How did you know?"

"Since you're a bit of a celebrity these days, it isn't as hard to keep track of you as it used to be."

"Okay, okay." Jason rolled to a halt at an intersection and used the opportunity to rub his eyes. The epic exhaustion that he had been successfully pushing away for the last few hours was finally beginning to seep in. "So why are you calling at this hour? Is something wrong?"

Noah's harsh laugh didn't convey the slightest trace of humor. "Are you serious?"

"Of course I'm serious. You're calling in the middle of the night. Is something happening at home that I need to—"

"Jason, has it sunk in yet that someone is trying to kill you? Are you getting that?"

"No Noah, I hadn't noticed. Thankfully, I've got you and your iron grasp of the obvious to point out—"

"Are you also aware that someone's house burned down because of you?"

"I didn't start the fire."

"But it wouldn't have happened if you hadn't been there."

"I'm well aware of that."

"And did you consider that those eleven stitches had been applied by some ER physician whose time and talents could have been better used for—"

"Yes, I'm aware of that, too. I'm aware of all of this. As far as the house the Wheeler house was concerned, it will be no trouble for us to compensate them at current market val—"

"*The money is not the point!*" Noah boomed, and Jason jerked as if he'd been punched in the face. "Good *God*, Jason, have you become so obsessed with solving this case that you've completely lost perspective on the bigger picture? Someone's *home* was destroyed. Maybe Denise Wheeler wasn't living in it, but I'm sure it held plenty of memories for her. How do we compensate her for those? What kind of, quote, market value, unquote, do you suppose they have?"

The light turned green, and Jason, tight lipped and fuming, continued through the intersection. His grip on the wheel had tightened until his fingers took on a corpse-like pallor.

"You might also want to think about how lucky it was that the blaze didn't spread to any of the other houses on that street!," Noah went on. "They're packed together like sardines, so you can count that as a major miracle!"

Jason had not, in fact, considered this possibility—and he shuddered when he was struck by the vision of Helen sleeping on a filthy folding cot in some gymnasium-cum-refugee-center.

"Then the fire department and the police had to go to the scene! Because, you know, in Vegas I'm sure they're just sitting around all day with nothing to do!"

Jason glanced into the rearview and saw an LVMPD squad car still tailing him. After he got his stitches at the hospital, Lisa asked the department if they'd give him some kind of protection as a personal favor. Jason didn't even want to imagine how Noah would react if he caught wind of this little tidbit.

"The house collapsed during the blaze. You know that, right?"

"Yes."

"Any one of those firefighters could've been inside when that happened. But they weren't. There again—nothing but *pure luck*. So tell me, how long until it runs out? How long until something happens that you can't fix with your checkbook? Just look at the facts, okay? Forget everything I'm saying right now and *just...look at...the facts*. What are they telling you?"

Jason pulled into the hotel parking lot and, following Lisa's advice, found a vacant spot under a lamp. The officer in the squad car—Jason didn't even get his name—waved once before driving off.

"What it's telling me," Jason said evenly, "is that I'm getting close to something big."

Noah let out a long, gloomy sigh, then muttered the granddaddy of all profanities, which he only did when he was frazzled to the breaking point.

"All these reactions," Jason said, "all this aggression and hostility, it's telling me that I'm getting near something that others want to keep under wraps. I can sense the fear, the feeling of being threatened."

"Then hand the matter over to the police and let them handle it!"

"They're not going to handle it because they've got a hundred better things to do! Even Lisa Sanchez agrees with me on that! Remember, this was her father's case, and these guys have cases of their own to deal with. I'm the guy who has to—"

"You have things to deal with here, today, this minute," Noah said, that razorlike tone returning in full. "The cost is becoming too great and the risks too high just so you can find the end point of some ancient mystery that no one—"

Now Jason lost it—"*Stop*, Noah! Okay? Just *STOP*! I'm going to see this through to whatever end, and that's that!"

"You're putting yourself and other people—*innocent* people—at constant risk!" Noah shouted back. "Someone could get killed, for God's sake! Don't you see that? Don't you understand it? What reward are you after that could possibly be worth that?!"

"You seriously don't know? You really don't?"

"What? That doing this as some kind of substitute for whatever void was left behind by the loss of your dad, mom, and sister?"

"You really think *that's* why I do this?!"

"It's either that or a death wish in the hope that you can be with them again!"

Jason laughed once to himself. "Are you hearing yourself? All this time, and you're still this *clueless*?!"

Noah said nothing to this.

"My God, Noah—after they were gone, I slipped into a very ugly place. You know that better than anyone because you were there. I had days that were so dark, that I didn't believe the darkness couldn't get any thicker—and then it *did*. There were days when I couldn't get out of bed, when all I wanted to do was wither and die. Yes, I admit it—die so I could see them all again! But I couldn't do that. For all sorts of reasons, I ultimately couldn't take that path. The problem was, I didn't know *what* path to take! The one I'd been on—immersed in my studies, hoping to become a happy-go-lucky history professor—never seemed less important. Nothing seemed important.

"And then, while I was lying in my bed in the middle of some wasted afternoon, stinking up the place because I hadn't showered in three days or whatever, I saw this documentary on Michael Rockefeller's disappearance, and something about it just spoke to me. It sparked something inside that I hadn't felt in...whatever it was by that time. Two years, maybe. And I felt this urge to do something about it. Michael disappears in 1961, a member of one of the richest families ever, and he's never found. So I thought, okay, I'll take a shot at it. I realize what a ridiculously overconfident, even arrogant notion that was, but I had it nevertheless. And more importantly, I absolutely believed I could do it. And I did. I *did it.* And you know what? It made me feel more alive than I had in ages, maybe more than ever! So when I had the chance to look into Amelia Earhart's fate, I couldn't say no. And when I cracked that one, too, it felt even *more* right. I kept thinking, *This is what I'm supposed to be doing...this is why I'm here....*"

Jason paused to catch his breath. Noah remained silent.

"I know you think I've been doing this, at least in part, for selfish reasons. For some kind of personal satisfaction or fulfillment or whatever. I wondered about that, too, at the beginning. But then I stopped wondering about it because every time I got involved in one of these things, what I really thought about was the people I'd be helping. The people who were finally getting the answers they needed so they could have closure. The whole time I'm in Texas working on the Kennedy thing, I'm thinking about Sheila and how frightened she was, how she'd never get any peace until everything was resolved. I thought about the surviving Kennedy family, too, especially Caroline. She had a right to know what really happened, and I felt particularly connected to her because of my own loss. The not knowing is what kills you, believe me.

"And if there *is* any part of this that gives me personal satisfaction, it's nailing the bad guys. They're always the same—the rich, the influential, trying to save their skins, trying to have things their way with no regard for anyone else. Arrogant elitists who are so wealthy they can afford to be wrong and get away with it. Look at Donald Trump, and the trail of destruction he left through this nation's political system. And for what? Because he only cared about what *he* wanted. You know how I've always felt about people like this. The kind of people my father dealt with. You know how uncomfortable I've always been with how he made his fortune, especially in the early days. That's why he and I fought so much. You know that, because you saw a lot of it. I know he turned around later on, that mom turned him to the good side. But that was long after he'd caused so much pain to others. People in high places always do. They reach that height because they stand on the bones of their victims. It's always the same, Noah. *Always.* And now I get to be an exterminator or something, ripping down walls and pulling up floorboards to expose an infestation, then wiping it out so all can be good again. I know how corny that sounds, like I'm Clint Eastwood or some comic-book hero or something. But I can't help it—I feel it. Who else can fight them? Who else, Noah? I'm providing balance, and *justice.* And I've been put into this incredible position where I can take dad's money and make a real difference in the world. I have come to believe that this is what God wants me to do, and because of that, I'm *obligated* to act. Like I said, it all feels right. It always has."

Jason paused here, feeling like a drain that's just had its clog blown out.

"I'm sorry, Jason," Noah said, "but I just don't agree with that. As long as you're taking all these unnecessary risks—not just with your own life, but the lives of others—I can't find it in myself to believe this is God's plan for you. I can't be a part of it."

"Huh? What are you saying? You're not going to help anymore?"

"I'll help you with anything else, but no, not this. I'm sorry."

Jason found himself in a rare state of speechlessness as a jumble of disjointed thoughts and emotions crowded together in his head.

"I'm sorry, too," he said finally. Then he ended the call.

Nineteen

Peace I leave with you
My peace I give unto you
Not as the world giveth
Give I unto you
Let not your heart be troubled
Neither let it be afraid

IT HAD LONG BEEN one of Noah's favorite prayers. And now, sitting in the humble little church, he recited it with the reverence of a schoolboy and hoped it would have some effect on the beleaguered soul he had always tried to love as his own. He had not slept, he had not eaten, and a feeling of hopelessness, usually so alien to him, had begun to blossom.

The rest of the congregation had already filed out, save for a few socializers by the door, leaving Noah as the lone figure among the rows of plain maple pews. He picked up his tweed flatcap and rose, following the aisle along the wall toward the exit.

Just before he got there, a voice called out—"Noah? Is that you?"

He turned and immediately recognized the couple coming toward him; he had known Frank and Laura Bridgeport for years.

"Hello there," he said more cheerfully than he felt.

"I was just saying to Laura that I thought that fellow sitting by himself looked a lot like you." Frank put out a hand that was richly tanned, of slightly larger-than-normal proportion, and belying its years through a visage of spots and wrinkles. The tan in particular created a somewhat arresting contrast to the lush white hair that hustled back in a heavy and dramatic sweep even as the man cruised through the latter half of his sixties. He was dressed in what Noah thought of as 'elite casual'—navy blazer with gold buttons, white-and-blue pinstripe shirt, and white cotton trousers. The outfit seemed to be standard issue among men of his age and financial standing.

Laura was quite a bit smaller than her spouse and dressed more simply in a cream-colored blouse and a white skirt that nearly skimmed the floor. The eyes behind the glasses ran counter to the platitude that they should be the 'window to the soul,' for hers gave away nothing. She also had a tight seam of a mouth, which created the faint impression that she was in a state of perpetual deliberation.

"It's nice to see you, Laura."

"Nice to see you, too." She said with a single, proper nod.

She looked to say more, but her husband got there first with, "So how are you making out these days? We haven't seen you in awhile." He had an immensely powerful voice, with a rough quality that made it seem as though he needed to clear his throat.

"I've been fine, thank you. Busy trying to get the property in order. We have a few projects going on at the moment. Renovations. They're taking up most of my time, although we're really still just in the planning stages."

"Is that right? We've been meaning to do a little work on our place, too—the one *here*." Frank pointed downward to indicate his own estate, about two miles north of Hammonds'. "But we've been traveling so much lately that we've barely had time to stop in and reload our luggage."

He had a good laugh over this stunted witticism. It reminded Noah of one of Frank Bridgeport's less-attractive qualities—his habit of steering conversations back to himself for the purpose of reminding you how frightfully wealthy he was. Noah already knew his story—born into old money, his great-grandfather having struck it rich not once but twice, first in silver, then in oil. The family fortune deteriorated over the next two generations, and by the time Frank came along, the Bridgeports had settled back into respectable middle-upper class but were no longer listed on many social registers. Then Frank got involved in banking and finance and carried the name back to prominence. Noah had to give him that—he was born into modest means and piled up millions through hard work and sheer force of will. The Bridgeports also had lineage to the Garfield family of Ohio, which included one US president—James Abram Garfield, who served just four months in 1881 before being assassinated by crazed office-seeker Charles Guiteau. Noah learned of this connection through Jason one day when they were discussing the Gilded Age, for which they shared a mutual interest.

Noah shook his head. "Renovations are so much work. So very much work."

"Tell me about it."

"And how is Jason doing?" Laura asked, again without the smallest degree of emotional registration. Noah knew bits and pieces of her story as well. She and a sister, Dottie, were the product of two hopeless alcoholics, both of whom died long ago. The mother, who was the violent one, died of liver failure. The father, a shivering worm of a man who was as emotionally dependent on his wife as he was his liquor, put a gun to his head seven weeks later. Two years after that, Dottie was killed by, of all things, a drunk driver, and Laura, nineteen at the time, was left to fend for herself. In spite of the wounds left behind by this protracted nightmare of a childhood, she threw herself into academics and won a scholarship to Duke University, where she met her very ambitious future husband.

Noah learned this part of the Bridgeport exposition from Jason's father on a frigid December night as the two of them drove home from a local party that the Bridgeports had also attended. Noah further learned that the reason Laura always wore long sleeves was because she had scars up and down her arms from the cigarette burns her mother had applied during fits of rage. Noah's final summation of the women was that she could easily have written the next depressing chapter in her family history, but instead chose to shove all the ugliness aside, focus on more worthwhile priorities, and make something out of herself. With all this in mind, her aloofness was quite understandable.

He smiled at her. "Jason's...fine. Just fine. Keeping busy, as always." He prayed that neither of them would push for more details.

"I heard about that thing with the Kennedy assassination," Frank said. "Crazy."

Noah nodded. It was his belief that Frank Bridgeport didn't think much of Jason or the way in which he lived his life, and the condemnation came from a lifelong addiction to conformity. Trotting around the globe trying to crack the greatest unsolved mysteries of our age, according to The Frank Bridgeport's Handbook, was something you simply did not do. Pure nonsense, the stuff of movies and television. Credible people went to school, got a job, got married, had children, and so on. Noah's opinion wasn't much different, yet he felt distinctly resentful of this man's disapproval. *I can criticize Jason*, Noah often thought, *but God help anyone else who does.*

"Yeah, it really was," he said.

"And Earhart before that," Frank said. "He's going right down the list, isn't he."

"It certainly seems that way. So, what about the kids? How are they doing these days?"

"Well, they're hardly kids anymore. Bill, who just turned thirty-seven, is out in California running his own commercial real-estate firm. He's doing very well, making money hand over fist."

"Good."

"And Maggie's working for Clarke and Simmons." This was a prominent law firm in the Boston area, but Frank said it in a way that presumed it was common knowledge to all. "She made partner three years ago and is finally pulling in the big bucks, which seems only right since they're making her grind it out seventy to eighty hours a week."

"Well, at least she's getting amply compensated for her troubles."

"You better believe it."

"And what about Katie? How is—"

What cut him off was the sudden appearance of a young woman from around the corner by the opposite exit. She was smallish with a slim frame, and dressed stylishly but without a hint of unseemliness. Beneath the classic wool beret, her golden hair fell straight down on either side. It was her eyes, however, that drew one's attention—or, more to the point, the liveliness that dwelled within them. Kathryn April Bridgeport radiated an effusion of warmth and cheerfulness, further augmented by the fact that there were lingering traces of the little girl in her aura even though she had, at least according to the calendar, recently crossed the border into her thirties.

"Hey, there she is," Frank said. "Speak of the little devil."

"Ha ha," she replied, and her smallish mouth puckered with pretended offense. Then, noticing her parents' guest, it spread into a pixyish grin.

"Noah?"

"At your service."

"Oh my goodness!" She came forward and embraced him. "Wow, I haven't seen you in forever!"

"At that barbecue you guys had right before you headed out west."

"That's right!" She took a step back and assessed him. "You look terrific!"

"An obvious lie," he said, spurring laughter all around, "but thank you. So do you. All grown up I see."

"She certainly is." Frank put an arm around her shoulders, and she responded by slipping one around his waist and pressing her cheek against him.

"Well, I'm getting there...." she said, rolling her eyes. "Trying to find my way at the moment."

When Frank saw Noah's look of puzzlement, he said, "She went back to school and got her MBA, but she's not sure what she wants to do with it yet. But she has natural organizational and financial skills, just like her old man. A millionaire in the making."

Katie blushed and sniffed out a tiny laugh. "It does seem that I have skills I can do something with."

"And now she's ready to figure out what that something is," Frank said, kissing her on the head. "Right, sweetheart?"

"I hope so."

Frank kept rambling, but Noah wasn't hearing any of it because inspiration had struck. When Frank finally paused for oxygen, he said to Katie, "Hey, let me ask you something."

"Sure."

"I was just telling your parents that we're doing some renovation work at the estate. Major overhaul of the structures, the landscaping, the area down by the dock, everything. And it's getting to be a bit much for me to handle on my own, so I've been thinking about hiring someone to lend me a hand. Would you be interested? I could really use a person with organizational skills. It would only be for a month or so at the most, and only part-time." He said this last to Frank and Laura.

"Isn't Jason helping you?" Frank asked.

"He...well, yes and no. He has been, yes. But he's...he's traveling at the moment, so I need help."

The silence that followed was more than a little uncomfortable. Noah went from face to face trying to read his audience. Katie was mulling over the idea, which was good, but Frank had his head back, frowning and looking down skeptically. Noah could just about read his mind—*Crazy Jason, off wasting his time and his father's money again.* The Bridgeports had been very kind following the loss of Jason's family, sending flowers, attending the memorial service, and offering whatever help might be needed. But in the years following the tragedy, rumors about what was happening in the house raged through the community—Jason attempting suicide, Jason drinking,

Jason taking drugs, on and on. Noah knew where the facts ended and the sensationalism began. But he also knew the Frank Bridgeports of the world often didn't bother to learn the truth before finalizing their conclusions. When Noah combined that with Frank's lofty hopes for his youngest daughter, he began to regret saying anything.

Katie shrugged and said, "I suppose it would be okay."

Her father set his hands in his pockets and stared at the floor.

Laura cut in with, "Well, let's get home and talk about it before you commit to anything."

"Of course," Noah said. "Think it over and let me know. And if you do accept and something else comes along—that magical 'something' you've been looking for—you are of course welcome to go ahead and take it with no hard feelings on this end."

Laura and Katie were nodding; Frank still looked decidedly unhappy.

"That's fair," Laura said. "Thank you, Noah."

"Of course."

Twenty

"YOU'VE GOT SOME NERVE showing up here," Denise Wheeler said through the screen door. She was nothing but a cigarette-smoking silhouette to Jason, who was standing on the warped boards of the front porch. "Especially after I told you not to."

"Ms. Wheeler, please. I just want to talk to you for a few moments, that's all."

"Any talking between us will be done through our lawyers." Her voice was mechanically steady, but the anger beneath was like a fish swimming under the ice.

"If that's the route you want to take," he said, "I can't stop you. But I assure you, whatever costs are not covered by your insurance, I will cover out of my own pocket."

"Oh yeah? And how will you do that? What're you, rich or somethin'?"

"I'll take care of it, I promise."

She put out a hiss that sounded like a can of soda being opened. "Trust a rich guy? How stupid do you think I am?"

"Just listen to me for a moment, please. As I was trying to explain on the phone—"

"You had no right to go near that house."

"I know that. But—"

"That was my sole source of income! Do you know how much money I'm going to lose?!"

"Again, whatever insurance doesn't cover, I will. I'll put that in writing, if you'd like. You did have insurance, didn't you?"

"Of course I did. You're not allowed to rent out if you don't. But the insurance people will try to stick it to me some way, I'm sure. That's how they get so rich in the first place—stickin' it to people who can't afford to fight back."

"I understand that you're upset about this, and I said I would help you in whatever way was necessary."

"I can press charges for trespassing. As a matter of fact"—she pulled a cellphone out of her pocket—"I can call the cops on you right now...."

Jason took a step forward and was able to see her in greater detail—pink t-shirt, jeans, bare feet. "Please don't do that," he said.

"I'm dialing."

"Just give me a minute. *One* minute."

"I'm dialing...."

"Ms. Wheeler, I was in your mother's house because I have some new information that may be connected with your brother's disappearance."

Her thumb froze over the keypad. Then she looked straight at him.

"What makes you think that's any of your business either?"

He put his hands up defensively. "It's not, okay? It's not. But it came onto my radar screen when I was investigating something else. Something entirely different. And through that, I may have found a connection."

"You may have found a connection," she repeated. "*May*. That's what made you come here today? That's what made you break into my mother's house and burn it to the ground? Do you know how many 'may's I've heard concerning Chase through the years? How many 'almost's and 'maybe's my mother and I had to deal with? I've heard that from cops, private detectives, judges, and a hundred others. And every one went nowhere. You know what I really think? I think you're just trying to distract me because of what you did to the house. As a matter of fact, that sounds like exactly the kind of thing some rich jerk would do so he wouldn't get sued."

"I assure you that's not the situation."

Nodding, she said, "Yeah, let's see how much you have to say about my brother when my lawyer is breathing down your neck." Then she began closing the inner door.

"Denise," Hammond said firmly, "I'm almost certain Chase's disappearance had something to do with Howard Hughes."

The door stopped about an inch short of its frame. A brief silence followed.

Then—"Are you making this up?"

"I am not."

"Because if you are, I swear—"

"I've almost been killed twice already, okay? Once in that fire, and another time on the highway the day before. You don't believe me? Here, look at this...." He lifted his shirt to expose the stitches he received at the hospital. They ran up his stomach on a crazy diagonal.

"And before me," he went on, "the people responsible for this also shot a little girl while trying to get hold of some of Hughes's notes. What all of this tells me is that there are some very nervous people out there, which means I'm onto something. And I now believe Chase was tangled up in it. So please, talk to me. Maybe we can help each other out. If not, I'll leave and you never have to hear from me again. Okay?"

Denise studied him carefully, her face giving nothing away.

"If you're lying about any of this," she said with complete conviction, "I'm going to make you regret it."

She unlocked the screen door and pushed it open.

****

As it turned out, Jason did lie about one thing—he required considerably more of Denise Wheeler's time than five minutes to tell her everything.

He came to the conclusion that although she was not well educated in the institutional sense, she was intuitively very sharp. If there had been any holes in his story, he thought, she would've caught them at once, and then grabbed him by the back of his collar and hauled him out the door.

"...and that's why I believe Chase was involved—and why there are people now who still don't want the will found."

Denise drew a final puff from her latest cigarette, then shook her head as she stubbed it out in an ash tray that was already overflowing.

"He would've said something to me if he'd had some kind of deal going with one of the richest men in the world. We were very close, me and Chase." She twined two fingers together.

"But it's well within believability that Hughes would've demanded complete secrecy from him. He did that with everybody in his life. He was crazy about privacy."

She shrugged and lit up another. "Maybe."

"That's why I wanted to speak with you. As I said, the police report is missing, so I need to know everything you told them back then. Or at least as much as you can remember."

She closed her eyes, took a long drag, then let it out noisily.

"He was nervous the day he disappeared. I remember that. Very nervous."

Jason took out a notepad and began scribbling. "How do you know that? Did he say something to you?"

"No, he never said when anything bothered him. He wasn't that kind of person. Just like our mother. He never wanted to burden anyone."

"So then how did you—"

"Junk food."

"I'm sorry?"

"There were candy wrappers and potato-chip bags and soda cans in his room. Whenever he was stressed, that's how he dealt with it. No drugs, no alcohol—junk food. That was the way we knew. We'd find stuff in his bedroom."

"But you didn't notice any of this until after he was gone that day."

"Not until the next morning. My mother didn't like going into his room when he wasn't around, but we did after he went missing. That's when we found it all."

"What do you remember from the day he disappeared? Can you give me a timeline?"

She shrugged. "There was nothing unusual about it. He got up around six thirty, took a shower, had breakfast, and went to work, same as any other day. I was already up because I was working, too, at a restaurant a few blocks away. I made him scrambled eggs and toast that morning."

"Did he say anything to you? Anything that struck you as unusual?"

"No. In fact, he was pretty quiet. He was never one to run at the mouth in the first place."

"So he didn't say anything about work? Nothing about Hughes or anyone else?"

Denise shook her head. "No. I've thought about our last conversation a thousand times. It wasn't much more than, 'Good morning,' 'What would you like for breakfast,' and 'Have a nice day.' Stuff like that."

"Okay, then what happened?"

"He got into his car—"

"The '66 Plymouth Valiant?"

Yeah. It needed the muffler fixed. Our neighbors used to complain about it waking them up. Jerks. If they wanted it fixed so bad, why didn't *they* offer to pay for it? Anyway, I went to work about an hour later. Then I talked to him on his lunch break. We always called each other on our lunch breaks."

"And how did that conversation go?"

"It was the last time I ever spoke with him." She looked away, her eyes rimmed by grief and rage that had been leeching their toxins into her for far too long.

"Did he say anything unusual then?"

She shook her head. "There was no...*feeling* in his voice. When I thought back on the call after he was gone, I could tell that something pretty heavy was on his mind. He said he had to run an errand after work."

"Was it normal for him to run errands after work?"

"Sure. If it wasn't something for himself or for me, he'd do stuff for our mom. Go to the supermarket or whatever."

She turned away then and looked to the refrigerator, which was covered with magnets holding up a variety of coupons, municipal notices, and children's drawings. Jason was curious as to what suddenly drew her attention over there, then realized she was trying to disguise the act of wiping a tear from her cheek.

"If I had known that would be the last time I'd ever talk to him...."

Jason smiled. "We can finish this up later, if you like. Or I can just call you."

"No, it's okay."

"Are you sure?"

"Yes. What else do you want to know?"

"Did he mention anyone during the call? Anyone he would be with?"

"No."

"So it was just a brief, ordinary lunchtime conversation?"

"Yes."

"He said he had to run some errands and that was it?"

"Actually, he said he had to run *an* errand. Just one. I remember that specifically."

"Any other details? Like where he was going?"

"No."

"How long it would take? What time he would be home?"

"No."

Jason kept scribbling. "Did he ever talk about anyone at his job? Did he have any friends there? Anyone he might have confided in?"

"He was friendly with everybody. They all liked him. People always liked him."

"Was he particularly close to anyone?"

"Not close, no. He didn't have time for friends. Every now and then he would mention someone, but only first names."

"Do you remember any of them?"

"Pepe, Maria, Felipe.... There was also a Rosalie, I remember that one."

"All Latinos?"

"That's right."

"And you don't recall any last names?"

"There weren't any."

"Excuse me?"

"They were undocumented workers. The last thing they were interested in was giving out their last names. When you went through those tax records, didn't you find it unusual that there were only a handful of employees working in a large and busy casino kitchen? Didn't it seem a little short-staffed to you?"

Jason hadn't considered this because he didn't take note of anyone employed by the Desert Inn unless their initials were 'CW.'

"No, but that makes sense. I'm assuming the police never talked with any of them?"

"They were the kind of people who walked the other way when they saw the police."

"And I suppose it's useless trying to track any of them down now," he said mostly to himself.

"They were gone like smoke in the wind a long time ago. Ghosts."

Jason sighed. "Okay, look...I went into your mom's house because I wanted to get into Chase's room and see if there was anything helpful in there. Since I obviously can't do that now, I'll just ask you—do you still have any of his things? Anything I could look through that might—"

"There's a box," she said. "One box."

"Would you mind if I took a look at the contents?"

She was already getting up. "Wait here."

Jason heard her go up a flight of uncarpeted stairs in the back of the house, then come back down a few moments later. The box was constructed from standard cardboard and of modest size, with four flaps folded over each other on top. She set it in Jason's lap almost bitterly.

"Here."

"You're sure it's okay if I look in here?"

"Why not?" As he carefully opened it, Denise continued with, "That's the fourth one."

"The fourth one? I don't understand."

"My mother went through his things so many times, just browsing and touching and holding, that she wore out three other boxes. I got that one from a recycling dumpster behind a convenience store less than a month before she passed."

There wasn't much inside—a few comic books, a half-filled bottle of cologne, a comb, a neatly folded Jimi Hendrix t-shirt, a pack of unopened guitar strings, and a translucent red light bulb.

Jason went through each page of the comic books, hoping a folded note would fall out or a phone number would be scribbled in one of the margins. None of the other items seemed to lend themselves to further examination.

"He loved that bulb," Denise said with a hint of a smile. "He'd put it on in his room and listen to psychedelic rock. He didn't care much for the psychedelic culture otherwise, but he loved the music."

"Me too," Jason said, smiling back. "Jimi Hendrix was one of the greatest guitarists in the history of the instrument."

He put everything back exactly where it had been and set the flaps in place.

"Nothing helpful, right?" she said.

"Not at this point, but you never know." He set the box on the table. "I don't suppose Chase ever talked about Hughes himself, right?"

"Sometimes he did. He found it pretty interesting that no one ever saw the guy. He thought it was neat that so many people were curious about him, yet he worked in the same building where Hughes was living."

"Did he ever mention having any kind of contact with Hughes, or with any of Hughes's executives?"

"No. I would've remembered that."

"Okay, let me ask you this—was there a point at which he *stopped* talking about Hughes?"

"Oh...well, yeah. I guess there was, now that you mention it."

"Is there any chance it was a relatively short time before he vanished?"

She looked at him squarely. "I'd say just a few weeks. How did you kn—"

"Because if my suspicions are correct, then I'll bet Hughes made him sign something. Like I said before, he was crazy about privacy. He had lots of people sign nondisclosure agreements."

Tears began running down Denise's cheeks again. "If this is true...if you're right...I swear...."

"I don't have the smoking gun yet, but I have a feeling I'm getting closer to it all the time."

"Rich people...it always comes back to someone rich, doesn't it?"

Jason flushed. "Well, not always. But yeah...a lot."

She turned back to him. "How much?"

"I'm sorry?"

"How much money are we talking about here? Hughes's estate? If it turns out that Chase was involved somehow, then how much money did I lose my brother for?"

"Billions."

Her eyes filled with so much sorrow now that Jason felt he was looking at the true soul—frightened and confused and helpless—that lay beneath the emotional armor she put on every day.

"You can't imagine what my mother through. She was *crushed.* I sat with her so many nights and held her as she cried more tears than I thought anyone could. She never stopped believing Chase would come home. She couldn't, because if she did, I'm sure it would've killed her. She kept his room exactly the same and made sure his car remained parked in the driveway for awhile—y'know, so when he came back he'd have it. Sometimes we'd get home from the store and she'd see it and say, "Oh, is Chase home?" as if he'd only been out for a few hours or something. She'd also make him dinner some nights, and then complain that she'd gone to all that trouble and he didn't eat it. There were times when I thought I'd have to have her put in an institution."

"And it hasn't been easy on you, either."

"I'm not exactly what you'd call a model citizen, as you can see." She held up her current cigarette. "I smoke, I curse, I don't have a job, I've got two divorces on my record." She shook her head again and looked around the room. "Quite a life I've put together."

"I don't think you should set too much of the blame on your own shoulders," Jason said. "A lot of people who've been through what you have ended up either in prison or addicted to drugs or whatever. You could've done much, much worse."

"I've never touched drugs. And I'm not a criminal. I've kept myself clean and tried to be straight with people, and this is where it's got me. Great old world, huh?" She took another long drag and said, "I'm sorry, I don't mean to turn this into a therapy session. I'm sure you're not interested."

He decided to take a chance here, reaching across the table and setting his hand on hers. "In fact I am."

She responded with a look of suspicious bewilderment, and Jason thought for moment she was going to yank her hand away and order him out of the house.

Instead, she said, "No one's like this. No one really."

"I am."

She searched his eyes for any signs of deception.

"I wish I could believe you."

"Then don't. If you can't find it in yourself, don't force it. But I'm not going to give up on this. I believe I'm onto something here, and if I'm right, then I'm going to find out what happened to your brother. You might not be thrilled by the outcome, because I think the worst has probably happened, and it probably happened a long time ago. I'm not going to lie and say I think he's living in Australia or something. But at least you'll finally know. At least you'll have that closure."

She took the half-smoked cigarette from her mouth and flattened it in the ash tray.

"You know when I'll have closure? When the people responsible are rotting in a cell somewhere, wondering where it all went wrong for them."

Jason nodded. "I couldn't agree more."

Twenty One

JASON LOOKED MURDEROUS as he stalked into Preston Hughes's office. Hughes's secretary, a bookish young woman in a beige skirt that almost reached the floor, trailed close behind. She had a stack of folders in the crook of one arm, papers sticking out like they were living things trying to wiggle free.

"You *cannot* go in there!" she squalled, reaching for Jason with her other hand but not quite getting there. "Sir!"

Hughes glanced up from behind his desk, made a quick appraisal of the situation, and smiled.

"It's okay, Nancy," he said, rising. "I've got it."

"Are you sure?"

"Yes, thank you."

She shot Jason a homicidal look of her own before withdrawing.

"She's very protective of her territory," Hughes said, "and like a demon from Hades when she's riled. Anyway, what can I—"

"I knew I shouldn't have fallen for that charm crap of yours. I knew it."

"What?"

"How dare you."

"How dare I what?"

"How *dare* you send that thug to burn the Wheelers' house down. Were you aware that the property was Denise Wheeler's sole source of income, not to mention the place that held all of her childhood memories? Did you think about any of that?"

Hughes had both hands up. "Hold on now, just wait a sec—"

"What about the other houses on the street?" Jason went on, stepping forward until his legs were pressed against the desk. "What if the fire had spread and taken out ten other homes?" He thought about the pitiful Helen, who had lived a full life and had so little to show for it. He slammed his fist on the desk. "Just for the sake of money! Of protecting your precious fortunes! What if someone had been *killed*, Preston?"

Hughes, still perfectly calm, opened his mouth to speak but was immediately cut off before the first syllable.

"And look at this," Jason said, pulling his shirt out of his pants and lifting it. There was a large gauze pad underneath, held on by multiple strips of medical tape and spotted with dried blood. Jason peeled it upward to reveal stitches that held the ugly, jagged laceration together. The flesh was red and swollen.

Hughes's eyes bulged and mouth fell open in an expression that struck Jason as absolutely genuine. Then he came around the desk in a rush.

"Dear God." He leaned down with his hands on his knees and examined the wound more closely. "I think it's infected, Jason!"

"It is."

Hughes looked up at him. "Are you putting some kind of ointment on it? Are you taking any medication, at least for the pain?"

Jason slapped the bandage back into place and let the shirt drop.

"I'm fine. You should be more worried about yourself. If you think you're going to get away with this, your out of your mind."

Hughes stood straight up again and sighed.

"You really believe I was responsible for what happened?"

"It makes perfect sense. You don't want the will to be found. If half the rumors about what Howard put in there are true, you and your whole family stand to lose quite a bit. Pretty much everything. And if it wasn't you, it was certainly one of your relatives. I've heard some of the stories. The drugs, the booze, the womanizing, the greed and arrogance. You've got some real gems in the family, and I have no doubt they'd do anything—*anything*—to protect their riches. And you'd protect them, too, because that's what *you* do, right? So yeah—all things considered, there's more than enough motivation here to believe either you or someone else in your bloodline did this. Or both. It's an entirely plausible scenario."

Hughes nodded. "I agree with you. No one would question the viability of such a claim. And you're right, I have put considerable time, energy, and thought into protecting them to whatever degree I can. I'm not denying that. However...." He went back to his chair and motioned with his finger for Jason to follow. "Come here for a moment, if you wouldn't mind. There's something I think you need to see."

He got behind his computer, cleared away the screen saver, and navigated through several apps until he came to a spreadsheet. The first column was a list of names, most of which Jason recognized as Preston's relations. There were others he didn't know, but nearly bore the Hughes surname. The second column was filled with high financial figures, the lowest being fifteen million and change. And in the third and final column were more figures, these only slightly lower than those before them in the previous column.

"What am I looking at?" Jason asked.

"These are all of my relatives who still benefit from Howard's fortune. The first set of numbers is how much they currently have in their accounts. The second is how much I've got tucked away for them in case the will is found and, as a result of the legal process that would follow, they lose everything."

Jason studied the data for a long time without saying a word, Hughes watching him with that perpetual grandfatherly smile on his face.

"You're telling me...no.... You mean to say—this is *real*?"

"Of course it's real."

"It's just a spreadsheet, Preston. I have a twelve-year-old niece in Virginia who's a math whiz and makes spreadsheets for fun. Anyone can do this."

Hughes laughed and shook his head. He navigated to another screen—an account in Nassau. Jason knew it was genuine the moment he saw it because a chunk of his father's money was in the same one.

"See that amount there?" Hughes said, pointing to the balance. It was $22,544,803.55.

"Yeah...."

Back to the spreadsheet. "Notice any similarity?" The cell he was pointing to now had the same amount, down to the penny. "This is Brenda, *my* niece. She lives in—"

"Toronto," Jason said. "Yeah, I know."

"And if you'd like to see the others, I'll be happy to—"

Jason waved him off. "No, no need."

He went to one of the guest chairs and all but fell into it. Then he leaned forward and covered his face with his hands.

When he removed them a moment later, he said, "So what are you telling me? That no one in your family would have any reason to try and stop the will from being found because they're not going to lose any money?"

"Well, they'd lose a little. About six percent each, by my estimation, if it was found today. But even that, I'd cover it out of my own pocket. So yes, that's what I'm telling you—the discovery of Howard's will at this point would have no measurable effect on their lives."

Jason was searching for any remaining evidence of deception and finding none. Unless Preston Hughes was the greatest actor since Laurence Olivier, everything below the surface appeared to be synchronous with everything above it.

"And just so you know," Hughes said, "they're already aware of what's going on here at the moment. This isn't the first time someone has made an attempt to find Howard's will."

"And they're nervous?"

"No, because they know I've got them covered. I've already spoken to a few of them on the phone, and I've assured them that, at the end of the day, they've got nothing to worry about. Jason, my relations fall into three categories where the will is concerned—couldn't care less, are concerned about the money but not that much because of the steps I've taken, and aren't concerned about the money but hate the idea of all the publicity that will inevitably follow. The last group is the most passionate, but that only constitutes two people."

"Joel and Lucinda?"

Hughes nodded. "My cousin and his daughter."

"They live in Singapore, I believe."

"That's right. Well away from the American media. But still...considering our lineage, you have to expect that a few of us are going to be obsessive about privacy and secrecy." Hughes laughed. "There are days when I think I'm the only person on Earth they speak with apart from each other and their housekeeping staff. Joel in particular makes Howard look more exuberant than Liberace."

Jason managed a smile that disappeared as quickly as it came. "All right, so then if it wasn't anyone named Hughes, who is it? Who else could possibly be trying to stop this?"

Hughes shook his head. "I have no idea. I mean, who would even care?"

"I don't know," Jason said. "I really don't know.

Twenty Two

THERESA RICHTER'S FACE was clear of all expression. Nashamura watched her from one of the winged-back chairs by the bookcase, the iPad in her lap momentarily forgotten.

"Where is your mind, Reese?"

"The will's out there. I know it is. I can feel it, in that intuitive place of mine. You know the one."

Nashamura nodded. "And I know it's been right often enough not to doubt it."

"I guess the media's going to be at my doorstep sooner or later."

"You'll get questions, yes."

"Such as?"

"One will certainly be what do *you* think is in the will? Are there any explosive revelations you might not want anyone to find out about? Something personal? Something professional? The journalists already know how secretive Howard was, so they're going to be curious. Secretive—and vindictive."

"I'll tell them I have no idea what might be in there, and that I don't want to speculate."

"Well, that's passable, but they won't like it. They could easily spin it to mean you know more than you're saying."

"Of course they will."

"They might ask about Jason Hammond, too."

"And if they do, I'm thinking I can go the straight route there. I've done a little research on him, so I now know as much as the public does. But I haven't contacted him, and he hasn't contacted me. I'm relieved to hear his injuries were minor, blah blah blah."

"That's a little better."

"Yes," Richter said, "but then there's the matter of him being attacked twice."

"I'm not sure what you mean. How could that be a problem for you?"

"You know how the public views these things—rich and powerful people trying to protect themselves, doing whatever they have to do no matter how nasty. Would it be that much of a leap for the average citizen to imagine I may have had something to do with Hammond's troubles? The person hoping to make her way to the highest office in the world?"

"That's the stuff of novels and movies," Nashamura told her. "Not reality."

"And we both know that, most of the time, reality is whatever the media decides it is. That people will still believe half of what they're told and all of what they read." She rubbed her forehead as a fresh migraine began to take root.

Nashamura leaned forward, looking remarkably tiny with her hands folded in her lap.

"Reese, why don't you tell me what's in the will that worries you?"

Richter shook her head. "I honestly don't know."

"But you're worried."

"I am."

"I'd like to believe I'm your most trusted advisor and closest friend."

"There's no doubt. You know that."

"Then let me help you. Surely there must have been some rumors about what Howard wrote."

"Well, rumors, sure. Always."

"Such as...?"

Richter shrugged. "Such as Howard smearing every person who ever stuck it to him. The possible location of a huge pile of cash and gold that he kept in some secret location.

And there was one, I remember, about his knowledge of a secret plot to dethrone America as the world's superpower."

Nashamura nodded. "And what about you? What did he know that might cause *you* trouble? You've told me a lot about the things you did in your early days. Things that neither one of us would ever want the media to know about. The real-estate deals, the bribes and kickbacks. You trusted me with that information, and I have never betrayed that trust. But is there anything else? Anything *worse*?"

Richter paused, then shook her head.

"It was almost forty years ago," she said quietly.

"The media doesn't care if it was four *hundred* years ago. They can spin such things so the voters feel it all happened last week."

"I know...I know."

"Reese?"

"Yes?"

"Tell me."

Theresa Richter took a deep breath, then removed the last dirty little secret from the depths of her soul and brought it up to the light of day.

"There was a young man back in 1970," she began, "named Chase Wheeler...."

Twenty Three

AT PRECISELY 8:32 AM the next morning, Grant got out of his car and walked to one of the back entrances to Jason's hotel. It was an unremarkable glass door located at the southwest corner of the parking lot, with a row of dwarf spruces on one side and the stockade enclosure for the hotel's central heating and cooling units on the other. Most guests never even realized it was there.

The call the night before had been brief. Grant expected it, expected his employer to be upset. But even he could not have prepared for the torrent of rage the man unleashed. This time the terms and conditions were direct, the threats fully clarified. *Hammond goes or you do*, he said, then used Grant's real name in full—first, middle, and last. That didn't just freeze him, it *frightened* him. He didn't think there was anyone left alive who had that information; he'd been certain of it until that moment. From there his own rage came charging to the surface, and it required the supreme effort of his life to keep a leash on it. He decided then to channel it in more productive ways. Namely, he would first kill Jason Hammond exactly as his employer had ordered. Then there would be some surprises.

He didn't dye his hair this time, but rather gelled it flat and covered it with a blond wig. Short around the back and sides, a bit piled on top. Ivy League perhaps, middle-upper class, respectable. Exactly the kind of person who would patronize the Four Seasons. The cotton trousers and pressed shirt also seemed about right, and the square-framed glasses added the perfect touch of erudition. Lastly, a prop—a copy of today's newspaper, which he read as he lingered there. The newspaper, the glasses, and the wig could be tossed in an instant—and it would come to that, he knew. It would most assuredly come to that.

Fatigue swelled through him. It had been a long night with very little rest. He had done all-nighters before; hundreds of them. But they were becoming more and more challenging. He felt sluggish and washed out, a recent development that signaled the overture to middle age. He was frankly amazed he'd lived this long. Gifted with an innate sense of timing, he acknowledged that the end of this particular career was looming. He didn't mind; he'd be doing this sort of business long enough. If all went as planned today, he would let the curtain fall and disappear forever.

Thus far, things had gone as well as could be expected under the circumstances. The bomb was tucked securely under Hammond's car, about two feet back from the driver's door and attached to the muffler with a pair of plastic ties. His employer had not specified the design of the explosive, so Grant used potassium chlorate. He had read somewhere that bombmakers in Afghanistan were now using this because fertilizer, their previous materiel of choice, was becoming increasingly difficult to acquire. Then the tripwire, attached to the base of the door itself. When the door was opened, the device detonated. It was that simple.

Building it hadn't been difficult, but planting it had. Local police sent a patrol car through the lot every thirty minutes or so in their ongoing effort to see that their billionaire guest didn't sustain further harm. Grant drew a certain degree of pleasure from the thought of the PR damage that the LVMPD would suffer in the wake of Hammond's death. If this had been one of the zillions of small towns across America, the authorities might have been able to assign Hammond a fulltime bodyguard. But this was Vegas, and it was amazing they were able to spare anybody. Grant imagined there were quite a few ruffled feathers back at the station, particularly in light of the fact that Hammond had the resources to field his own, private army. Regardless, he was able to set the IED in place and then take his position at the rear door without being detected. And just in case the tripwire failed, he incorporated a second detonator that could be activated from his cellphone.

As soon as the bomb went off, the second part of the plan—*his* part of it—would begin. Through the back entrance and to the right were a set of fire stairs. He would take them to the third floor, and from there the door to Hammond's suite would be the fifth on the right. It would be magnetically locked, but Grant had a set of six universal keycards that he'd acquired years earlier from a master thief in Florida. Once inside, he would grab Hammond's laptop, notebook, and iPad. Those were the priority items, plus anything else that looked important. Down the stairs again and back outside, then into the parking lot of the restaurant next door, where his car would be waiting. From there he would take up Hammond's search for the will, and he would find it. Then he would get in touch with his mysterious overlord and the blackmail would begin. *As much as I want*, he had decided. *Millions.*

He expected the entire operation to take no more than two minutes, three max. In the confusion and horror that followed the explosion, it would be more than enough time. He had already emptied out his own hotel room and programmed his GPS to take him to another in Indian Springs, a safe distance north of here. He would leave with more money than he ever imagined and never look back. And he would keep a copy of the will handy in case anyone got cute. Perhaps he would even retain the original. He was dealing with the megawealthy, after all. Experience had taught him they could be quite vindictive.

With his heart pounding, he checked his watch—7:36. Hammond would be coming out any minute. He had called Lisa Sanchez the night before and arranged an eight o'clock breakfast meeting at Corrigan's, which was fifteen minutes away.

Hammond appeared at the opposite end of the lot. He was dressed modestly, in a white button-down shirt and black trousers. As he crossed between the first row of cars, Grant took the keycard from his pocket, his hand trembling from the adrenaline rush. It wasn't until his target reached the third row—one shy of the vehicle in question—that he realized it wasn't Hammond at all, but one of the hotel valets; a well-groomed young man in his early twenties. He lifted a fob into the air and pressed one of the buttons. When Hammond's car flashed its lights and let out a single electronic chirp, Grant stiffened. He never even considered this possibility.

He considered calling out, but being the immeasurably selfish individual that he was, his survival instincts squelched the idea so he wouldn't risk being seen. He decided the only option he really had was to blow the bomb early. There was nothing in his soul that felt even the slightest apprehension toward wasting an innocent life, but the calculative side of him knew it would cause further complications in a situation that now looked as though it would produce no rewards.

He took the cellphone from his pocket and pressed the third speed-dial button. The car exploded in a thunderous ball of flame, spraying glass and metal everywhere as the remaining hulk lifted off the pavement and flipped neatly onto the car next to it. The valet, no more than ten paces away, was blown backward with galactic force. He smashed into the windshield of a pickup truck, then went up and over it. His body landed with a muted thud in the next lane, rolling twice before coming to a stop. After that, it did not move.

Grant stood frozen for what seemed like an impossibly long time. Reality took on a ropy, elastic quality, as if his consciousness was trapped inside some kind of psychedelic warp. He was aware of people screaming, of others running to the site of the blast. He heard car alarms wailing away, blurring together in a crazed, discordant cacophony. And somewhere along the fringes of consciousness, he was aware that all had been lost.

Through the haze of incredulity, those survivalist's instincts once again burst forth, screaming down a message of unyielding vicissitude—*get moving NOW*.

He turned and began walking swiftly away.

Twenty Four

NOAH PULLED the front door back and found a smiling Katie standing on the flagstone stoop. She was clad in a mid-length wool coat, all eight buttons done up to the neck, and a wide belt cinched around the middle.

"We have enough Girl Scout cookies already," Noah said.

Katie made a face. "*So* funny."

Smiling back, he said, "Come on in."

She stepped across the threshold. "Thank you."

"Take your coat?"

"Sure." She undid the buttons and slid out of it. Underneath, black jeans and matching boots were combined with a floral blouse just visible behind a violet mélange cardigan. An onyx pendant hung from a string necklace.

"Would you care for a drink? Soda? Juice? Bottled water?"

"Water would be fine, thank you."

The hallway he led her down had the darkest hardwood floor she'd ever seen. The mirror shine was badly faded, and she could smell the bare grain that lay exposed in some places. The pea-green wallpapering was in passable condition, but the white ceiling had visible cracks, chips, and water stains. There were open doorways on either side, through which she caught a glimpse of a well-stocked library on the left and an expansive living room on the right. Some long-sleeping memories were stirred by the sight of the latter. A little further on, a carpeted staircase ascended along the left side, an antique carriage light hanging from the slanted ceiling.

The hallway terminated in a kitchen that seemed out of place compared to everything else she'd just seen. The tile floor was beautifully rendered in light gray stone, and there were narrow windows all around with the microblinds turned open to permit as much light as possible. The appliances were stainless steel and fully modern, as was the selection of cookware that hung from an open frame over the island. Behind a pair of sliding glass doors, there was a handsome patio with a wrought-iron table and chairs, the latter with blue cushions and protected by a large umbrella.

Noah opened the refrigerator—which contained mostly fresh fruits and vegetables—and handed her a bottle.

"Thank you," she said, twisting the top. "This is a very nice kitchen."

"It is."

"I can't imagine it's part of the renovation."

"Oh no. Actually this is the most modernized part of the house. It was redone about five years ago. Before that, it hadn't been touched in over three decades."

"Some of the things in here look unused."

Noah leaned against the counter and crossed his arms. "We don't use it as much as we could. We have a cook staff when Jason's around, but when he isn't I usually handle the cooking myself."

"Is most of the property in need of renovation, or is it modernized like this?"

"Most of it is in *desperate* need of renovation."

"When I walked in, I couldn't help noticing how familiar some things looked. I was here once when I was little. I think it was..." She noticed Noah's widening grin. "What?"

"I was wondering if you'd remember."

Her eyes widened. "You were here then?"

"I was. Probably my first year, certainly no later than my second. I was just the groundskeeper at the time, making sure the grass was cut and the flowers bloomed." He chuckled. "What do you recall about that day?"

"I was being babysat, right?"

"Right."

"My mom was called away suddenly. I think it was the time my Aunt Carol went to the hospital after she slipped down the stairs and broke her ankle. Mom couldn't get a hold of our normal babysitter, so she called Mrs. Hammond, who invited me to come here."

Noah nodded. "That's exactly right. I remember your mother dropping you off at the door, the very same one you just came through."

"It was raining, right?"

"Pouring. And there you were in your little yellow slicker and boots, holding your mother's hand. The rain was dripping off the brim of your hat and you looked absolutely miserable."

"Was I crying?"

"No, but I could tell you wanted to. Your mother wasn't sure when she'd be back to get you, and Linda—Mrs. Hammond—told her not to worry about it. Then she brought you inside. I don't know about anything after that. I'm sure I had things to do."

"I remember we played board games upstairs. Joanie came in and played with us for awhile. Then we had lunch. After that it stopped raining and the sun came out. Mrs. Hammond took me down to the dock. She said the best time to see life along the shore was right after the rain." Katie smiled. "I caught a frog with a little net."

"Linda loved nature."

"We were only there for a short time before it started to rain again. It was just a sunshower, but by the time we got back we were soaked. Mrs. Hammond made a fire in the living room, and we sat drinking cocoa and playing the favorites game. You know—what's your favorite food, what's your favorite movie."

"That's one of the rooms we'll be working on. Shall we go take a look?"

"Sure."

He led her back down the hall and through the open doorway on the left. Missing pieces of her memory fell into place with such emotional force that she had to pause to catch her breath.

Although the stylings were as outdated as those throughout the rest of the house, it was still a lovely space by any standards. It was mostly white—carpet, walls, columns, ceiling—with varnished oak trim. The hearth stood five feet high, with a giant beam of roughcut timber as a mantle. There was a spiral staircase next to the sectional couch, and Katie remembered running up and down a few times, giggling madly, while Linda looked on. At the back, standing on a slightly elevated stage, was a grand piano with its lid propped at an angle. A run of tall windows stood behind it, affording a broad view of the estate's rolling south lawn. A single access door was on the left.

"We came in from the rain through that door," Katie said. "We were running and laughing, trying to keep our heads covered. I stopped on the mat because I didn't want to come inside. I thought Mrs. Hammond would get mad if I came in all wet. But she didn't care at all."

"No," Noah said, "she wouldn't have. In all the years I knew her, I never once saw her lose her temper."

Katie went to the piano and set a hand on it. "Mrs. Hammond had to take a phone call, so she sent Jason in to watch me. He was very sweet. He could tell I was a little afraid of him, so he sat down here and started playing."

"He can play magnificently when he feels like it."

"He was just fooling around, playing the kind of goofy things you'd hear at a circus or something. And he was making jokes, too, trying to set me at ease. After awhile I sat on the bench next to him, and he taught me something simple."

"'Chopsticks'?"

"No, something else. I'm sure you've heard of it. Everyone has."

"Do you think you'd remember how to play it?"

She turned to him, the smile growing a little wider.

"Seriously? You want me to try it now?"

"Why not?"

She laughed and shook her head. The bench groaned on the floor as she pulled it out, and when the long lid protecting the keys bumped against the fall board, the old strings vibrated collectively, issuing a discordant note that somehow underscored the dusty, hollow character of the household. It was the echo of lost years and empty spaces and once-wonderful things that had lay forgotten far too long.

Katie sat and began playing a melody familiar to millions as the piece from the 'FAO Schwartz Piano Scene' in the Tom Hanks movie *Big*.

"I think it's called 'Heart and Soul,'" Katie said.

"Yes, that's it. Sorry the piano's so out of tune. No one's touched it in a very long time."

"Jason doesn't play it?"

"Never."

"What about you, Noah?"

"I'm afraid I don't have that particular gift."

"I didn't know *I* did until Jason helped me find it. We kept working on the song until I could get through it without making a mistake. He was so patient. And he was such a perfectionist, too."

"Oh yes, that's him."

Katie set her hands in her lap. Then she looked over at Noah and said, "I can't believe what happened to the Hammonds. I just...can't believe it."

"I know."

"How is Jason doing?"

Noah paused to consider his response.

"Let me answer by first asking, what have *you* heard about him?" When she responded to this with a look of polite hesitation, he quickly added, "Don't worry, you're not going to say anything to offend me. I know all the rumors."

"That he was on drugs. That he was an alcoholic. That he was often violent. That he had become a recluse."

"That all sounds about right."

"It's true?"

"Other than the reclusive part, no. He did stay in this house for a very long time, only rarely venturing off the property. But the rest of the stories—the drugs, the drinking, all that—are products of people's imaginations. Rumors and gossip from those who are bored with their own lives and need something spicy to focus on. You want to know the truth? What really happened to Jason after the others died?"

"What?"

"He crawled inside himself and stayed there. He's very much like his father in that way. When he's suffering, he shuts down and lets the emotions fester. And there were so many bad ones back then—the guilt from being the only survivor, the fear, the confusion, the anger...he just sat and broiled in it day after day."

"But he's not like that anymore, is he? I mean, he travels all over the world, working on his investigations."

Noah shrugged. "I don't know, it's hard to tell with him. It probably seems like he's getting better because, as you say, he's out there keeping busy. But that doesn't mean he's getting out from the dark places inside *himself*. I feel like he's just using that work as another way to remain in hiding, another means of escape."

"It's so sad."

"It really is," Noah said. Then—"Your father isn't too thrilled that you've agreed to come here, is he?"

"Not particularly."

"You don't have to do this if you don't want to. It's really okay."

"No, it's fine."

"Are you sure?"

"Very sure."

"Okay." He had to admit he was impressed by this small measure of rebellion against a man known for his titanium willpower. "Would you like to take a tour of the estate so I can show you what's going on?"

"Absolutely." She got up, closed the keyboard lid, and slid the bench back into place. "Let's get to it."

"We'll start out back at the dock, where you caught your frog."

"Sounds good."

As they passed through the hallway once again, Noah said over his shoulder. "By the way, I'm not expecting you to do this for free. Just tell me what kind of compensation you're looking for, and I'm sure it'll be fine."

"How about what I was making at the Sagamore?"

"How about what you were making at the Sagamore plus ten percent?"

"No argument from me on that one."

"Done."

They returned to the kitchen, and Noah headed for the sliding doors that led to the patio. He paused mid-stride, however, when a single musical note rang through the house's integrated speaker system.

"Uh oh," he said under his breath.

"What's wrong?"

"I don't know—" he turned and breezed past her "—but I'm sure it's nothing good."

She followed him to the other side of the kitchen and down a different corridor, this one much narrower than the first. He turned and entered a cluttered office occupied by an enormous L-shaped desk and matching filing cabinet. He got into the chair and studied the screen for a moment. Then all the color drained from his face.

"What?" Katie asked, coming up behind him. Then she saw it too, and her mouth fell open. Under the CNN 'BREAKING NEWS' header was the following—

One Presumed Dead in Las Vegas Car Explosion

And beneath that, in smaller letters—

Possible Connection to Latest Jason Hammond Inquiry

The parking lot was shown in real time from a helicopter perspective. A few cars were still burning around the blast site, the smoke rising in gray columns. Police cars and fire trucks were parked everywhere, their lights swirling. There were officers along the fringes to keep the crowds back. And an off-screen female reporter was giving the update—

"...but authorities have not released the victim's name as of yet or given an update on his condition. What we do know is that he was unconscious when he was taken away in an ambulance a short time ago. The first witnesses to the scene said that his body was covered with blood, and much of his clothing had been literally burned away from the force of the explosion."

"And what about the restaurant security video?" asked another disembodied voice, this one male.

The screen switched to a blurred image of the parking lot in front of the restaurant next door. All movement—cars, people—was in a jerky, step-by-step fashion, underscoring the low frames-per-second capability of the equipment. Grant's as-yet-unidentified figure appeared on the left, emphasized for viewers by an arrow over a highlight box.

"This is the person police are most interested in at this point. If you notice, he is walking away from the scene very quickly. Then he gets into a car and heads for the nearest exit."

"No clues yet as to who it might be?"

"Police are only willing to say they are following several leads."

"What about Jason Hammond? Have you had the chance to speak with him?"

The screen switched back to the helicopter perspective, this time with the inclusion of a head shot of Jason in the upper righthand corner.

Katie gasped again, and this time it was quite audible.

"Is that him?" she asked. The phone rang at the exact same moment.

"Yes, that's him," Noah said, snatching the handset off its base. He checked the caller ID, saw that it was Reuters journalist David Weldon—the only member of the wider media that Jason would speak with—and thumbed the 'ANSWER' button.

Noah launched into a longish conversation with Weldon, and the CNN report continued. But Katie was barely aware of either. She was unable to pull her attention away from the image of Jason's drained, tormented face.

Twenty Five

JASON SAT HUNCHED FORWARD in one of his suite's luxuriantly upholstered chairs, eyes wide and staring. They were glazed with fatigue, completing the tableau of tangled hair, unshaven cheeks, and wrinkled clothing. Lisa sat opposite and watched him judiciously, unable to get a read on the man. Uniformed officers moved around them in every direction, but he seemed oblivious.

"You can't put this on your own shoulders," Lisa Sanchez said. "You did not plant that bomb. Some lunatic did."

"It wouldn't have been there if I'd just gone home, like Noah suggested a hundred times."

"That doesn't make it your fault. I've dealt with enough attempted murders, so I know what I'm talking about. Don't waste your time with transferred guilt."

"Did you see the hatred in his parents' faces? Did you hear the things they were saying?"

These were rhetorical questions, as Lisa had been with him at the time. They went to the hospital to visit the boy, and as they approached his room, his parents emerged. They were an early-to-mid-forties couple, respectable blue-collar types. The father, who worked in a machine shop, had a down-to-the-skull crewcut and was built like a bull. The mother, much smaller and a bit wide around the waist, worked in the cafeteria of an elementary school. The moment they recognized Jason they came at him like wolves. He stood and took it without reply, and all of the things he wanted to say suddenly seemed ridiculous—*I can't tell you how sorry I am.... I wish there was something I could do....* And, most absurd, *I'll be happy to cover all of your medical expenses*. He was beginning to understand how useless money was in certain situations.

Lisa moved swiftly to intervene, although she understood the importance of allowing the parents their say. A crowd of nurses, doctors, and other spectators gathered. Finally a pair of security guards came and broke up the assemblage. Just before the parents disappeared around a corner, the father jabbed a finger in Jason's direction and said, *And I don't want him anywhere near my son!*

Jason took a deep breath. "Do you think the boy's going to make it?"

"Well, the next forty eight hours will tell us. That's the critical period. He's got burns and lacerations and broken bones, plus he went into deep shock. But the worst thing is the punctured lung. On the other hand, he's young and strong, so there's a good chance his body will bounce back."

"Will there be any *permanent* damage?"

"I'm sorry, I just don't know the answer to that."

Jason shook his head. "Why was he going to my car in the first place? How did he even get a *key*?"

"We haven't figured that out yet. We probably won't be able to get to the bottom of it until he regains consciousness and we can question him."

"The media's have a good time making a story out of it. They're suggesting that I sent him out there on purpose, to act as a kind of buffer or something. I never even saw him before. And my car keys are *right over there*!" He pointed to the accent table by the door, where they lay next to his wallet. "So how did he get a set in the first place?"

"We're making inquiries. Give us time."

Preston Hughes came into the room, minus his suit jacket but otherwise dressed and groomed immaculately. He was holding up a clear plastic bag and shaking it. At the bottom was a small circular object.

"They found another bug," he said. "It was attached to the end of the little knob on the nightstand lamp."

Lisa examined the contents without opening it.

"Best eavesdropping equipment in the world," she said. "Ultra-modern and very expensive."

"Just like the others," Preston added.

"Whoever planted these was very well funded," she went on. "And at least that solves the mystery of how the guy knew everything you were doing."

"Savages," Preston said. "Absolute savages. Any clue as to who it might be?"

"Down at the station they're tossing around theories about a few of the local pros. Their list of 'usual suspects,' you might say. But I'm not too hopeful about that. This is pretty advanced stuff—the bugs, the bomb, the disguises. My gut tells me this is someone from out of town, someone who came here for just this reason. We've been beating the bushes, but no one seems to know anything. We can usually scrape together some leads, but in this case we're coming up empty. That alone tells me I'm probably right. And with this kid getting hurt, I'll bet the guilty party is long gone."

"And what about that search *you've* been doing for the will?" Jason said to Lisa. "Has anything useful come up there?"

"No, I'm afraid not. I've gone through the records of literally thousands of safe-deposit boxes, and nothing fits the criterion we discussed."

This was to be one of the central topics of their breakfast meeting—he possibility that Chase Wheeler had hidden the will in a local safe-deposit box. Lisa limited her search to banks that had been in business in 1970 and had boxes opened within two months prior to both Chase's disappearance and Hughes's flight to Acapulco.

"I'll keep on it," she said, "but I'm not too encouraged. Frankly, a safe-deposit box is a little too obvious a hiding place."

"Howard used them all the time," Jason said. "People were still finding his stuff in safe-deposit boxes around the world years after he was gone."

"But it would've been Chase who opened it," she pointed out. "Right?"

Jason buried his face in his hands. "I suppose."

She reached over and patted him on the back. "Hey, listen...."

"What?"

"It's time, Jason. Time for you to go back home. You've done all you can here."

"I'd love to argue that point, but.... I've gotten innocent people injured, destroyed hundreds of thousands of dollars' worth of property, alienated Noah, nearly got killed myself, and I've made no significant progress on this case. Yeah, I've really done great things."

"You've made some very bad people very nervous," Preston told him. "That means something."

"I agree a hundred percent with that," Lisa added. "Now let us handle it from here. I'll keep you in the loop, I promise. Just take a break and let things cool off. When you're ready to come back and help, you'll come back and help."

Jason sat there for a long time, his drawn and haggard features giving away nothing.

Finally he rose and said, "Well then, I guess I should pack."

****

Grant stepped back from the window. The great majority of the bottom pane was gone; what remained were glass fangs of varying sizes around the inside of the rotting frame. The long curtains, once white but now filthy, were swaying gracefully in the desert winds.

The little house was one in a subdivision of twenty two, all basic ranches built from the same set of blues, and all abandoned before completion following the foreclosure crisis. The development sat six miles outside of Vegas proper, accessible only by a dirt road off the highway and surrounded by rocks and sand and the specter of failure. Grant chose this particular home in which to cloister himself simply because it was the only one that had a door on the garage. The car that he would never drive again was already stored inside.

He kept careful watch on the main road, which was miniaturized in the distance. It wasn't particularly busy right now; people going about their lives, oblivious to the fact that today's most wanted man was so close by. He kept expecting a squadron of police to appear, lights going and sirens screaming as they flowed down here in a prelude to a bloody firefight. Grant would just as soon avoid such a scenario. But if it did unfold, he'd resist until the last bullet, which he'd use on himself if necessary. He would not be incarcerated under any circumstances.

His phone rang, and an uncharacteristic touch of nervousness pinged inside him when he saw the number on the screen. He wanted this call, yet he didn't.

"Yeah," he said flatly.

There was nothing from the other end for a moment. Then, "You're finished."

Grant's jaw tightened, and his free hand curled into a white-knuckled first. "If you try that, I swear I'll find out who you are and hunt you down like an animal. Do you understand me?"

No response.

"*DO YOU UNDERSTAND ME?!*"

There was a weak *blip* as the caller terminated the connection.

Grant screamed like a madman, grabbed a two by four was lying among a pile of other discarded building materials, and proceeded to demolish all the sheet rock that separated the room he was in from the three that surrounded it.

Twenty Six

THE MAN WHO APPROACHED Jason as he sat in the small airport's main office two hours later was wearing a neatly pressed uniform that consisted of dark navy trousers and a white shirt with a gold nametag on one side—J. GRIFFITH—and 'Henderson Executive Airport' embroidered in a modest script on the other. His tie, shoes, socks, and belt were all black, and his russet-colored hair, kept short along the sides and combed to perfection, completed the image of sobriety. He seemed almost paradoxical in these otherwise industrial surroundings—a huge Quonset hut with ruggedly corrugated walls, a worn concrete floor, and the drifting scents of gas, oil, air tools, and propane.

Jason stood, and Griffith put out his hand. There was a clipboard in the other.

"Good to meet you, Mr. Hammond."

"You too."

The clipboard came up. "We have all your paperwork here, and everything appears to be in order. There will be a short delay while we get some of our other pilots on their way. I'm sure you've experienced this before."

"Sure."

Griffith flipped through the first few pages, then lifted the clip and removed two sheets in particular.

"These are for you."

"Right."

"And we keep the rest. That's about it. Please have a seat, and you'll be called in turn."

"Thank you."

Jason looked over the forms briefly, then tucked them into his blazer and reseated himself. He made a quick survey of his surroundings—just a handful of other people, windows and doors propped open as the afternoon warmth drifted in.

The anger, the frustration, the anxiety...it all continued to ebb and flow like some psychotropic toxin. He had never experienced defeat on this level before, never left so wide a field of debris in his wake. *And for what?* he wondered. *That was the price paid—but what were the rewards?* The discovery of a potential connection between the will and Chase Wheeler's disappearance, it seemed to him, was about the only shiny object in an otherwise smoldering pile of failure. And even that was circumstantial at best. *It wouldn't be the first wild coincidence uncovered in the course of an investigation*, he reminded himself. And while it was true there had been people making a clear effort to stop him, their identities remained as much as a mystery as they had been at the beginning. Would the LVMPD really devote resources to tracking them down? *Even if they did, it won't be a priority*. There was so much else going on in Sin City. No one would push to put this at the top of the to-do list.

He thought about Denise. He felt obligated to update her, so he called her on the way to the airport. The conversation had not gone well, and the guilt of being responsible for the latest in a seemingly endless line of setbacks in her life sat in his stomach like a small boulder. He had desperately wanted to be her savior on this. And just like the incident with the valet's parents, he absorbed her firestorm of rage without uttering a word.

He had wanted to talk to Noah so many times, wished for his insight and wisdom, and—if Jason was to be completely honest with himself—the comfort of his voice. There was no one he loved with deeper affection. He knew that his debt to Noah was incalculable; he shuddered at the thought of where he would have ended up if Noah had not remained at his side during the darkest days. The man had a strength that Jason dreamed of finding in himself one day.

The focal point of their discord was the simple question of, *Is this what I'm supposed to be doing with my life?* Jason found he was no closer to settling on an answer than ever. Since his communion with former Cuban assassin Galeno Clemente two months earlier, he had pondered this every day. The proverbial 'road ahead' had not been a mystery in his youth—elementary school, high school, college, a fruitful and productive career, and so on. After his family was taken from him, a new path, also clear, presented itself—grief, suffering, and then escape into a new endeavor. And with every conundrum that followed—Michael Rockefeller, Amelia Earhart, John F. Kennedy—it seemed as though an invisible hand was guiding him. There were struggles to endure and challenges to overcome, of course; he never expected any of it to be easy. But there had also been progress...categorical evidence that he was moving in a direction that just felt *right.* He was not feeling enough of that now, however. It wasn't there in his bones like it had been before. *So is Noah right? Is this God trying to tell me it's time to move on to something else?*

He considered it for a moment, then wondered if, in fact, he had been receiving the signs all along and chose to ignore them. That sentiment vibrated with an uncomfortable note of accuracy. He thought again he pyre that consumed the Wheeler house, the couple on the highway who were almost run off the road, the family in the minivan who could've been wiped out, and the fresh bruise that had been put on Denise Wheeler's already stiffened heart. Then he thought about the young boy lying in a hospital right now, his life hanging by a thread....

He buried his face in his hands, and in that moment made the decision to let it all go.

****

"Mr. Hammond?"

Jason looked up to find Mr. 'J. Griffith' standing there once again.

"Yes?"

"Could you follow me, please? There's something we need to take care of before you can depart."

"Is there a problem?"

"Not at all. Please, right this way."

Griffith first led him through the main hangar—a team of mechanics tending to a single-engine Cessna took no notice of them—then to a tarmac that seemed to stretch on forever. The wind rolled down from the surrounding mountains, offering a minor abatement from the midday sun. As Griffith continued onward, walking with almost military precision and saying nothing, Jason realized where they were headed—about fifty yards on, a private jet stood alone like a massive white insect at the very edge of the pavement. The cabin door was already open and the steps unfolded.

Griffith turned and gestured for Jason to go in. "Please," he said with a tiny smile. In spite of the unease that was raging within him, Jason complied. Griffith then walked off as unceremoniously as he had come.

Although somewhat cramped, the interior was nonetheless luxuriously designed, with thick carpeting, lacquered woodwork, and wide, comfortable seats. There was a couch on one side complete with pillows, and in a far corner was a wet bar and fridge. Jason also saw a copy of the day's newspaper lying on a small table next to a stationary vase that held a single red rose.

"Hello?" he said firmly. When there was no response, he added, "I assume I'm not here by myself, right?"

Still nothing, and his uneasiness began to escalate.

Then he heard a rustle of clothing from the flight deck, followed by the unmistakable sound of a seat belt being undone. His host rose from the pilot's seat and turned in his direction. As the lithe figure stepped beyond the shadows, Jason made the recognition and went cold.

It was Howard Hughes.

Twenty Seven

JASON STUDIED HIM from top to bottom. All the traditional Hughes accoutrements were there—the banded fedora, the leather flying jacket, the loose-fitting cotton trousers. And then the man himself—tall and slender, almost fragile, with a longish oval face that was somehow boyish and manly at the same time. The mouth was small but well-formed, the nose prominent. But the eyes were the real giveaway, dark and trenchant beneath the heavily rendered brows. The only element missing was the scant mustache, but then Hughes didn't always have that anyway. In his last known photo, a corporate shot taken some time in the late 1950s, he was clean shaven. So was the person standing before him now. Jason had seen traces of Howard in Preston Hughes as well as other relatives whose images he'd found online. But this wasn't a faint copy. This was a rubber stamp.

"You can relax, Mr. Hammond," the man said. "I'm not a ghost."

The voice was similar, too—high and thin, with the same halting, stop-and-go style of speech. Jason did not, however, detect Howard's characteristic Texas accent.

"No," Jason said, "I can see that."

"Would it be easier if I was?"

"Maybe."

The man gave a little chuckle and settled into one of the large swivel chairs. Jason noted that he moved with a fluidity that seemed almost choreographed. That, too, set him apart from Howard, who had an awkwardness that made him seem uncomfortable in his own body.

"You're welcome to sit down if you like."

"Thanks."

As Jason went to one of the other swivel chairs, he watched his host the way a mouse watches a snake.

"I'm not a professional Howard Hughes impersonator, if that's what you're thinking."

"No? You should consider it."

"I have to admit, I *have* made offhanded comments about the resemblance from time to time, for the purpose of smokescreening."

"Smokescreening?"

"Yes. Misdirection as part of a lifelong secrecy campaign. Secrecy is, as you know, encoded in my family's DNA. You see—" the man leaned forward and held out his hand, "—I'm Howard Hughes's son."

Jason observed the hand as carefully as everything else—there was a small scar running across the thumb just below the fingernail—but did not go to shake it. Nevertheless, Hughes's cherubic little smile never faltered. He pulled back and removed a folded sheet of paper from the breast pocket of his flying jacket.

"You might want to take a look at this."

Jason unfolded it and found the topsheet to a DNA report dated February of 1999. He had seen these before, specifically during his search for Michael Rockefeller. Everything on this one looked correct; from the laboratory logo to the raised seal from the State of Illinois. In this case, a tissue sample from the late Howard Robard Hughes had been compared with that of the same from a 'John Doe.' The certainty of the resulting match was listed as 99.99999998 %. The only part of the report that seemed questionable was the fact that the signature of the attending lab technician had been blacked out.

Pointing to that in particular, Jason said, "What's this about?"

"Simple—that was my half-sister. She had a different father, in case you're wondering. She worked in that facility at the time, and I needed someone I could trust. I'm sure you can understand that. She ran the tests and then destroyed all evidence of them. Labs always claim total privacy with their archiving, but these things have a way of slipping out. I covered her signature because I would prefer to keep her identity to myself."

"More secrecy."

"I'm afraid that's out of necessity."

Jason refolded the paper and handed it back. "Anyone can falsify a document these days."

"Yes, I suppose that's true."

The man turned away, and his resemblance to Howard in profile was so absolute that it seemed as though one of the old photographs had come to life.

Jason said, "When the court battle for Howard's estate began, there was a massive effort to determine his true heirs, including potential offspring. Millions were spent and literally thousands of hours devoted by teams of legal professionals. And yet, no children were ever found. I've been researching the man off and on for a few years, and I never once encountered any mention of a son or daughter beyond the occasional wacko theory put forth by the crazies in that informational wasteland known as the Internet. If you further consider that we live now in a world of disposable privacy, your claim seems—"

"Is that really the case, though? It seems a lot of people are bandying about the notion that privacy has been a casualty of technological progress, but I have found that you can still retain as much as you please in most regards. True, you have to go to greater pains to secure it. But to imply it's hopeless...no. I don't believe you're right about that. I think you're basing your position on misguided pop mythology."

Jason appeared mildly annoyed. "Oh?"

"Let me ask you—how old do you think I am? Take a guess."

"Early fifties, maybe."

"You flatter me, but that's close enough. Here's the salient point—I was born in an age before DNA tests and Internet searches and cellphones, which have afforded the ordinary person the ability to film a terrorist act on the spot while it's happening and send it to someone on the other side of the world in seconds. Back in a time when privacy, as you say, was not a disposable commodity. So hiding my origins would not have been that difficult. Now, further consider that my mother was deeply concerned about concealing my identity. My father was, too, actually. They both knew what a nightmare my life would be if the truth got out, but it was my mother who led the charge in this regard. She put a false name on my birth certificate. She also moved us to a new town and made up a back story. My father was very supportive and helped out where he could, giving us money and visiting from time to time. If anyone understood and appreciated the value of secrecy, it was my father. The only remaining issue, then, was my appearance. But even that could be handled."

"How's that?"

The man removed his fedora and raked his fingers over his head. "First, I don't have the same hair color—mine's a medium brown, whereas my father's was nearly black like yours. And I never wore it the same way he did. I was very careful about that. Second, when I was younger, I looked much more like my mother than I do today. That was obviously a blessing while it lasted. And third, I usually use these...." He took a pair of square-framed eyeglasses from the pocket of his jacket and put them on. "I started wearing them in my twenties, when the resemblance to my father came on strong. They didn't have corrective lenses at the time, but now they do. It's amazing how one's appearance can be altered by glasses, isn't it?"

The resemblance to Howard had faded considerably. "I'd say so."

"And then there's that old theory that we all have an exact double walking around somewhere. I don't know if that's quite true, but there are certainly people who come close. I have a friend who looks more like Dean Martin than I do my father. He can't sing a note, though. Anyway, you'd be surprised how few people have commented on it through the years. After my father passed away, the public went on to other curiosities. People tend to forget yesterday's news pretty easily."

"Thank God for that."

"Amen."

Jason smirked. "All right, so let's say for the moment I believe you. Why this meeting? Why take the risk and reveal yourself to me? Should I just assume the obvious?"

"The obvious? What would that be?"

"That if the will turns up, you want to make absolutely certain your name is on it so you can get your share of the inheritance?"

Hughes laughed. "Oh no, you've got it all wrong, Mr. Hammond. All wrong."

"I do?"

"Absolutely. You see, I already know I'm in the will. My father assured my mother and I of that a very long time ago, and I have no reason to doubt he was lying."

"So then what—"

"If you find it, I want to know if you'd do me the favor of taking my name *out* of it."

****

After a longish pause, Jason said, "Excuse me?"

"I came to see you today to ask if, in the event that you do locate my father's will, you would be good enough to remove all mention of me from it. If that particular section is nestled in one paragraph among others, tear that paragraph out. If it's neatly compartmentalized on just one page, rip that page to shreds. Or burn it, or throw it into the sewer. I don't care. Just get it out of there."

Jason's stare carried a healthy allotment of suspicion. "I'm not following you."

"It's a simple procedure, Mr. Hammond," Hughes said, making tearing motions with his hands. "You just take the page and—"

"No, I get that part."

"So what's the problem?"

"As the sole true heir, you would be entitled to Howard's—or, I guess at this point I should say 'your father's'—entire fortune. We're talking about billions of dollars."

"I'm aware of the amount, at least in general terms."

"And you don't want any of it? That's basically what you're saying?"

"That's *precisely* what I'm saying."

Jason tried to get his mind around this. When he found himself in the same position following the loss of his family, the notion of rejecting his inheritance never occurred to him. This was not out of greed but a range of other reasons. His father had dedicated his lifetime to building a business empire, and Jason felt obligated to keep it in the family. He'd had plenty of offers to sell it, some of them staggering sums. But he thought beyond the present and considered that, should he ever have children of his own, they might want it. Also, he knew that such a powerful mechanism could be calibrated to produce enormous good in the world. His father had already begun working with various philanthropic causes, and Jason expanded this effort since taking the helm, branching into child safety products, interest-free educational and home-building loans, pharma development for diseases of low profile but high impact in developing nations, and so on. He believed the issue of wealth was not merely about how much you had but what you did with it. The fact that Hughes seemed to be of an entirely different attitude was perplexing.

"Would you mind my asking why you feel this way, if only to satiate my curiosity?"

"I'm not trying to set myself on a higher moral plane than anyone, if that's what you're thinking. And you needn't take it personally either, Mr. Hammond."

"Personally?"

"I know your story. I did some research before I came here, of course. I am aware of the tragedy that took your family—I am so very sorry, by the way—and of the enormous endowment that came to you as a result. I'm not making a judgment on that, believing that you should have given it all to the Red Cross before taking a vow of poverty and living out your days, monklike, in a cave somewhere. No, there are two reasons for my choice. The first is that I'm happy with my life as it is. My mother, my siblings, myself...we're content, and that's not something money necessarily guarantees. I'm not a millionaire, but I don't go to bed hungry, either. As a student of my father's history, you might be interested to know that I'm in the aeronautics field. I inherited my love of it from him. If you've really scrutinized his life, then you've probably drawn the conclusion that he would've been a much happier man if he had simply become an engineer working in the burgeoning airline industry."

"Based on everything I've read, I'd say that's accurate, yes."

"What I did not inherit from him was an unwieldy fortune like the one he received when his own father passed away."

"You make it sound like a handicap."

Hughes shrugged. "As I say, I've been happy, and I see no reason to alter that."

"So what's the other reason?"

"The other reason concerns you as much as it does me, Mr. Hammond."

"Excuse me?"

Hughes leaned toward him and dropped his voice. "You're getting close."

"Close?"

"Close to finding it. There are serious people trying to stop you. This nut who shot the little girl—you think he's just some over-enthusiastic collector trying to one-up his rivals?"

"Of course not."

"Right. He's a professional, which means he's working for someone. Someone who can afford to hire a professional, someone who knows how to *find* a professional."

"A lot of people fit that description. They're all over the world, I'm sorry to say. And by that reckoning it could be a member of your biological family too. Anyone would believe it, considering they have a lot to lose if the will—"

Hughes was shaking his head.

"No?" Jason said. "Why is that so hard to believe?"

"It's not hard to believe. But it'd be easy to prove. The motivation, the means, the opportunity...all the elements are there. I can't imagine any of my relatives doing something so obvious, even the stupid ones. The authorities would be on them in the blink of an eye."

"I know that, I was merely speaking hypothetically. Your family would be the obvious first place someone would look."

"But Preston showed you the light, right?"

Jason's mouth dropped open.

"You know about that?"

"Preston is the only member of the family who knows of my existence. My father once said, 'If anything ever happens to me, go to Preston. He's the only one I trust.' I figured if he had earned my father's trust, then he must be beyond reproach."

"I have to admit, I find him a most remarkable individual."

"He is," Hughes said, nodding. "He's everything he appears to be. An incredible man."

"I've come to the same conclusion," Jason agreed. "Okay, so then who else could be behind this?"

Hughes turned serious. "I don't know who they are exactly, Mr. Hammond, but I'd be willing to bet every penny of my potential inheritance that it's the same people who scared the daylights out of my father."

"I'm sorry, I don't really understand."

"I saw my father for the last time in June of 1966. It was a Friday night—I don't know why I've remembered that it was a Friday, but I do—and there was something very unusual about the visit."

"What's that?"

"He arrived to our home without warning. Mr. Hammond, my father *never* did anything without careful planning. Even as a little boy I realized how meticulous he was about things. Sometime to the point of madness"

"He had severe OCD, as I'm sure you know."

"Actually it was a fairly mild case. There are examples much worse out there. A man in Oregon in the 1990s used to go around and around on highway jughandles, unable to break the loop. And a woman in Michigan had the habit of cleaning her bathroom, then taking a shower because she was dirty from the cleaning, then clean the bathroom again because she'd taken a shower, then shower again, on and on and on, until her children had to go over and force her out of the pattern. With today's medication, my father's condition would've been entirely manageable."

"That's pretty sad if you consider it."

"And I have, many times. Anyway, on that summer night in '66 he arrived clear out of the blue, disheveled and with more fear in his eyes than I've ever seen in anyone. When he sat down at our kitchen table, his hands were shaking. My mother gave him a glass of milk—he loved milk—"

Jason nodded. "Yes."

"—and he spilled quite a bit of it because he couldn't hold the glass steady. When my mother asked him what was wrong, he said, 'I wanted to stop in and see our boy, because after this I won't be able to for awhile.'" He said he had to stay out of sight, and that he was doing it for our safety as much as his own. He gave us a brown bag loaded with cash—I think it was around a hundred thousand, which was a small fortune in those days—and said we should use it if we had to leave in a hurry. That's when my mother started getting scared, too. She kept pushing him for an explanation, and he asked me to leave the room. I did, but of course I stayed near the doorway to listen. They were talking in whispers, so I couldn't hear much. But I do know he said something about being asked to take part in some kind of financial scheme. Something international. And he wouldn't. He said he refused to do it, so he was afraid the people who asked him were now going to come after him. He called them, 'The most evil people I've ever encountered.'"

"Who were they?"

"If he said as much, I never heard it. I doubt if he did, because he kept saying to my mother, 'The less you know, the better.'"

"What then?"

"Then he came out into the hallway to find me. He knelt down, gave me a smile, and kissed me on the cheek. I still remember the scent of his aftershave. I know history has drawn him as something of a machine, Mr. Hammond. Unfeeling and calculating and ruthless. But he did have a heart. He was hesitant to show it, but he did."

"I know that. I've heard the stories about some of things he did for people anonymously. So, after that visit he walked out of your life for good?"

"We received a few notes from him over the next ten years, but that was it."

"Nothing more about the people he was running from?"

"Not a word."

Jason shook his head. "He disappeared from public view altogether around that time. Quite a coincidence if you ask me."

"I agree."

"Was there anything else he said that night that might lend a clue as to who was after him? Anything at all?"

Hughes considered the question carefully. "I remember him saying, 'Our boy will be okay as long as you don't let anyone know.' I doubt that sheds any light on their identity."

"Not much."

"He said he would try to get in touch again when he could."

"Okay. That's it?"

"He said something about Glenn Odekirk."

"His chief aeronautical engineer."

"Yeah, and Robert Maheu."

"The lawyer who oversaw most of his business dealings in Vegas."

"Right. There was someone named Rafael that he mentioned. He didn't seem too happy with that guy. And someone else named—are you okay?"

Jason's mouth was hanging open.

"Could you repeat that?" he asked.

"What?"

"About someone named Rafael."

"He mentioned someone by that name, but I didn't hear a last name."

"And you said he seemed unhappy when he talked about him?"

"Yeah, very."

"What did your father say, exactly, that made you think that?"

"He said something like, "I'm not interested in that damn Rafael." Or maybe, 'I don't want anything to do with that damn Rafael." It was something along those lines."

"My God."

"Why?"

"My...*God*...."

"You look as white as a sheet, Mr. Hammond."

Jason eyed him squarely. "I'm sorry, but I have to go."

"You...okay, of course. Of course you can go."

They both rose, and Jason put his hand out.

"I'm sorry, Mr. Hughes. I'm sorry to cut this short."

"It's all right."

"Thank you very much."

"Is this 'Rafael' person important?"

"I don't know. Maybe. I need to...I need to call someone right away."

Hughes nodded. "Well, please just remember my request to remove any mention of me from the will. Can I count on you for that?"

"No problem."

"And I pray you will keep my existence a secret. I feel I can trust you to do so."

"You can, don't worry."

"Good enough. Please don't let me delay you any further." Hughes gestured toward the exit.

Jason went to it, took one step out, then turned back.

"How can I get in touch with you if need be?"

"We won't be seeing each other again," Hughes said matter-of-factly, "but don't worry—I'll know what's going on."

****

Jason watched Hughes's plane taxi around to the nearest runway, then motor forward and lift into the sky. It occurred to him that Hughes had made at least one error in hiding his identity, in that the plane's registration number could be traced with relative ease. Then he saw that all the identifying marks on the outside had been covered over.

Walking swiftly toward the airport, he took his phone out of his pocket.

Twenty Eight

NOAH GOT DOWN on one knee, which hurt like mad, and stretched the tape measure horizontally across the third step. Then a second measurement, vertical this time, and finally the depth.

"Forty two, fourteen, and ten," he said to himself, allowing the tape to reel back into its case. He got up with a groan and removed a small piece of paper from his pocket so he could jot down the figures. The staircase in the front hall desperately needed new carpeting, and he wanted to have the numbers ready when he called for estimates. He was calculating the total area when his cellphone rang. Taking it from its holster, he saw Jason's name on the screen and took a deep breath.

"Hello?"

"Noah, I need you to look for something."

"I'm busy measuring the front staircase at the moment." The present carpeting was worn away to nothing in some places, revealing the wood underneath. "It needs recovering, as I'm sure you'll agree."

He waited for Jason to take the bait but had already decided not to mention Katie. That information could wait for another time.

"I'm sorry, I know you're busy. But this is very important."

"So's this. These steps are getting dangerous."

"I'm sure it'll take no more than a few minutes."

"Jason, I still have things to get done today—" he checked his watch and saw that it was just after three—"and it's going to be dinnertime soon. Now if you're not going to help me with—"

"I need you to find a lockbox that belonged to my father. A *blue* one."

Noah's mouth snapped shut. He said nothing.

"Noah?"

"Yes?"

"Do you know the one I'm talking about? It's about the size of a shoebox, and it has a digital—"

"Keypad instead of a dial or a keylock."

"That's the one."

"It's a deep, steely blue."

"Exactly."

"But how do you even—"

"Have you seen it lately? Do you know where it is?"

"Not at the moment," Noah said, which was the truth. "I haven't seen it since...well, since before the accident. Then again, I haven't gone through much of your father's things, per your request."

"I understand. But you need to find it and let me know what's inside. I don't know if my father ever told you the combination. But if he didn't, you should break the box open. Use whatever means necessary."

Noah didn't think it would come to that. Alan Hammond had left a list of all his passwords, pin numbers, combinations, bank accounts, and similarly sensitive material in a Word document that was, in itself, encrypted. And he had entrusted the password for that file to just two people, the other being his late wife Linda. Noah had no doubt the correct numeric sequence was in there.

"Do you mind if I ask why you need it? Perhaps what you're looking for is somewhere else."

"Maybe," Jason said, "but I want to start there."

Noah eased into a sitting position on one the steps, which was a challenge as his knees were screaming now.

"Jason, I've got so much going on with the renovations right now. And frankly, you know I'm not thrilled with what you're doing out there in the first place. The worry for your safety is just about killing me." He paused, then added, "And if I'm being totally honest, I'm not thrilled with the way we've been...*communicating* lately, either." Noah leaned his head against the wall and closed his eyes.

Silence dominated the line again, then Jason sighed and said, "Look, I'm sorry, okay? I'm sorry for all of it. I know everything that's happened has been my fault."

"Well, no, I wouldn't go that—"

"And I'm sorry for the breakdown between us. That was my fault, too. I'm particularly sorry I raised my voice to you. I've never done that before, and I'm ashamed of myself."

"Jason, take it easy."

"You held me together during the worst days of my life, and I've never said thank you. But I'm saying it now—*thank you*. Thank you for...well, for everything. I don't think I'd even be around today if it wasn't for you."

"Okay, I'm sure that's not the case."

"And for whatever it's worth," Jason said with a quick laugh, "I'm really happy to hear your voice again."

Noah smiled. "I'm happy to hear yours, too."

"Look, I wouldn't be asking about the box if I didn't believe it was important. I was all set to come home an hour ago. I was going to give up and come crawling back to you to admit that you were right and I was wrong. Then something happened."

"What's that?"

Jason told him about the encounter with Hughes's son. When he was finished, Noah said, "That's incredible."

"I know it is. And when he told me the part about his father mentioning someone named 'Rafael,' it sparked a memory of my father doing the *exact same thing*."

"When was this?"

"Maybe a month before the accident. It was late at night and I couldn't sleep. I was going down the hall to the stairs, heading for the kitchen. That's when I heard my father in his office, talking to someone on the phone. I thought it was strange because, you know, he never stayed up very late."

"Never."

"And yet this was around one in the morning. He was trying to keep his voice low, but I could tell he was pretty ticked off. He said something like, 'I wouldn't touch that Rafael if my life depended on it.' He didn't notice me when I walked by because the door was mostly closed. But through the crack I saw the blue lockbox open on his desk. I never saw it before that, and I never saw it again. But Noah, there has to be a connection. It's just too coincidental."

A surge of thoughts raced through Noah's mind; so many things he wanted to say but couldn't. The one at the top of the list was, *I know exactly which box you're talking about, Jason, because I've seen it myself—on more than one occasion.*

"I agree it's quite a coincidence," he said finally. "But are you sure it was the blue one? Absolutely certain?"

"Yes, I'm certain. Could you please find it and get it open?"

"I'll start looking right away."

"Great—thank you very much. I'll call you back in a little bit. And if you find it before then, please let me know."

"I will."

Noah ended the call then, got to his feet, and began up the staircase.

Before he even reached the top, he realized with burgeoning surprise that he was feeling more awake, more alert, and more *curious* than he had been in a very long time.

****

All appeared perfectly normal in the airport office upon Jason's return; no indication that anyone had a clue as to his rendezvous with Hughes. Travelers and pilots and mechanics came and went in routine fashion, paying him no mind. 'R. Griffith' was nowhere in sight.

He took the same seat he'd had before. His leather shoulder bag was still lying on the seat next to it, he noted with relief. He'd forgotten all about it. He had no idea what to do now; for the first time since he'd arrived in Nevada, the road ahead was unclear. The urge to ride into Denise Wheeler's life on a white horse and put to rest the painful question of her brother's disappearance remained strong. In fact, his fundamental love of mysteries still had as much blood running to it as ever. Even now, with all the struggle and heartbreak that had come from this case, the thought of tying up all the loose ends and bringing the bad guys to justice still stirred him into euphoria.

But the other side of the issue could not be ignored. He *had* caused substantial suffering to others, and could not shake the feeling of responsibility. His money, intelligence, focus, determination, good intentions...it all paled in comparison to an injured young man, a defeated sister, and the tortured family of a wounded little girl. The fact that he had not made the kind of progress he was accustomed to only compounded his despair. He accepted that he would face challenges with each venture. But so was gathering little bits and pieces of the puzzle along the way until you formed a cohesive picture. That still hadn't happened here. How could he justify getting back into it now?

He set his chin in his hands and remained that way until another uniformed man, this one slim and curly-haired, came up to him.

"Mr. Hammond?"

"Yes?"

"You're all cleared. You can go as soon as you're ready."

"Okay, thanks."

He took a deep breath and made his decision. *Maybe something in the lockbox will make me come back,* he told himself. *Maybe....*

He got to his feet and began walking toward the main hangar again. His plane was on the far side of it.

Then a voice called out—"Uh, excuse me."

He turned and found an attractive woman of perhaps forty two or three dressed in a gray business suit. Her blonde hair was pulled back hard and twirled into a tight little bun.

"Yes?"

"Can I have my bag?"

"What?"

"My bag," she said, pointing. "You just picked up my bag."

He looked down and saw that he was toting a women's carryon with a black and tan checkerboard design.

He smiled. "Oops—sorry about that." He slid it off his shoulder and held it out to her. "Yeah, you might as well take it. It's not really my color."

The woman smiled back in a manner that underscored her lack of interest in all things comical.

"Thanks." She pulled it over her own shoulder before turning and walking briskly away. Then she joined up with the rest of her companions—three men of about the same age, also clad in dull boardroom fashion.

If one of them mates with her, Jason thought, *he better be careful she doesn't kill and eat him afterwards.*

He went back and found his own carryon still sitting there. He took it by the handles this time and made a second attempt for the exit. The business woman, meanwhile, had stopped in front of a bank of lockers. While her harem waited, she opened one, set the carryon and another bag inside, then shut the door and ran a magnetic card through the lock. A little light went from green to red, and she walked off pulling a wheeled suitcase behind her.

Jason stopped short, his eyes and mouth widening in perfect sync.

"Oh, wow...." he whispered.

It all came to him then, every piece of the puzzle flying together as if in a film being run in reverse.

Yes...YES.

He gasped out a breath as joy overwhelmed him, then he did something for the first time in ages—he laughed.

"That's it," he said out loud, which earned him a few curious glances. "That's *it!*"

He ran back to the counter, where the curly-haired man was sifting through a pile of paperwork.

"Sir? Forget about my flight."

"What?"

"My flight, just cancel it."

"Are you sure? It could be awhile before—"

"I'm sure—*thanks*."

He moved rapidly toward the exit.

Twenty Nine

RUDD CAREFULLY REMOVED the lid from his coffee as he walked through the basement gym. He blew on it, took a pensive sip, and judged that it was still undrinkable. They always served it too hot at the Starbucks around the corner, but he wasn't willing to drive another two miles to the next one. He needed the caffeine fix every morning without fail.

A routine that may be changing soon, Rudd considered as he passed through the laundry room and slid aside the door of the storage closet. *It's getting to be about that time.*

Since he began his career in cyberterrorism, he had not remained in any one venue for more than ten months. Computers were, at their core, mathematical devices, and one of the foundations of mathematics involved two related elements—constants and variables. Rudd, being a predominantly mathematical animal himself, viewed most of life in the same way. And when he applied this perspective to his current profession, he knew that one of the factors that had to remain variable was his location. In the good old outlaw days of the Internet, a diligent hacker could assure his anonymity from the comfort of his bedroom. But as technology improved, so did the response capabilities of the government, as well as hordes of watchdog NGOs. Rudd had seen countless friends and colleagues get picked off in sting operations, their freedom invalidated and the fruits of their labor stripped away. He vowed this would not happen to him. There was no concrete method of knowing when trouble was near; it was simply a matter of paying heed to one's instincts. His own appeared to be quite good, as they had saved his skin several times in the past. And they'd been nagging at him recently. *The next move is coming*, he thought as he slid away the back wall and entered his cryptic domain.

A fist rocketed out of the dimness and struck him squarely in the face. He saw a bright flash, the coffee slipping through his fingers, then fell dizzily to the floor. Even through the torrent of pain he immediately knew the identity of his attacker.

He was hauled off the floor and thrown into his swivel chair. Then Grant leaned in close, slamming his hands onto the armrests. His eyes were glazed with madness.

"Don't *ever* speak to me like that again, you understand?"

The smell drifting off the man was terrible, as if he hadn't washed in days. His considerable beard growth appeared to support this.

Rudd had been expecting him to show up. He thought back to the phone conversation from a few days earlier—

Grant: *I need that information, junior. I need the name of the guy on the other end.*

Rudd: *I finally cracked it—but I require payment for it.*

Grant: *You'll get your payment, just give me the info.*

Rudd: *Payment first. That's how it works. That's how it's always worked. I'm not a charity organization.*

Grant: *How about I don't tell the Feds where you are? How's that for payment?*

Rudd: *You're at liberty to try that, of course—but it still won't get you what you want. Which brings us back to my first point—when I get my payment, you'll get your information. Otherwise, I'll be happy to sit on it forever. Your choice.*

He hung up then, and he ignored the constant ringing that followed. He knew there would be retribution for it. Guys like Grant weren't known for their tolerance of snot-nosed kids. The problem was that Rudd *loved* being a snot-nosed kid. Working his way under people's skin and then watching them blow their corks had been a lifelong pleasure. It had gotten him into hot water so many times he'd lost count. He treasured each of those incidents with a twisted brand of nostalgia. Pushing someone to their breaking point, to where they seemed on the verge of blowing every blood vessel in their brain, was better than drugs, booze, and women mixed together. And it probably lay at the core, he had theorized, of his love for his current profession. It really was the best of all things—frustrating random people and getting rich while remaining irritatingly out of reach.

The only downside to such arrogance, he had come to learn, was when one of the people you ticked off became fixated on revenge—and found you.

Blood streamed from both nostrils, as if a pipe had burst somewhere in his head. Covering his nose, Rudd said mutedly, "*You broke it, you slime! You broke my—*"

Grant slapped him hard and Rudd went silent.

"I'm going to make this real simple for you," Grant said, sweat dripping off his face. "I want that name and number *now*. If I don't get it, one of us is going to become very sorry very quickly."

"All right, all right! But look—it took me a long time to break through that firewall." A part of him was screaming *Are you out of your mind?* but a stronger part—the one that was hopelessly addicted to exasperating others—urged him to forge ahead. "I really have to insist on our agreed price of—"

Grant removed a handgun that had been tucked inside his belt and fired at one of the flatscreen monitors, which disintegrated into a zillion sparkling pieces.

The fright in Rudd's eyes elevated to blazing horror. "*YOU'RE CRAZY!!!*"

Grant pointed the weapon at Rudd's right hand. "Next time it won't be something you can replace, and I'm not kidding."

It wasn't the sentiment that turned Rudd cold but the conversational manner in which it was delivered. *This guy's a psychopath*, he thought dazedly. *Not just a little nuts—a true head case.*

"Okay, Jesus...I wrote it down someplace. Let me look...."

Grant kicked the chair away, slamming Rudd into the desk. Rudd then flipped through piles of papers, his hands trembling.

"Here, here it is." He spun around, holding it out.

Grant snatched it from him and looked it over. The tiniest of smiles appeared in the corner of his mouth.

"Good, very good."

Rudd was yanking tissues out of a box and stuffing them up his nose.

"One thing, though," Grant said.

"What's that?"

"If this information is wrong—" Grant leveled the gun squarely between his eyes "—you're dead. You got that?"

"Y-yeah."

"Good."

Grant turned as if to leave, then spun back and struck Rudd with the butt of the weapon. Rudd collapsed onto the floor and lay still, a fresh line of blood coursing from his temple.

****

When he regained consciousness a short time later, he found Grant gone and a parade drum beating inside his skull. He stumbled out of his lair, up the basement steps, and into the bathroom on the first floor. He almost fainted when he looked in the mirror. When he touched his nose with a peroxide-soaked cotton ball, he let out a scream that rattled every window in the house.

He returned to the basement and was about to toss his dirty clothes onto the pile that had been accumulating in front of the washer machine. Then he noticed a stain on his jeans left behind by Grant. It was small, round, and dark.

He took out his cellphone and dialed a number that was not in the phone's memory but had never left his own. The call was answered on the second ring.

"Hey Pam, it's Danny. Yeah, I'm fine. Listen, I've got a question—can you get a good DNA sample from perspiration in fabric? Good...no, great. All right, I need a favor from you, a big one. And right away, too...."

As he hurried out of the house, he ran down a mental list of everything he needed to do afterward.

****

Parked at the curb early the next morning, Jason scanned the area for anyone who looked suspicious. He was wearing the quickie disguise of a baseball cap and sunglasses. The only person in view was an elderly woman coming down the sidewalk with her dog, a small bichon frise with a red bow on the top of its head.

He used cash and one of his false IDs to secure the new rental car and hotel room. The latter was a far cry from his previous digs, but it was clean enough and, more importantly, well off the beaten track. In spite of the continuing swirl of all things Jason Hammond in the media, no one had recognized him. Maintaining that anonymity—and, more to the point, the illusion that he had gone back to New Hampshire, which the local journalists were already reporting—was crucial now.

He got out and went up the walkway to Denise Wheeler's front porch. He rang the bell twice, and as he waited he removed his cap and deposited the sunglasses in his shirt pocket. The door opened a short ways, then came to a dead stop.

"What are you doing here?" she said. "I thought you'd tucked your tail between your legs and scurried back to your billion-dollar estate like the coward you are."

Jason smiled. "I changed my mind."

"Yeah, why's that? No one back home for you to toy with?"

"I have a question."

"I think you know what you can do with your que—"

"During my last visit, you said you showed me everything that belonged to your brother. But I don't think that's quite true."

"Pardon me?"

"I think you failed to show me something—something very important."

"You saw *everything*. Everything that was his has been kept in that box since—"

"What about his keys?"

"His what?"

"His keys. You know, keys?"

The woman's anger began to visibly dissolve, replaced by a look of contemplation.

"You said your mother kept Chase's car in the driveway," Jason went on, "back at the other house. That means she also had to have his keys. When she moved here, I can't believe she didn't take them with her. Even after she finally gave up the car, I'm sure he had other keys. Everyone has more than one. So they must be around somewhere."

Denise Wheeler's expression modulated again, this time to dawning realization.

"Oh my God."

"Yeah, I thought so."

She unlocked the door and let him in.

Thirty

LESS THAN TWO HOURS later, Jason strode into the lobby of one of Vegas's most storied hotels and was hit with the greeting before he even opened his mouth.

"Good afternoon, and welcome to the Flamingo!"

The concierge looked to be in her early twenties and was as bright and shiny as the lobby itself, with its garish celebration of all things marble and gold.

"Good afternoon to you as well," Jason replied. The baseball cap was still in place, but the shades had been replaced by a pair of low-magnification reading glasses so he wouldn't appear quite so creepy.

"How may I help you today?"

Jason held up a brass key. It was tarnished and spotted but otherwise in good condition. It had a simple round bow with a hole near the top. Just below that, an ornate capital 'F' had been stamped into the metal.

"Where will I find the lockers for this?"

The girl took it from him and looked it over. "Wow, that's an old one. Are you certain it's from here?"

"Yes, I checked online. You wouldn't believe how many sites there are for key collecting. That is definitely a Flamingo key." Jason pointed. "See the 'F'?"

"It certainly looks like our 'F.'"

"It belonged to the younger brother of a friend of mine, and he passed away some years back." Jason had already decided he wouldn't lie about the back story, but he was willing to leave out a few details.

"Oh, I'm so sorry to hear that."

"Thanks. We found this among some of his things, and I've been helping out, trying to tie up a few loose ends."

"I understand."

"So, would you happen to know where the lockers are? This place is a bit of a labyrinth."

The girl chuckled and nodded. "I know, it can be confusing. Let me see...." She got behind a computer terminal and began tapping away at the keyboard. "Okay, well...we have lockers for patron use in several areas, and I do have this floor map—" She reached under the counter and produced a colorful tri-fold document with the words 'How to Get Around The Flamingo' on the front. She did some more keystroking, then shook her head. "However...."

"However?"

"I'm not sure about something." She stuck one finger up, which had a longish nail at the end. "Please just give me a second."

"No problem."

She disappeared into a back room for a few moments, then reappeared with a male colleague in tow. He was slightly heavyset and, in spite of pure silver hair and a matching beard, did not appear to be any older than his early forties. He was dressed in the same uniform as the girl, adjusted to suit his gender.

"Good afternoon, sir, my name is Paul and I'm the head concierge." His smile was brief and insincere.

"Nice to meet you."

"And you as well. I understand you're trying to locate the lockers that accept this key." It now lay in the palm of his hand.

"Yes, that's right."

"I'm sorry, but we no longer have lockers of this type at the Flamingo."

"Oh no?"

"The interior of the resort has undergone several remodelings over the years, and the ones we have now use electronic passcards. In fact, this is my eleventh year with the company, and I have no recollection of ever seeing a key of this sort." He set it down on the counter as if fearful it might give him some kind of infection.

"Umm...there aren't *any* of them left?"

"I'm afraid not."

"Not even repurposed? Maybe as storage in the basement or something?"

"No, I'm sorry sir."

Jason took the key back and sighed. "Okay, thank you."

He turned away and headed toward the exit without a clue where to go next. A nightmare scenario played out in his mind—the locker with Hughes's will being ripped from the wall and heaved into a dumpster, then deposited in one of the local landfills or, even better, incinerated for recycling purposes. *And one of the most important documents of the 20th century went with it, gone forever.* He felt sick at the thought of it. There was always the possibility someone had checked through the lockers beforehand, just to make sure they were empty. But that would mean the will would have been found, and Jason doubted such a discovery could've been kept quiet for so long.

As he drew closer to the exit, he passed a small gift shop. It had all the usual convenience items—candy, gum, bottled drinks, travel packs of common medications—as well as Flamingo-styled novelty items such as hats, t-shirts, and cheap jewelry. The entrance was a broad archway, and on either side were recessed display cases with glass shelves and bright halogen lights. These held the more expensive knickknacks.

Jason came to a stop when he noticed them.

Collectibles....

"Oh wow," he said, "hang on a minute...."

He turned and went back to the concierge station. Paul was finishing up a conversation with his younger colleague and was just about to return to his lair. When he saw Jason, he took a step back.

"Yes?"

"This might be a longshot, but is there any chance the lockers weren't thrown away, but rather taken by some collector, or maybe by a dealer who sells to collectors?"

"A collector? You mean for...what? People who collect *lockers*?"

Jason laughed. "No, I mean people who collect casino items. Since I've been here, I've noticed that just about everything related to the casinos has some kind of collector value. There are antique shops all over town, and about a million items on eBay. When I was on Las Vegas Boulevard, I saw a sign for a place called the 'Neon Museum.' Vintage signs lying around a big piece of land, just rotting and rusting away. But, apparently, it gets lots of visitors."

"Yes, I admit that's a very popular tourist attraction."

"I have a friend who even got her wedding pictures taken there," the girl added.

"See?" Jason said. "There's a whole other dimension to the consumer demand for Vegas stuff beyond the gambling. I don't think it's too much of a stretch to believe people would be interested in the lockers. They seem to collect everything else, so why not?"

"I suppose it's possible," Paul said.

"Is there any way I could find out if some antique dealer or collector came and took the lockers when they were removed during the remodeling? Is there anyone here who might know about that?"

Paul pursed his lips and appeared to give it some thought. Then the girl said to him, "You know who might know? Tim Stryker."

"Oh yeah...maybe."

"Tim Stryker?" Jason asked.

Paul ignored him and picked up the phone, turning away so he wouldn't be overheard.

"He's one of our execs," the girl said. "Very high up. He's been here forever and knows everything about this place."

The conversation was brief, and when Paul hung up he said, "I'm impressed by your instincts."

"Oh?"

"Mr. Stryker says he clearly remembers selling the lockers, along with a hoard of other items, to several different dealers in the area."

"*Different* dealers?"

"Yes. Apparently, this has become common practice during the remodelings. Instead of throwing out the old stuff, the casino sells it to wholesalers in huge lots. Some of the items will then be immediately resold to retail shops, others will go into storage until demand begins to grow."

"So does Mr. Stryker know who these dealers were?"

"Not off the top of his head, but he does have the information somewhere."

"Would it be possib—"

"He's already expecting you." Paul pointed with his pen. "Down the hall and to the left, you'll see a set of elevators. Take them to the 11th floor and go right. Mr. Stryker is in office number nine."

Paul smiled then, but Jason got the impression it was only because their discourse was finally at an end.

Jason smiled back at him. "Thank you for your help."

****

Theresa Richter sat upright in bed with her knees pulled to her chin. The book she'd been reading for the last four days lay nearby, facedown and forgotten. She wasn't really here at the moment, anyway. Not in her thoughts.

She was back in that grubby little office in July of 1982. A grubby office not even suitable for a councilwoman. But that's what she was then. At the formative age of twenty nine, she had the plan all mapped out—first mayor, then governor, then president. It was a big dream, she knew, but not unattainable. She had told no one other than Bill—because those in the political arena who revealed their dreams would almost assuredly never see them fulfilled—and he'd been unswervingly supportive. He never joked about it, either, e.g., "So, how's my future president doing today?" or some other ridiculous comment people dealt out that betrayed how idiotic they thought the ambition really was. No, Bill stood by her, doing whatever was required to move her closer to the mountaintop. How she had truly loved him, and how her soul had been crushed when the cancer came and chopped him down inch by inch.

But he'd been alive and well and as healthy as a thoroughbred when the note about Chase Wheeler appeared on the grubby little desk in that grubby little office. And *appeared* was the right word because she didn't know then—and still did not know now—how it got there in the first place. She had a secretary, Jan, who was twice her age and as engaging as a nest of yellowjackets. But she was fiercely protective of her territory, and there was simply no way someone could have slipped past her and into Richter's domain. If someone tried, Richter believed, the woman would've pulled a gun out of her purse and started firing. It was also unlikely that Jan would have delivered the note herself without grilling the messenger first—*Who is this from? What does it concern? What contact information should be used to reply?*

Yet there it was, lying in the center of the blotter when Richter returned from lunch that day. An ordinary # 10 envelope with the name 'Theresa Anne Richter' printed across the front. The font had been rendered with a common typewriter, as this was before computers had conquered the world.

Jan had already left for her own break, so Richter couldn't ask her about it. The woman took lunch at precisely twelve-thirty every day, no variation. If she was on her way out the door and President Reagan pulled up with a cadre of Secret Service agents, she would've told them all to wait in the lobby until she returned.

Richter sat down and slit the top open with a sigh. Inside was a single sheet of plain paper. And on it, in the same typewriter font, was two lines—

I know where the body of Chase Wheeler is located. Go to the Holiday Inn on Route 17 at 7:00 PM tomorrow night and wait by the pay phone.

Richter's first reaction was that it was a joke. Then logic squelched this idea. The only person who could have put the note here—or so she believed at the time, although that was another notion on its way to the ash heap—was Jan, and Jan would never do something like this. When God ran Jan Birch's initial programming, he had opted not to install a sense of humor. In the two years she had worked here, Richter never once heard her laugh. Even her smiles, which were rare enough, were awful. They made her look like the grizzled old swamp woman in a southern-Gothic horror movie.

Richter's next thought was of her enemies. She didn't have too many yet, but there were a few. She ran through the list in her head and couldn't imagine which ones would even know about Chase Wheeler. Heck, even *she* knew very little about him. His disappearance had been big news around town for awhile, riding on a wave of countless rumors—that he took off to the mountains of Oregon; that he fell in love, got an overnight marriage at one of the Vegas chapels, then flew off with his new bride to Europe; that he drove to the middle of the desert and blew his brains out.... Then the public found something else to suck on, and the matter faded into obscurity.

There would have been some political value, Richter knew, in leading the charge to the discovery of his body. Wheeler's mother, Val, was a beloved and tragic figure in her neighborhood. The kind of feelgood drama that could unfold would be priceless if exploited from the right angle. But there were risks, too. Some people might think she had known about Wheeler's death all along. Pretty convenient that she had suddenly uncovered the body after two seasoned detectives could not. Maybe she had something to do with it, people would say. She was a politician, after all, and politicians were ruthless. They wiped out anyone who opposed them. And if a life or two was lost along the way, well, that was the nature of the game, right? Backs got stabbed, toes got stepped on, and throats got cut. That's how you acquired power in this world.

No, she ultimately decided, there were too many unpredictables in the equation. 'Too Much Risk, Too Little Reward.' She'd measured almost everything in her adult life by this simple platitude, and it had worked. She'd come far in a relatively short time, and she planned to go a lot farther. And when she reached her greatest ambition, she would do great things. That would justify all of her previous sins. All of them.

Those were her thoughts then, and they were her thoughts now. Four decades later, the goal remained the same, as did the singleminded focus. She had crumpled the note and thrown it away that day. And if something else came up concerning Chase Wheeler, she'd deal with it then. But it hadn't. The boy's mother gradually lost her will to live; Richter knew this because the local papers would run a human-interest piece on her at least once a year. And she hated herself a little more with each one, marinating in the guilt that came with wondering if she could've eased the woman's suffering to some degree. Locating Chase's dead body might not be the result Val Wheeler had prayed for, but there would be closure. At least Richter could have given her that. But she didn't. She *chose* not to. And she said more than a few prayers of her own, pleading that no one would ever come forward about the note, that no one else would ever know about it. That the person who had left it would eventually be as dead as Chase himself. Then the matter would be closed, and she could let the horrible burden of her indifference die as well. And for four decades—a long time by any human measure—that seemed to be exactly what would happen.

Until yesterday, with the news that someone was looking for Howard Hughes's will. Someone rich. Someone smart. Someone *determined.*

The intervening years vanished, and it was 1982 all over again. She realized the pain of it had been right there all along, so very close. Maybe hidden under a layer of denial, but a very thin layer, and not very far from her core thoughts in the first place. That protective layer dissolved like tissue paper when all the pieces began linking together—Chase Wheeler (Desert Inn employee), Howard Hughes (Desert Inn owner, thus his employer, and someone that Richter had irritated in order to gain media attention on many occasions), Hughes's legendary lost will (likely to contain revelations about many of his enemies, per his equally legendary vindictiveness). It was all too impossible to believe...and yet, in the strange way that life sometimes worked, all too likely. When the prize was enough money to tell the rest of the world to go scratch, you could buy a million lottery tickets and never come close. But when the prize was a fatal blow to your life, it was amazing how easily you seemed able to beat the odds.

So she told Kelli everything about Chase Wheeler. And Kelli did as she always had—she sat quietly, allowed her finish, then assured her everything would be fine. They would talk in greater detail in the days ahead. Kelli would have a plan for all contingencies, and it would be a good plan; they always were. Perhaps most importantly, Kelli did not judge her. She always understood. She understood that an ugly thing sometimes had to be done in order to achieve a beautiful one. That Richter's heart was a good heart, and that she would do good things when she reached the fabled land of the American presidency. That the end really did justify the means sometimes. And if you really did make a positive difference, much would be forgiven.

That's what Theresa Richter had always believed.

Thirty One

KATIE HAD PASSED by the photos in the upstairs hallway several times in the course of her duties. But now, standing there alone, she took a moment to really look them over.

They hung on the wall just outside Alan Hammond's office suite. Four were black-and-white portraits—formal studio shots of each family member. She guessed Jason to be in his early to mid twenties at the time. Every hair was combed into place, the back and sides kept short and the top swept to one side in the standard Ivy League style. He was looking directly into the camera, the smile tight-lipped and confident. He had that same expression in a group shot of the family down at the dock. Everyone was dressed identically in white cotton pants and light blue oxford shirts, their hair a little windblown. Linda Hammond stood between her son and her husband, holding hands with both of them, and Joanie was lying on the sand in the foreground, propped on one elbow. The remaining shots were candids, random captures that someone had judged good enough to hang. In one, a very small Jason was standing by a Christmas tree in the living room downstairs, holding up a toy railroad engine and beaming as only a little boy can. In another, an adolescent Jason was giving Joanie a piggyback ride out by the patio. The stirringly handsome man he would one day become was just beginning to emerge in that young face, Katie noticed.

She was still struggling to digest the fact that the blissful setting portrayed in these images was the same one she'd been visiting for the last few days. She'd found no evidence to support the rumors that Jason had become addicted to drugs or alcohol, taken on violent tendencies, or any of the other apocryphal contrivances of local chatter. But that didn't mean the realities were much better. Nearly every inch of the property could be neatly filed into two categories—badly outdated or neglected to the point of near-ruination. The interior of the main house was the primary victim of the former, more like a museum than a living space. Katie got the distinct feeling most of the rooms were never actually used. Jason had a housekeeper who came in four days a week, but she never seemed to have much to do and spent most of her time watching television in a small anteroom just off the kitchen. This struck Katie as particularly strange when, standing in the upstairs hallway one afternoon, she watched Noah step briefly into Joanie's bedroom. The bed was unmade, a bath towel was hanging over the back of one chair, and there was an empty glass on the nightstand. When Noah closed the door again, Katie asked if someone was living in there; perhaps a visiting relative or something. Noah explained that Jason had asked for his sister's room to be left exactly as it was on the day she died, and his parents' room as well. Katie would soon learn that Jason maintained the same policy with almost every other part of the house.

Outside, the years of neglect had taken a heavy toll. While Noah tended to simple landscaping chores, the rest of the property had fallen to a deplorable state. There was a greenhouse that, according to Noah, had once been Linda Hammond's pride and joy, producing flowers for decoration and fragrance, plus fresh fruits and vegetables for the family. Now the windows were opaque with mold and other filth, and ugly vines crept over everything. There was a small pond on the west wide of the property named 'Nearly Oval Pond' for its near-perfect shape. That shape had been distorted by overgrowth so wild that it now looked more like a giant puddle. When they went down to the boat launch in the bay, the long run of zigzagging steps creaked and groaned with such articulation that she feared for her safety.

"Hey," Noah said as he appeared in the hallway.

She hadn't noticed his approach and was mildly startled. Turning away from the photos, she said, "Hey to you, too."

He opened one of the paired doors to Alan Hammond's office and went in. A light went on, and he said, "You can come in here if you like. I'm just looking for something."

She entered and found exactly what she expected—a place trapped in time. The furniture and decor were all beautiful but at least a generation removed from the present. *Like a museum*, she thought again. *A bygone era kept in a vacuum.*

Noah got behind the desk and opened one drawer after another with a set of tiny keys. Katie noted that most of the paperwork on the desktop appeared to be current. Then something caught her eye.

"Oh my goodness."

Noah looked up. "What?"

"Is that Mr. Hammond's?"

Noah followed her gaze to an unusual paperweight—a small Lucite cube with shiny pennies inside. He picked it up and gave it a cursory inspection.

"This thing? Yes. He bought it at a gift shop in Florida. Why?"

"I remember it."

"You're kidding."

"No, from the day I stayed here. Mrs. Hammond brought a cup of coffee up to Mr. Hammond when he was working in here, and she took me with her so I wouldn't be by myself. When Mr. Hammond saw me looking at it, he handed it to me and told me I could keep it. But I felt bad and left it downstairs when my mom came to pick me up."

Noah laughed and held it out. "Well, do you want it?"

She took it and said, "Oh no, of course not. I just...I had forgotten all about it until now."

"Ah...." Noah said, and went back to the drawers.

She turned it over in her hands, once again overwhelmed by the memories of that day. And then it came to her, the realization that had been gradually coalescing from various points across her consciousness ever since she had come here.

It wasn't just Jason's family that died that day—he did, too.

There had been no progress, no maturation. His travels around the world were merely lateral maneuvers, circumventions to quiet the demons. In turn, he was compounding and prolonging his suffering. *And how he suffers,* she thought. She had known little in her own life, but she had a gift for sensing it in others. *How horrible it must be, fighting off that torment day after day.* He was alive in one sense, through the simple passage of time. But to truly live, one had to grow—and for Jason, she realized, there had been no growth in uncounted years. *He's wasting away. Everything I've seen here is proof of that. And soon, there will be nothing left of him. Nothing left of that once-sweet little boy except—*

"Katie?"

She looked over and saw that Noah was now standing in the doorway.

"Hmm?"

He smiled. "I'm all done in here."

"Oh, sure. I'm sorry...."

"That's quite all right."

"Did you find what you were looking for?"

"No. The search goes on."

"Very good."

She put the paperweight back in its place and turned to go out.

"Are you sure you don't want to keep it?" Noah asked.

"Very sure."

Thirty Two

A SILVER BELL JINGLED over the front door as Jason entered Mr. Morton's Memory Emporium. It was by far the smallest of the four shops he'd visited. It was also the nicest. There was actual carpeting here—a badly outdated pea green and a little worn in the high-traffic zones, but still in one piece. Muzak was streaming quietly from an unseen source, wafting through the scents of dust and age.

Jason didn't see any of the Flamingo lockers from his vantage point, and the knot in his stomach grew tighter. Then he noticed the broad archway leading to a second room and began toward it.

"Good afternoon," someone said.

He halted again and turned. There was a long display case loaded with smalls—silver spoons, porcelain thimbles, rings and brooches—and on top was a beautifully ornate cash register. The man standing behind it could've stepped out of a book called *Classic Americana*, in the chapter entitled 'Shop Owners of the Mom and Pop Era.' He had a round and friendly face beneath a slanted mat of fine white hair. His bifocals hung from a black cord against his plaid shirt and were further supported by his slightly swollen belly. He even had a lint-specked cardigan sweater, which he kept unbuttoned.

Jason needed a moment to register the fact that he had just received a formal greeting. He had not experienced the same kind of civility with any of the other dealers today.

He nodded. "Good afternoon to you, too."

"How are you today?"

"I'm all right, thank you."

"Can I help you find something?"

"I just want to browse around if you don't mind."

"Of course not, take your time. If you need help, let me know."

"I sure will."

Jason passed into the second room, which was startlingly different from the first. The ceiling was twice as high, the lights brighter, and the carpet a rich gold color, like something out of a 1970s home-interiors catalog. All of this made him think the long archway had at one time been a solid wall separating two distinct businesses.

There were thousands of items here—standard casino-related goods like ash trays, hotel keys, poker chips, and slot machines, as well as more familiar junk-shop relics such as quilts, lamps, vases, clocks, framed prints, and a variety of vintage furniture. Jason walked to the center of the room and took note of all these things. What he did not see, however, was a set of lockers that had once belonged to the Flamingo Hotel and Casino. The knot in his gut now hardened into a fist, his nerves fraying to the point where he began to tremble slightly.

Please...please tell me it's here somewhere...this is the last one.

The day before, he had followed the concierge's instructions and met with the infamous Mr. Stryker. Stryker was a bit of an antique himself, with wasted, almost corpselike features and the slow-but-purposeful movements of a tortoise. His mind, however, was still quite sharp, with a prodigious memory for details. He correctly remembered that there had been four dealers interested in the lockers in spite of the fact that the remodeling in question had occurred nine years prior. A humorless and straightforward sort, he never asked Jason about the reasons for his inquiry; he simply read the dealers' names from a printed list and sent him on his way.

Jason's main concern was that any or all of the four could easily have gone under in nine years' time; the failure rate for non-gambling businesses in Vegas, he had come to learn, was remarkably high. But when he returned to his hotel room that evening, he discovered all four listed on the Internet. He called the numbers and discovered one had been disconnected, which caused a minor cardiac event. When he checked several other online sources, however, he found that they had simply moved to a new location closer to the Strip.

The plan for the next day was to visit each in order of proximity. The first, which turned out to be the one that had moved, was filthy and depressing, with a beer-bellied, cigar-smoking proprietor who didn't so much as look in Jason's direction because he was too busy playing a video game online. The only time he pulled his attention from it was to yell at the two small children of a tourist couple.

Jason found the first bank of lockers in the confines of the cramped second floor. There were sixteen total, arranged in a four-by-four grid. They had thick, porcelain-plated doors with the chrome locks on the right. Above each keyhole was a tiny tin plate with a number. Jason took out Chase's key, but he found no corresponding number on it anywhere. *No*, he thought irritatedly, *that would be too simple*; the Flamingo's patrons were apparently expected to remember on their own.

His heart pounding, he brought the key up to the first door, in the upper lefthand corner. Might as well go methodically from left to right, he figured. The key didn't seem to want to enter the slot, he noted with some alarm, then realized it had to be turned over so the teeth were up rather than down. Once he did that, it slid in without a fuss. He applied gentle pressure, first left then right, but the cylinder didn't budge. He gave the key a little shake and tried again but got the same result. *Didn't really expect it to be the first one*, he told himself. He thought about putting a bit more muscle into it, but the thought of twisting or even breaking the key's shaft filled him with dread. He went on to locker number two...then three...then four.... It took less than five minutes to discover Chase Wheeler's key didn't turn any of them.

The second location was a warehouse large enough to store an airliner, with junk piled into little mountains in some places. The owner was an overwhelmed looking kid in his late twenties who explained that he had inherited the business from his father following the latter's fatal heart attack earlier in the year. He had only scant knowledge of the inventory—his dad apparently kept that information in his head, along with where everything was located—and was looking to unload the whole business when the first reasonable offer came along. Jason was concerned the lockers might have been sold off already, or perhaps they were so deeply buried that he'd have to spend hours, even days, digging through everything. He thanked the heavens when he finally found them standing back-to-back against two china cabinets. This time there were twenty eight boxes instead of the previous sixteen—but again the key did not grant access to any of them. Speaking to the owner just before he left, he learned that the father had cut off one vertical row—the reason for their being twenty eight instead of thirty two—and tried further dividing those four into individual units with the hope of selling them off one at a time. "But all he did was mangle the heck out of them," the son said with a shrug, "so he just ended up throwing them in the dumpster."

Jason's third port of call was an auction house on Charleston Boulevard. They had also been unsuccessful in landing a buyer for their share of the Great Flamingo Locker Haul—another set of thirty two, this time unmangled by an overambitious and underqualified handyman. But Jason didn't need to even remove Chase's key from his pocket. The owner, a man of equal parts girth and joviality, had given up all hope of selling them and had the locks replaced so the cubbies could be used by his employees. When Jason asked—casually, he hoped—if anything interesting had been found inside, the owner's reply triggered a second mild cardiac event—"Oh, some little junk, stuff people forgot about, y'know. If it was important, they would've come back for it. I'm pretty sure we tossed it all." Jason walked out as numb as a rock and headed for Mr. Morton's Memory Emporium.

As he stood in the center of the Emporium's vast second showroom, a sinking feeling began to creep in. He did not see any lockers, nor did he see any indication there were more rooms to explore; no second archway or set of dusty wooden steps going up or down. There were two doors about fifty feet to his right. One bore a placard that read 'FOR EMPLOYEES ONLY' and the other 'RESTROOM.' As he continued scanning, his fatalism began taunting him—*They've been sold off...either that or the owners finally got tired of waiting for a buyer and dumped them...this is a mom-and-pop business, and they've got limited floor space. They can't afford to hang on to stuff that doesn't sell....* He tried countering this by reminding himself that if someone had, in fact, acquired the lockers and found the Hughes will, it was unlikely the discovery would've remained a secret. *So that means they were probably thrown out....*

He returned to the first room. Mr. Morton was still behind the counter, sitting on a stool and reading a *National Geographic.*

"Excuse me."

Morton looked up and smiled. "Yes?"

"Are these the only two rooms that you have?"

"That's it. This is the full extent of my vast kingdom."

"Okay, thank you."

He gave the tiny first room another good long look, although he knew it was ridiculous to do so—unless Morton had successfully managed to cut the lockers into single cubes and had just one left hiding somewhere, there was no chance Jason would miss them. He went back into the larger room and returned to his strategic centerpoint.

They're not here...they're not here....

He was just about to go with his final option—asking the owner about them, something he had not wanted to do unless absolutely necessary—when his eye caught a narrow vertical stack by the two doors. He hadn't noticed it earlier because an armoire was standing in front of it. Walking over there, he found a final set of eight lockers tucked between the armoire and the bathroom door. There was a junior fire extinguisher mounted on the wall nearby.

Just eight—that makes sense, he thought, digging the key out of his pocket. *Limited room, mom and pop....* The idea that the will would end up here, in this forgotten corner of town, struck him as ridiculously amusing.

"Sure, why not," he said out loud, starting in the upper left again.

The first one didn't open, nor the second. There was a boxy *click* when he turned the key to the right on door number three, but it didn't go any further than perhaps a millimeter or two. *Worn cylinder*, he thought. Four and five didn't budge, nor did six. Now he began rationalizing—*Of course...Chase would've put it in one of the lower ones. People generally don't use those.* He got down on one knee and slid the key into number seven. It, too, produced a thin metallic click and gave a little before coming to a hard stop.

No way, Jason thought, shaking his head. He slid the key into eighth and final slot, then turned it firmly.

Nothing happened.

"No...." he said angrily. "*No!*"

He got back on his feet and went through all eight again. This time he jiggled the key like mad, turned it both ways with greater force than before, even tried grasping the lockers doors along the edges and pulling on them. They remained defiantly in place.

He sat down on the floor, pulled his knees up, and lowered his head. Closing his eyes, he went over everything—*Stryker said there were four dealers. He had the list. He couldn't have gotten it wrong off the list. If he'd been relying purely on memory, then I could believe he'd made a mistake. But he pulled a list out of a file and read the dealers' names to me. I visited each one...each and every one. I put the key every locker. I turned it both ways, applied as much pressure as I reasonably could. What did I miss? What other possibilities could there be?*

There were many, and he knew it. Any of the dealers could've sold off a bank of lockers and forgotten they'd done so. There could have been other dealers that Stryker didn't know about, or that someone had failed to note. There could have been other lockers at the Flamingo that no one wanted and ended up being thrown out after the auctions were finished. And there was still the possibility that someone had already found the will and was laying low with it. *Or someone had forced the information out of Chase, gotten their hands on it, and destroyed it. Which means this would've been a wild goose chase from the start.*

"Certainly wouldn't be my first," Jason said wretchedly. He felt as though he didn't have enough vigor left to blow a cloud of smoke out of his way.

So now what?

He remained in a folded-up position for a time, then started to get to his feet. He stopped halfway when he saw Mr. Morton standing there with his benevolent shop-owner's smile.

"Are you okay, son?"

"Hmm? Oh...yes. I'm fine."

Morton put a hand on his shoulder. "Are you sure? Do you feel ill?"

"Well, I do. But not in the way you probably mean. Just having a bad day."

"Is there anything I can do to help?"

Jason's instinct was to politely decline. He had been raised in the New England tradition of taking care of one's business on one's own. He was much like his father in this way. But there was something about this man he found endearing and trustworthy. In spite of the fact that he was a businessman by trade, Morton didn't seem like the for-profit type. Jason was already under the impression this shop was nothing more than a retirement gig, something for Morton to do in order to stay active.

Besides, what have I got to lose at this point?

"Well...maybe." He held up the key. "I've got this, and I believe it belongs to one of these lockers."

"Ooo..." Morton took it from him and examined it over his bifocals with a mad-scientist gleam in his eyes. "Yes, one of the old Flamingo keys."

"That's where these lockers came from, right? The Flamingo?"

"Correct. I've had them for years."

"I know, you and three others in town."

Morton looked at him with delighted surprise. "You've really done your homework!"

"I have, yes."

"Where did the key come from that it's so important to you, if you don't mind my asking?"

"Someone I knew who passed away. We found it recently among his things, and now we're just curious as to what he might have left in there, if anything."

"A little mystery, huh?"

Little, yes, Jason thought bemusedly, *or perhaps big enough to deviate the course of American history. One or the other.*

"Maybe," he said.

"Well, let's see if we can solve it for you. You tried the key in these lockers already?"

"Yes, every one."

Morton turned and slipped the key back into the first slot. "They stick sometimes," he said. "And you have to shake them." He did so with much greater force than Jason had.

"Uh...please be careful with that, would you?"

As if he hadn't heard, Morton then gave a little grunt as he tried to force the key left and right.

"Please," Jason said, "don't try to turn it too hard."

Morton went to the next box and then the next, using the same degree of force each time.

"Mr. Morton, I really have to get going. Could I please have th—"

Morton reached the last one—he was down on one knee—and said, "Wow, tough little buggers, aren't they?" Even with Jason's help, it took him an eternity to get back up.

"Yes, very tough. Listen, I need to get going, so if I could—"

"Hang on, hang on." Morton waved his hand. "Young people and their impatience...." He opened the door with the 'EMPLOYEES ONLY' placard and rumbled around for a few moments without turning the light on while Jason assembled a contingency plan in his mind—*Back to Stryker and see if there were any other dealers or if any of the lockers went unpurchased and got thrown away. Then go ahead and buy all those that are available and just break them open. Take them out to an empty lot or something with a hammer and a crowbar and—*

"...in each one. That helps sometimes."

Jason's trance evaporated as he realized Morton had already come back out and slipped the key into the first lock again. There was a spray can of some kind in his other hand.

"I'm sorry, what?"

"I said sometimes it helps—no, it's not that one—with these old locks if you squirt a little WD-40 into the keyholes. They sit for—no, not number two—years and years, and moisture gets in there and rusts the mechanis—"

There was a *pop!* sound from the module in locker number three—left row, second down—as the key turned.

"Ahh..." Morton said, looking over his shoulder and grinning. "You see?"

He stepped back, beaming, and Jason came forward. He reached up and pulled the little door back; the geriatric hinges squealing like a coffin lid in a horror film. The inside of the box was still as smooth and clean as the day it came off the manufacturing line. For a flicker of an instant, Jason thought there was nothing inside. Then he saw that the locker's singular item simply had the same buff coloration as the interior itself.

"Oh my dear God," he said.

It was a large envelope.

Thirty Three

RUDD PULLED THE DOOR tight, then tried the knob to make sure the lock had caught. The keys were inside on the dining room table as the landlord had requested, and the alarm system was active. There was no turning back now.

His hands were shaking; everything, in fact, was shaking. He looked left and then right, then did it again. He had never felt so vulnerable, not even when he got out just minutes ahead of the Feds in San Diego a few years ago. That was folly, going there in the first place. He'd heard nice things about the city so he thought he'd give it a try. That stay lasted only three months. He'd been here for much longer than that and, for the most part, felt reasonably comfortable. Never so comfortable that he'd consider staying for the long run; that wasn't an option under any circumstances. But there was something about Vegas that seemed fitting for someone in his line of work. Now, however, his comfort level had evaporated. At least in San Diego he knew who was coming for him. The entity he feared here was more phantom than human. Rudd didn't care for people he couldn't manipulate, people who had no presence on the digital grid.

He moved off the porch and merged into the darkness. It was windy this night but otherwise quiet; the neighborhood was fast asleep. That meant nothing when you were dealing with a lunatic, of course. The fact that Rudd now knew so much more about the man had amplified his fear to the Nth degree. 'Lunatic' wasn't even the best word. Savage, psychotic, barbarous, malevolent.... Rudd was expecting Grant to jump out and slit his throat at any moment. The hectic nature of the day had certainly depleted him, but the emotional strain had been far worse. He could not recall a time when he had felt so frightened, at such a frantic level, for such a sustained period.

He got to the driveway and pressed a button on the keychain. The lights on the minivan flashed once as the doors unlocked. Everything he needed was packed into the back—his CPUs and monitors and cables, plus several changes of clothes and basic toiletries. He had already cleared out all other evidence of his presence, wiped down all surfaces for fingerprints, vacuumed every room twice. The landlord never knew his real identity and never seemed the slightest bit suspicious. Rudd had several functional aliases, and using one this time had been particularly easy because the landlord owned more than a dozen homes in the area and, with the local housing market still struggling, was thankful for any tenants who came along. Rudd paid his rent on time and didn't complain about anything. He didn't want the hassle or, more to the point, the attention. He wanted to remain invisible.

The minivan was his, whereas the BMW had been a lease. The van was the 'coming / going' vehicle, which he always put into storage when he arrived at his next destination. Earlier today, the BMW had been returned to the dealer along with a month's payment in advance so the guy wouldn't give him any grief. Then Rudd had a taxi drop him off around the corner from the storage facility. The van started up without any trouble, and he returned to the house to pack it.

He climbed into the driver's seat, closed the door, and reactivated the locks. Then something moved in the seat behind him and he screamed. When he realized it was nothing but shadows from the trees as they danced in the nightwind, he set his head down on the steering wheel and took several long, measured breaths.

He started the engine, and as he waited for it to warm up he reached below the passenger seat, pulled out the little storage tub, and retrieved his laptop. The screen came to life as soon as he lifted the lid, and the email program was already running. He went into the 'Drafts' folder and opened the single message waiting there—

To Whom It May Concern,

This email is being sent to you to establish the identity of the man you have been seeking in connection with the attempted murder via the recent bomb detonation at the Four Seasons....

Rudd then checked to make sure the supporting attachments—which included a collection of photos, fingerprints, official documents from an unbelievable array of locations around the world, and the DNA report he had commissioned—were still there. They were.

He paused, wondering again if he was signing his own death warrant. He shoved these thoughts aside, moved the cursor over the 'SEND' button, and clicked. A moment later he received confirmation that the email had arrived with its intended recipient.

He shut the lid and stored the laptop back under the passenger seat. Then he put the van in gear and started forward. He countered his fear by reminding himself that he would be back in business within a week or so. *Lay low for a little while, use the laptop just to keep the fires burning, then head to the new place and set up shop.* This time it would be Colorado, for no other reason than he'd always wanted to try his hand at skiing.

He reached the intersection at the end of the street and turned east, never once looking back.

****

At the central headquarters of the Las Vegas Metropolitan Police Department, a young officer carrying his third cup of coffee of the night eased back behind his desk. In the same moment, Rudd's email landed in his inbox. The kid had only been with the force a few months but had already developed a fair degree of expertise at distinguishing the bogus tips from the good ones, and the subject line immediately caught his attention—IDENTITY OF MAN IN FOUR

SEASONS BOMBING. The fact that there was no name in the 'Sender' field—something he had only seen on two other occasions—amplified his curiosity. He wasn't a tech pro, but he knew this wasn't something easily accomplished.

He set the coffee down and clicked on the message. When he was finished reading, he opened the attachments as well. He saved everything to the hard drive and did a second read-through, just to be sure.

With his heart pounding, he picked up the phone.

Thirty Four

JASON BURST INTO the hotel room like a fugitive, which he was in some ways. Then he locked it, closed the blinds, and tossed aside his cap and glasses. The former skipped off the bed before disappearing over the other side. He sat down at the little table with his iPad, magnifying glass, a Walgreens bag, the Hughes notes Randy Miller had found, and the large buff envelope.

He'd already opened the envelope, as soon as he got back into the car. There was no force in the universe that could have prevented this. First and foremost, he wanted to make sure the contents were as he'd hoped. When he saw the familiar handwriting, and further that it was rendered on Hughes's beloved yellow legal sheets, he chuckled with delight. He resisted the urge to begin reading on the spot; something instinctive told him this had to be done in private, free of distractions. On the way back to the hotel, his imagination began pumping out all sorts of disturbing scenarios—being recognized and followed, getting into a car accident that would climax in a fiery blaze, or that lunatic catching up to him cutting his throat. When he made the stop at Walgreens, he brought the envelope with him. Las Vegas was one of the nation's leading cities for car thefts.

From the Walgreens bag he removed a smaller bag, which he ripped open. A pair of white cotton gloves fell to the table without a sound.

He'd already decided he would get his own lawyers involved if necessary, if only to assure that the will's presentation and processing was carried out in the appropriate manner. From a legal standpoint, Jason knew, his primary obligation was to deliver it to the nearest probate court—but not just yet. He unbent the clasp, worked his hands into he cotton gloves, and carefully removed the pages.

He took the magnifying glass in hand. All the little characteristics lined up perfectly—the right-leaning tilt...the curly capital 'I's that looked more like 'J's...the fullness, bordering on chubbiness, of most of his embedded lowercase 'l's...and the roughly three-space indentation that marked the start of each paragraph. Particularly pleasing was the tidiness of Hughes's penmanship. One didn't need to be a professional graphologist to realize the man had gone to great pains to assure its legibility. He certainly hadn't burdened himself this way when he was going through his free-thinking machinations on the pages Randy Miller had found.

My God, this is really it, Jason thought as a warm tingling spread over his back and shoulders. *I'm holding Howard Hughes's lost will in my hands.* He took a deep breath, suppressed another cackle, and began reading.

At the very top of the page, in title-case letters and underlined, was the legend—*Last Will And Testament.* It had been rendered above the first rule and ran down at a slight angle. This struck Jason as typical Hughes fare—a document of such import being written out as casually as a love note. No fine linen paper, no letterhead from an elite law firm. Just some guy with his legal pad and fountain pen.

Jason read the first line of the first paragraph—

I, Howard Robard Hughes, being of sound mind and body...

Right away he saw the legal weak spot—it was common knowledge that both Hughes's physical and mental state had been deteriorating for awhile by the 1970s. Opposition counsel, whoever they turned out to be, would have a field day with this. There was, of course, no way of proving that Hughes was illucid at the time, but it wouldn't stop them from trying.

...declare this to be my final will and testament and revoke all previous wills and codicils I have made.

Once past this boilerplate preamble, Hughes went right into the guts of it—

Concerning the disposition of my estate...

The first benefactor didn't surprise Jason in the least—more than 95% of Hughes's immense fortune was to be passed to the Howard Hughes Medical Institute. This had been the rumor all along, and now it was there in black and white. *That one sentence*, Jason thought, *is going to rock many people's worlds.* The Institute was founded by Hughes in 1953 as a tax haven, although he claimed at the time that its primary purpose was research aimed at understanding the fundamentals of human existence. It did receive tax-exempt status as a charity, even after Hughes transferred all of his stock of Hughes Aircraft—a highly profitable defense contractor—into its holdings, and in doing so channeled millions away from the IRS. Hughes had said repeatedly that he planned to continue utilizing the Institute in this manner after his death.

...but more importantly, it is one of the great regrets of my life that I did not do more for my fellow man. I know I have been selfish in many of my endeavors. Even when making films for public entertainment or trying to improve the city of Las Vegas or furthering the science of aeronautics, I was ultimately driven by my own desires. I hope this in some way compensates for that. It is my wish that the Institute makes good use of the funds in their effort to combat, and one day altogether wipe out, the most wretched illnesses that riddle mankind...

Jason was warmed by this minor confessional, seeing a glimpse of humanity in a man accused by many of having none.

The remaining 2% percent of my holdings is to be divided among the following as noted...

The first on the list was Noah Dietrich, the financial genius who became Hughes's go-to man in all business affairs from 1925 until their falling out in 1957. Many considered him to be the true architect of Hughes's epic success, and there was abundant evidence to support this.

...could not have built my empire without his hard work, talent, and dedication. As a gesture of my gratitude, I leave him a full 1% of my estate along with my apologies for the manner in which we parted ways years ago.

Jason found the sentiment both touching and saddening. Dietrich died in February of 1982 without having exchanged another word with his former boss. In spite of the business nature of their longtime alliance, they seemed to be genuinely fond of one another. It made Jason think about his own Noah, who sometimes hesitated to push him too far for fear of permanently damaging their relationship. If Noah knew the full width and breadth of Jason's affection for him, that fear would scatter to the wind.

Jean Peters was next. She and Hughes had been married for fourteen years, and the union was anything but traditional. Hughes went into seclusion not long after they took their vows, and there were times when their only contact was through handwritten memos. On the rare occasion when they were together, Peters pleaded with Hughes for a life of normalcy. Hughes would repeatedly promise the large and beautiful home, the regular schedule, the outside possibility of children, and so on, but he never delivered. Peters tolerated his eccentricities as long as she could, but ultimately filed for divorce in 1971. She asked only for a modest alimony payment—even turning down more when Hughes offered—and never spoke ill of him in the years after. Many Hughes experts believed she was the true love of his life.

There was only a single paragraph on the second page, and it concerned itself entirely with his illegitimate son.

...and if he and his mother are willing to accept this gift following my demise, I would be glad to give it to them...

Hughes had earmarked another 1% of his fortune—tens of millions in today's dollars—and yet he had obviously known that there was a chance they wouldn't accept it. This also must have been the reason, Jason guessed, that Hughes included this part of the will on its own sheet of paper—so it could be removed without a trace. Jason marveled again at the providence of the man that many claimed to have a sixth sense for the future. If the son and his mother refused the offering, Hughes wrote further, it was to be included with the Institute's bequeathment.

Hughes continued with some of the men and women who had worked with him through the years. Most were high-ranking executives who, in Hughes's own words, '*...have served me honestly and efficiently and asked for no more than their paychecks and their occasional bonuses.*' One of the non-execs was Glenn 'Ode' Odekirk, the amiable aeronautics engineer who was instrumental in the development of the H-1, H-2, and D-2 models, as well as the H-4 Hercules, *aka* the 'Spruce Goose.'

The last entry on that page began as follows—

Finally, I would like to leave one tenth of one percent of my estate to my employee Chase Wheeler, without whose courage and trustworthiness....

"Oh wow," Jason said, "even that fractional amount translates into millions." *Hey Denise, you might find you have a very different attitude toward wealthy people when you wake up to find you're one of them.* He smiled and went to the next page.

So began one of the most significant turning points in his life.

****

There was new header along the top—*My Testament*. Under that, in small letters, Hughes added, *Written this day, November 3rd, 1970, in Las Vegas, Nevada.*

Then the preamble, which Jason found fascinating in itself—

I have lived a life of uncommon privilege, and as a result I have been in the company of people of tremendous wealth and power. Some have used their advantages productively, whereas others have indulged the worst sides of their nature. Business on the highest level is usually a harsh affair, and those who play this game often end up battered and bloodied. I have never taken any of my rivals to task for exploiting the opportunities at their disposal as long as their objectives were clear and their methods understandable. In a few instances, however, I have witnessed tactics so appalling that I have decided to keep a record of such transgressions in order to share it with the world after I was safe in my grave. The information in question is no longer the most important part of this testament, but I still wish to include it here:

Each revelation was more astonishing than the last, touching upon every power sector of the nation, from the gambling, aeronautics, and movie industries to the numerous layers of local, state, and federal government. Jason quickly found himself dizzied with disbelief—

Concerning the Mafia's involvement in the Las Vegas casino industry....

Concerning the true motives behind the blacklisting of certain Hollywood figures in the 1940s and 1950s....

Concerning the manner in which government contracts have been awarded in various years within the aeronautics industry....

Concerning the people at the base of influence in the Internal Revenue Service....

Concerning Richard Nixon's presidential election of 1968....

Many of the people Hughes mentioned were long gone, but the legacy of their actions still had wide-ranging significance and effect in the modern world. *The lawsuits will begin immediately*, Jason thought. *Howard won't be the only one looking to settle the score.*

Then came a second preamble—

There is one final matter I wish to set forth; one that will likely affect the very course of humanity. This information should be handled like the potentially explosive material that it is, with due delicacy and wisdom. And if my conclusions are in fact accurate, then I can only say I find tremendous relief in knowing that I will not be here to witness what follows.

There were two paragraphs, and Jason would remember every syllable for the rest of his life—

I was approached in the summer of 1961by three people I'd never seen before....

Once I discovered their true objectives, I refused to cooperate further, which infuriated them....

I became suspicious and sent private investigators to follow up. Some of them were never heard from again....

This, I have concluded, is the reason I have been kept prisoner, unable to communicate with the outside world, all these years....

They began controlling me with codeine injections until I developed a dependency....

And then the last line, which landed in Jason's mind like a bowling ball—

I can only conclude that their goal is to replace the United States as the leading power in the world.

"My God," he whispered. Something moved in his stomach then, and he barely made it into the bathroom in time to drop in front of the toilet and flip up the lid. After all of his stomach's contents were jettisoned, he remained in that position for a long time. A part of him didn't want to go back out there—'there' being not just where the will lay with its radioactive content on the table, but the courtyard beyond, the entire state of Nevada, and the rest of the world. He was already beginning to understand the full width and breadth of his discovery.

He forced himself onto his feet and washed off in the sink. Then he returned to the table and took numerous high-resolution photos of every page with his iPhone. These were uploaded to a personal cloud server.

A media-alert message appeared on his iPad with a soft ping. He tapped it with his forefinger, which opened the browser to the site of the *Las Vegas Sun*—

PARKING LOT BOMBER IDENTIFIED

Jason read the article twice, then returned to the bathroom for a glass of water. He stood with his hands on the sides of the sink as he calculated the best path forward. After he did, the next thought that came was *I don't think I'll tell Noah about it just yet.*

He looked up to face his reflection.

"Okay," he said to the haggard image staring back. "Time to gear up."

Thirty Five

NOAH STEPPED INTO the second-floor hallway and closed the door behind him. Setting his hands on his hips, he said to himself, "Okay, it's got to be *somewhere*, right?"

He'd looked in all the obvious places up here—Alan Hammond's office, the parlor where he and Linda watched television in the evenings, and the suite in which they'd shared a bed for twenty-nine years. He'd been meticulous, opening every drawer, moving every dresser, looking beneath every chair and every couch. In the bedroom's private bath, he even lifted the lid off the toilet tank.

What made it all the more frustrating was that Alan Hammond had maintained a very limited range in his own household. There were just a handful of rooms he occupied each day, so the box should have been relatively easy to find.

No such luck.

Where else? Where else did he ever go?

Both the basement and the attic offered a multitude of hiding spots, but Noah considered those longshots at best. The attic was a dusty mess of old furniture, bags of clothes, and holiday decor, and the basement reeked of dampness due to a high water table that the original builders hadn't considered. Then there was the fact that he had never actually witnessed Jason's father carry the lockbox into his office. *The few times I saw him with it, he was already at his desk*. But how it got there in the first place was unknown.

Noah looked down the carpeted hall and thought about each stop along the way. There was Joanie's bedroom, which wasn't even worth checking—both Alan and Linda Hammond believed their children had as much right to privacy as anyone else and never violated their personal space. The hallway then turned left, with three doors at even intervals along the right side. The first led to Jason's room. Then there were a pair of guest suites, each with—

"Whoa," Noah said, "hang on a second...."

The memory came back vividly—Alan Hammond getting up from the dinner table in a huff and ascending the enclosed staircase at the rear of the house because Linda told him the 'white room' was going to be occupied that night. Linda occasionally ran the estate like a homeless shelter, offering a solid meal, a hot shower, and a place to stay to whatever needy person she encountered. Alan never seemed to mind these kindnesses before, but something about this one clearly got under his skin. Noah, who had been eating with them at the time, never forgot the incident.

Noah strode down the hall and turned, moving past Jason's door and the first of the two guest quarters. The second room, rarely used now, had wide windows to allow plenty of sunlight, a brightly colored comforter on a four-poster bed, and walls painted simple white.

He went to the dresser first, pulling out each of the six drawers and finding them empty except for six separate mothball packets. The drawers on the nightstands didn't produce much more; there was a pencil in one and an aging telephone book in the other. He got down on all fours and looked under the bed, finding only an extra wool blanket in a zippered bag. Beneath the sink in the small bathroom was an array of guest soaps still in their wrappers and collected in a wire basket. There was also a roll of paper towels, a spray bottle of glass cleaner, and a can of air freshener.

Returning to the bedroom, he slid the closet door back. All the empty hangers on the pole—about a dozen—were pushed to one side. The top shelf had a spare pillow with no cover. And in the darkened opposite corner, a cardboard box held two sets of clean linens. Noah slid it over and dug down to the bottom, which also proved fruitless.

"Shoot."

He replaced the box in the corner and got up. He was almost back to the hallway when he came to a stop.

The access panel.

He pivoted on one foot, paused for further consideration, then went to the closet again. The door on the left was slid aside this time. And when Noah sunk to his knees, he didn't so much as wince. His mind was too occupied.

The box with the linens was dragged out and set aside. All that remained in the corner now was the light Berber carpeting and two lengths of wainscoting connected at a firm right angle.

"It's here," he said to himself. "I know it is."

He got down on all fours again, set his palms flat, and began pushing and pulling. At first the carpet held tight. Then he tried closer to the corner, and the nap shifted as if it there was nothing holding it in place.

As he went about prying the carpet away from the wainscot, he made another pleasant discovery—it came up easily, as if it had been left unattached on purpose. A natural fold-line had even developed...

...because Alan had been doing the same thing, over and over.

His heart racing, Noah peeled the carpet back as far as it would go. Then he looked down and grinned.

"Bingo."

There beneath him, set neatly into the solid maple boards, was small access door.

It didn't have a latch or a handle, but rather a hole about the size of a quarter. He stuck his forefinger into it and lifted. The panel swung all the way over until it rested flat on the floor. Then he removed the small flashlight he kept in a holster on his belt and clicked it on.

There were two pipes, both copper and still shiny. Each was about an inch in diameter and had a valve for restricting or releasing flow. He remembered having them installed to replace the older pipes at least twenty years ago. The previous pipes had greened with verdigris patina and were beginning to leak.

The red rubber coating on the valve handles was also in good condition, as was the wood in the support beams, and the pink insulation below the pipes that neatly filled the space between them. What Noah did not see was an anodized blue lockbox.

"Oh, come on...."

He leaned in closer, twisting his neck until it hurt. There was nothing ahead but more beam, more insulation, and more pipe.

When he shined the light in the opposite direction—illuminating the gulley that ran directly beneath him—he saw the same thing. More wood, more pink insulation, and more copper piping.

He also saw a lockbox of modest size, cast in an anodized blue.

Thirty Six

ON THE TELEVISION—an old CRT model with a fine layer of dust on top—a middle-aged reporter in a suit and tie stood in a briefing room that was emptying out rapidly. There was a lectern a few feet behind him, and on the wall behind that was the seal of the Las Vegas Metropolitan Police Department.

"...say they are widening their search for Bruce Jax, the man who up to this point has been calling himself 'Robert Grant,' and that the FBI will now take part in the investigation. They don't know yet if Jax's presence here has any connection to the recent rumors that billionaire Jason Hammond was also in the area searching for the lost will of the late Howard Hughes, but they think it's a possibility."

Then a male voice off screen—"And what else can you tell us about this Jax? He seems to be a very slippery figure. False names, false identities, living in various places around the world."

The reporter nodded. "He is that, Brian, in every sense of the word." The screen faded to a slideshow of old photos—a teenage Jax in a filthy t-shirt with a cigarette hanging from one corner a self-assured smirk, the official military photo of Private Jax just days after his enlistment, and a slightly older Jax holding up a letterboard following his arrest by military police for shattering an officer's jaw with the aid of a bar stool. In this last image, the arrogant smirk wider than ever.

"...spent a year and a half in a military prison for repeated charges of insubordination as well as three incidents of assault, after which he was dishonorably discharged."

"Colorful," the off-screen voice commented, and the reporter chuckled.

"Indeed. After the military gave him the toe-end of their collective boot, he disappeared for a time. There are rumors that he changed his name and went to South America to fight with a variety of guerilla organizations, and that he may have even received terrorist training somewhere in Middle East. Apparently he was on several watchlists, but since he was never found, many believed he had been killed."

"Incredible."

Jax grabbed a chair and went to smash the screen, then stopped himself. He could hear a Latino couple fighting in another room down the hall; the walls were paper thin here, and he didn't want to draw any unnecessary attention to himself. He arrived last night, certain that nobody had recognized him, and wanted to keep it that way. The only one who got a good look at him was the grizzled old fossil at the front desk, and he didn't seem to know what day it was. This wasn't so much a hotel as a way station for the walking wounded—addicts, alkies, gamblers, etc. A cesspool of society's runoff set in a xeric dead zone approximately thirty miles outside Nevada's most storied city. The other patrons were too consumed by their own demons to take note of the guy who currently occupied the room at the end of the first-floor hall.

Jax went to the window and moved the curtain back an inch. It was a beautiful day, calm and quiet. But *they* were out there, too, and they were on the move. He could feel it. They hadn't found him yet, but they would if he became complacent.

He turned back to the room—cracked plaster, bare bulbs, threadbare carpeting—and the anger inflated further. This wasn't how it was supposed to be now. He should be lying on the deck of a sailboat in Antigua while the freshly acquired millions were piling up interest in some offshore account. And up until forty eight hours ago, the plan to turn that dream into reality had been unfolding just fine. The rapidity with which it fell apart was astonishing.

He knew he couldn't dwell on it; the priority now was the immediate future, particularly the question of what came next. He paced around the room licking his lips.

I can't stay here. Sooner or later they'll check this place out. And with the Feds involved, they'll get here even faster. I need to move.

Even that was dangerous, but there was no other option. He had to go somewhere. *But where?*

Returning to Brazil wasn't possible. He had burned too many bridges there, left too many bodies. It was a very different world down there, especially in the wild. He didn't even feel safe when he was one of their friends. Now that he wasn't....

He thought about the person who had brought him back here in the first place; the 'mystery man' on the phone. Jax suspected from the start that the guy must be a Hughes-family insider. He knew things about them that an ordinary person wouldn't. He had gained their trust, discovered a few of their secrets. And somewhere along the way, Jax assumed, they had tried to screw him. People like that lived in a jungle of their own, followed their own code of savagery, and did so with a holy air of self-righteousness. The man promised they would take the Hugheses down together using a potent combination of his insider knowledge and Jax's unique talents. It all sounded so good. Then the bastard tried to brush him off like a fly. When Jax finally made the ID, he realized it should have been obvious all along. But that, too, was in the past and not to be dwelt upon. What mattered now was making something out of what was left.

"...is also purported to be a master of disguise," the television reporter went on, "and the FBI have released these images of what Bruce Jax might look like in disguise."

There was a time when this type of a speculation was dependent upon the limitations of sketch artists and their imaginations. But now, with the aid of computer simulation, they were able to move within range of authenticity. There was one of Jax dressed as a police officer, and it was so reminiscent of a job he did in Argentina that it sent shivers all through him.

Another, of him trying to pass as some kind of ordinary suburbanite, was near-flawless reproduction of the persona he'd adopted less than two weeks ago. A third, him in a business suit with his hair slicked back, was so close to the figure he was planning to cut when he walked out of this room that it was as if someone in the bureau had reached into his mind.

"...FBI are asking all area residents to stay alert and contact them immediately if they see—"

He sat on the edge of the bed and buried his face in his hands. He considered simply disappearing again, as he had on so many other occasions. Steal a car, switch the plates with another, and drive to the coast. Then hop a boat to wherever. Or maybe head down to Mexico, perhaps to Baja via southern Cal. A fresh start. Shave his head, lose some weight, find one last job.

But then what? Start the cycle all over?

No—*no.* The whole point of coming back here was to net enough cash to end the cycle, then hustle off to a world of blissful comfort. Sandy beaches, beautiful women, a free-flowing supply of drugs and booze. Was it all still possible?

Maybe....

An idea that had occurred before came to the surface again. He had nixed it previously because it seemed dubious. Now it appeared to be the best shot he had left.

Grab him.

He had the guy's name now, had done some research on him. He knew the home address, knew he was unmarried. Most critically, he was wealthy. And that was the decisive point, wasn't it?

I'll have him share a little of that wealth. In fact, I'll make him beg me to share it.

He could get the little weasel alone, just the two of them. He had that talent. Then he would use his powers of persuasion. He had that talent, too.

And if the cops come? Or the Feds? Or both?

"Then I go down," he said aloud, "and that'll be that."

He went back to the bedroom and picked up his revolver from the table, checking to make sure the magazine was full. Then he inspected the silencer and blew through it. It went into the left pocket of his jacket, the gun into the right. Everything was ready; now it was just a matter of waiting for darkness.

He pulled a chair to the window and was just about to sit when he heard a faint crackle of static followed by the sound of a shriveled voice coming through a tiny speaker. Turning around, his first thought was, *The TV's still breathing?* Then he followed the noise to the earpiece that lay on the table next to his cellphone.

"What the—?"

He picked it up cautiously and could feel the vibrations through the plastic casing. Then he set it gently in place, and when he began to hear the words clearly and realized the person speaking was Jason Hammond, his mouth fell open.

"...found it yesterday afternoon.... Yes, I read though it, of course.... What.... Oh sure, of course.... Yes, yes I will...."

He's in his car, Jax realized, *where one of the bugs I planted was never found. Jesus....* Then he figured out the reason for all the pauses in Hammond's speech—*He's on the phone. Probably talking to Noah Gwynn.*

"No, it's incredible.... You cannot believe the stuff that's in there. All sorts of dirty little secrets about the government, the Federal reserve, Hollywood, the Mafia and their involvement in the gambling business...."

Jax smiled for the first time in days. "He found it. He actually found it."

"I can't even begin to imagine the number of people who are going to freak when this thing hits the streets, not the least of which will be the family.... Howard cut them out, all of them.... "What's that? No, no—

I'm going to do it here.... Later today, in about an hour or so. There's a probate court downtown, in the municipal building...."

Jax stiffened. *Oh no...that's no good—*

"But I have to get into the shower first. I haven't taken one in two days and I'm pretty, y'know...ugh."

"Okay, better," Jax said. "Take your shower, pal. Kill some time."

"Then I'm going to get down there.... It's about three miles away according to MapQuest.... I'm at this place called the SandPiper.... Huh? No, nothing like the Four Seasons. Far from it, but nobody would think to look for me in a place like this...."

Jax leaned back in the chair and marveled—*Hammond has been here the whole time. He just let everyone* believe *he had gone back home. That way, he could keep looking for the will without any distractions. That's brilliant....*

He really wasn't some rich kid skipping around the world blowing Daddy's money because he had nothing else to do, Jax realized, then made the correct assumption that others had underestimated him in this manner and lived to regret it. *Maybe Hammond even realized this would happen, and he allowed it on purpose.* It seemed believable. The mark of true genius was being able to think on a level inaccessible to everyone else, and to reach conclusions that others could only comprehend long after the fact. Hammond, Jax decided, was of these. In spite of Hammond's occasional missteps, the guy had been a few moves ahead of everyone from the start. For someone who had spent the bulk of his adult life walking the knife's edge between life and death, Jax couldn't help but admire that.

His admiration, however, wouldn't stop him from exploiting this new information.

Thirty Seven

WHEN JASON WAS FINISHED, he dropped the small surveillance device into the outside pocket of his blazer. It was the last one found in the Four Seasons, where he spotted it behind the light above the bathroom cabinet. He meant to give it to Lisa and her colleagues, but some deeper intuition told him to hold onto it. He neutralized it by wrapping it in tissues and then tucking it deep in his shoulder bag. Now it seemed like to smartest thing he'd ever done.

Or the stupidest, he thought as he pulled the curtains back just enough to survey the parking lot. *We'll see.*

There was no one in sight, but he had a feeling that would change soon enough. He prayed for strength and courage and wisdom.

And for protection.

****

He stepped into the beating sunshine two hours later and pulled the door shut. The click of the lock had a sinister finality to it. He could turn around and go back in, of course, but that wasn't really an option. It would lead to the same end one way or another. Carrying Chase's envelope was like having a bullseye on his chest, but he needed it to be visible.

He surveyed his surroundings. The room itself had been passable, but the hotel grounds not so much. There were a few scraggly pinyon pines and some sagebrush, and nestled in the latter were some rusted steel corpses—an old Chevy pickup riddled with bullet holes, a doorless refrigerator, a jumble of oil drums. The mountains stood impassively in the distance. It was a clear day and the wind was whistling low and eerie. *Just like in the movies*, he thought.

He began toward the car, a nondescript sedan. His body grew tighter with each step. He expected the sound of a gunshot followed by the rush of darkness, and he was surprised to discover he was actually frightened by the idea. He hadn't felt such fear since....

Come on, admit it; at least to yourself. Since before the crash.

When, he wondered, had this change in his psyche occurred? What subconscious process had unraveled that rekindled his fear of dying? And how would it figure into the future?

He pushed these thoughts aside for the time being. The distance from the hotel to the car was perhaps thirty feet, but it may as well have been thirty miles. When he finally got there, his throat was as dry as a chimney.

He reached for the door handle, then stopped.

What if it's wired? What if there's another bomb, just like at the Four Seasons?

No, he realized after smearing some logic on the idea. *Blowing me up would also incinerate the envelope and its contents. He wouldn't do that—he wants the will in one piece.* At least that's what Jason was assuming.

He pulled the handle back slowly, every sense on heightened alert. The door popped opened, nothing more, and he got into the driver's seat before he collapsed. When he turned the key and the engine started up without incident, he closed his eyes and tried purging all the angst from his system in a single breath. He wished he'd thought to bring along a bottle of water, if only to roll it across his forehead.

There were few cars on the road. *The further you get from Vegas itself,* he thought, *the more Nevada looks like the surface of Mars.* Of all the routes back to town, he intended to take the most remote. When he reached the first intersection, he turned right instead of rolling straight through. The latter would've taken him to Interstate 15 eventually, and from there it would be smooth sailing to the heart of the city. The right turn, on the other hand, took him down a hard-packed but still unpaved byway, probably just an access route to wherever. But in this world it was still considered perfectly legitimate—it had shown up on Mapquest, where it bisected with more blacktop a few miles on.

If nothing happens, Jason reminded himself, *I'll have to do this all over again. As many times as it takes.* Then he glanced into the rearview mirror and realized that probably wouldn't be necessary.

The other vehicle, a black sedan that looked like a police cruiser minus the lights, had also turned down this far-flung thoroughfare. It looked positively sinister in the wavy afternoon heat, the dust blowing out behind it. It was accelerating at an exponential rate, and Jason already knew who was behind the wheel. He kept his own speed level to maintain an incurious appearance.

Jax roared up alongside him and made a sharp cut across his bow, driving him into the sagebrush. Jason allowed the car to bump and bounce to create the illusion that he was trying to regain control of it. He came to an abrupt halt and sat for a moment so his pursuer could pull beside him. When Jax jumped out with his weapon already in hand, Jason could see the psychosis in his eyes.

"Get out," Jax demanded, moving within a few feet of the door. "Let's go!"

Jason did as he was told, holding his hands up. He was deliberately sluggish, however, as if weakened or injured.

"Come on, come on! Let's move!"

The moment Jason was fully out, Jax spun him around and frisked him.

"I don't have a weapon, Bruce," he said dully, adding a few coughs afterwards.

"All right, turn around."

"How did you find me?" he asked. "No one knew I was out here."

Jax's self-satisfied grin was a terrible thing to see. This was a man thoroughly in control of the situation, the balance of power heavily tilted in his favor, and he was clearly enjoying every moment. *How does someone become like this?* Jason wondered. *Is it genetic? Environmental? A little of both?*

"You're smart, Hammond," Jax said. "But I'm smarter. Now let's go, give it up."

"Give what up?"

"Don't play with me. Today's not the day for that."

"I really don't know what you're—"

Jax fired once, and sand leaped up in a spurt between Jason's legs as the sound echoed around them forever.

"The will," Jax said. "I want it, and I mean right now. You've got two choices—you can reach into the car and get it for me, or I can blow your brains out and get it myself."

Jason studied him for another moment, then turned back and reached through the open window.

"Slowly," Jax instructed. "Very slowly."

"I already told you I'm unarmed."

"I'd just as soon not take your word for that."

Jason came back out with the envelope. "Here, take it."

"Drop it on the ground."

"Sure."

It hit the ground with a little puff of dust, and Jax came forward. The two men remained locked in a staring match that neither wanted to lose. The moment Jax looked down, however, Jason made his move.

The kick to Jax's right hand struck its target neatly and squarely, and the gun went flying off like a deranged bird. Then Jason delivered an open-palmed blow to Jax's surprise-covered face as he came back up. This, too, found its intended point of impact, causing Jax to stagger back a few steps while blood began flowing out of both nostrils. But it didn't knock him off his feet as Jason hoped, which would have afforded just enough time to retrieve the weapon. Years of close-combat experience enabled Jax to regain his bearing with impossible speed and then regain the offensive. He lowered himself and charged like a bull. Jason tried sidestepping but wasn't quick enough, taking Jax's shoulder full in the stomach. They grappled like wrestlers, each trying feebly to get a firm hold on the other. Then Jax brought a fist up to Jason's chin, causing Jason's head to snap back savagely and send him sprawling. He smashed against the car and bounced off, and Jax's fist was there again. All the cartilage and bone in Jason's face seemed to stretch inward to accommodate it. He saw a quick flash of light, then collapsed to the ground. The dizziness that followed carried a sense of vulnerability and helplessness that was utterly terrifying.

As his senses began to clear, he could heard Jax's approaching footsteps. Then the unmistakable click of the gun's hammer being set in place, following by the cold touch of the barrel as it was pressed to the top of his head.

"Make it quick, please."

"If I didn't think half the world would come after me..." Jax said.

Then a bolt of white-hot pain exploded in Jason's skull as he was struck with the butt of the gun. The swirling began anew, pulling him deeper and deeper into nothingness until all was quiet.

****

"It's me," Jax said from his car minutes later. He was back on the main road, heading toward the city at a brisk pace, but not so much that it would catch the attention of Nevada's finest.

"You should not be calling. We're finished. In fact, I will be terminating this number before the end of th—"

"I've got the will."

There was a pause. *That's good*, Jax thought. *That's very good.*

"I don't believe you."

"I don't care what you believe. I have it. I just got it from Hammond. Large envelope, multiple pages of yellow legal paper, clearly Howard Hughes's handwriting. It's all here." Jax picked it up from the passenger seat and shook it. "Hear that? And I read it, too. Lots of interesting things. It'll blow *your* life away, that's for sure."

"You don't know anything about my life."

"Don't I?" Jax said—then added his name.

There was another pause, much longer than the first. *I got him*, Jax thought, and could not remember a moment of such antagonistic delight.

"What do you want?"

"I want all the money I was promised, plus $10 million more."

"You're insane."

"Yeah? How much do you stand to lose if I decide to drive this thing over to a probate court? Quite a bit more than that, I would imagine."

A final hesitation, and then the words he'd been waiting for—"Where and when?"

Thirty Eight

JASON AWOKE WITH a bitter, coppery taste in his mouth and a headache that could kill an elephant. He drew himself onto all fours, spitting away the sand that had dried on his lips.

He got to his feet and was struck by a fresh wave of dizziness so profound that he almost went down again. He took two wobbly steps to the car and leaned against it for support. When his cheek touched the hot metal of the roof, he sprung back with a yelp. He was fully alert now.

He reached into his pocket for his phone but it wasn't there. He tried the other pockets, then went through the car, including the bags in the trunk.

Did I leave it in the room?

No, impossible. He'd used it as a GPS to get to the intersection that led to this middle-of-nowhere spot in the first place.

Then where...?

It was on the ground—or at least what was left of it. Jax had blasted it to bits.

"Terrific," he muttered.

****

He'd passed a convenience store on the way. Now he drove back to it and bought a prepaid phone along with a bottle of water and a packet of buffered aspirin. One small mercy was that his Bluetooth earpiece, which Jax hadn't reduced to dust, paired with the new phone without any trouble.

Back in the car, he went to call home. When it came to entering the number, however, he drew a blank.

It's in speed dial...or at least it was. He couldn't remember the last time he'd actually tapped it into a keypad.

He flogged his memory until he came up with what he thought was, at least, the right group of numbers. It took three tries and two fairly disgruntled New Hampshire citizens before he finally got the sequence correct.

Even the third seemed off the mark—

"Hello?" asked a cheerful young woman.

"Hello, yes, is this...uh, is this the Hammond residence?"

"Yes."

"Really?"

"Yes...?"

"Who is this?"

"I think I should ask you the same question first."

Jason held the phone out and examined it curiously for a moment. *Noah's having a woman over?*

"This is Jason."

"Jason who?"

"*Hammond.*"

A pause, and then, "I don't think so."

"Excuse me?"

"I'm pretty sure he'd know the number of his own house."

Jason grunted. "I lost my phone and it was in speed dial, and I couldn't remember it because normally I don't *have* to remember it."

"That's a pretty good story."

"It's not a story, it's the truth. Now who is th—?"

"If you're really Jason, then tell me what picture is hanging next to the refrigerator."

"What?"

"I'm in the kitchen right now. What picture is hanging next to the refrigerator?"

Jason rolled his eyes. "There are two, actually—paintings of disproportionately shaped cows. And the frames are green, Kelly green. Ugliest things you ever saw, but Noah finds them hilarious."

A pause, and then, "Um, okay...I guess it's really you. Sorry."

"That's all right, but now tell me who *you* are."

"It's Katie!"

"Katie?"

"Bridgeport."

"Katie Bridgepor...from Sandingham Road?"

"That's right!"

"What in the world are you doing there?"

"Gee," Katie said, "try not to sound too thrilled."

"Oh no, I'm sorry. I didn't mean to—I would love to chat, but I need Noah right now. It's an emergency."

"He's not here."

"He isn't? Do you know when he'll be back?"

"I don't."

"Shoot."

"Is there anything *I* can do?" she asked.

"Well...actually, I need some help."

"Are you hurt?"

"No, no. I need technical assistance. Do you know your way around a computer?"

"Sure."

"Okay. There's an office on the first floor, just down the hall from where you're—"

"I'm there," Katie told him.

"You are? I thought you were in the kitchen."

"I was," she said, "now I'm in the office."

He held the phone out and stared at it again. "How does she knows about the office?" he mumbled.

"Huh? What?"

He brought the phone back. "Nothing, nothing. You'll see a computer in there, with a really big screen. You have to shake the mouse to bring it out of—"

"I did. It's awake."

"You'll need the password to—"

There was a rapid clatter of keys. "I'm in."

"What?"

"I'm in the system. I'm ready."

"You know the *password*?"

"Yes, it's 'Beatles.'"

"And how would you know that?"

"Noah told me," she reported.

"Did he now?"

"Yes."

Wasn't that generous of him. "All right, whatever. On the desktop you'll find an icon for a program called 'Panic Tracker.' It's part of a new product line we're developing."

"Should I launch it?"

"Yes please."

"Okay...it's open."

"You should see a one-dimensional map of the world."

"I do."

"Good. Now, there's a pulldown menu called 'Devices.'"

"I see it," Katie said.

"Click on it, and you should see four serial numbers."

"All starting with 646."

"That's right. Click on the first one."

"K.... I'm getting a dialog box telling me it's acquiring the signal, please wait."

"That's what it's supposed to do."

"What are we tracking here?"

"A ring."

"A *ring*?" she asked.

"Yes. It's part of a line of what we're calling 'Panic Jewelry' for kids. All they have to do is press down twice on some part of it, and it sends out a signal via satellite. I'm hoping it'll cut down the number of child abductions by half or more."

"That's *great*."

"Let's hope so."

"My God, is this an abducted child you're tracking now?"

"No. Long story short, I wanted to track some guy, so I got into a fight with him on purpose. It was a hand-to-hand combat situation, and I stuck the ring in his pocket."

"Aren't you clever."

"You'd think so, but I almost got killed in the process. He had a gun."

"Jason!"

"It was a calculated risk, but I was willing to take it."

"Still, should you really be doing such things?"

"Oh Lord, not you too...."

"Huh?"

"Nothing. Are you getting the signal yet?"

"Yes...the box just disappeared and I'm getting a blinking red dot in the western United States."

"Click on it, please," Jason said.

"Okay.... Now the map is zooming in."

"To what depth? Can you see street names?"

"No, not that close."

"On the right side of the screen there should be—"

"A magnification slider?"

Jason nodded. "Yes, exactly. Slide it up toward the plus sign until you—"

"Got it—I can see street names now. The blinking dot is on Highway 15."

"Moving in what direction?"

"Southwest. It's almost to the intersection of 579."

Jason got back onto the road and gunned the motor. "Excellent, thank you. Keep watching the signal, please."

"I will. Is this Bruce Jax, by any chance?"

"You know about *him*, too?"

"Noah and I have been following the story on the news."

"Great, the news.... That should make this a *lot* easier. Has he reached the intersection yet?"

"Yes, reached it and passed it. Still on 15."

"Okay."

"Where are you in proximity to him?"

"I'm not sure," Jason said. "I don't know the area that well."

"Do you have one of the other devices with you?"

"What other devices?"

"There were four serial numbers in the 'Devices' pulldown menu. I'm guessing that means there are three others."

Jason pulled the car off the road. "As a matter of fact I do. The other one I have is a watch. I was testing it with Noah when I flew here." He pressed the trunk button under the dash and got out. "That's pretty good thinking there, Katie Bridgeport from Sandingham Road."

"Thank you."

He dug through his suitcase and found it—a standard men's design, stainless steel band with black face and little hash marks for numerals. There were three tiny buttons along the side.

He shut the trunk and climbed back into the driver's seat. "Okay, I'm pressing the panic button now."

"Which serial number should I use?"

"The last on the list."

"Ending with 4775?"

"That's it."

A few minutes after Jason got back on the road, Katie said, "Hey, there you are."

"The screen split into two separate maps?"

"Yes."

"Good, the software engineers were having some trouble with that."

"It appears to be working fine."

"So where am I in relation to Jax?"

"You're about twelve miles behind him."

"Twelve? Okay, time to floor it...."

****

On the computer screen, Katie watched Jax cross into Vegas, turned east onto Charleston Boulevard, then northeast onto Maryland Parkway.

After he made another turn onto Calumet Street, she said, "I think he's stopped."

"What makes you say that?"

"He's not moving."

"Could be at a red light."

"I don't think so. He's been stopped for over a minute now. That's a long light."

"What's the address?"

"Hang on...." Katie said.

"Use the magnification slider to—"

"I know."

"Sorry."

"He's at....422," she told him. "You're not that far behind him now."

"And what's at that address? Could you try to—"

"I'm doing a Google search right now."

"I was going to suggest that, but I didn't want to offend you."

"It'll take more than that."

"Give me time, I'm sure I'll find a way."

Katie laughed. "There's something to look forward to. Okay...it's a casino called 'The Gold Mine.'"

"Really? He's going into a casi—"

"It's been out of business for four years."

"Ah, okay. That makes sense."

"It does?"

"Yeah. Hang on, I'm going to floor it again...."

****

Jason careened onto Maryland Parkway, weaving in and out of midday traffic, then made a sharp right onto Calumet. The Gold Mine was about two miles down, surrounded by a rusting chainlink fence. He saw why the place hadn't been able to stay afloat—it was a free-standing structure set in the middle of what looked like a demilitarized zone. He was beginning to realize that it was nearly impossible to maintain a business in this town without the blood flow from the Strip.

He found Jax's car half-perched on a curb around back. There was a gap in the fence, providing access to the sub-level parking garage.

Katie voice came through the earpiece—"Jason? What's happening?"

"Hang on," he whispered. "I'm getting out...."

"Oh, please be careful."

"I will...."

He moved through the break in the fence and down the entrance ramp, staying close to the wall so one of his flanks was covered. Then multiple gunshots echoed like cannon fire.

"Oh no."

"Jason! Was that—?"

"Hang on, hang on—"

He immediately registered one stunning detail—the shots came in two different pitches, thus from two different weapons. He began running in that direction.

"Jason, what's happening?!"

About a hundred feet further on, he discovered a grisly sight—Jax on his back, motionless, with blood spreading rapidly beneath him. Three holes were clearly visible in his shirt.

Jason knelt down beside him. "Bruce, can you hear me? Bruce!"

Jax's eyelids fluttered, the eyeballs rolling around liked oiled marbles.

"A man..." he said through a clogged throat.

"What man?" Jason asked. "Who was—"

Jax went on as if he hadn't heard him—"It...supposed to be a man. But it was a *woman*. She...she...."

Two more shots came, one so close that it sounded like a bumblebee zipping past Jason's ear.

He grabbed Jax's gun and scrambled behind one of the concrete columns. Peering around, he saw a bright flash in the darkness as a third shot was issued. He jumped back, then reached around the corner and blindly fired several rounds, each echoing like thunder. Silence came when the thunder faded, then the slam of a car door followed by the squeal of tires.

Jason bent low and peered around again. The vehicle in question was a nondescript sedan, perhaps a Nissan or a Ford. He couldn't make out the license plate in the darkness.

He went back to Jax and knelt down. Jax's eyes were closed, his head pitched to one side. Jason pressed his fingers against the man's carotid to find a pulse. There was nothing.

Thirty Nine

"JASON, ARE YOU out of your *mind*?" It was Noah's voice coming through the earpiece now.

Returning to the hotel, Jason threw the door to his room open and began stuffing things into his bag.

"I know, I know," he said into the earpiece, "it was a little crazy."

"A little?! Baiting yourself to a professional killer? That's not craziness—that's *lunacy*."

"I suppose."

"You could've been killed."

Jason went into the bathroom and grabbed his toiletries bag. "And that would've left you with tons of paperwork to do. How thoughtless of me."

"Please don't make light of this."

Back in the bedroom, he took his iPad from the nightstand and wrapped it in a shirt for protection.

"I'm not making light, believe me. And to prove that, I thought you'd like to know that I'm coming back home."

"Seriously?"

"Seriously. I'm packing up my stuff right now and, like a shepherd in a hurricane, getting the flock out of here."

"When?"

"Immediately."

"I can't believe it."

Jason smiled. "Your wish has been granted, my master."

"If you don't mind my asking, what made you change your mind?"

He leaned down and yanked his phone charger from the outlet.

"Mainly that I'm forced to admit I still have no clue who I'm dealing with. At first I thought it was just this guy, Bruce Jax, and whoever was pulling his strings. That could've been anybody—a member of the Hughes family worried about losing his or her share of the inheritance, some politician that Hughes was going to expose, or a businessman who crossed him in an old deal. Someone along those lines. But then Jax gets shot and killed, and that suggests there's more than one faction at work. Multiple people who want to get their hands on the will. I mean, they actually *killed the guy*, in cold blood, right there in an abandoned parking garage."

"They tried to kill you, too."

"That's just because I showed up unexpectedly. If they really want to do it, I'm sure they could have. If they were good enough to take down a psycho like Jax, I certainly didn't pose much of a threat."

"Then just thank God they didn't."

"I *am* thankful," Jason said breathlessly, "believe me. What may very well have saved me was the simple fact that they got what they wanted. The will's in someone else's hands now, and I haven't the foggiest idea who that is. So until I get a little more information, I'm going to come home and regroup."

"Regroup? That means you're not done yet?"

"Not even close."

Noah sighed. "Okay...."

Jason made one more scan of the room, then hurried out.

"Very quickly on another topic," he said, "can I assume Katie Bridgeport is the person you've hired to help with the renovations?"

"Yes, yes she is. I ran into her and her family at services a few days ago. She's looking for work, so I figured she'd be perfect in the interim. Are you okay with that?"

"Yeah, sure." He dropped the bag in the back seat and got behind the wheel. "I assume she's doing well?"

"She's smart as a whip and a quick learner. And she's very enthusiastic."

"That's one way of putting it. Where is she now?"

"Checking out the landscaping and the greenhouse. Both of those fell under your mother's jurisdiction, so I figured they could use a woman's touch."

"I have to say, when she helped me chase Jax down, she was very levelheaded. I was worried she'd freak, but she didn't."

"No, she's quite composed," Noah said with a touch of pride.

Jason got onto the road, heading north this time. The sun was beginning to settle into the horizon, casting the sky in shades of red and yellow in that strangely beautiful way that is at once dusky and luminescent. Jason would've taken the time to appreciate the magnificence of it under ordinary circumstances, but this luxury couldn't be permitted at the moment. Every vehicle that passed by had to be considered a threat.

"And what about the lockbox?" he asked. "What's the latest there?"

"Well, it took some doing, but I did manage to find it."

A smile flickered briefly onto Jason's lips. "That's great, Noah."

"It wasn't easy. You're father went to great pains to hide it."

"Oh?"

Noah recounted the search in detail. When he finished, Jason said, "So what's inside?"

"I haven't gotten that far. It has a digital lock, and none of the combinations in your father's password file have worked. I went through them twice just to be sure."

"That tells me there's something pretty important in there."

"Possibly."

"So what are you going to do?"

"Take it to the shop, as you suggested. That's where I was headed when you called. I'll get it open, don't worry about that."

"Good." The lights around the airport appeared in the distance. "Well, I'm almost to the plane, so I'm gonna go. Whatever you find in the box, please let me know right away."

"I will. Have a safe flight."

"Thanks."

****

Sitting in Alan Hammond's chair with the lockbox on the desk and the password file on the screen, Noah took a deep breath.

"If you have any secrets to tell," he said to the box as if it was a living, breathing thing, "I hope they're not too dirty. I have a feeling, however, they might be."

He lingered another moment, wishing beyond all things that he didn't have to do this. Then he rose with the box in hand and went out.

Forty

THERESA RICHTER LOOKED downright presidential through the limo's darkened rear windows. The clothes, the hair, the makeup, all done up to perfection. It was the digital age, when high-def visual clarity elevated some careers and sent others tumbling. She was lucky in this regard because the cameras liked her, and that was a blessing to be thoroughly exploited. She'd chosen a dove-gray power suit with a white blouse and black accessories. Pants instead of a modest-length skirt, and ankle boots with heels to offer a touch of provocation. There was no necklace, a point that she and her handlers had argued about. She almost went for fine chainlinks with a round onyx pendant, but ultimately decided it was too fragrant with undertones of bondage. America was shopping for a tough woman, but not in that way. They wanted one who wouldn't think twice about pressing the button if Iran or North Korea got out of hand, not one who was unable to reach heights of physical pleasure without the aid of something purchased at a hardware store. It had taken years to project that balanced image of steely and soft. She wasn't about to upset it now.

The swirling lights and sirens from the escort vehicles no longer fazed her. As the skyscrapers zoomed by, she thought about the last time she was here in San Diego. Bill was very much alive and still a few years off the cancer diagnosis that changed everything. It was supposed to be a vacation, although it felt like they spent nearly as much time on their phones and laptops as they did back home. But there were moments—the candlelight dinner in Little Italy, the ensuing passion a few hours later at the hotel; even the trip to the famous San Diego Zoo had been fun. The city did live up to its reputation. The people were friendly, the infrastructure efficient, and the weather immaculate. The only other time she'd set foot in this town was in August of 1996, for the presidential nomination of former Kansas senator Bob Dole. She was a nobody then, still trudging her way through the Nevada state senate, and was treated as such by the party's big wheels. Now they were at her feet, paving the way for what appeared to be a relatively smooth journey to the most powerful office in the world. She'd dreamed of it, worked for it, and believed in her heart she was ready for it.

What she wasn't feeling was the elation one would expect on the day of their imminent nomination. The convention would be broadcast around the world with an expected viewership of more than thirty-five million. That shattered the previous record by a solid twelve to fifteen percent. America's first female president, a historic figure before she even took the oath. She possessed a bearing that was nothing short of iconic, at least on the surface. The emotions churning beneath that cultivated exterior, however, were another matter.

She reached into the pocket of her blazer and pulled out her private cellphone just far enough to see that Kelli's name still hadn't appeared on the screen. *No call, no text, nothing....* They had worked so long and so hard for this, endured a tireless onslaught from fellow Republicans who wanted the nod instead of her, a media that hammered her around the clock because that's what the public craved, and more assassins from the opposing party than they'd ever employed before. She felt as though she'd been stripped, gutted, and hung in the town square. Nothing was sacred anymore, no territory off limits. And yet she had withstood all of it, with Kelli at her side. Ever faithful, ever loyal.

Although that's not completely true, is it? a small voice in her mind said to her. *Not quite.*

Kelli had made abrupt disappearances before. Not many, but a few. They were explained the same way each time—*I had some urgent business to take care of.* Business, always business. And she meant it in the literal sense, not like some people used the word. Theresa was always understanding. She knew she wasn't the only focal point in Nashamura's life, knew she served more than one master. But that didn't stop it from bothering her.

From there Theresa made a startling realization—she had developed something of a co-dependency on the woman, and that was not good. Not because she didn't feel Kelli was worthy of it, but rather because she had sworn off such attachments long ago. After the emotional beating she took during Bill's illness, followed by the immeasurable nightmare of its aftermath, she swore she would never allow such vulnerability again. Her heart would be stored in a black box and the rest of the world viewed with cool detachment. She would put on whatever airs were necessary for professional advancement, but truly investing herself was off the table.

Or so she had believed.

She glanced at the three people sitting across from her. Three *kids*, really, because political operatives seemed to be getting younger all the time. There was one girl and two guys. The girl was Andrea Mott, just four years out of Brown and only one on the job as her personal aide. Bright, pretty, and cheerfully serious in that off-putting way only Ivy Leaguers can be. Theresa could see her career trajectory as clearly as fireworks on a summer evening—hang around the White House after November's victory in some relatively minor capacity, use that as a springboard to something more substantial in the DC jungle, then get into position for her own run, perhaps as a representative from her home state of Illinois. That's where she'd hit the ceiling, Theresa thought. Not because she was a woman, but because she had a fatal streak of naïveté that would likely never dissipate, and because she wasn't particularly quick on her feet. On the second point alone, any experienced opponent or hostile journalist would make a meal of her.

Of the other two sitting there, the first guy was a logistics whiz, the second a writing whiz. Their names were Ted and Bobby, respectively, but Theresa didn't know much more about them. She wasn't even certain why they'd jumped into the limo with her in the first place. They'd been on their cellphones ever since.

Andrea Mott was looking at her plaintively. "Do you need anything, ma'am?"

"No, I'm all set. Thank you."

This came out with a quiet and commanding confidence that Kelli had taught her early on. There were days when Theresa wondered if this one trait hadn't been the turning point in her career. In America—and pretty much everywhere else, she came to understand—it wasn't about who you were but rather who you appeared to be. Whatever persona you projected at any given moment, that would be the basis for the public's response. "Be commanding and you will command," Kelli told her as the two of them stood for uncounted hours in front of a mirror in Kelli's home, in Theresa's in home, her office, and even a few public restrooms until the act was refined to perfection. It was at once exhilarating and a little frightening; exhilarating because she knew intuitively that it was her ticket to success; frightening because she sometimes worried that the 'real her' would be smothered by it. In time she realized the latter wasn't truly possible—what actually happened was that the 'public her' simply had to step forward once in awhile to do its thing.

Mott smiled. "You look just right," she said, and Richter knew she meant it. The girl's sincerity would get her batted around pretty good in the years ahead, but it was valuable here.

"Thank you."

"Would you like something to drink? A bottle of water, maybe?"

"No, I'm okay."

"Something to eat?"

Richter smiled back at her. "Are you going to cook it here in the car?"

Mott sniffed out a little laugh. "I have some power bars in the bag." These were among Richter's favorite on-the-fly snacks.

"Oh, I see. No, but thank you. I'm fine."

Mott's eyes shifted around for a moment, as if she was trying to decide where to bring the conversation next. Then she surprised Richter by saying, "Do you want me to try Ms. Nashamura for you, ma'am?" She already had her cellphone out.

"Hmm? Oh...no. Thank you, Andrea. She'll check in sooner or later. She always does."

Mott nodded and replaced the phone in her pocket. But Richter could feel the disappointment—no, *disapproval*—drifting off her.

Ted the Logistics Whiz finally detached his phone from the side of his face. "Okay, we're just about there," he said to no one in particular.

Richter peered out the window again and saw the convention center looming in the distance. The brilliant lights made it seem more like a venue for the reunited Beatles than a glorified political gathering. People had begun to appear along the route, queuing for even a transient glimpse of their presumptive new leader. Male and female, young and old, black and white, but all with one thing in common—they were looking to Theresa Richter to resuscitate the fabled American dream for them.

She knew they couldn't see her in detail because of the smoked windows, and she knew she'd get an earful if she opened one. (She wasn't even sure if she could; the Secret Service certainly had the authority to disable them.) But she was sure they could see her silhouette, so that would have to do. She began waving and was delighted to see many wave back. Bright bursts of light jumped from cameras and cellphones. She felt the urge to stop and get out, shake hands as so many presidents had done before her, talk to them, learn their greatest dreams and deepest fears. But that was quite impossible, and she knew it. But she also knew she was going to work like mad to make life better for them once she got behind that desk. Moved by their enthusiasm and support, she vowed not to let these people down.

I will not.

She turned back to her associates, all of whom seemed gripped by mild anxiety.

"Don't be nervous," she said.

Mott laughed again. "Aren't you?"

"No, and you shouldn't be, either." She swept her hands up to her chest dramatically. "And *breathe*, two, three...," she said in a devastating impression of Richard Simmons that had reduced others to tears on many occasions. "Come on, you can do it...remember, you're all beautiful! Let's *go!*" As her mini-entourage became inebriated with laughter, she said, "Okay, that's better. So what do I have to know?"

Bobby the Writing Whiz said, "The speech will be on the teleprompter when you take the stage."

"I won't need it," she told him, tapping her temple, "but thanks. It's all up here."

Bobby smiled. "I have no doubt of that. The prompter is just a backup, ma'am."

"Good. What else?"

Ted was in mind meld with his phone again, this time to read a text message. "The chairman is going to greet you as soon as we get there," he said, "in a few minutes."

She nodded. "Got it."

They arrived at the center's rear entrance moments later.

"Are you ready, ma'am?" Mott asked.

What flashed through Richter's mind just then was a highlight reel of all the years, all the planning, and all the toil it took to create this moment. It had been a brutal journey, and she couldn't help thinking about the person who did more to make it possible than any other.

"I am," she replied.

The longing for Kelli's comforting presence found its way to the surface again. As if out of pure reflex, Richter reached for her phone one more time. Before she got to it, however, the limo rolled to a stop and the door was opened by some faceless operative.

The American people were waiting.

Forty One

NOAH LIVED ON the north side of the estate, in a small cottage propped on a cliff overlooking the Atlantic Ocean. The house and surrounding grounds were as neat and tidy as the man himself. There was a white picket fence with a gate, and a flagstone path that led to a small backyard. Handmade birdboxes stood on poles within the colorful tangle of wildflowers by the patio. More than once on a warm summer evening, amid the drowsing scents of mint and honeysuckle, Noah would lay on the chaise lounge with his hands folded over his considerable belly and watch the stars until he dozed off.

Just east of the cottage were two smallish outbuildings—one a storage depot, the other a workshop. The centerpiece of the latter was a large and lovingly worn oak table set under a broad sheet of pegboard, upon which hung an array of hammers, wrenches, pliers, screwdrivers, and so on. Other features of the room included a free-standing drill press, band saw, miter saw, lathe, and rotary sander. And tucked into one corner under a hanging light with a conical aluminum shade was an ancient writing desk that was used by Alan Hammond during his four years at Dartmouth. It had been moved between several rooms in the main house before finally passing to Noah when the workshop was first built. Taking a deep breath now, he set the lockbox down on it.

It feels like there's a snake inside, he thought, *just waiting for the chance to bite.*

He inspected the box carefully, turning it this way and that. The keypad was set into the lid, and he knew better than to think simply prying it up would provide access. The lid's hinge couldn't be cut either, as it was riveted on the inside and not even visible. And the box *felt* solid, so much so that he got the feeling he could throw it off the cliff in the backyard, and when it struck the rocks below it still wouldn't loosen up.

Solid like something NASA would use. Or the Treasury Department. Or Alan.

Alan Hammond had always been a very careful man; careful and reflective and meticulous. To his mind, every detail mattered. If he felt the need to acquire a lockbox of this strength, keep it so well hidden, and withhold the password even in the event of his death, then....

"It's important," Noah said with a sigh. "Whatever's in here is very important."

A snake...waiting to bite....

He propped up his iPad in its folding case and hopped on the Internet. Instructions on how to get into a box with a traditional lock were plentiful—some as simple as using a paper clip or a penny—but there was almost nothing concerning a keypad. One blogger suggested contacting the manufacturer, but Noah had already determined that the company who manufactured this box had gone out of business a few years ago. Another advised resigning yourself to the fact that every four-digit combination—a total of ten thousand possibilities—could be tried without *too* much trouble. Noah had calculated that each attempt would take about three seconds, and thus every possibility could be covered in twelve and a half hours. The problems with that approach, however, were numerous. First, what if he missed a few combinations along the way and skipped over the right one? Second, what about the inevitable mistakes that he did catch? They would add more time to the total, prolonging an already tedious task. And third, the mere idea of sitting and trying every possible combination for more than half a day sounded about as fun as a root canal without anesthetic. *Life's too short*, he told himself.

He picked up the box and seesawed it next to his ear. This produced two distinct noises—a sandpapery swish and a rattling thunk.

The swish is from papers of some kind sliding around in there, he thought with a fair degree of certainty. *The clunk, however....* He couldn't be sure what that was, but he knew it was now lying at one side of the box—which gave him the idea for what to do next.

It took twenty minutes to change the blade on the band saw—he always kept a blade handy specifically for metal cutting—and reduce the speed to almost a tenth of that required for woodwork. The guts of the machine had to be oiled because it hadn't run in ages. Noah was deeply relieved when it sparked to life without any fuss, and he felt a rush of old excitement at the prospect of undertaking a new project in here. He hadn't come into the shop much since the accident and realized how much he missed the peace of it. The steady methodology of the work produced its own kind of comfort.

He put on gloves and safety goggles, then set the box on the cutting surface. The moment the steel met the blade, sparks began spewing out in a brilliant shower. Some landed on his flannel shirt, sending up tiny tendrils of smoke.

The plan was to shear off just the one side. Progress was agonizingly slow, but eighteen minutes later the box's right wall, along with a short length of its still-hinged lid, fell to the floor with a clatter. It looked like a discarded clapperboard on a movie set.

He killed the power and removed the goggles. He also took off his gloves while the blade spun down and set them aside. Then he carried the back box to Alan's old desk and sat. He put on his glasses and tipped the box at an angle to let the contents slide out.

"Oh my God."

****

There were four items—two sheafs of folded papers held together by binder clips, one small spiralbound notebook, and a USB flash drive. Neither the drive nor the notebook bore any kind of labeling. The papers, however, grabbed Noah's attention for the simple reason that he was the one who had provided them to Alan Hammond in the first place. The material had been taken off the Internet and printed from the laptop in Noah's cottage many years ago.

He unfolded the first and looked it over. At the top was the following title—

Transcript of Dr. Nouriel Roubini's Lecture at the Meeting of the Interntional Monetary Fund, September 7, 2006, Washington DC

He flipped through the pages and found that Alan had highlighted some sections with a yellow marker—

I have been quite outspoken about the fact that I believe we're going to have a recession.

We're going to have a hard landing rather than the soft landing that most people believe.

If the U.S. goes into a mild slowdown or a severe one, the rest of the world could decouple, with growth in Asia and Europe picking up while the U.S. may be slowing down.

What are the main three bearish forces in the U.S. economy in my view that are going to trigger this recession? The first is a housing-sector bust.

I think the effects of the housing bust will be larger than those of the tech bust.

I believe that commodity prices are going to collapse, you are going to have a huge slack in the labor market, and slowdown in wages.

My concern today is that the bursting of the housing bubble—we have not seen it yet—is going to lead to broader systemic banking problems. It is going to start with the subprime lenders—they are already in trouble because of increases in delinquencies and foreclosures—and then it is going to be transmitted to other banks and financial institutions all over the country.

I see essentially a recession coming by next year. I give it a very high likelihood. I argue that housing today, like the tech bust in 2000-2001 will have a macro effect; it is not going to be just a sectoral effect. I argue that U.S. consumers are now close to a 'tipping over' point given all the vulnerabilities I have discussed.

The second set had the U.S. Securities and Exchange Commission seal at the top and bore the following headline—

Alternative Net Capital Requirements for Broker-Dealers That Are Part of Consolidated Supervised Entities

In the very first section, titled 'Summary,' Alan had highlighted two lines—

We are adopting rule amendments under the Securities Exchange Act of 1934 that establish a voluntary, alternative method of computing deductions to net capital for certain broker-dealers.

We are amending the risk assessment rules to exempt a broker-dealer using the alternative method of computing net capital from those rules if its ultimate holding company does not have a principal regulator.

Alan had asked Noah to search for and print these texts. Noah thought nothing of it at the time because Alan asked for Internet printouts all the time, as he wasn't particularly tech savvy. And although he had been in his office later than usual in both instances, it was routine for him to spend most evenings reading through financial literature. There was nothing even remotely unusual about these requests.

Noah brought the notebook over and flipped the cover back. Each page was dense with Alan's handwriting, a small and upright hybridization of both print and script. A wave of nostalgia washed over him, along with a heavy dose of melancholy. He thought of Alan every day, the old schoolmate who appeared like a guardian angel years after they'd graduated and pulled him out of the darkest place he'd ever known. Seeing these writings in Alan's distinctive hand elevated his emotions to another strata. He thought back to the little notes Alan would leave for him from time to time—'Noah, please give Linda a hand in the greenhouse today because her back is bothering her. Thank you.' Or 'Noah, please bring Joanie to the store so she can buy a new laptop for the coming school year. Thank you.' Or, 'Noah, please help Jason figure out what's wrong with his car. I don't want him tinkering under the hood by himself. Thank you.' And there was one which Noah kept in his wallet to this day—'Noah, I sometimes worry that we don't say it enough, but this family and this household couldn't function without you. Thank you.'

He felt the sting of tears and fought it back, refocusing on the notebook's content rather than the manner in which it was rendered. There was more financial commentary, seemingly random and disjointed in some places. There were dates and times, accounts of phone calls and email conversations without any mention of the participants' names, and free-floating observations like "*credit default swaps without initial collateral?!*" and "*obvious cracks in the foundations of the shadow-banking system!!!*" Alan had also drawn charts and graphs, made calculations that stretched over multiple pages, and even rendered a few maps.

With only a fundamental understanding of fiduciary matters, Noah felt like a cork afloat on the restless ocean of his old friend's mind. He tried hopelessly to find some kind of harmonic thread but was unable to do so.

Then it struck him—*Alan was doing this on purpose. He had created a kind of shorthand that only he could understand in case this was ever found.*

"But by whom?" he wondered aloud. "Who was he worried about?"

He continued thumbing through the pages, so overwhelmed by the weight of the material that his mind merely skated over it. Then he came to one of the last entries, and his eyes riveted on a name.

"Oh my God," he said for the second time. "Good...*God*...."

When he took his phone from his pocket, his hands were shaking.

****

Cruising at about twenty thousand feet, Jason was not as attentive to the control panel of his Gulfstream as he should have been. The city of Albany twinkled across the landscape as evening settled, with a caliginous beauty that stretched to the horizon. Jason saw all of this without really registering it, just as he was barely aware of the hiss of the oxygen compressors, the baritone hum of the engines, and the faint odors of gas and oil that informed the tiny fuselage. His mind was still out west.

He was unable to envision what should happen next, and that worried him. The will was gone, at least in its original form. True, he had the images of it taken with the cellphone and safely uploaded to an online server. But it was doubtful anyone beyond himself would accept its legitimacy; certainly it would hold no value in a court of law. He had no leads regarding the fate of Chase Walker, and he still doubted the Las Vegas police would give the matter much attention; a fact he still had not conveyed to Denise. Bruce Jax, who could have been a wellspring of information, was lying on a slab somewhere, his silence assured for eternity. The identity of the person who shot him was a complete mystery and further complicated matters as it implied there might be multiple parties at work. Whoever the shooter was, they now had the will in hand. And if it was worth taking a life, then there was a good chance it would never see the light of day. Jason wouldn't be surprised if it had already been tossed in a furnace or shredded into confetti.

His thoughts turned to Katie Bridgeport, and not for the first time, either. It brought along an altogether unexpected sense of comfort, of preordination, and of familiarity that had lain dormant for ages. He generally regarded 'The Past' in wholly negative terms, something to be set aside whenever it came to mind. He always knew that was an oversimplified, perhaps even downright ignorant, way to view it. But considering the magnitude of the pain that came with any form of reminiscence, he allowed that ignorance to form a protective layer around his psyche. He had so forcefully synonymized the loss of his family with all things prior that there were times when he felt as though he didn't even have a personal history. But Katie, he discovered, had a curious effect on all of that. Even though she was markedly a part of days gone by, he felt none of the misery or hopelessness when she strolled into his thinking. She provided a kind of emotional immunity borne from a presence so bright and pure that it drilled through the stiffened crust of his sorrow. She had been so detached from the loss of his family; she was away at school when it happened, and Jason wasn't even sure if she'd reached out to him. He had plunged so deeply into an ever-thickening darkness at the time that he wouldn't have noticed in the first place.

What shook him from this reverie was an alert through his headphones that a call was coming in.

"Hello there," he said, seeing Noah's name in bold letters on the screen.

"How's the journey?"

"Smooth and uneventful."

"You should be getting pretty close by now, yes?"

"I am." Jason checked the board, then his watch. "A little over an hour and I should be there. I'm canvassing Albany at the moment."

"Weather looks good?"

"Very clear. No problems. Are you calling about the box?"

"Yes."

"And?"

"It's open."

Jason grinned. "How'd you manage that?"

"The bandsaw in my workshop. I just sheared off one end."

"Excellent. And the contents?"

"Some printouts, a small notebook, and a USB flash drive."

"Have you gone through all of it?"

"Not the flash drive yet, but the other stuff. The printouts were actually made by me at your father's request years ago. A lot of financial material I didn't understand at the time and don't understand now."

"Like what?"

Noah told him, reading the headlines and some of the text Alan Hammond highlighted.

"Like I said, I don't have a head for money matters like your father did, so I can't—"

"It's about the crash," Jason said. "My God, it's about the financial meltdown that occurred in 2007 and 2008."

"You mean the 'Great Recession'?"

"Yes, the one that brought the United States within inches of going over the cliff. *Inches*, Noah. It would've been mayhem on a scale you can't even imagine. Blood would've been running in the streets, and I'm not kidding."

"But I made these printouts in early 2007, so how could he...."

Noah's voice trailed off, followed by a brief silence.

Then he said, "Oh God, your father—"

"—saw it coming. Yeah. He knew, Noah. He *knew*."

Jason heard the sound of riffling pages.

"Then some of the things he wrote in the notebook make sense now," Noah went on. "Not all of them, but some. At least to me. You'll be able to translate everything much better, I'm sure."

"I'll have a look as soon as I get there." Jason swallowed into a dry throat. "And what about this Rafael character? Was there any mention of him?"

"Yes there was."

"Tell me."

"Before I do, I want you to promise me something."

"What's that?"

"That you won't get crazy behind the controls afterward. That you'll keep your head."

Jason took a deep breath. "Okay, sure. I'm calm. Now, who was he, Noah?"

"Rafael isn't a person, Jason. It's a thing."

"What?"

"A thing, Jason. Not a man."

"I don't under...okay, what thing?"

Noah told him, and then there was more silence.

"You're not *serious*," Jason said.

"That's what it says in your father's own handwriting."

Jason went into a thousand-yard stare, and the plane began losing altitude. He didn't correct it until an alarm went off on the panel.

"What's that?" Noah asked.

"It's nothing. Don't worry about it."

"Jason, keep your eyes on the skies."

"I am...."

"Seriously. I don't want you to—"

"You have no idea what's on the flash drive?"

Noah let out a sigh. "No."

"Would you take a look?"

"I'd rather wait until you've landed."

"Please?"

"When you land."

Jason nodded. "Okay, I'll be there shortly."

He gunned the engine.

Forty Two

THE VEINS ON Frank Bridgeport's neck were standing out like cables.

"You are not going back there!" he said sharply, jabbing a finger through the living room's cool, filtered air. "And that's *it*."

"Yes I am!" Katie countered. She was a foot shorter than her father and looked particularly demure in her beret and black leggings. But her intensity was every bit as fierce. "I'm not ten years old anymore, daddy! I'm perfectly capable of making decisions!"

He pointed to the TV screen, where an update on the parking lot bombing was on CNN.

"You want to get tangled up with *him*? A man who's being targeted by professional *killers*? That's your idea of a smart decision, is it?"

Katie's mother stood nearby in silent arbitration. She seemed to be waiting for her daughter's attention to shift to her—a familiar sign of uncertainty—but it never did.

"I can make a *real* difference there," Katie went on. "Noah and Jason are suffering, and they don't even realize how much because they've been stuck in it for so long. But I can see it. That place isn't a home anymore, it's a mausoleum. It hasn't had any spirit since the rest of the family died."

"You can't fix that by carpeting the floor or painting on the walls, Katie." Her mother said. Her tone was firm but sincere, and without a trace of condescension.

Katie nodded. "I know, mom. But I'm helping in other ways too."

Her father set his hands on his hips and did an eye roll

that seemed out of place on someone so polished. "So you're an expert in crisis therapy now?"

"They don't need a therapist, daddy, they need someone to breathe fresh air into their lives. When I'm with Noah, you should see how he perks up. The difference in him from when I get there each day and when I leave is unbelievable. And when I was on the phone with Jason—" she had told them about the call from Vegas but neglected to mention certain details, like the real-time shooting death of Bruce Jax—"he sounded like the Jason I knew when we were kids, not the one you hear about around town."

"He's whacked in the head."

"He's *depressed*, daddy. Very deeply."

"Same thing."

Her eyebrows rose. "Really? I don't remember you being this insensitive when it came to Aunt Eleanor."

He jerked as if slapped hard, and his wife drew in a breath with the faintest whistling sound.

"The situation with my sister was diff—"

"How?"

"It just was."

"No, daddy. It was no different. She was drawn into a dark place and couldn't find her way out, so she took her own life to ease the pain. Maybe Noah's not that bad, but Jason is. He's scrambling, trying to find anything that'll make him feel better. That's why he goes off on these crazy adventures. To numb himself from the loss. He's not running toward anything, he's just running."

"And you can make all that pain disappear, can you?"

"I know I can *help*."

"Why do you even care so much? What are you, sweet on him?"

Katie's mouth opened and shut again, followed by a brief, icy silence.

"I am not sweet on him, daddy. I am trying to make a difference."

Her father was shaking his head. "I didn't pay for you

to attend the best schools so you could waste your time on crap like this."

Katie's jaw tightened. "It's not going to be forever. This is not going to become my career."

"You're right about that," he sniffed. "How could it? They're not even paying you much."

"This isn't about money."

"Oh please—don't be naive."

"I can get a paycheck anywhere. I can't do *this* anywhere."

Her father turned back to the screen. The valet who'd been injured was being interviewed from his hospital bed. There were bandages around his head and half his face. The other half looked as though it'd been beaten by Rocky Balboa. The caption on the bottom read, 'Lot Attendant Will Survive, But Lost Spleen In Emergency Surgery.'

"Look at the trail of destruction this guy leaves. Look at it! Do you want to be the next casualty?"

"He didn't mean for that to happen."

"But it did happen! That's my point, Katie. The guy is like a cyclone—you get too close and you get destroyed."

"It won't happen to me," she said.

"What, you think you'll be *immune* to it?"

She stood rooted to the floor and said nothing.

Her father lowered his voice. "You are not to go over there again, do you understand? Not tomorrow, not the next day, not ever."

"No."

"Yes."

"*No.*"

"YE—"

"You will *not* live my life for me!" she roared back, then turned and stalked out.

A moment later, the front door slammed shut.

****

"Yeah, this is all about the financial crash of '07 and '08," Jason said, sitting in the first-floor office and thumbing through his father's notebook. "No doubt about it."

He read over a page, turned to another, and then another.

"He knew. He *knew* it was coming. Like here, he writes, *Housing sector clearly peaked in 2004, then the defaults began en masse due to all the ridiculous SP and ARM lending.*"

"I understood about half of that," Noah said.

"He meant that home sales and their relative prices reached a high point in 2004, then began to fall. The 'SP' and 'ARM' acronyms stand for 'subprime' and 'adjustable-rate mortgage,' respectively."

"Okay...."

"In very simple terms, millions of people were talked into signing up to buy homes they couldn't afford. A significant part of the economy's foundation at the time was the housing market. In order to maintain it, lenders and agents had to get as many live mortgages going as possible. People were being conned into believing they could purchase a home worth half a million dollars on a salary of thirty or forty thousand a year."

"How is that even possible?"

"They were told their salaries would rise over time because, hey, that's what salaries did, right? And we'll just ignore the fact that wages for the average American worker have been at a standstill for the last few decades. Even the annual cost-of-living increases haven't been able to keep up with the *actual* cost of living. The amount of money someone makes—the actual number—is meaningless. It's what they make in relation to what things cost that matters. And in that regard, the dollar's buying power has shrunk to a fraction of what it used to be. Think about it—a generation ago, one parent could earn enough money to support a family of four, have two cars, take an annual vacation, and put whatever was left over into savings. Now both parents work and they're barely able to tread water."

"I get that much, yes. It's the norm now."

"And yet, millions of people were told they could own the home of their dreams when they really couldn't. And they did—for awhile. In just a few years, however, the lie behind the whole scheme came into play, and the deterioration began. Those buyers didn't get the wage increases they needed to maintain the ballooning payments. Taxes kept going up, the cost of repairs, the cost of utilities, everything...except their paychecks. By that point, the brokers who'd convinced them to sign on the dotted line had pocketed their commissions and disappeared. Scores of these toxic mortgages went into default. And I don't mean a few thousand. The American economy could withstand a few thousand bad mortgages. But these...they were defaulting by the millions. Think of the economy like a living, breathing body. When blood is flowing, everything's fine. But what happens when there's air in the veins?"

"Cardiac arrest."

"Exactly. For our economy to be healthy, we need cash to keep flowing through it. These fantasy mortgages started out with real money—provided by the lenders—going into the purchases. But then the borrowers—the people who lived in those homes—couldn't manage the payments, so the blood flow stopped. That led to the economic equivalent of a massive heart attack."

"I think Warren Buffett said something like that, didn't he? Something about a great athlete who's suddenly had a heart attack."

"Yes, and it's a perfect analogy."

"And your father saw it coming."

"He did." Jason went back to the notebook. "There's a clear progression in these pages, a growing awareness on his part. He was putting all the pieces of the puzzle together. Here he writes, *More and more institutions are taking advantage of recent deregulations by accepting riskier investments while reducing their ability to absorb them should those considerations go south.* And then, right under it in big capital letters, he puts, *WHY TAKE RISKS OF THIS KIND WHEN YOU'RE ALREADY MASSIVELY PROFITABLE???*"

"I saw that."

"A few pages later, he says, *Talked to JJ (BOG) in April.*

No concern."

"I saw that too. I have no idea who—"

"John Jordan, a member of the Board of Governors."

"Board of Governors?"

"Of the Federal Reserve."

"Fed...you mean *the* Federal Reserve."

"Yes."

"As in Alan Greenspan?"

"He was the chairman at the time, yes."

Noah shook his head. "I didn't even realize your father knew people on that level."

"He didn't know Greenspan, but he and Jordan were friends from years back. They sat on a few commissions together in the old days." Jason looked over another page. "It appears as though my dad tried to convince him there was a big problem coming, and Jordan disagreed. *He's going to do nothing but sit on his hands*, dad wrote, *I cannot believe it!*"

"He tried talking to a few others, too, right?"

"Yeah—there's a DN mentioned here, and an LR. I don't know who they are. But in every instance, his warnings were ignored. Here he says, *That idiot thinks everything's just fine. We've learned nothing from 1929 and 1873.*"

"I know about the crash in 1929 that led to the Great Depression, but what happened in 1873?

"A different crash, which triggered a different global depression."

"You're kidding."

"I'm not."

"I've never even heard of it," Noah said.

"Most people haven't. We tend to forget these things, which is why history keeps repeating itself. Making a mistake is understandable. That's human. But not learning from a mistake—that's just plain stupid." A few pages on, Jason said, "My father talked to Jordan one more time, then it seems like they had a falling out. He wrote, *I'm finished with JJ and he's finished with me. He won't listen, so I guess I have no other choice.*"

"No other choice? To do what?"

"He doesn't say. Maybe he—"

Jason came to a halt, his eyes widening.

"This is where—"

"The Raphael, I know."

He looked at Noah.

"My God."

"Yeah."

"*I was offered Raphael's 'Portrait of a Young Man' today, in return for keeping my mouth shut about the current situation. I did some quick research. It was painted in the early 1500s. Various owners since then, including royalty. Stolen by Nazis during the Polish invasion in 1939. Last seen in Kraków in 1945. Rumors for years that it was still around.*"

"This would've been the art equivalent of discovering a lost Beatles album," Jason said.

"No kidding."

"*I didn't even know who was calling*, my dad goes on. *A man who sounded middle-aged. He said the arrangement would be that I would purchase a warehouse just outside Berlin that was supposedly abandoned, and the painting would be 'accidentally' found inside. That way I could claim ownership by German law. This mystery caller said it would be worth at least $100 million. That estimate appears to be accurate.*"

"A hundred million dollars," Noah repeated.

Pointing to the notebook, Jason said, "I remember this conversation. It was late at night, much later than my dad usually stayed up. He was on the phone in his office, and I was walking down the hall to go downstairs. I could hear him trying to stay quiet, but he was really mad. *I'm not interested in any Raphael!* he said. I can hear it in my head even now."

"And you said that Howard's son claims his father had a similar conversation with his mother?"

Jason nodded. "Very similar. His father's words were along the lines of, *I don't want anything to do with that Raphael!* He said his father sounded agitated. Very, very similar."

"Do you really think it could be the same thing? The same painting?"

"Why not? It's been lost for a long time, but a lot of

people believe it's still out there. With so much mystique surrounding it, it would be a very hot property if it suddenly turned up. All the hype has driven up not just the price but the intrigue. If it really does still exist, I'll bet the person who has it is uneasy about it. That kind of thing happens all the time—someone steals something of great value, figures they'll hide it for awhile until the dust settles, then quietly unload it. But every now and then a kind of legend builds up, and the dust never has the chance to settle. At that point, whatever was stolen essentially becomes worthless to the thief, because the moment he tries to pass it on, he cuts his own throat. So yeah, I can see the reasoning behind not wanting to take ownership of it."

"Did your father make any guesses as to who had it?"

"Let's see...." Jason turned a few more pages, then stopped again.

"What?" Noah asked. "What's wrong?"

"There's nothing else in here." He held up the notebook and fanned through the remaining sheets, which were all blank. "He didn't write anything further after—oh no...."

He flipped back to the last entry, locking on one spot in particular. Then all the breath seemed to go out of him.

"Jason?"

"The date, Noah." He held the notebook up again. "Look at the *date*."

In the upper righthand corner, Alan Hammond had written the date in neat blue pen.

Noah shrugged. "So? He did that with all of them. He always—oh...wait. Oh wow."

"Yeah.

"That was...."

"One week before we all left for the Caribbean."

"Jason...."

"And a week after that, they were all dead." Jason looked like a dragon ready to breath fire. "Bit of a coincidence, wouldn't you say?"

"Jason, do you really think—"

"It all fits. My father was very distracted in the days before we left. He was more tense and irritable than usual. The trip had been planned months earlier, and he'd been looking forward to it. Then he suddenly didn't want to go. But my mom insisted. She kept pushing him, y'know, in that gentle way. The way that only she could get him to do things he didn't want to do."

"Sure, of course."

"He finally gave in. But he never really relaxed down there. He was on his laptop a lot, I remember. He didn't want to talk to any of us. He and I were fighting more than ever." Jason's jaw tightened. "The last conversation we ever had was him telling me to leave him alone, and me saying *No problem.* Those were the last words I ever said to him—*No problem.* As snotty and arrogant as ever...."

Noah shook his head. "Don't do this to yourself. There's no way in the world you could have known what would happen next. Absolutely no way. And if your father felt like he was in danger, it was his responsibility to tell the rest of you."

Jason nodded, but without conviction. Then he stopped with a frightening abruptness and his eyes widened again.

"What is it, Jason?"

Jason picked up the flash drive. "I think I know what's on here."

"You do?"

"Yeah."

He swiveled in the chair and inserted the drive into one of the empty ports. Then he cleared away the screen saver and went into Windows Explorer.

"Brace yourself, Noah."

****

He clicked on the 'USB DRIVE (E:)' icon, and a new box opened—a box that had nothing in it.

"It's empty?" Noah said. "That can't be—"

Jason put up a finger. "Hang on."

He went into the 'Organize' pulldown menu and chose 'Folder and Search Options.'

"This is a little trick my father showed me a long time ago. He wasn't the most computer-literate person in the world, as you know, but he did figure this out. And you'll understand why in a second."

Jason clicked the 'View' tab from 'Folder Options,' which opened a scrollable list. A short way down was an entry for 'Hidden Files and Folders,' and there were two choices—one for showing them, and one for hiding them.

The second one had been chosen.

"I didn't even know that was there," Noah said.

"Most people don't."

Jason clicked on the 'show' option, and a single file appeared in the main box—

alanhammond11april.mp4

"My God," Noah breathed, "that's..."

"A video."

"Made two days before you all left for Nassau."

"Yeah."

Jason set the cursor on top of the file, then paused. His eyes were bugged out again.

"Hey, I can watch it if you don't wan—"

"No, I can do it. I *need* to do it."

"Okay, sure."

He launched Windows Media Player, and Alan Hammond's office immediately came into view via the tiny camera perched atop the monitor—specifically, it showed the area behind the desk, which included a walnut bookcase, a filing cabinet, and a small refrigerator. In the foreground, the top of a leather swivel chair was also visible. The quality of the video was fairly good, although the lighting in the room could've been brighter.

Jason's father abruptly entered the frame and sat down. He was handsome in a simple way; a way that would be easy to miss without looking close. The resemblance to his son was there but not overwhelming. They both had the same black, satiny hair, the same small mouth and narrow chin. The eyes were different, but the well-defined eyebrows were a match. Alan Hammond was clearly much older, with flecks of grey along the sides, and lines etched around the mouth. But he was otherwise in excellent shape for a man in his early fifties.

"Hi dad," Jason said in a near whisper, his eyes rimming with tears.

Alan got into the chair and cleared his throat, then checked his watch.

"Okay—it's twelve thirty-five on the night of April 10th. Or the morning of April 11th, to be more precise."

"Wow," Noah said, "Alan up at that hour. A man who went to bed at nine religiously."

"The rest of my family is asleep right now," Alan continued. "Kenny and Valeria went home awhile ago"—they were, respectively, the estate's cook and housekeeper—"and Noah has gone back to his cottage. So I have the house to myself."

He paused a moment to look just past the camera—at the paired doors that led to the hallway—then back in the lens.

"I'm making this video for a variety of reasons. One, if you're watching, then you also have the notebook that accompanies it, and there are a few critical things I'd like to add that aren't in there. Reason two, if any of this material ever needs to be used in a court of law, this video will serve to strengthen the existing evidence. And three, to be quite frank, I'm a little frightened by some recent developments."

Noah and Jason looked at each other.

"Scared?" Noah said. "I didn't realize he knew the meaning of the word."

"Me neither."

The video continued—"If you've read the diary, then you know I've been very concerned about the economic progress of this country in recent years. No means of genius enables a person to foretell the future, but I have studied enough financial history to know the makings of a disaster when I see it—and it is my adamant belief that the United

States is heading toward a disaster of tremendous magnitude.

"Per my notes, I believe these conditions began in the housing sector through the scores of untenable mortgages being sold by the thousands to consumers who have been deftly manipulated. There are other contributing factors as well, but I'm not going to reiterate them here. The point I need to make right now is this—after expressing my concerns to those in positions influential enough to steer the nation clear of the catastrophe, I was casually rebuffed. When I pushed harder, I was rebuffed more forcefully. And when I still refused to let the issue drop, I was threatened."

Noah mouth fell open. "My God." Jason said nothing.

"That threat was delivered by phone two days ago. I received the call in my car, on the way home from my office, which I find too coincidental to disregard—I had the distinct feeling the caller knew my schedule and waited until I was isolated. He was not the same anonymous person who attempted to buy my complicit silence through the promise of the Raphael painting. If I had to guess, I would say this individual was fairly young, perhaps no more than his mid to late thirties. His voice was rough; a 'tough-guy' voice, clearly meant to intimidate. There was no accent that I could detect—he was American, and almost certainly from the Northeast. The conversation lasted less than a minute, and it was not so much his promise to take my life that rattled me. People in my position have to deal with threats from time to time; it's part of the ethos of being wealthy. But it was the words he used. He said, 'If you continue to press this issue, *the only option will be to put you down like a dog*.' It unsettled me so much because I'd heard this exact phrase before....

"In the summer of 1997, I was in the UK on business with my wife. And on the evening of July 1st, we encountered Diana, Princess of Wales, at the centenary celebration of the Tate Gallery in London. Linda and I had met the princess on several other social occasions and maintained a very friendly relationship with her. This particular date also happened to be Diana's birthday, so she drew an even greater amount of attention than usual. And although the cheerful public Diana was there for all to see, in her few quiet moments she seemed very troubled. When I asked her if anything was wrong, she pulled me aside and confessed that she had been receiving death threats ever since the rumors began that she was pregnant with the child of her then-boyfriend, Dodi Al-Fayed. None of these threats reached her directly—they were relayed through various assistants. She also confided that she was not, in fact, pregnant, and assured me that she and Dodi were being guarded by security provided by Dodi's father, Mohamed. But one person had nevertheless managed to reach her on her cellphone—a number that, she said, was changed at least once a month and given only to a handful of close friends and family. The caller told her that if the rumors of her pregnancy were true, she was to have an abortion immediately. If she did not, then he would—and these were the exact words she told me, because I've never forgotten them—have no choice but to 'put you down like a dog.'"

Noah took on an expression of sheer disbelief, but Jason's steely, focused gaze did not change. "Now we know why my subconscious kept sending up those images of the princess. Mom and dad used to talk about her once in awhile."

"Diana was badly shaken," Jason's father continued, "not just by the threat but also that the caller managed to get the number in the first place. She thought maybe someone in her inner circle had betrayed her, which made her even more frightened. 'Either that,' she said, 'or the man was a professional. Someone very good at these sorts of things.' After Linda and I returned to New Hampshire, I got in touch with Diana in early August to see if she was okay. She told me that the same person had called two more times, in both cases to see if she'd gone for the abortion. She insisted she was not pregnant, but the caller didn't believe her. She said Mohamed Al-Fayed's security people were going crazy trying to figure out how he kept getting her number, which was being changed with even greater frequency and secrecy than usual. She also described the caller as having, in her words, 'A very hard voice, very mean.' A few weeks later, she died in Paris in the accident we all know about."

"God Almighty," Noah said.

"I reported all of this to the authorities during their investigation," Alan said, "for whatever good it did. I'm not suggesting there's a definitive link between the person who kept calling her and her sudden death. Nor am I saying the caller was the same person who contacted me. Diana's death has been investigated on multiple occasions, and no evidence of premeditated murder has been found. But the fact that both callers were male, both managed to find cellphone numbers that were just about unobtainable, both had an intimidating demeanor, and both used the exact same euphemism for murder strikes me as far too coincidental to disregard."

"I'd say so," Noah commented. "Wouldn't you?"

He turned and found Jason still unmoving and still silent, now with a look of homicidal loathing on his face.

"For that reason and all the others I have explained," Alan Hammond concluded, "I wanted make this video as a kind of insurance policy in the event that something should happen to me. Hopefully, however, that won't be necessary."

Alan reached for his mouse, gave it a single click, and the screen went blank.

****

Jason didn't react for a long time. The seconds stretched into minutes, and those felt like hours.

Finally, he turned to Noah and said with savage calm, "He was murdered. They all were—dad, mom, Joanie. The plane crash wasn't an accident. It was the work of professionals, just like the princess said. Didn't we all think it was strange that there was virtually no debris found in the water? How long did the search team look? How much effort was put into that? No debris from the plane, no bodies—as if someone had cleaned up the site before the authorities had the chance to get there. As if it had all been planned out very carefully."

"Jason," Noah cut in quickly. He was hoping to keep

the man's rage to at least low boil. "The investigators said there was a strong possibility much of the debris was swept away by currents, especially if the plane exploded in the air as they believe. If it did happen that way, then the bodies...well, I'd rather not say it. I'm sure you understand."

Jason was shaking his head. "That's not my point. Even if the investigators were right—even if that's how it happened—I'm talking about *why* it happened. And it's all right here." He was pointing at the blank screen. "It fits together seamlessly. Like dad said, there's too much coincidence to be ignored. He saw what was happening. He tried to do something about it. Then they stopped him. You heard what he said—when he pushed hard, he was threatened. After that he was dead. That's a little too coincidental for me." Jason's eyes were reddened with fury. "His instincts were right. Millions of people got hurt in the crash of 2008. Maybe *billions* if you consider the ripple effect it had around the world. But a few—a very select few—ended up extremely rich. And most of them were already in positions of privilege. That's also a little too coincidental. No, these weren't accidents or cosmic bad luck or a product of the law of averages or whatever. Not the financial crash, not the death of my family...probably not even Diana's death. Or, for that matter, even Chase Wheeler's. I don't believe any of it was either incidental or accidental. There's a common thread here, I can feel it. Look at the evidence. Look at what we know and tell me you think it's all purely coincidental."

Noah considered everything he'd heard over the last thirty minutes. From there he considered a thousand further details he'd absorbed in recent years. When it came to theorizing, all you had was the information in front of you and your intuition. Theories didn't become facts until you had proof, and there wasn't enough of that here yet. But in his gut...seeing the way many of those details came together...how some fit seamlessly...like pieces in a jigsaw puzzle....

"My God, do you really believe it?" he asked almost timidly. "Do you really think it's all somehow connected?"

Jason locked eyes with him and nodded. "I do. Maybe I'm dead wrong. Maybe it's an outlandish idea, and I just can't see the outlandishness of it yet. But something in here—" he tapped his chest "—is telling me I'm right. This isn't a whacked-out conspiracy some nut posted on a blog. If you do the math, so much of this adds up. Like I said, too many coincidences. Too much that fits together."

Noah searching his mind for anything he could use to stick a pin in Jason's theory. Something that neatly and conclusively debunked evidence of the evil he was alluding to. This was the kind of evil that usually only dwelled in books and movies, and the mere thought of which kept good people awake at night. He desperately wanted to be able to dispel all possibility that this was the type of malevolence at work here—but he couldn't.

"So what are you going to do?" he asked.

There was real hatred dancing like fire in Jason's eyes. "I'm going to track down whoever's behind all this. I'm going to root them out, expose them to the light of day, and make them face whatever punishment there is. I don't care how long it takes, what it costs, or what I have to do. I will work tirelessly. This is my mission now. *This* is my life goal—to learn the truth, find those responsible, and make...them...pay."

"There's no need to do all that," said a new voice to the conversation. Jason and Noah jumped and turned together in an almost choreographed synchronicity. A small Asian woman who looked vaguely familiar to both of them stood in the open doorway. Neither could summon the name of Kelli Nashamura because she had appeared so few times in the media. But it wasn't Nashamura that commanded their immediate attention—it was her male companion, crewcutted and massive, who held a pistol with accompanying silencer in hand, leveled steadily at Jason's chest.

"I'll be happy to ease your minds," Nashamura said to them sweetly.

Forty Three

THE GUNMAN, WHO'S NAME turned out to be 'Ellis'—Jason couldn't determine if that was his first or last—gave the second pair of handcuffs a tug to make sure they were tight enough. Then he went back to his place behind the perpetually smiling Nashamura. Jason got the impression this was his usual station in the dynamic of their relationship.

They secured their prisoners in the living room by handcuffing them together in separate chairs, back to back, with one of the Romanesque columns between them. The cuffs had been ratcheted to maximum tightness. Between that and the sharp, unnatural angle at which their arms were stretched, Jason found himself in considerable pain. That being the case, he thought, he couldn't imagine how much Noah was suffering. There hadn't been so much as a moan from him, and Jason sensed that this was because he didn't want to give his captors the pleasure. That Cheshire cat's grin on Nashamura's face was particularly irritating, and he never felt so proud.

Ellis handed Nashamura the gun and walked out of the room.

"Where's your buddy going?" Jason asked.

"You'll find out soon enough."

By any measure, this woman appeared as inoffensive as they came. She couldn't be more than five feet tall. She was sleight in frame; maybe not anorexic, but small enough to tumble over in a strong wind. She was dressed unremarkably, in polyester slacks and a basic cotton turtleneck. A single Japanese character printed on a round jade pendant hung from a chain around her neck. Jason recognized it as the kanji symbol for strength and power. The most striking feature about her, however, was the eyes. On the surface they appeared warm and inviting, even maternal. But he kept seeing flashes of something more. Something ugly and bitter, bordering on crazy. And that's when he remembered her.

"You work for governor Richter," he said. "You're one of the advisors of her presidential campaign. I've seen you on television."

"That is correct."

"So how does that fit into all this? Is Richter part of your consortium?"

She shrugged. "Beats me."

"I thought you were going to ease my mind. Isn't that what you said before? Since you're obviously going to kill us, why would you be worried about revealing anything?"

"There are some things I don't share," she replied, "regardless of circumstance."

"In case we get out of this?"

She laughed, and it wasn't a pleasant sound. High and strangled, like a chuckle that might come from turkeys if they had a sense of humor.

"You won't be getting out of this. You want to know where Ellis went? To put an explosive timer on your gas line."

"Jesus," Jason heard Noah say, his voice haggard. "There's that reserve tank downstairs. They'll blow this place to pieces...."

"That's right," Nashamura said. "And we'll remain here until the last possible minute to make sure neither of you wanders off in the meantime."

"We have security—"

"Cameras. Yes, we know. The first thing we did was disable your surveillance system."

Jason stared at her with the undisguised loathing he reserved for those who held no regard for human life. And from there, another bright revelation materialized.

"It was you in the parking garage in Vegas, wasn't it." This was not a question. "You killed Bruce Jax."

"Correct again. You're on a roll today."

Before he had a chance to employ the internal censor that governed his mouth, he said sharply, "You're quite the little psychopath, aren't you?"

"Jason—" This was Noah.

For just a moment, it appeared as though the jibe would bounce off her. Then the priggish grin dropped as if its strings had been cut, transformed into an angry snarl, and she came forward rapidly. She raised the pistol above her head, spinning it around with practiced fluidity so the butt was now at the fore, and brought it down hard. Jason saw fireworks as it connected with his cheek, sending blood and bits of flesh cascading in all directions. He let out a cry that was impossible to repress, although he still hated himself for doing it.

When he turned back, he found Nashamura leaning over him like an enraged teacher. And in her eyes he saw a blazing hatred equal to his own.

"You have no place to judge me, you arrogant bastard! How dare you!"

She really is crazy, he thought through the dissipating fog of agony. *Certifiably deranged.*

She pressed the barrel of the silencer to his temple. This was followed by the distinctive click of the hammer as it was thumbed into place.

"Please don't!" Noah cried with surprising strength.

"Shut up," Nashamura told him. Then, back to Jason— "You're still alive right now because of my good graces, nothing else." Her words rode atop a wave of labored, hysterical breathing. "I've been told to eliminate you and destroy this property, but the method I use is entirely at my discretion."

"Since you're going to do it either way," Jason said evenly, "I'd be interested to know who gave those orders."

She put a knee on his thigh and pressed the gun down harder. Jason's head tilted to such a sharp angle that it felt like it might snap right off. She was hovering close enough for him to catch a whiff of her perfume, and the jade pendant with the power symbol struck him once on the bloody cheek. It remained fixed there for just a moment before peeling free.

He was certain she was going to pull the trigger, and a brief, makeshift prayer flashed through his mind—*God, please forgive me for every stupid thing I've ever done.* Then she pushed off him and backed away, and he released the terrified breath he'd been holding.

The grin returned to her face as if it had never left; as if the unhinged maniac that dwelled behind it had never made this brief exhibition. But the gun remained leveled, the hammer cocked, and Nashamura's finger curled around the trigger.

"Okay, rich boy, I'll tell you some things. Not all of it, just because I want to enjoy the thought of you going into oblivion tormented by the knowledge that some of your questions remain unanswered. But I'll throw you some crumbs. Does that sound reasonable?"

A dozen wiseguy replies came to mind, all jumping and kicking like wild horses, but he held them back in the interest of survival. *Something will happen*, he told himself. *Please God...please let me catch a break here. Please...anything....*

"Sure," he replied, going out of his way to leave out even the tiniest hint of sarcasm.

Her pompous smile widened, and in the process it had the remarkable effect of making her uglier rather than prettier.

"Okay," she said, "Go ahead, ask your questions. And if a few of my answers burn you like acid, so be it."

Forty Four

KATIE OPENED THE front door and stepped in quietly, wiping away the last of her tears. It had taken a few tries to get used to the idea of entering the Hammond household without knocking or ringing the bell, but Noah had been insistent. "You're working here now," he had told her. "It's perfectly fine. And besides, you're like family anyway." She had come to adore the man in a relatively brief time. And yes, he was right—the relationship felt more familial than anything else. Noah was like the affable uncle all the kids hoped to see at holiday functions and birthday parties, the one who always had candy in his pocket and gave the toddlers horsey-rides on his knee.

It was unusual for her to come by during evening hours, but not unprecedented. She'd dropped in twice to make dinner—once when Noah seemed particularly exhausted after the day's work, and again when he banged his knee on the corner of a coffee table and had to sit with an ice pack on it. She also checked in on him occasionally, uncomfortable with the idea that he was on the estate by himself. Once they played gin rummy until midnight. Another time it was Yahtzee. He never questioned her visits, just welcomed her with a gentleman's hospitality and good cheer. So when she stormed out after the confrontation with her father, she was drawn here like a moth to a porchlight.

She didn't call out to him after she closed the door; that wasn't the routine they'd developed. Instead, she paused in the foyer and waited for any audible indication of his whereabouts—the jingle of silverware in the kitchen or chuffing of slippers in the upstairs hallway. Tonight it was voices drifting out of the living room.

Does he have guests? she wondered, and immediately regretted the decision to come. She turned back toward the front door and was about to make a silent exit when she caught a few notes of what she believed to be Jason's voice. Noah had told her he was coming back, but she'd forgotten about it after the domestic meltdown with her father. Now, the thought of seeing Jason produced a pleasantly animated stirring in the pit of her stomach.

She crept back toward the living room's broad entranceway under the pledge not to engage in official eavesdropping. If it was just Jason and Noah, she thought, she'd knock softly on the doorframe and wave. If there was anyone else with them, she'd disappear like she'd never been.

It was Jason's voice for sure, and that stirring in her stomach swelled like an ocean wave. Then she realized something wasn't right; the conversation, although unclear, carried an unsettling resonance.

She moved up to the edge of the entranceway and, the no-spying pledge already forgotten, turned until one ear reached a position of maximum reception.

"...want to enjoy the thought of you going into oblivion tormented by the knowledge that some of your questions remain unanswered," she heard someone say. A woman, older. Katie had no idea who this was. "But I'll throw you some crumbs. Does that sound reasonable?"

Then Jason, curtly—"Sure."

So he did have visitors, Katie thought. But the conversation unfolding here was not a friendly one.

"Okay," the woman said, "Go ahead, ask your questions. And if a few of my answers burn you like acid, so be it."

What the heck...who is this?

With excruciating caution, Katie leaned over just far enough to acquire a visual. She captured the unbelievable scene in essentially the same way a camera would—with one brief click of the shutter—then pulled back. It took a moment to register all of it—Jason and Noah handcuffed back to back around one of the columns, the latter with his head hanging down and looking like he might be dead, the former conversing with a small Asian woman holding a handgun. It took Katie another moment to realize the gun's barrel was so long because a silencer had been screwed onto the end of it.

This can't be happening, she told herself. It looked like something out of a movie, not real life. *But it* is *real...and wishing it wasn't won't make it go away.*

Two things occurred to her in that instant. The first was that almost anyone in her position would be panicking—but she wasn't. An odd kind of calm had been called in from some unknown quarter of her being. The second was that all of her senses were rapidly elevating. There was still genuine fear coursing through every vein, but it had somehow been deprioritized so she could react to the situation rationally.

As she considered her options, she also kept listening.

Forty Five

"HOWARD HUGHES WASN'T really a recluse, was he," Jason said. "A private man, yes, but not a true hermit. He was being held captive. Too wealthy and well-connected for your people to murder, so you just took control of him and his empire. The minders, the codeine injections, all of it. Am I right?"

"You're exactly right."

"And that's because he knew."

"About...?"

"About there being some kind of master plan to bring America down. To remove this country from the number-one position in the world."

Nashamura nodded pridefully. "Most Americans feel it every day, but they don't know there's an invisible hand guiding it. It's been going on for a long time now, long before I was in the picture. It's been working, too. Slowly, yes. But it has been working. This country's been in charge of the world long enough."

"That's why you're here now? Because I'm starting to figure it out?"

"Basically."

"Things like the economic crash of 2008."

"Oh, much more than that." Nashamura looked off to some faraway place. "The saturation of sexual and violent content into all forms of media—movies, television, music, journalism. The decay of traditionally reliable institutions like religion and law enforcement. The struggles of the education system...skyrocketing drug and alcohol use...expanded welfare and other costly social programs...and much, much more. So much you'll never know about it." Her smile broadened until she looked as though she might burst from the sheer joy of it. "It has taken a long time, but we have accomplished a great deal."

"I think you're full of it," Jason said flatly.

"What?"

"You're lying. No one criminal organization could possibly be so powerful. You're talking about the kind of stuff the conspiracy loonies write about on the Internet."

He watched her reaction carefully, and a shudder went through him when she appeared genuinely relaxed and unshaken.

"Think whatever you like. There have been others who tried to sound the alarm bells, and public reaction has always been the same as yours. 'That's just crazy!' or 'A paranoid fantasy!'" She chuckled. "I'll let you in on a secret."

"What's that?"

"One of the greatest advantages we've had over the years has been people's refusal to believe such a thing is possible. It has given us a shield behind which to operate safely. The more people who won't allow themselves to think this can really be done, the easier it is to do it."

"I see. So you're saying that you and a group of others have been singlehandedly responsible for all the ills of American society since the 1970s? That's what you're claiming?"

"Basically. Not every single thing that's gone wrong, of course. But a lot of it. Some very big things."

"That's ridiculous."

"Why?"

"No group, no matter how powerful or influential, could possibly do that much damage without being found out. You'd need thousands of agents working in all critical sectors of—"

He stopped because Nashamura was holding a hand up and waving it.

"Where do you get this number, 'thousands'? Why do

you say that?"

"How else could so much be accomplished? There are more than three hundred million people in this country, and our infrastructure is very well established. We have systems in place that have been operational for decades, not to mention the safeguards that have evolved from past problems. There's no way some small faction of twisted minds could bring all that to ruin."

Nashamura looked at him with a brand of arrogant pity that is the exclusive property of those who are thoroughly convinced of their superiority and, as an unfortunate coefficient, are forced to occasionally interact with those who are not.

"Why would you need so many people?" she asked. "Does every beam in a house need to break for it to come crashing down? Does every part in a car need to fail for the car to stop running?"

Jason saw it all in that moment—first a flash-image of the whole picture, then the unthinkable details that brought it into reality. His father's voice echoed in his mind—*After expressing my concerns to those in positions influential enough to steer the nation clear of the catastrophe, I was casually rebuffed. When I pushed harder, I was rebuffed more forcefully. And when I still refused to let the issue drop, I was threatened.*

"No...." he said feebly. "There's no way." He looked at Nashamura with wide-eyed disbelief. "There is no way you had the Fed in your back pocket. That's not possible."

"Why? Because those people are above suspicion? Because they're too principled? Too moral?"

"Yes—*yes.* I absolutely believe that. At that level, with that much responsibility and so many lives dependent upon your every decision, you'd have to walk the straight line."

Nashamura shook her head. "More of that glorious naïveté; I really do think we would've failed without it. Just about anyone can be manipulated, you idiot. Whether it be through bribery or threats or whatever, at the end of the day it's easy to get others to do what you want. And yes, that includes people in the so-called 'high places.' Such people are still only human. They may hide their vulnerabilities better than most, but they have them. Everyone has them."

Noah finally re-entered the conversation at this point by saying, "So that's what you did? You threatened people in positions of influence?"

"Threats weren't necessary in most cases, Mr. Gwynn," Nashamura said. "Usually we just needed to find the right number."

"You mean you bought them off," Noah said.

"Yes, we bought them off. We agreed on a number, whether it be a flat figure or a percentage going forward. Everyone has a number, an amount of money that they want."

"Or a painting," Jason said, "like a supposedly lost Raphael masterpiece, for example?"

Nashamura shook her head. "We haven't been able to give that lousy thing away."

"And if bribery didn't work," he went on, "then you threatened them?"

"That's it." She said this as matter-of-factly as if she was reciting the best method for making hard-boiled eggs. This sociopathic side of her sent chills through his body. "We try to be reasonable at the beginning. But if that doesn't work, we always have alternate methods."

"At which point the first choice suddenly doesn't seem so bad," Jason said.

"Now you've got it."

"And what was Chase Wheeler?"

"A very stubborn young man."

"Not stubborn," Jason grinned. "Loyal. I'll bet your people didn't like that."

He saw a shadow of irritation pass over Nashamura's face, and it was deeply satisfying.

"Well," she said, "his *loyalty* cost him his useless little life."

"I suppose your fingerprints are all over that murder, too?"

"No, I wasn't in Nevada at the time."

"Then how do you know about it?"

"Because I've been entrusted with the information since, both metaphorically and literally, it can be useful in the right circumstances."

"What, exactly, does that m—?"

Nashamura's cellphone binged, and she removed it from her back pocket without taking her eyes off her prisoners. Then a quick glance at the screen to read the text.

"He's almost finished with the explosives," she said. "Apparently you have some large acetylene tanks in your basement in addition to your main gas line." She giggled like a little girl. "We certainly have to get those involved. Then it's time for the big show. So tell me, how does it feel to know you've only got about five minutes left to live?"

Noah, who had been quietly praying for awhile, said, "You're an animal. There's nothing human left in you. And I say this as a dedicated followed of God who believes all life has value."

Jason made sure Nashamura could see the bemusement in his eyes. "I couldn't agree more," he said, and Nashamura's face clouded with anger. For a moment Jason was sure she would step forward and give him another shot across the face.

So be it, he thought. *If I'm going down, I'm doing it knowing I had the last laugh.*

Forty Six

NASHAMURA'S AFFIRMATION echoed in Katie's mind—*five minutes left to live...five minutes left to live....*

She considered calling the police, but they couldn't possibly get here that fast. Even if they did, their lives would be in serious danger. And the other person involved—the mysterious 'he'—was, according to the Asian woman, in the basement.

No, I have to take care of this myself. There's no other choice.

Katie turned and went through the dusty, moonlit library, then into the dining room. A small section of the kitchen was visible through the doorway in the opposite corner, and beyond that she could see the basement door standing open with the glow of a bare bulb coming up from the stairwell. She could even hear someone moving around down there. *Planting the explosives...my God, this really is happening.*

She forced all emotion aside and went back through the library, then crept up the stairs to the second floor while reciting the plan in her mind—*Get the gun from up there, force the guy to kill the explosives*—she guessed they were connected to some kind of timer or remote control—*and hold him and the woman at bay. Then the police can come.* She prayed she wouldn't be forced to shoot either of them. She had a strange certainty that, under the right circumstances, she could. *If it comes down to them or me, Jason, and Noah,* she told herself, *I'll do what I need to do.* She was both surprised and comforted by the strength of this previously untapped fortitude.

The weapon in question was a shotgun that belonged to Alan Hammond and was stored in the closet of his bedroom. She'd noticed it when Noah gave her a tour of the property and pointed out that some rooms on the second floor had, by Jason's insistence, remained untouched since the day of the accident. Alan and Linda's suite held all the telltale signs of a couple still very much alive—the unmade bed, the bathrobe draped over the footbench, the half-empty bottle of water on one nightstand, the pair of slippers on the carpet below...and the closet door that stood almost all the way open. Beneath the neat row of hanging dress pants, one could just see the butt of the Winchester Super X3 tucked in the back corner.

Katie had to open the double doors that led into the suite because, also by Jason's decree, they were kept closed at all times. The knobs were quiet enough, but the hinges let out a series of high-pitched squeals in various registers. She paused, her heart going like a pulverizer at a quarry, and waited for the explosives guy to come charging up the stairs. When this didn't happen, she closed her eyes and let out a long, silent breath.

The suite was a land of darkness, populated with undefined shapes backlit by the vague luminescence of indirect moonglow. She negotiated her way to the closet mostly by memory, praying she didn't trip over anything along the way. When she got there, she felt along the molding both inside and out in the hope of finding a light switch, but there wasn't one.

She got down on one knee, removed her iPhone from her pocket, and launched the flashlight app. The butt of the Winchester came immediately into view, a spooky image in the phone-light's monochromatic radiance. She also spotted a small box stashed behind the butt, tucked snugly into the corner. It was mostly silver, with a large 'X' as well as the word 'Winchester' printed on the side in bold red letters. *The shells*, she realized. *Good.*

She remove the rifle first, easing it out gingerly and feeling for the safety to make sure it was on. Then she set it on the carpet behind her and turned back for the ammo—and as soon she lifted the box, she knew she was in trouble.

It weighs next to nothing...oh no.

She lifted the lid and found a full complement of shells inside, but they were all empty. Alan Hammond was a recycler, she realized, meaning he likely refilled them with lead shot so they could be reused.

She utilized the phone-light to search the rest of the closet floor. There was a pair of leather loafers, an unopened tube of blue racquetballs, and a braided belt that seemed to have been dropped down here inadvertently and was now forgotten. But no more ammo.

Moving to the shelf above the clothesrack, she discovered an empty toiletries bag, a Ralph Lauren Polo shirt with a ripped collar, three glass Mason jars loaded with coins, an Indiana Jones-type fedora that Katie couldn't envision Alan Hammond wearing even as a joke, and a small and well-used pair of Zeiss binoculars.

But no shells. Not even one.

She hated to admit it, but this really did make perfect sense. Alan Hammond was a careful and responsible man who would've readily adhered to one of the cardinal rules of firearms safety—that when a weapon is kept in the home, the ammunition must be kept well separate from it. Her own father observed this protocol religiously, keeping all of his guns in a locked cabinet in the basement while the ammunition stayed in a safe on the second floor. *And I'm sure Alan observed rule number two as well—never leave your gun loaded when not using it.* To confirm this, she broke the weapon and peered into the barrels. Both were empty.

"So if there are more shells," Katie said softly, "they could be anywhere."

She glanced around the suite, tempted to dig through the drawers and feel between the mattresses. Then the words the Asian woman spoke to Jason came to mind again—*So tell me, how does it feel to know you've only got about five minutes left to live?*

She checked the clock on the iPhone.

"No time left to look around," she said matter-of-factly, her face clear of any particular expression.

She picked up the Winchester, hefting it in both hands as if to gauge the weight of it. She had always been a good shot; her father saw to that long ago. She'd never killed a living thing, but she could go ten-for-ten with clay pigeons before she was a teenager. That talent didn't seem particularly significant now.

"Time for a new plan," she said into the darkness, with no clue what that might be.

Forty Seven

"SO," JASON WENT ON, "judging by your current post, is it safe to assume you've got your hooks into Theresa Richter?"

"I haven't stayed close to her because I find her company so delightful."

"And if she becomes president, what then? She pressures Congress to rewrite a few laws so big business can fleece ordinary citizens even more than they already are? She gets a pointless war going with some largely defenseless country so a few thousand more bodybags can be sent home? What?"

"Something good, believe me. Too bad you won't be here to see it. It'll make the 2008 crash look like a light sunshower on an August afternoon."

"My God," Noah chimed in, "if you can really do that, you'll destabilize the whole w—"

"And what if Theresa Richter doesn't win?" Jason went on. "Are you telling me you can rig an American presidential election? What a crock."

Nashamura let out another shrill, discordant laugh. "Can you possibly be this naive? No, you're right, we have no control over how the voters react. That's why we've got *both* candidates under our thumb."

"You can't seriously expect me to believe that."

"They're just people," Nashamura said. Then, tapping the side of her head, she added, "Lousy, revolting, disgusting *people*. Why can't you get that?"

Jason thought he was seeing the core of personality in that instant. *That's it—she's a misanthrope. Somewhere along the way, she has come to hate every living human on this Earth. That's the fuel running this lunatic's engine.*

All but certain of this new theory, Jason made a point of saying, "Because I'd like to believe most of us are fundamentally decent deep down."

Her laugh this time came out in a tiny sniff. "That's so ignorant I won't even waste time on—"

"Who's at the top of your organization?" he cut in rapidly, and did so on purpose. She froze for the briefest moment, but it was long enough.

He smiled. "You're scared. Whoever it is, they scare you."

"There is no 'organization,'" she said. "No name, no headquarters, no paperwork. It's invisible, which is why no one's ever been able to—"

"You're changing the subject. Now why would that be?"

Nashamura didn't respond.

"Yeah, they scare the daylights out of you. I'm dead right about that, aren't I? I'll bet th—"

She turned the gun around and held it up. "You want this across the other side of that pretty face?"

"Okay, fine. So what's in it for you?"

"That's my business, not yours."

She turned when Ellis reappeared. He took note of the irritation on her face and said, "Is everything all right here?"

"Yes, fine," she replied. "Are you done?"

"Yes."

"How long?"

He checked his watch; a ridiculously oversized chronograph with a knobby black band. "Three minutes."

"Good."

She turned back to Jason, but before she had a chance to speak, he said, "Can I assume you killed Princess Diana?"

"I had nothing to do with that."

"But your *organization* did."

"Yes."

"Why?"

"Because, like you, she found out a little bit more than she should have. We're still not sure how."

"She was a saint in the eyes of millions. How dare y—"

"I'd love to keep up this conversation," Nashamura told him, "but I have to go. Enjoy what's left of your glorious mortality."

As she headed for the door, Jason said tonelessly, "Did your people kill my family?"

The question hung in the air for what seemed like a long moment, and Nashamura, halfway out the door, came to a halt.

"Ma'am, come on," Ellis urged.

She ignored him and turned back, her smile as wide as ever.

"Maybe," she said with a shrug.

A rage of mythic proportions boiled into Jason's soul, and in that instant he was capable of killing her with his bare hands.

"*I hope you burn in hell!*" he screamed.

Nashamura's smile vanished as her arm swung up with the revolver. Then a blast filled the room.

****

The weapon flew away from Nashamura and slid down the hall where Ellis had emerged moments earlier, the barrel now twisted and useless. Nashamura screamed and looked down in horror as blood poured from what remained of the fourth and fifth fingers of her right hand.

Katie entered the room and pumped the shotgun before leveling it again.

"Do not move," she said.

Noah's eyes grew so wide they looked like they might roll out of his head. "Katie?"

Jason, seeing the scatter of small silver circles that now lay all over the carpet, said, "Are those...*dimes*?"

"Yeah," Katie replied as she moved closer to her targets. "A trick my grandfather taught me—and my father made me promise I'd never actually do."

Nashamura addressed her with a name that was unrepeatable in polite company. Katie ignored this and said, "Turn it off."

"What?"

She adjusted her aim slightly; Ellis was now in the crosshairs and seemed to realize it.

"The timer for the explosives. Turn it off, or I'll make your face look like her hand."

Please, God, don't let them call me on this. She hadn't even really wanted to harm Nashamura; only get the gun away from her. That she *had* turned her hand into a bloody mess did lend credibility to the bluff, as did the fact that they didn't know her and therefore had to gamble on a large degree of uncertainty. *But will it be enough?* she wondered. And hoped.

"There *is* no way to turn it off!" Ellis growled. His eyes kept shifting from the woman holding the shotgun to his boss and her injury. The latter's lavender top was rapidly becoming soaked a deep scarlet. Ellis seemed as though he wanted to comfort her but was holding himself back.

He checked his watch. "There's only two minutes left!"

Praying that he was bluffing every bit as much as she was, Katie said, "Turn...it...off.... If you don't, then I guess we're *all* going to d—"

Ellis pulled Nashamura out the door and turned her around. Then he got behind her so his body would act as a shield if another shot came.

It did—Katie fired again, and the massive plate-glass window next to the door disintegrated in a glittering spectacle. Nashamura and Ellis were running now, the darkness quickly enveloping them. Katie pumped the gun once more and sent the next round through the empty frame and high into the air.

"What the heck are you—" Jason began.

Katie turned and came alongside them. "Pull your hands apart."

In perfect unison, Jason and Noah said, "What?"

"Your hands on this side of the column! Pull them apart as far as you can!"

They did as ordered, and Katie put the end of the barrel on top of the handcuffs' three small links.

"Wait it second!" Jason said. "Do you think that's a good—"

BOOM!!!

The cuffs snapped apart, and a hole about the size of a watermelon appeared at the base of the column. In a quirky phenomenon that would have been comical under different circumstances, one of the dimes that did not become embedded in the smoking cavity bounced away at high speed and shattered a porcelain bud vase that stood on a nearby end table.

"That's it," Katie said, tossing the shotgun onto the couch next to it. "No more dimes, no more rounds. Let's go...."

She grabbed Jason by one hand, and he grabbed Noah's with the other since they were still cuffed together on that side. They'd taken just a few steps when Noah stumbled and went down, coughing and gagging like a chain smoker. Jason gathered him up in his arms fireman style, and they continued through the living room, down the hallway, and out the front door.

They were no more than a hundred feet away when the detonators went off, triggering three different explosions and blowing the house to pieces in a colossal fireball. The force of it drove them forward and onto the ground, where they rolled like children on a hillside. Flaming debris rose lazily into the night sky before showering down everywhere. A broken length of timbered beam landed near them, plunging torpedo-style into the Earth. The other half continued flaming like some giant tiki torch.

As they got to their feet, Katie assessed the burning wreckage and realized there would be nothing left by morning. *The foundation and the chimney*, she thought. *That's it.*

She came up next to Jason and put a hand on his arm. "I'm so sorry."

Noah went to his other side but said nothing. He couldn't imagine the emotions that were at work now.

With a perfect poker face, Jason said, "Well, I guess that takes care of the renovations."

Unsure of how to react, Noah pursed his lips and nodded. "I guess so."

"And I guess I'm out of a job," Katie added. "Again."

Jason turned to her. "Not if you don't want to be."

"Oh?"

"There's lots of work to do now. Important work, maybe the most important of my life. And I sure could use some help, if you're interested."

She smiled. "You bet I am."

He turned back to Noah. "And what about you?"

The outrageous events of the last few weeks flashed through Noah's mind in a bright and colorful rush. Then they were eclipsed by the following two lines of dialogue that would never be forgotten—

"Did your people kill my family?"
"Maybe."

With more determination, more willpower, more *spirit* coursing through him than he'd felt in a very long time, he said, "You can count on it."

Jason nodded once, then looked back at the glowing remains of what had been the only home he'd ever known.

"Good. Then let's get going."

"What's first?" Katie asked.

"First we disappear," Jason told her. "Fast."

Forty Eight

THERESA RICHTER STOOD in the midst of the chaos with her hands in her pockets and a carefree smile on her face. It was critical to appear composed on this night; a night she had dreamed of since childhood. All eyes would be upon her—not only those of the twenty thousand who had come to the Staples Center in downtown Los Angeles to attend the convention and see her nominated, but also the estimated fifteen million who would be watching on their televisions, tablets, and phones. And then there was the staff, whose core included her campaign manager, chief strategist, political director, media controller, congressional liaison, and four policy advisors, as well as nearly two dozen assistants. All were present in the echoey locker room except for one of the advisors, and it was a struggle for Theresa to keep her concern for the recently vanished Kelli Nashamura under the surface.

A makeup artist approached with palette and brushes in hand. Theresa's reaction was to go perfectly still so the woman could do her duty; a habit that had developed slowly over the last year but was now second nature. On the monitors, the current president was out there whipping the crowd into a near-hysteria that, even down here in the bowels, could be heard through the walls and felt through the floor. He was the last of a litany of marquee speakers that included four congressmen, three senators, the current secretaries of state and defense, two Civil Rights leaders, and a former First Lady.

As soon as the makeup artist withdrew, Theresa's personal assistant appeared. Nicki Hill was thirty four, with a masters from Stanford and a buoyant spirit that the outbreak of World War III couldn't dampen. She was, as always, appropriately roboticized for someone in her position, with two cellphones holstered on her belt, a blinking Bluetooth headset in her ear, and an iPad cradled in her arm.

"Twenty minutes," she said, "then it's all you."

Theresa had insisted on this casual language between them; it was the kind of rapport she wanted with all her people. If she couldn't think of them as friends, then how could she trust her future to them?

"Okay, no problem."

Nicki plucked a dot of lint off her shoulder, then inspected the rest of her.

"You look good. Really good."

"Thanks."

"Do you need anything?"

Theresa shook her head. "No, I'm all ready. If I'm not ready now, I'll never be."

Nicki chuckled. "I guess that's true."

The question pulsed in Theresa's mind, dying to be asked—*Have you heard from Kelli?*—but she held it. No one had said a word to her directly on the subject, but there had been whispers and veiled comments. The media hadn't picked up on it yet because Nashamura had been something of a phantasmal figure all along, so she seemed MIA most of the time anyway.

"Everything will be on the teleprompters," Nicki told her, "if you need them, which is doubtful."

"I can recite the speech in my sleep."

"It's excellent. The crowd's going to go crazy."

Theresa glanced at the monitors again. *We stand at a crossroad in history*, said the current president, his words echoing like a voice from the heavens, *and it is now our solemn responsibility to choose the best way forward for this storied nation....*

Nicki said, "You're going to set this place on fire."

Theresa unveiled the full smile that had been seen by literally billions of people, and magically transformed her from ordinary human into charismatic leader.

"Oh yes—have the fire trucks ready."

"You are. It's going to be a night to remember."

"And it couldn't have happened without you."

They embraced like sisters, then Nicki melted back into the human beehive. All of Theresa's staff knew she preferred to be alone in the last precious minutes before any major public address. They remained close by in case she needed something, but otherwise they treated her as though she wasn't there.

With fifteen minutes to go, her personal cellphone vibrated inside her blazer. She retrieved it and lost a few heartbeats when she saw Nashamura's name on the screen.

She answered by saying, "Hang on a sec, Kell," then went into a small anteroom that had been designated just for her and closed the door.

"Thank God you've called, I've been worried like mad. Where are you?"

There was nothing but silence for a moment. Then a male voice she'd never heard before said, "Kelli Nashamura is temporarily unavailable, so I will be handling her duties for the time being."

Theresa's face clouded with irritated confusion.

"Who is this?"

"You need to make some last-minute changes to your speech," the caller told her.

"*What?*"

"And I strongly urge you to abide them."

"Why on Earth would I do that?"

"Chase Wheeler," he said, which led to another pause. "That's one reason. You were given a chance to be the hero and close the case back in 1982, but you turned it down."

Theresa's face drained of all color. "Christ...." she said raggedly.

"Paul Perkins, that's another. And the Henhaffer real estate project in 1984. There are others, as you know. But Chase Wheeler is at the top of the list. I could tie you to him now with ridiculous ease, but I'm going to guess you don't want that. Do I need to go on?"

Theresa felt the world around her begin to spin, melt, fade away. She thought she might faint; or, at the very least, throw up. *This isn't happening*, one part of her said. *A bad dream, nothing more. This cannot be happening.* But another part knew it was real—and reality, she had learned over the course of her lifetime, was better confronted than ignored. If one ignored it, one got bitten. And the longer the denial, the harder the bite.

"Ms. Richter?" the caller asked. "Are you ready for the changes?"

She swallowed into a throat as dry as the desert sands back home. The idea of simply ending the call and going forward with the speech as planned—as she had rehearsed for what seemed like a thousand times over the last four weeks—occurred to her. Then the idea was as quickly dismissed because she had the undeniable sense that it would be an act of pure lunacy.

"Yes," she said tacitly, thinking back to all the times she told herself she'd be able to buy back her soul one day.

She'd been so sure of this.

Forty Nine

CHASE WHEELER'S BURIAL service was a modest affair, with no more than a dozen in attendance. Denise sat by the silver coffin in a black sheath dress, conversely wiping tears away and looking homicidal. Next to her were her two children; Dylan, twelve, and Courtney, nine. They had never known their uncle, but they'd heard their mother speak of him enough times to sense the weight of the occasion.

The priest was the same one who had officiated Valeria Wheeler's funeral years earlier. He was the rector of the church where Val had attended services. She sometimes went with Karen Paulson, the elderly neighbor who aided Jason after Val's house burned down. Paulson stood among the tiny congregation, swaying slightly as the first of the day's alcohol seeped into her system. Nearby, Lisa Sanchez recited each prayer from memory due to all the services she'd attended in the past. And lingering at the back was Preston Hughes, somber and dignified in his dark suit. He had anonymously given the bright spray of flowers that lay in a round wreath on the coffin, which bore a ribbon with the words 'Beloved Son, Brother, and Uncle' across the front. The same attribution had been engraved on his headstone, which stood a few feet next to his mother's.

When the service concluded, Preston first went to Denise to give his condolences, then back to his limousine. He slipped in quickly, not wanting the door open any longer than necessary.

"She asked me to convey her gratitude to you for covering the funeral expenses," he said to Jason. "That felt like a strange thing to say since you were sitting here the whole time."

Jason nodded. "I wanted to be present for the burial." He watched the last of the proceedings through the tinted windows. Father Galloway guided Denise and the children away from the grave while a pair of young men with shovels, their boots and jeans already filthy from two earlier services, kept a respectful distance in anticipation of their duties.

As the limo pulled away, Preston said, "So, did you see them?"

Jason held out his iPhone, where the photo album was already open. The first image showed a Lincoln Continental with the same type of darkened windows. It was parked about fifty yards away, obscured under a cluster of elm trees.

"You mean this car?"

"Yes."

"It arrived with all the others," Jason said, "but no one ever got out of it. And if you look back there now—"

Preston turned to see out the rear windshield.

"It's gone. Wow...."

"As they say here in Vegas, I could've made book on that bet," Jason told him.

Turning back, Preston said, "And the man with the cane?"

"Got him, too."

Jason fingered through a few other pictures until he came to the freeze frame of a video, which he launched. It showed a gray-haired man appearing from behind a stand of arborvitaes, moving past the burial party, and continuing on until he reached a large garden mausoleum. He went behind it and disappeared.

"Oh, I'm sure he was just taking a walk," Preston said with a smile.

Jason chuckled. "Please—the limp and the cane were pure theater."

"No kidding. I've had an arthritic right knee for years now. Most days I can manage with it no problem. But every now and then, especially when the temperature drops or the barometric pressure rises, it hurts like heck and I have to use a cane a little bit. I've become familiar with the physical affectations that go with it, and I'm certain that man was faking. Either that or he had just recently started using it and didn't have the method down yet. But what are the odds of that?"

"Zero to none."

Preston shook his head. "My God, I really do think they arranged for Chase Wheeler's body to be found in the hope that you might show up for the funeral."

"I have no doubt about it," Jason said. "None at all."

The note had been found in Lisa Sanchez's mailbox five days earlier. There was a plain white envelope with only Lisa's name printed on the front, and inside were directions—the standard Times New Roman font on ordinary twenty-pound paper—leading to the location of Chase Wheeler's body. The language had been straightforward, dispassionate, and precise, and the corpse was found and exhumed the next morning. Chase had been rolled in a wool blanket and buried about four feet down in the desert sand three miles north of Vegas city limits. A gas-station-convenience-store combo had been erected close to the site in 2002, but authorities only needed to tow a long-dead Dodge Dart out of the way. The body had become essentially mummified and thus unrecognizable, but there was more than enough tissue for DNA confirmation. Cause of death had also been determined as asphyxiation due to choking. Repeated tests on the note and the envelope were less successful, as if neither had ever been touched by human hands.

"Did you find out anything about Kelli Nashamura?" Jason asked.

Preston nodded as he took a sheet of folded paper his jacket pocket.

"You could say that. Have a look at this...."

Jason unfolded it and found three photos printed at the top. The first, a grainy black and white, was of a small Asian girl with a filthy face who looked absolutely miserable. The second was of a beautiful young woman in a silk dress standing amidst a crowd at some kind of high-class function. The third was of Kelli Nashamura in her early days with Theresa Richter, couched in the shadows behind the stage as Richter gave a speech. But it wasn't these sequential photos that wrapped a cold hand around Jason's heart—it was the bulleted list of data points beneath them.

"Good God," he said plainly.

"What?" Noah asked.

Preston answered—"We're almost positive her real name is Kaori Nakano. Born April 11, 1939. Her father was a successful businessman who owned, among other things, a munitions plant. He was about as gung-ho as they came, thought Hideki Tojo was Japan's Messiah. And the only people he loathed more than Chinese were Americans."

Noah shrugged. "Okay, but a lot of Japanese thought that back then. How exactly does this—"

"They lived in Nagasaki," Jason said, his eyes still fixed on the page.

"Oh no. Don't tell me...."

"Yeah—her parents were killed when the bomb dropped in August of 1945. She was just six years old and apparently wasn't with them when it happened."

"She was found by police almost three weeks later," Preston added, "living in the woods."

"Lord Jesus," Noah said hoarsely.

Jason had considered the possibility that he was being paranoid about Nashamura and her claims, that she was nothing but a lunatic with a hyperactive imagination. But something deeper had been telling him different all along, and this new information clinched it. Everything she had said—about the murders, about the manipulation of the American economy, about the alliances with people in high places, and about the overall objective of bringing America to ruin—now had a sickening feel of undeniability. *She loathes us*, Jason thought. *We took her family from her, her future from her. The hatred was planted right from the beginning.* And of course she'd take part in some kind of plot to bring America down. In fact, Jason realized, she would have been the perfect recruit to get involved in such a thing once she was the right age and the hatred had time to root itself deep.

And the plot itself—millions of people losing their homes, their jobs, their savings, and their dreams. In recent years, Jason had the recurring feeling there really was a plan in motion. It all seemed so directed, so *intentional.* The rising cost of everything in contrast to the shrinking of incomes wasn't some quirk of cosmic phenomenon—some person or group made these things happen. The crushing price of gasoline during the recession...the skyrocketing cost of education...the deterioration of salaries and health benefits and 401Ks...all these things occurred because a once-sturdy equation was being altered. Every time Jason learned of yet another way in which the average citizen was getting shafted, he would think, *This can't all just be coincidental. No one has a run of luck* this *bad. This is being orchestrated...it has to be.* The scenario also aligned seamlessly with the revelations Howard Hughes set down in his final testament. *He was kept prisoner all those years, when the rest of us thought he was just some monk-like weirdo. Jesus....* Who could wield enough power to accomplish such a thing? To keep one of the wealthiest people in the world captive for decades...control men and women in positions of great influence...murder a beloved princess....

And kill an innocent young man, successfully hamper the ensuing investigation until it went cold, then, nearly fifty years later, lead authorities to resolve it in one day.

"Y'know, I wasn't sure before," Jason said, "but now I think everything Nashamura said is absolutely accurate. Why would she lie when she was convinced we were going to die anyway? She's a classic antagonist, the kind of person who gets a charge out of making a bug squirm under a magnifying glass before squishing it."

"I've known people like that before, and I've always wondered how they got that way," Preston said. "In this case, however, I think it's pretty clear."

Jason nodded. "I agree. I'm also growing in my suspicion that she does know something about the death of my father, mother, and sister. I don't think she was just being coy to get under my skin. I think it's very likely her little syndicate had something to do with it."

Preston looked at him gravely. "Then we're talking about some very dangerous, and very *evil*, people."

"Which is why I have to go after them. I have no choice. Who else will? Who else is in a position to do this? Look what happened to Howard. If you don't play along, they get you by the throat. They're growing far too powerful. Soon they'll have everyone on the planet in chains." The determination on his face was immovable. "I *have* to do this."

"But you don't even know who it is. That puts us at a tremendous disadvantage."

"If you want to change your mind about helping, there will be no hard feel—"

Preston put a hand up. "No, I absolutely want to. Please don't misunderstand me. Howard and I weren't particularly close, but he was still my cousin. And Howard had a very good side that most people don't know about. He gave a lot of money away to people in need, and he truly was a patriot. It was his refusal to sell out his country that got him into this mess in the first place."

"I know all that," Jason said. "I know he a decent streak. And let's remember that I'm a patriot, too. America may have made its mistakes through the years, but the *good* that we've done—why doesn't anyone ever talk about that? About scientific advancements and peace deals and humanitarian aid. Did you know we conducted more flights during the Berlin Airlift—to make sure a whole population caught under the oppressive hand of that psychopath Joseph Stalin would be adequately fed and clothed—than we did in the whole of World

War II? More than three hundred thousand flights carrying over two million tons of cargo."

"Yes, I remember that. Incredible, isn't it?"

"What about American aid to Iran in 2003?"

"Aid to Iran? You mean during the Bush administration?"

Jason nodded. "In December of 2003, a massive earthquake struck the Iranian province of Kerman, killing more than twenty six thousand people. And what did we, the Great Satan of the planet according to them, do in response? We sent more than eighty crisis professionals to help out—on military planes, I should add—along with critical supplies."

"I didn't know about that," Preston said.

"That's because the international press did a good job of burying it. And here's the punchline—Iran's central media agency went out of its way to accuse us of interfering with domestic matters!"

"Nice."

"Yeah...."

Jason looked pensively out the window as the desert landscape rolled by. They were moving quietly along Interstate 95 now.

"You know what gets me the most?"

Preston turned to him. "What's that?"

"I got really lucky in that I was born into a wealthy family, and I've never take that for granted. I thank God every day. But for the average American, where did the dream go? My father started with nothing and became rich. That right there has, in my mind, been the definition of the 'American dream'—work hard, walk a straight line, be patient, and you'll get ahead. Maybe you won't become a billionaire like ol' Alan Hammond, *but you'll get ahead.* Now, it's as if the system has been turned upside down. People doing horrendous things are reaping huge rewards, and people doing terrific things are being punished. When did right become wrong, and wrong become right? When did *that* happen?"

"If I had a dollar for every time I've asked myself that exact question, I think I'd triple my fortune."

"People are piling up credit-card debt in order to buy food and gasoline. If someone amassed a huge pile of personal debt because they just had to have twenty more pairs of shoes, you could at least say, 'Well, it's not like you needed them to survive.' But, my God, families are submitting themselves to interest rates of 18% or 22% or whatever just so they can eat. I mean, my God—*a whole generation has been cheated."*

****

They got off 95 at the exit for Boulder City; a quiet, upscale community with calendar views of the surrounding landscape and, by legal mandate, no presence of the gaming industry.

"So you think Paris is the first step?" Preston asked.

"I do. I think I'm going to find some answers there, specifically by digging a little deeper into the—" Jason used air quotes here, even though he generally loathed doing so "—'accidental' death of Diana."

"A dangerous undertaking, my friend."

"I'm sure."

"Your life will be at risk, I have no doubt. Very serious risk."

Jason turned back to the window without a word.

"Are Noah and Katie going with you?"

"No. Noah has to stay here and take care of some things. There's the whole business with the house; or, I suppose I should say, what's left of the house. And then we're going to launch a new, privately funded investigation into the accident that killed my family. Federal authorities were never able to draw a conclusion because no wreckage or bodies were ever found."

"I know," Preston said. "I remember."

"I took their word as gospel at the time. I wasn't in any condition to do much else. Those were some very dark days."

"I know about that, too, Jason."

"Well, that was then and this is now. Time to get some closure—on many things."

"And what about Katie?"

"She'll stay here and help Noah. As much as I'd like to have her come to Europe with me, things might get a little rough. It's bad enough she's got to hide in the shadows back here."

"I'm sure her parents are delighted with that."

"They're livid," Jason said, "and they blame me directly. I think Frank Bridgeport would love nothing more than to see me go to France and fall off the top of the Eiffel Tower."

The limo pulled up to a modern two-story home with lush and extensive landscaping that seemed out of place in the Nevada desert It was one of many rental properties owned by the Hughes Corporation in the area.

"Get some rest," Preston said, "and I'll talk to you in a bit."

"I will. And thanks for everything, really."

"No problem."

Jason got out and shut the door. When he was halfway up the walk, Preston rolled the window down.

"Hey."

"Yes?"

"Did you say you'd *like* to have Katie come with you to Europe?"

The tiniest of smiles formed on Jason lips. It stood in stark contrast to the way his brow furrowed with uncertainty. "I don't think so." A pause, and then, "Did I?"

Preston smiled back at him. "I think you did."

Fifty

JASON WAS AWOKEN by his iPhone at precisely 3:00 AM and slid up onto his elbows. Fear came in a bright charge along with the unfamiliarity of his surroundings—a lavishly furnished bedroom with a sitting area, small fireplace, and private bath. All very nice...*but this isn't my home.* Then the last of his sleepiness fell away and the blanks filled in rapidly—Chase Wheeler's burial, the ride with Preston Hughes, and the fact that he *had* no home anymore.

He tried to throw the covers back, then realized he'd never gotten under them. In fact, he was still fully dressed.

I showered last night. Showered and dressed so I could get right up when the alarm went off. Then I laid down for a minute....

He got up and went to the closet. There was nothing inside but a black deerskin backpack on the floor. He hefted it onto the bed and folded the flap back to perform a quick inventory—three changes of clothes, basic toiletries, a bag of power bars, a cellphone with a new number, a Dell laptop, a wallet containing five thousand in cash, another three thousand in travelers cheques, and two Hughes Corporation credit cards. There was also a false passport—Preston refused to reveal its source, but it looked flawless—in case things got really hairy. Jason's alias was Craig Meyers.

"Okay, Craig," he said to himself. "Time to get moving."

He went into the bathroom to wash his face and brush his teeth. When he came back, Katie was standing in the doorway leading to the hall. She was dressed in gym shorts and a t-shirt. Both had been obtained—like everything in Jason's backpack, as well as the backpack itself—by Preston and his oldest son, Brett, in a marathon shopping spree the night before.

"Time for you to go?" she said. Her voice was steady and her eyes clear. She'd been awake for awhile.

"It's time," Jason told her. He checked his watch. "The car will be here in twenty minutes."

"And then it's off to Paris?"

"Yeah, on Preston Hughes Airlines."

"He doesn't seriously own—"

"No, it's just a private plane of his. I can't go through a normal airport. I'll show up on the grid as soon as I reach the first security checkpoint."

"Can't he get in trouble for helping you travel overseas *in cognito*?"

"He can, but let's stay positive. Once I'm in the air, I'll get in touch with David Weldon, too."

"The only journalist you trust," Katie said matter-of-factly.

"How'd you know that?"

"Noah told me."

"Of course he did. Yes, that's right. David's about the best there is where the international media's concerned. He could be very helpful with what's ahead."

"And you spoke to the Millers last night, didn't you."

"I did."

"And?"

"Their daughter will be fine. They'll all be fine...eventually. But for now, both they and I have agreed that it'll be best for them to remain out of sight. Noah will look after them."

Katie smiled in a way that was clearly forced, drew in a theatrically deep breath, then released it.

"I'm worried about you, Jason. *Very* worried."

A horde of conflicting emotions thundered through him—fear and joy, anxiety and affection, yearning and relief. It had been a long time since anyone aside from Noah expressed this kind of direct, sincere concern; so long that he had trouble processing it now.

"I appreciate that a lot, but I'll be okay."

"You know there's no certainty of that."

"All right, I *believe* I'll be okay."

"Jason—"

"And by the way, I never properly thanked you for...wow, where do I even begin? For helping me when I was chasing Bruce Jax. For keeping Noah company. For helping him on the estate. And what else, hmm...? Oh, that's right—*for saving our lives.*"

She smiled again, in full color this time.

"I'm happy about that, too."

"Not as happy as *I* am!"

They laughed together then, but whatever cheer it provided was gone in an instant.

"I'm sorry you've been dragged into this," Jason told her. "I'm sorry you have to hide out here, cut off from your family and the rest of your life back home."

"It's the way it has to be right now," she said flatly.

He came over to her, put his hands on her shoulder. "But not for long, I promise. I'm going to go over there and get to the bottom of this. I'm going to get these people, and I'm going to end this nightmare. I'm going to end *them.* If they really did kill—"

A single tear rolled down Katie's face, and she threw her arms around him.

"Jason, don't. Just stay here, and we'll figure something out. You, me, Noah, Preston...we'll figure a way out of this. Make a deal with them or whatever. But don't do this. Your life will be on the line, and you know better than anyone how dangerous these people are."

With a war of urges storming inside, he reached around and returned the embrace.

"I have to, Katie," he said in a near-whisper. "For my family, for the princess, for Chase, and for God knows how many others. I can't just stand by and do nothing. I'm sorry, but it's the way I'm programmed." He felt tears of his own rise to the surface, but he held them at bay. "I don't expect you to understand. Nobody does."

"No, I do. Believe me, Jason, I do. That's why this is so hard for me. I know what you want, but I can also see the price of getting it."

"I have to try," he said. "I *have* to."

He felt her nod against his chest, and he put his hand gently on her head.

"Thank you for...for caring."

She looked up at him, about to say more. Then their lips were together, and they stayed that way for some time.

****

The front door opened with a squeal, and Jason walked out with the new backpack slung over his shoulder. The roads were deathly silent and illuminated only by the somber glow of neighboring porch lights. Then the hum of a car rose through the quiet, growing in volume until the halogen beams splashed through the darkness. The same limousine from the day before rolled up to the curb.

Jason turned and smiled. "I'll be back, Katie. You'll see."

"I hope so."

"I will. Have faith."

They kissed again, only briefly this time, before he walked away. When he reached the limo door, he looked back at her. They waved to each other, then he was gone.

Katie stood there until the sound of the engine was consumed by the high desert winds.

****

She paused by Noah's bedroom door, which was opened just a crack. He was snoring peacefully.

She continued to her own room, where she closed the door and locked it. Then she sequestered herself in the bathroom and took out her cellphone.

The number she'd been told to use seemed impossible—six zeroes followed by a two and a four, then the pound key. It did not ring, but rather beeped just once. Then, although Katie had no way of knowing it, the same unidentifiable male voice heard a few days earlier by Theresa Richter, and by Bruce Jax well before that, came on the line.

"Well?"

"He's taking a private plane owned by Preston Hughes out of the Henderson Executive Airport." She was finding it nearly impossible to keep her voice steady. "The flight leaves Nevada at 4:45 and lands about thirteen hours later in Paris."

"Good."

"Look...please. I told you what you wanted to know. Please promise me—" the tears came now "—you'll leave my family alone."

The line went dead.

JASON HAMMOND

WILL BE BACK

IN

The Diana Directive

SUMMER 2018

Made in the USA
Middletown, DE
30 December 2017